By Joseph Heller

Catch As Catch Can

Portrait of an Artist, as an Old Man

Now and Then: From Coney Island to Here

Closing Time

Picture This

No Laughing Matter

God Knows

Good as Gold

Something Happened

Catch-22

Plays

Catch-22: A Dramatization

We Bombed in New Haven

CATCH AS CATCH CAN

CATCH AS CATCH CAN

The Collected Stories and Other Writings

JOSEPH HELLER

Edited by Matthew J. Bruccoli and Park Bucker

Scribner

First published in the USA by Simon & Schuster, Inc., 2003
First published in Great Britain by Scribner, 2003
An imprint of Simon & Schuster UK Ltd
A Viacom Company

3 5 7 9 10 8 6 4 2

Simon & Schuster UK Ltd
Africa House
64-78 Kingsway
London WC2B 6AH

www.simonsays.co.uk

Simon & Schuster Australia
Sydney

A CIP catalogue record for this book is available from the British Library

ISBN 0-7432-3978-4

Printed and bound in Finland by
W. S. Bookwell

ACKNOWLEDGMENTS

Susan C. Pyzynski, Librarian of the I.L.S. Development and Special Collections, Brandeis University Library, provided copies of Joseph Heller's unpublished stories. Shiny Hsu, New York University Archives, patiently sought and located the issue of *Apprentice* with Heller's contribution. Patrick Scott, Thomas Cooper Library, allowed us to plunder the University of South Carolina Collection of Joseph Heller. The Interlibrary Loan staff of Thomas Cooper Library supplied necessary photocopies. Charles Adams of Simon & Schuster backed this volume.

CONTENTS

Contents

FOREWORD

Joseph Heller published thirteen short stories between 1945 and 1990—eight of them before his first novel *Catch-22* established him as a major literary figure in 1961. Of the remaining five stories, "World Full of Great Cities" (1955) was written in 1949; two—"Love, Dad" and "Yossarian Survives"—are *Catch* spin-offs; and two—"Yossarian Lives" and "The Day Bush Left the White House"—are previews of *Closing Time. Clevinger's Trial* dramatizes an episode from *Catch-22.*

There are twenty unpublished short stories in the collection of his manuscripts Heller gave to Brandeis University. Most of them appear to have been written in the forties and fifties while he was a student at the University of Southern California, New York University, and Columbia University, and a composition instructor at Penn State. Five of those buried stories have been rescued here. This volume ends with five nonfiction pieces related to *Catch-22.*

Joseph Heller forsook the short story form when the success of *Catch-22* allowed him to concentrate on novels and plays; but he had worked hard on stories for fifteen years. He started the process in 1945 while in the Air Force awaiting discharge, as he reported in *Now and Then* (1998):

> The subject matter of all the short works with which I was now busying myself and had been busying myself even earlier was not founded on experiences of my own. I hadn't had any then that seemed worth translating into

. . . I borrowed the action and the settings from the works of other writers, who may—I didn't consider the possibility then—in turn have been borrowing from the works of still others. These experiences, which I as author dealt with knowledgeably, were vicarious and entirely literary, gleaned from wanderings as a reader, and they ranged from the picturesque whimsies of William Saroyan to the hard-nosed, sexist attitudes, particularly toward women and marriage, of Hemingway and Irwin Shaw, embodying as well implicit assessments of materialism, wealth, Babbittry, and ideals of masculinity and male decency that I ingenuously accepted as irreducibly pure and nullifying all others.

In the immense replacement depot in Constantine, Algeria, where I spent a few weeks with the crewmen with whom I had flown overseas in our small B-25 before being assigned to Corsica, my primary inspiration as a neophyte writer was Saroyan. He appealed to my taste and seemed easy to emulate and well worth copying. (The stories that seemed easiest to emulate and most worth copying were short ones with few descriptive passages written in literary vocabulary and with a large proportion of vernacular dialogue.) In one of his collections was a story titled (I am working here from memory) "Did You Ever Fall in Love with a Midget Weighing Thirty-eight Pounds?"* In one of the stories from my Algerian period (working still from memory) was a young man in New York romantically involved with a girl who walked around on her hands. I have no recollection of my title. (I can imagine now that I imagined then the title "Did You Ever Fall in Love with a Girl Who Walked Around on

---

*"Ever Fall in Love with a Midget?"

Her Hands?") Where she walked on her hands and where the story went I have also mercifully forgotten.

By then I was familiar with most of the work of Hemingway, Irwin Shaw, and Jerome Weidman. Jerome Weidman's prewar collection of short stories from *The New Yorker* called *The Horse That Could Whistle Dixie* was another favorite of mine, as were the two novels of his I'd read. . . . These were *I Can Get It for You Wholesale* and its sequel, *What's in It for Me?*, and I thought them marvelous, as I did Budd Schulberg's *What Makes Sammy Run?* The Studs Lonigan trilogy of James T. Farrell was another sophisticated favorite of mine and everybody else's, mainly for the realistic action and realistic words. James Joyce's *Ulysses* floated briefly into the Coney Island apartment also, no doubt borne there, I recognize now, by the notoriety of the court victory over its banning. *Ulysses* sailed back to Magrill's drugstore unread by any of us, although I still can tingle with the *frisson* of astonishment I enjoyed coming upon two forbidden words in the very early pages, one of which describes the green color of the sea, the other the gray, sunken state of the world. John O'Hara was known to me also.

In one of these [Armed Services Editions], a collection of short stories, I found a work by Stephen Crane, "The Open Boat," and in this tale of shipwrecked sailors adrift in a lifeboat is a line of dialogue repeated by a man at the oars like a Wagnerian *leitmotif* (although I did not learn about Wagnerian *leitmotifs* until later): "Spell me, Billy."

From this sonorous reiterated chord, which I pondered in my tent, and perhaps from a one-act play of Saroyan's called *Hello, Out There* that I might already have read, could have sprung the notion of the short story to be titled "Hello, Genoa, Hello, Genoa," which would be related entirely in brisk intercom radio dialogue between a bomber pilot, or a few of them, and the control tower at the air base in Corsica. It is (even to this day, I feel) an engaging notion with a beguiling title, and I never tried writing it (or have no recollection that I did).

Instead, I wrote a short story in a day or two that I called "I Don't Love You Any More." It is about two thousand words long, and like everything from my Algerian and Corsican periods, it is based on things I knew nothing about except from my sifting around in the works of other writers. Consequently, it reflects the style and point of view of many of the malign and histrionic fictions by American male authors of that time and ours: A married, worldly-wise serviceman, with whom we are intended to sympathize, feels temporarily, upon finding himself back home, and offering no specific complaint, that he no longer wants his marriage and no longer loves his wife. (Whatever that last was meant to mean, I truly had no idea. It was a convention.)

I don't know how it happened, but after I was back in the states and just out of the service, the story was submitted as an unsolicited manuscript and accepted for publication in *Story*, a periodical then publishing fiction only and held in very high esteem. By pure luck in timing, the war in Europe being just over, it chanced that the magazine was devoting an entire issue to fiction by men and women from the services.

The stories Joseph Heller wrote and submitted to magazines in 1945–46 while attending the University of Southern California were all rejected until *Esquire* sent a note of acceptance for

"Beating the Bangtails"—retitled "Bookies Beware!"—written
as a freshman English theme:

> Assigned the subject of describing some kind of method
> or device, I had invented a series of sure-fire systems, all
> of them foolish, for always winning money at the race-
> track.
>
> And with the note had come a check for $200!
>
> I was now, at twenty-two, a certified young author of
> fiction and, with *Beating the Bangtails*, of nonfiction also
> (an illustrious distinction in 1946, two years before Vidal,
> Capote, Mailer, and others came rolling onto the national
> scene and made me feel backward, aged, envious, and
> derelict).

When Heller transferred to NYU in 1946 he took Maurice
Baudin's fiction-writing course:

> Hardly a workday went by that didn't find the postman
> delivering to 20 West 76th Street at least a few of my
> stamped, self-addressed manila envelopes returning man-
> uscripts of mine with rejection slips. *The New Yorker* then
> was as admirably efficient in editorial procedure as it was
> superb in editorial content. I used to joke—and it wasn't
> much of an exaggeration—that a story I would mail to
> *The New Yorker* in the morning would be back with its
> concise, slighting rejection slip in the afternoon mail that
> same day.
>
> Sometime during my second or third semester with
> Baudin—I took a third semester without credit because I
> wanted to keep working with him—he chose four short
> stories of mine and delivered them for consideration to his
> literary agent. The reader's report from there said that

none in the group was suitable for publication. Of the four, three were subsequently accepted by magazines when submitted by me as unsolicited manuscripts.

A comment I always seemed to get back from Baudin with each short story, regardless of other notes of praise or criticism, was that I was taking too long to begin, dawdling at the opening, as though hesitant to get going and move forward into what I had in mind. It's a quirk of mine, perhaps a psychological flaw, that has lasted. I have cogitated over it in the closest secrecy, secrecy until now, as a quality that might credibly be described as anal retentive.

In the margin of one story of mine in college, "Castle of Snow," Baudin asked why I simply didn't begin at the top of page four and instructed me to start there when I read it aloud to the class. It went well that way, to my grateful astonishment, and I began on my original page four when I typed a clean copy.

Mailed out by me to the "Fiction Editor" of the *Atlantic Monthly* with that revision, it was rejected, but with a personal letter from a woman there who signed her name and seemed to be implying that with several small alterations it might be accepted if resubmitted. (I wish she had suggested one more, for the choice of Chaucer as the favorite author of an East European immigrant forced to sell his books jars the teeth now with its blatant improbability.) I made the changes, amending what was amiss, providing what was lacking (I welcomed text suggestions then, and I've welcomed them since), mailed the revised manuscript directly to her, and the story was ac-

cepted for publication as an "Atlantic First." Coinciden-
tally, in the issue of the magazine in which it finally appeared was a story by the equally young James Jones, also
presented as an Atlantic First. (Neither of us was fortu-
nate enough to win the semiannual bonus prize for the
best of the Atlantic Firsts in that period.) I was paid $250.
With a contact now at the magazine, it was not surprising
that sooner or later I would place another work there, and
I did. For this second one I received just $200, since it
wasn't as long as the first one (and not as good, or even
much good at all).*

Much the same process was simultaneously going on
between me and a benevolent editor at *Esquire* magazine
who finally signed his name George Wiswell in elabora-
tion of the initials to the penciled notes of encouragement
he had been adding to the formal rejection slips. Eventually he rejected a story regretfully, lamenting some defect
in motivation or characterization and virtually pledging
that he would recommend it for publication if that fault
could be remedied. I made the attempt, the story was accepted, and for this one I received $300.† Sometime later
they took another one and paid me less, because the second one was shorter than the first (and not as good, or
even much good at all).‡ As I advanced in college, I ac-
quired standards and learned to be more critical, and before I finished I also learned that, apart from their being
mine, there wasn't much distinctive about all but two or

---

*"A Man Named Flute."
†"Girl from Greenwich."
‡"Nothing to Be Done."

three of the stories I was writing at this time. I now wanted to be new, in the way that I thought, as I discovered them, Nabokov, Céline, Faulkner, and Waugh were new—not necessarily different, but new. Original.

A flattering consequence of my collegiate fame was that I was prevailed upon against my better judgment to submit a short story to the college literary magazine just getting started, and I did. For those who care, it was called "Lot's Wife" and was about—oh, never mind that!—the wife was icily indifferent and petty in regard to the victim of an auto accident, the man thoroughly sympathetic but no match for her.

Of more interest is the unflattering aftermath of that charitable gesture, which was a patronizing review of the story in the college newspaper by a fellow student with literary ambitions who condescended to find it pallid, riddled with faults, lacking any compensating merit.

That should have steeled me against unkind critiques in the future, but nothing does.

However, at just about that time I was ecstatic to learn that one of my stories, that same "Castle of Snow," had been selected for inclusion in the Martha Foley annual anthology of best short stories.

That was ameliorating! There was no doubt I was on my way.

It took longer than he anticipated.

Heller set out to become a professional writer and became a literary genius. He studied in the classroom and at the local newsstand, learning what kind of stories sold to *The Atlantic, The New Yorker,* and *Esquire.* His early stories were crafted to fit the requirements of realistic fiction, emulating the style, material, and technique of Shaw, Saroyan, Algren, O'Hara, and Weidman. Heller was an apt student. In stories of bookies, addicts, and failed marriages, he replicated Shaw's dialogue, Saroyan's pathos, and Algren's poolrooms. "Castle of Snow" is an act of homage to Shaw. For a creative-writing assignment to write an O'Haraesque story, Heller could have turned in "Girl from Greenwich" and received an A.

With publications in *Esquire* and *The Atlantic*, Heller was a moderately successful "rising young talent" of the late forties. But he never achieved the status of a full-time professional short-story writer. A product of Depression-era Brooklyn, Heller began as a proletarian writer. He wrote stories of urban naturalism without the satire, parody, and surreal humor that identify his novels. His apprentice stories are written in what came to be labeled "New York Style"—a quasi-reportorial vernacular prose. Not until "MacAdam's Log" (*Gentlemen's Quarterly*, 1959) did Heller break through the conventional magazine formula. Written during the composition of *Catch-22* (1961), the story blurs fantasy and reality as "Captain" MacAdam enters a Mittyesque existence, escaping his oppressive family life by means of imaginary transatlantic voyages.

Heller's early stories don't break any rules; they don't experiment with point of view or challenge reader-editor expectations. They're safe. They lack the sad hilarity and sane lunacy that identify his fulfilled work. His early heroes experience as much despair as any character in *Catch-22*, without the concomitant hilarity.

This volume is not Joseph Heller's wastebasket. He worked hard and long on his short stories; the ones that were published appeared in respectable magazines before he became a celebrated novelist. They will instruct and gratify Heller loyalists.

Apprentices may take encouragement from observing Joseph Heller's apprenticeship, during which he learned how to write like Joseph Heller.

The previously unpublished stories are printed here as written by Joseph Heller; the other texts are printed here as they were published. Dead writers cannot approve editorial alterations in their work. No improvements have been made here except for the correction of typographical errors, spelling inconsistencies, and punctuation.

M.J.B.
P.B.

I DON'T LOVE YOU ANY MORE

Joseph Heller is twenty-two years old, born and educated in Brooklyn, New York, and, after three years of service in the Air Corps, is planning to enter the University of Southern California. He says, "I was stationed on the Island of Corsica with a B-25 squadron of the Twelfth Air Force and flew sixty combat missions as a bombardier, earning the Air Medal with seven oak-leaf clusters and a Presidential Unit Citation. I was discharged from the Army in June under the point system and have been comfortably rehabilitating myself ever since. At present, I am busy trying to get a play produced."

She stood in the center of the room, her arms folded across her ample bosom and he could almost see the fires of anger flickering within her. She was doing her best to control them.

"You aren't being very considerate, you know," she said quietly.

"I know," he replied, "I'm sorry."

"I don't believe you are sorry," she said. She waited for him to answer but he remained silent. "Are you?"

"No," he said. "I'm not."

She didn't answer him immediately; she didn't know what to

Story, vol. 27, September–October 1945, pp. 40–44; reprinted with new headnote by Heller in *Story*, Spring 1992, pp. 116–20.

say. It wasn't working out right. He had been home three days now and it was getting worse. The first day they had been uncomfortable, very cautious and considerate, feeling each other out as prize fighters do, not being themselves at all, and hoping to pick up the thread of happiness from where it had been dropped almost a year ago when he left. The second day should have been better, but it hadn't been. She was still considerate, too much so, and he found that something in the routine was getting on his nerves and making him bitter. And now they were quarreling; not yet, but he could see it coming because he was deliberately bringing it on. He was being cruel purposely, not really wanting to be, but nevertheless deriving some perverse pleasure in seeing her unhappy. He had been thinking about her for ten months, thinking about how nice it was going to be when he got back to her, and now he was back and it wasn't nice at all.

He fingered the Chinese puzzle in his hands unconsciously, two metal rings, and without being aware of it, he deliberately thwarted himself each time from separating them. He caressed them with his hands, enjoying their cold firmness as he waited for her to speak.

"Harry and Edith are coming over," she said finally.

"That's nice."

"Will you put some clothes on?"

"No."

"Why won't you?"

"I don't want to."

"What do you want?" she implored.

He looked up at her while he thought it over. He was lying on the davenport completely naked except for a pair of shorts he was wearing, his thick, close-cropped hair uncombed and wisps of it standing out in all directions. He drank in the sight of her as she stood with her arms folded and he wondered why he had ever married her. It was her build, he decided. She was tall, taller than average, and everything about her was big, but she was put together in excellent proportion and was well rounded so that she possessed a strong physical attraction.

"I don't want to meet anybody," he said. He hadn't left the apartment since he had arrived. "I don't want to meet my family or your family, or any friends. I don't want to sit in a room filled with people who are all beaming at me as if I were some marvelous mechanical toy, and play the modest hero. I don't want to tell anybody what it was like and smile shyly as they tell me how wonderful I am."

She unfolded her arms and let them fall to her sides. She moved a few steps toward him. "What do you want to do?" she asked.

"Just what I am doing now," he said. "I want to lie here relaxed and comfortable and drink beer. Will you go downstairs and get me a pitcher of beer?"

"I will not," she said indignantly. "I'm your wife, not a servant. What did you marry me for? It would have been cheaper to hire a maid."

"I know," he said. "I married you because it was part of the dream."

"It hasn't been easy for me," she said, and asked, "What dream?"

"The sugar and tinsel dream of life," he said smirking. He didn't want to smirk but he left the expression unchanged. "The *Reader's Digest* beautiful panorama of a beautiful life. You were a pretty girl, I was a good-looking boy; we are both just a trifle oversexed, so we got married. It was the thing to do, wasn't it?"

"I'm doing my best," she said plaintively. "If you would only tell me what you do want, perhaps I could be more of a help. I know that you are disappointed but I don't know why. What did you expect to find?"

"I want to do what I want to do," he said.

She refolded her arms. "That makes sense," she said bitterly. "That makes a lot of sense."

"You don't understand," he said in a patronizing voice, still fumbling with the puzzle. "I want to do what I want to do when I want to do it. Is that better?"

"No," she said.

"I'll try to break it down for you. If you miss some part of it let me know and I'll repeat it. Right now I want to lie here exactly as I am doing. Two hours from now I may want to go to the Stork Club. I don't know. While I am there I may want to sing aloud at the top of my voice, but right now I want to lie here without any clothes on and drink beer."

"You know it hasn't been easy for me."

"I know it hasn't. I'm sorry."

She walked to the side of the room and sat down in an armchair, once again not knowing what to say next. She didn't want to surrender to the anger that she was trying to repress, but she could feel it swelling within her as if it were something having physical dimensions.

"You've changed," she said softly.

"I know," he said. "You've said that several times before, but it's the truth." He waited for her to reply but she made no motion to speak. "I don't like George Gershwin any more," he said, "so don't feel too badly about it."

Now he was becoming brutal, and he could feel himself filling with self-contempt for it. He knew what she would say next and he felt a glow of pride as she obliged him.

"What does George Gershwin have to do with it?" she asked.

"I used to think about his music all the time. How much I missed it and how when I got home, I would sit down and listen to him for hours. Well, I got home finally, and I listened to his music and I found that I didn't like it."

"I don't see it," she said.

He turned on his side so that he could look her fully in the face. "It's the same way with you, Anne," he said slowly. "I don't love you any more."

She sat up quickly as if the words had slapped her across the face. "That's not true," she said.

"No, it isn't," he said. "But I don't. That's the way it is and as long as it is that way, we might as well face it now. There isn't any point in dragging out something that is unpleasant. The kindest use a knife because the dead soon grow cold."

He studied her features to see if she was going to cry and he saw that she wasn't. He noticed it with disappointment. He became conscious of the rings in his hands and he grated one against the other mechanically as he waited for her to speak.

"That's nice," she said. "That's very nice."

"That's the way it is."

"Do you want a divorce?" she asked.

"No," he said, "I don't want a divorce. I have been leaning upon you for support too long a time. Psychologically, I am dependent upon you."

"Good God!" she exclaimed in desperation. "Then what do you want?"

A mischievous smile played with his mouth.

"A pitcher of beer," he said.

She rose to her feet and walked from the room. He turned over on his back and stared at the ceiling, feeling unhappy, wanting something and not knowing just what it was. He heard her come back into the room, but he continued to lie there without moving.

"Will you please get dressed?" she said. "We'll talk about it some other time."

"No," he said.

"Harry and Edith will be here soon. I can't very well entertain them in the hallway."

"Send them in." He turned to his side and looked at her. "I'll see them."

"Put some clothes on, then. You're naked."

"Harry and Edith have been married for five years. If she

5

isn't familiar with the anatomy of the male by this time, then she has been missing a hell of a lot and it is my duty as a friend to enlighten her."

"Will you at least put a robe on?" she asked. Her voice was low and her words were carefully pronounced, and he could tell that the break was soon coming.

"No," he said. He turned over on his back again and looked down at the puzzle in his hands, watching her carefully through the corner of his eye. She stood motionless for a few seconds, looking at him. Then she let a long, loud breath escape her and her mouth formed a resolute line. She turned and walked to the clothes closet.

"Where are you going?" he asked. His tone wasn't smug any more. It quivered with alarm. She didn't answer. She removed her coat from the closet and put it on. She opened her purse, fumbled inside it, and withdrew a bankbook.

"Here is your money," she said.

"Where are you going?"

She set the bankbook down on a table and left the apartment.

"Damn!" he said explosively. He heard a slight click and he looked down at his hands. The rings of the puzzle had come apart. He sat up. "Oh, hell, what's the matter with me!"

He rose from the davenport and walked into the bedroom quickly. He sat on the edge of the bed and put his socks and shoes on. He went into the bathroom and washed his face and combed his hair. He didn't need a shave. He returned to the bedroom and finished dressing, fastening the buckle on his blouse with a strong tug. Then he went to the phone and called her mother.

"I think Anne is on her way over," he said. "Will you tell her to call me as soon as she arrives?"

"Is anything the matter?"

"No, nothing is the matter. I have to speak to her. Tell her to call me as soon as she gets there."

"What's wrong?"

"Nothing is wrong. I just want to talk to her as soon as she gets there. Before she does anything else. Will you tell her? It's very important."

"All right."

"You won't forget, now. As soon as she gets there."

"All right, I'll tell her."

"Thank you."

The doorbell rang a moment after he hung up. It was Harry and Edith and they flurried about him as soon as he opened the door, Harry shaking his hand and pounding his back, and Edith coming to his arms and kissing him, both of them gushing with questions which they gave him no time to answer, and he knew that he was glad to see them. They moved into the living room and even before they were seated they were asking the questions he knew they would ask and he found a joy in answering them. It was many minutes before either of them noticed Anne wasn't there.

"Where's Anne?" Edith asked.

He hesitated an instant. "She's over at her mother's."

"Listen," Harry said, "we canceled our bridge appointment as soon as Anne phoned us. We're going on a party and you're coming with us."

"Me?" he asked stupidly.

They looked at him strangely. "You and Anne."

He rose to his feet. "Anne isn't here," he said. "We had an argument and she left." They started to speak and he cut them off. "I don't think she'll be back."

They were silent for a few moments as the surprise seeped in.

"It isn't anything you can't patch up, is it?" Harry asked. He noticed that Edith was looking at him queerly.

"I don't know," he said. "I don't think so. I hope not. You two go out on your appointment. I'll try to straighten it out. I'll call you tomorrow, Harry."

"All right," Harry said, his exuberance gone. "Look, don't be foolish. It isn't any of my business, but use your head whatever you decide to do."

"I will, Harry," he said. "Thanks. I'm sorry I had to spoil it. I never was much as a host."

"That's okay. I wish you would patch it up. I'm rather fond of both of you."

"I'll try," he said, and they rose to leave.

They walked slowly to the door. Before they could reach it, the latch clicked and the door opened. Anne came in, backing into the room at first so that she did not see them immediately. When she turned, they saw that she wore an angry, inflammable look. For a moment she stared at Harry and Edith in surprise and then her face softened as she noticed them looking at her, and saw him standing there beside them, looking smart in his finely cut uniform with his hair combed and his face shining and wearing a sad apologetic smile. She saw him grin like an erring schoolboy when he noticed the pitcher of beer in her hands, and she smiled sheepishly.

BOOKIES, BEWARE!

January 4, 1946, is a memorable date in the history of man's grim battle with the bookmakers. On that day the art of selecting horses through the medium of pure science was born. The pioneer behind the science was a precocious twenty-year-old student of a California college, Marvin B. Winkler. His scene of operations: lush and lovely Santa Anita race track, death stage for many a Hollywood bank roll.

On the above deathless date, Marvin B. Winkler arrived at Santa Anita race track carrying a large, square carton, and took his seat in the grandstand. It was, according to accurate observers, about thirty minutes before post time for the first race. As soon as he was settled, he removed from the carton an odd assortment of scientific paraphernalia, which he set up. Then he donned a pair of thick, horn-rimmed glasses and began to work over his equipment.

Since everybody at a race track is regarded suspiciously by everybody else as a possible repository of "Sure Information," the unusual behavior of Mr. Winkler soon caused a stir among the spectators. A large crowd gathered about him. Word quickly reached the ears of the track authorities, and two Pinkerton detectives were immediately dispatched to the scene, and a call was issued for an expert in atomic energy to ascertain if the activities of the young student represented a menace. Nothing came of

Esquire, vol. 27, May 1947, p. 98.

this, as all the scientists in the country possessing knowledge of atomic energy were in Washington at the time appearing before congressional committees.

Meanwhile the student continued with his work. He gazed over the heads of the crowd and shot the sun with a sextant, carefully entering his data on a complicated computer. The staring crowd, mesmerized with curiosity, drew closer about him, until finally a racing tout, known in betting circles as "Bad Breath Harry," pushed through the crowd to where the young man was working.

"Say, pal," said Bad Breath Harry, according to competent witnesses who were in the vicinity, "what are you doing?"

The young man looked up at him briefly from a barometric seismograph.

"I am picking the winner of the first race," the student replied, according to the competent witnesses.

"Well, how are you doing it?" asked Bad Breath Harry, sweeping his hand over the array of instruments and almost knocking over a vial containing an emulsion of silver nitrate suspended in a solution of phenol red.

"Scientifically," replied Mr. Winkler.

"Scientifically, huh?" said Bad Breath Harry. "I use a scientific method myself, but I never saw any of this stuff before."

"I mean pure science," Mr. Winkler said with a deprecating smile, as he computed the density of the ultraviolet rays. "I have determined the dew point, the barometric pressure, the resistance of the air and wind, the cubic weight of moisture in the air, and the surface tension of the turf. Upon looking over the entries in the first race, I find that only one horse has ever before raced under these conditions, and then it did quite well. I conclude therefore, that this horse will win by two and three-sixteenths lengths."

"And which horse is that?" asked Bad Breath Harry, as all the competent witnesses leaned forward so as not to miss the reply.

The student looked about him doubtfully. "I hesitate to impart this information for fear of bringing the price down, but in the interest of scientific research, I will make that concession. The horse's name is Oatburner. He cannot lose."

At this, everyone within hearing distance broke into laughter, for it was common knowledge that the horse Oatburner was a hopeless flop and would probably go off at about two hundred to one. The young student was not at all disturbed by this reaction.

"Would you keep an eye on my andlocosmicneutrophile while I place my bet," he said to the gentleman sitting next to him, and pushed his way out toward the betting windows.

News of the student's choice spread throughout the track, and he was at once dismissed as an erratic clodpate. When this information reached the paddock, the jockey of Oatburner, who, it is rumored, had placed a sizable wager on another horse in the race, died laughing and had to be replaced. The horse's owner guffawed heartily and filed a mental memo to pluck his son out of college at once. Even the horse, it is reported on reliable authority, repressed a chuckle.

The young student was virtually forgotten as the race began. When it was over and Oatburner had triumphed exactly as predicted, he was besieged by spectators who flocked hopefully about him, the prayer of the leper in their eyes. And thus a new weapon, the pure science method, had been added to the age-old onslaught of the bookmakers. Let the latter answer as they may.

LOT'S WIFE

The night hung obliquely about them, depthless, quiet, and cold, growing quieter and colder as the minutes passed. The only noise was the chirping of crickets in the fields adjoining the highway, but unless you were thinking about it, it merged with the silence and was lost in the darkness. The only light came from the headlights on Sidney Cooper's car. Louise still sat inside; she hadn't left it, and when he looked at her now she was smoking. The headlights were growing dim and the yellow glare fell weakly around them, leaving the asphalt black but illuminating Cooper and the man who lay on the road before him and stared up at the black night with a wooden, inscrutable expression and the automobile the man had been driving which was now crumpled around a concrete road post.

"What time is it?" the man asked.

Cooper pushed back his sleeve and turned his watch to the light. "He left about fifteen minutes ago," he said.

"How far did he say it was to town?"

"About eight miles," Cooper answered. "They'll be coming soon." The man didn't say anything. He had been awfully nice so far and Cooper was genuinely sorry for him. "Do you feel all right?" he asked.

"I feel fine," the man said, without rancor. "I'm in the pink."

"I'm sorry," Cooper said. "I shouldn't have asked that."

Apprentice, vol. 11, January 1948, pp. 3–4.

The man turned his head slightly and smiled. "Just innocent sarcasm," he said. "I'm full of innocent sarcasm."

"Would you like a cigarette?" Cooper asked.

"No. I don't think I should. You go ahead and smoke though."

"That's all right. I really don't want one."

"Is your wife all right?"

Cooper turned and looked at her. She sat motionless behind the wheel, her head turned away from them as she stared out the side window. "She's all right," he said slowly. "A little shaken up from the shock, I imagine. It's her first accident."

"It's mine too," the man said.

"Is there much pain?"

"It's gone down. My leg is numb and I can't feel it so much. Occasionally a muscle twitches and there's pain, but it isn't too bad. How did my leg look?"

"I don't know," Cooper said. "I didn't really look at it."

"Is it broken?"

"Yes," Cooper said. "It's broken."

He had always wondered how a leg looked when it was broken and it had only taken one glance for him to know. The man turned silent and Cooper heard the clatter of the crickets approach and the croaking of what he thought was a bullfrog. The noise of the crickets was really quite deafening when you concentrated on it, and it grew very cold in the country at night even though the days were hot. He could feel the cold air on his skin but inside he was burning. He was worried about the cold. He knew that an injured man should be kept warm, otherwise shock would set in, and he had taken every precaution to keep the man warm. He had his own overcoat, and fortunately there had been a blanket in his car which Cooper had placed carefully beneath him. Then he had removed his coat and covered the man with it. He was going for Louise's coat when the man had stopped him, saying he would be all right.

"Are you warm enough?" he asked now.

"I'm all right," the man said. "How about yourself? You must be chilly."

"No," Cooper said. "I'm all right."

The man was about his own age, he judged, with a mature, competent face. All through life there had been people with mature, competent faces, and he had always admired them. There was a gash on the man's forehead that had stopped bleeding, and one side of his lips had swelled up like grotesque blisters.

"How did it happen?" the man asked. "You know, I haven't any idea how it happened."

Cooper didn't know how it had happened. He was asleep and Louise was driving. Then there was a jolt and Louise's scream, and then that loud, abrupt thud and the grinding crunch of metal and the tinkle of showering glass.

"I don't know how it happened," he said. "My wife was driving."

"It reminds me of a cartoon I once saw in a magazine. It was a picture of a big desert with one tree on it and a car had smacked into the tree, I thought it was funny at the time."

"Yes," Cooper said. "It's very funny."

"Do me a favor. Ask her to come out for a minute. I want to talk to her. I want her to tell me how it happened."

Cooper hesitated for a moment and rose. "All right," he said. "Will you be all right?"

"Sure," the man said. "I won't run away."

Cooper turned and walked to the car. The man turned his head to watch him. It was uncomfortable and he turned back again and stared up at the night as he waited. Cooper spoke to Louise in a low voice through the window, then he opened the door and sat down beside her. A few minutes later he walked back alone to the man and squatted beside him.

"She was starting to pass you. She ran over something and thought it was a blowout. She slammed the brake on and turned the wheel."

"Just like that, huh?" the man said.

"Yes," Cooper said. "Just like that."

"Is she all right?"

"Yes. She's all right."

"Why wouldn't she come out?"

Cooper was afraid of that and he didn't know what to say.

"I must look pretty bad."

"You look all right. Just a little blood, but it's all dry."

"Did you tell her that?"

"Yes," Cooper said. He turned and looked at Louise who sat in the automobile and stared fixedly out the side at the dark fields. "She's that way about everything. She can't stand anything morbid."

"Morbid!" the man exclaimed. "Do I look morbid?"

"That's just the way she is. It's the same with everything. She won't go to a movie unless it's a comedy or romance. That's the way she is."

The man didn't speak and Cooper felt lame and awkward. At that moment he hated Louise for the way she was and he despised himself because she was his wife and he was so closely involved with her. He stood up slowly and looked down the road.

"Do you see anything?"

"No," Cooper said. "Not yet."

"I wish to hell they'd come. It's getting cold."

"Are you?" Cooper said with alarm. "Maybe I should move you into the car."

"No. It's all right."

"I think I'd better move you there anyway. I'll be very careful and I'm sure she won't mind."

The man turned his head and looked at him with surprise. "It isn't that," he said. "I don't think I should move. I feel like I'm bleeding inside. It's probably a rib."

"Do you feel any blood in your mouth?"

"I don't know. I've been swallowing. What does that mean?"

"I don't know," Cooper said. "I know it means something. Turn your head and spit and I'll see."

The man turned his head and spat on the ground. Cooper bent to the ground and looked. It was too dark. He held his hand before the man's mouth. "Go ahead and spit," he said. The man spat into his hand. He turned to the light and saw with relief that there was no blood. "There's no blood," he said, and wiped his hand on his trousers.

"That's good," the man said. He was silent for a few moments, and then, with quiet disgust, he said, "Lot's wife! She reminds me of Lot's wife."

"I'm really terribly sorry," Cooper apologized. "It's just the way she is. Some people are like that."

"I know," the man said. "I didn't mean anything. I'll take that cigarette now."

"Do you think you should?"

"It's all right. It won't hurt."

Cooper took his pack from his pocket and lighted two cigarettes. He handed one to the man. The man inhaled deeply and held the smoke a long time before exhaling.

"Be sure and wash your hands when you get home," the man said, without moving his eyes from the sky.

"I will," Cooper said. "Why?"

"You'd better use Lysol," the man said.

"What do you mean?"

"Spit is very morbid," the man said. "Spit is exceedingly morbid. I once saw someone spit and I was sick for days. I couldn't eat. It was morbid all right. It was worst than when my mother died."

Cooper didn't reply and they smoked their cigarettes and waited without talking until the ambulance came.

CASTLE OF SNOW

My Uncle David was a sober man, and my Aunt Sarah, an earthy, practical woman, lived uncomplainingly with him in what seemed to be a perfect and harmonious relationship. When he was reading or occupied with his thoughts, she was always busy with the housework. Occasionally he would find himself tedious, and she seemed able to anticipate these infrequent excursions. When he would look up from his book and remove his glasses, she was always at liberty from her chores and ready to provide the relief he desired.

"Reading," she would complain. "Always reading. How can you waste so much time with your books?"

"I'm not wasting time," my Uncle David would reply defensively. "There is knowledge here in these books, and knowledge is a very great thing."

"What's so great about it?" my Aunt would demand. "You can't leave it to the children. It's something you have to take with you when you go."

"It's the same with all great things," my Uncle would answer. "You must take them to the grave with you. You cannot leave great things behind."

"If you take all the books in your trunk," my Aunt would scoff, "there won't be room for you."

Atlantic Monthly, vol. 171, March 1948, pp. 52–55.

"It's not the books," my Uncle would try to explain. "The great things are what they create. Great things are here," he would say, tapping his forehead slowly. "And here," he would add, a little more loudly, and tap his finger over his heart.

The great tragedy in my Uncle's life was the failure of the revolution in Russia. He was born in a small village not far from what is today Leningrad. He was an active socialist in his youth—so active that he had been forced to flee the authorities. He was good at figures, and when he came to this country he found employment as a bookkeeper with a manufacturing firm, working there until the great depression threw it into bankruptcy.

He watched the revolution from this country, and he rejoiced when the Czarist government was overthrown. He had faith then that in Russia would soon be found the culmination of all that is beautiful in mankind. When the original aims of the revolution failed to materialize and were abandoned for ends that were more prosaic and more easily achieved, my Uncle's faith was questioned. He watched the betrayal of his hopes in the following years, and when the reality could no longer be ignored, he turned silent and went to his books for solace.

The first effects of the depression struck close, throwing many of our friends and neighbors into unemployment immediately. I was attending elementary school then, and I was just barely able to understand the implacable laws of economics and the harsh punishments of poverty.

One morning my Uncle David took me to the city for a winter coat. Autumn was turning bitter, and the coat I had worn in previous seasons had been diverted to the use of my younger cousin. It was a cold, gray afternoon when we returned, and as we walked up the street to the house, we came upon a pile of furniture stacked desolately in the street near the curb. We stopped to look and my Uncle answered my questions, explaining the tragedy to me in a low, unhappy voice. It was my first experience with eviction and I was horrified by such a drastic circumstance.

"But that's terrible!" I exclaimed.

"Yes," my Uncle agreed. "It is terrible." He placed his hand on my shoulder and we resumed walking. "It's terrible for someone to be put out on the street. And it's terrible and frightening to be unable to help."

2

The next week my Uncle lost his job. When I came home for lunch one day, he was sitting by the window reading. He glanced up briefly at me when I entered, and returned to his book without a word. My Aunt put a finger to her lips, motioning for silence, and when I sat down to eat, she told me that the firm had closed and he was without work.

There must have been some money saved, for he was unemployed for almost three months and we continued to live on the same standard. My Aunt Sarah was a thrifty manager and an excellent cook, and if she economized on the food, it passed without notice.

My Uncle went looking for work every day. He would be gone when I awoke in the morning and he would return late in the afternoon or sometimes in the evening long after we had eaten. He would enter wearily, seat himself at the table with a dejected sigh, and announce his failure. My Aunt would set some food before him, and he would eat in silence, staring despondently at some point on the kitchen wall. After eating, he would sit awhile. Then he would rise, go to the trunk for a book, settle in the living room, and read late into the night.

My Aunt showed great concern for him and she would sometimes entreat him to leave his book and come to bed. He always refused, and if she persisted, he would grow annoyed and move into the kitchen, where she would have to raise her voice to be heard and risk awakening the children. After a while she allowed him to stay up without protest, but she suffered terrible anxiety over his health.

Finally, after three months, he found work. It was a temporary job on a construction project that fortunately lasted for seven months. Several weeks after it ended, we were forced to sell some furniture. My cousin was moved into my room, and his bed was sold along with several chairs and lamps and a miscellaneous assortment of other household articles. My Uncle made arrangements for the sale, and everything that was to go was moved into the foyer.

The man came in the afternoon. He entered respectfully, and throughout the entire transaction regarded us with practiced solicitude. He examined each article thoroughly, making whispered calculations to himself, and then retired to a corner of the kitchen with my Aunt to haggle over the price. They were there a long time, arguing stubbornly in low, muttering voices. When my Aunt returned, she wore a petulant expression. She announced obstinately that she was not going to sell.

"How much will he give you?" my Uncle asked. She told him and he smiled sadly. "Give them to him," he said. "These are bad times, Sarah. You will not get more any place else."

"I won't do it," my Aunt argued resolutely. "I'll get a job first. I'll go out tomorrow and get a job."

"Where?" my Uncle David asked. He smiled at her with sorrow and spoke in a soft, pitying voice. "Where can you find work?"

"I'll do what I used to do. It isn't so long ago that I used to work and I am still in good health. I'll work as a waitress or I'll serve drinks in a cabaret. I can still do it."

"No, Sarah," my Uncle said, shaking his head slowly.

"Why?" my Aunt insisted. "Why not?"

"You're not a young girl any more."

"But I can do it. I'm strong for a woman."

"They don't want you. When they hire girls they want a young girl with fire in her eyes and firm hips that will roll when she walks. That isn't you any more."

My Aunt was a pathetic figure as she groped for a reply. She was near tears and her naïve sorrow saddened us all. My Uncle put his hands on her shoulders and smiled into her eyes.

"But when you were younger!" he exclaimed. "Then it was a different story. You could walk into any place then and they would be glad to have you."

My Aunt was not mollified, but the furniture was sold, and in the weeks following, other articles moved from the house in small, stealthy groups. Clothing was mended and remended until wear was no longer possible, and all the schoolwork was completed in the afternoon so that a minimum of electricity would be used after darkness.

One day my Aunt Sarah went out and visited the neighborhood laundries, and she secured work mending shirts, turning frayed collars and cuffs and sewing rents in the fabrics. She would bring the work home with her, and when she was not busy with the housework, she would sit in the kitchen sewing. My Uncle would chide her with a broken, self-pitying humor, and she would respond to his teasing with indignant perseverance, but in all his heavy raillery, he never once attempted to dissuade her.

Our misfortunes prolonged themselves in a way that was unintelligible to my young mind. It was like a string of rubber being stretched beyond its limits, growing thinner as the tension increases with no promise of respite, and I was aware that a point was being approached at which everything must suddenly and disastrously snap. Relief must come or else a rupture occur that would hurl us all into a maelstrom of confusion, chaos, and tragedy. Then one day, without a word beforehand, my Uncle returned with a stranger, a man who had come to buy his books.

I remember the figure of my Uncle kneeling by the closet before the open trunk. He removed the books singly, each one with both hands, glanced at the title soberly, and passed it to the strange man, who appraised it in a moment and added it to the mounting pile behind him. My Aunt was stunned by this latest development, and she stood motionless, watching the proceeding with profound regret.

From my Uncle's actions it seemed that he had been determined to sell them all and had then wavered. Midway through the pile, he hesitated over one book and placed it on the floor behind him. Near the end he withheld another. When all the others had been sacrificed, he picked up the two books and considered each thoughtfully. Then, with reluctance, he handed one to the man and rose. It is interesting to note that in this, possibly the moment of his greatest tragedy, he chose the humor of Chaucer in preference to the comforting promise of the Bible.

He received a pitiful sum for them, four or six dollars, accepting it without complaint, and then gratuitously offered the trunk with the books. When the man had departed, my Uncle faced my Aunt and handed her the money. The poor woman was too confused to speak. She wanted to upbraid him, and yet she seemed to know that his sacrifice could not be avoided.

3

The next week he found a job. He came rushing into the house with wild exuberance, too excited to remain still or speak coherently, and we were transformed to a gleeful mob by the good news. When we were calm, we learned the details. He had been hired by a large bakery as loading supervisor and traffic manager. The pay was good, only ten dollars less than what he had been paid by the manufacturing firm, and, as he was quick to inform us, since prices had dropped, it was really much more. He was to begin work the next day, and we took the snow that had begun falling that afternoon as a good omen.

We left together the next morning and he walked with me as far as the subway. The snow was still falling and it was deep and dry on the ground. He kicked it up with his feet as he walked jauntily with the unleashed energy of a young boy, talking giddily and happily, unwilling and unable to suppress his enthusiasm. He inquired into my schoolwork and my ambitions for the future, and he prophesied a lawyer's or a doctor's office for me and talked about putting money away for a small home. We parted by the station and I walked on to school, feeling at peace for the first time in almost a year.

The snow stopped falling sometime during my morning classes. At three o'clock we were dismissed. I walked home alone, because for some reason I wanted to hurry.

When I turned the corner, I noticed some people in front of the cigar store staring up the street with amusement. As I continued, I saw that all along the street people had stopped and were looking toward a group of young boys playing around a large pile of snow. I peered ahead, but I could discern nothing from the distance. Then, when I approached the snow pile, I stopped with astonishment, for seated in the snow among the boys, and completely at ease with them, was my Uncle David.

They were erecting a fort, packing the snow into blocks and passing them to another group who set them into a wall that was appearing around the pile. One of the larger boys there had assumed command and was directing activities with loud, belligerent orders, and my Uncle David was complying with cheerful abandon. He was laughing as he worked with the other boys, and his dark face seemed younger and more content than I could ever recall. He was wearing his suit, and I noticed his overcoat folded up on the sidewalk. He looked up suddenly and saw me.

"Bobby!" he greeted loudly, raising his arm to wave. "You

are just in time. Put your books down and come play. The snow is good and clean."

I flushed with shame and a dreadful fear seized me. I stammered something unintelligible and ran to the house and up the steps. I tore into the house with a cry, startling my Aunt Sarah.

"Uncle David!" I cried. "Something's the matter with Uncle David!"

Her hand leaped to her face with alarm. "What? Where is he? Where is he?"

It was too much for me to explain, and I pointed frantically to the living-room window. She rushed across to it and threw it open. I followed her slowly, catching my breath, and waited behind her. When she turned, the fear had gone, and her face was set in a tight, angry expression. She went to a closet, put a coat on over her apron, and walked out, motioning me to follow. We walked downstairs and down the street to where they were playing in the snow. Some more spectators had gathered immediately about them, and my Aunt Sarah pushed through until we were standing right above my Uncle. He was busy with the snow and he did not see us.

"David," my Aunt said. "Come upstairs."

He saw us and his face broke into a welcoming smile. "Sarah!" he exclaimed with delight. "I was just thinking that maybe I should go upstairs and call you. Come, Sarah, come play in the snow."

"Come upstairs," my Aunt said firmly.

He looked at her with surprise. The boys, sensing a conflict, had stopped playing and were drawing slowly away. All the noises in the world ceased suddenly as the whole universe focused eyes upon us.

My Uncle's hands played unconsciously with a snowball as he looked up at her. "Forget your housework for a while, Sarah, and come play. It will be like old times again. Do you remember when we used to play in the snow years ago?"

"David." Her voice was low and determined. "Come upstairs."

"Do you remember the time when we went into the country and found the old farmhouse? It was snowing then, and there were you and I and a girl named Sonya, and Peter Grusov. I built a castle for you from the snow. You were fifteen years old then. I built this fine castle for you and you helped me. Then we all went into the woods to look for rabbits, and when we came back it was late and the castle had frozen solid, and we all said it would last forever. It was too late to go back that night and we stayed in the old farmhouse, and when we went out the next morning, the sun was shining and it was warm, and the castle I built for you from the snow had melted and couldn't be recognized. Do you remember, Sarah? Try to remember."

"Come upstairs."

"And when we got back that day and you told your father, he chased me with a stick, and I hid in my cellar and he wanted to fight with my father. Try to remember, Sarah. Please try to remember."

"David. Come upstairs."

The calm on my Uncle's face disappeared, and he looked strained and anxious. "All right," he said. "I'll come upstairs. But first tell me if you remember. Think back and try. Do you remember?" He watched her with desperate hope. When she spoke, his face fell.

"Come upstairs," she said.

A great shadow came over him and his body went limp with disappointment. He rose listlessly, retrieved his coat, and walked after her to the house. She walked ahead. He did not try to catch up, but followed meekly behind, and I, puzzled and frightened, kept several yards in the rear.

When we were upstairs in the apartment, my Uncle dropped in a chair by the kitchen table. My Aunt hung her coat in the closet and returned to the kitchen. She stood across the table from him, her expression sternly demanding an explanation. My Uncle sheepishly avoided looking at her.

"What happened to the job?" she asked at last.

"They were striking. That's why I was hired. They wanted me to scab."

"You didn't take it?"

"They were picketing when I got there. They were walking in the cold with large signs in their hands and picketing."

My Aunt didn't speak. Her lips began to twitch with despair.

"I couldn't go in, Sarah. They were men like myself. I couldn't go in and take their jobs."

"I don't care about the job," my Aunt said, speaking rapidly, as though she feared her voice would choke at any moment. "Then what is it?"

"In the street," she blurted out. "Like an idiot. With the children in the snow like an idiot."

My Uncle shook his head as though he were in a stupor and ground his knuckles into his eyes. "I was coming home," he said, softly and sadly, "and I had only bad news for you. I passed the children playing in the snow and I remembered how I used to enjoy it when I was a boy. I wanted to play with them, so—I took off my coat and played with them."

My Aunt turned to the stove and peered into a simmering pot. Then she began to knead some dough that was laid out on a wooden chopping board, her unforgiving face disclosing her anger. My Uncle rose and moved into the living room, abject and silent.

He remained in the house the rest of the day, keeping carefully out of her way and glancing at her meekly from time to time. My Aunt Sarah worked ploddingly in the kitchen, never once meeting my Uncle's gaze. She was angry and hurt, and most certainly baffled, for she was unable to understand why a grown man should want to act like a child.

GIRL FROM GREENWICH

Duke stood across the room, waiting, his eyes fixed on the girl from Greenwich. She was pretty and he admired her clean, young beauty, but it was her faint, enigmatic smile that intrigued him.

Sidney Cooper and some others were standing around her talking. Someone said something funny and they all laughed, all but the girl from Greenwich, whose remote smile reflected the amusement without taking shape. Then they moved off. She was alone, and Duke crossed the room, coming up behind her quietly and leaning against the back of her chair. She sensed him after a moment and turned slowly.

"Can I get you a drink?" he asked.

"Do I know you?" She spoke with a normal inflection of curiosity.

"It's all very proper I assure you," Duke said. "We were introduced before."

"Oh, I'm sorry." She looked over the room slowly at the buzzing horde of guests that milled noisily about the Cooper apartment. "It's terribly exciting, isn't it?" she said with enthusiasm.

"What is?" Duke asked.

"This." She raised her hand in a small gesture that encircled the entire gathering.

Esquire, vol. 29, June 1948, pp. 40–41, 142–43.

"Oh," he said dryly.

"It's a wonderful party, isn't it?"

"Yes," he said. "Let's leave it."

She raised her head and looked at him with new interest. "I'm afraid I've forgotten your name," she said inquiringly.

"It's Arthur Clarke," Duke said. "And you haven't forgotten. You probably never heard it."

"You mean we weren't introduced?"

"It can be arranged if you find the present relationship offensive."

"That won't be necessary," she said, and laughed lightly. "Tell me, do you write?"

"I've published several books. None very successful. Do you?"

"I've just finished my first novel," she told him. "They're going to publish it in the spring."

"Well, congratulations. I hope it goes well."

"I'm sure it will," she said happily. "It has already been chosen by one of the book clubs." She watched him expectantly.

"That's very nice," he said. "It really is. This isn't your reception by any chance, is it?"

"No," she replied, her face brightening. "Will I have one?"

"It's customary," he explained, and studied her as she assimilated the information in silence. "How about that drink?" he asked again.

"All right," she said, consideringly. "A martini."

Duke spied a maid with a tray, selected Scotch for himself and returned. She took the drink from him and stared at it reflectively. Standing beside her, he studied the soft slope of her cheek and the full lips fashioned in the arch, introspective smile, and he saw that she was very young, and very happy, and very much afraid.

"Well, here's luck," he said, and emptied his glass. He saw she was staring at hers with the same serene contemplation.

"A martini," she said softly, when she saw him watching her. "Would you believe it? I never drank martinis before."

"Do you like them?"

"Not particularly," she admitted. "Are you supposed to sip them or drink them fast?"

"You do whatever you like."

"Then I'll just go on staring at it for awhile."

"Not for long," Duke said. "I think our hostess is coming to take you away."

He had noticed Louise Cooper, her eyes fixed purposefully upon them, moving through the numerous groups crowding the room, her smile appearing every time someone caught her eye.

She said to the girl, "There's someone to see you, my dear."

"Who?" Duke's companion asked quickly.

"A man," Louise said. "I didn't know whether to admit him or not. I have him in the foyer."

The girl's face darkened as she looked toward the door. "What does he look like?"

"He's rather young, with blond hair, and he's wearing a trench coat."

The girl's face, staring thoughtfully toward the foyer, showed recognition. "Oh, yes, I know him." She smiled up at Louise in apology. "Could you tell him I'm busy and can't see him now?"

"I'm afraid it's too late for that," Louise said. She said it regretfully, but in a firm voice. "I think you had better see him."

The girl nodded and rose reluctantly. She excused herself with an embarrassed smile and walked toward the door. Duke stared after her, even when she had turned from the room, scratching his chin in a slow, unconscious movement. Then he turned to Louise and they chatted about nothing, and when someone called her away he wandered across the room, talked to another critic for awhile, had another drink, and looked around for her. She was still gone.

The jumble of conversations around him made him uncomfortable with a sense of idle loneliness. He scanned the room for Cooper and saw him in a corner with the others. He walked up behind him and tapped his arm. Cooper looked around, recognized him, smiled, stepped back and said, "Hello, Duke. Everything all right?"

"No, Sid. Everything's all wrong. Why do you throw these parties anyway?"

"It's good business," Cooper said laughing. "Where've you been?"

"Talking to your new writer. The pretty one with red hair."

"Oh, Arlene Edwards. How do you like her?"

"Is she any good?"

"She'll sell a hundred thousand copies in three months."

"That's not what I asked," Duke said. "Is she any good?"

"No," Cooper said evenly. "It will sell, but it isn't any good."

"Whose party is this anyway?"

"Max Winkler's," Cooper said.

"That hack!"

"You gave him a good review," Cooper argued. "Why don't you congratulate him."

"To hell with him."

"Go ahead. He's standing right behind you."

Winkler was a grave, middle-aged man who had moved Scarlett O'Hara and Rhett Butler to the Alaskan gold rush, thereby finding his own fortune. At that moment he was very pleased and proud and trying not to show it. Duke walked up to him and they shook hands.

"I'm grateful for your kind review," Winkler said.

"It was a pleasure to write it," Duke lied. "I enjoyed your book." It had been a pleasure because it pleased Cooper, and Cooper was his own publisher. "Are you working on anything new?" he asked.

"Well, yes," Winkler said, choosing his words with caution.

"At the moment I am planning my next book. A serious work. Something with more depth than my last one. Something more significant."

Someone began talking with Winkler, and Duke drifted away unnoticed. He wandered through the room aimlessly, avoiding anybody he knew, his eyes returning often to the wide entrance opening into the foyer. They were all going to do serious works someday, he thought cynically.

There was still no sign of her. He recalled suddenly that she hadn't wanted to see the man, and it occurred to him that something might be wrong. He found them standing together in a corner of the next room. They seemed to be arguing vehemently. The girl looked up at the door for a moment and caught his eye. Duke caught the distress in her glance and moved forward.

"It's gone far enough," the man was saying as he approached. "It's gone too far."

"You'll just have to trust me a little longer," the girl said. "I wish you would try to understand."

"I understand," the man said. "I understand that it's out of my hands and there's nothing I can do. I wonder if you understand."

"Anyway, this is no place to discuss it," the girl said.

"I can see," the man said, as Duke joined them.

He faced Duke resentfully, his thin, tired face regarding him with hostility. He was wearing a grey, military trench coat that was a bit too large, and he had that sharp, cunning look that Duke remembered from poolrooms and prize fights. Duke smiled at him sweetly and turned to the girl.

"I'm sorry to interrupt, but you're wanted on the phone."

"You see," she said to the man triumphantly. "I have to go inside."

"I'll wait."

"Please don't. I'll call you as soon as I have time."

"It isn't a question of time. It's something I have to know now."

"I'll call you tomorrow. I promise."

The man glared at Duke with anger, opened his mouth to speak, then changed his mind and, without a word, strode from the apartment. When the door had slammed behind him, the girl smiled with relief.

"A very nice character," Duke observed. "Where did you meet him?"

"I won't apologize for him," the girl answered, pressing his arm confidentially. "And I want you to promise not to ask."

"I'll promise," he agreed. "Because right now it's none of my business." They were walking back to the living room. "Do we have to go back?" he asked.

"Why, of course."

"Let's not. There's no climax to these parties. They occupy the same level of monotony from start to finish."

"You're very cynical," she said, with amusement. "I love parties, especially this one. I think it's glorious."

Duke was incredulous. "What's so glorious about wasting an afternoon with a lot of talkative people who have nothing to talk about?"

"That's not true," she protested. "They're very entertaining and I think it's wonderful being here with all these famous people and being in New York and everything else."

"Haven't you ever been in New York before?"

"Oh, yes. But I never lived here. Mr. Cooper gave me a gorgeous suite at a hotel and when my book comes out and I have money I'm going to live there all the time and go to parties every day and be the happiest person in the world."

There was a clear, wholesome beauty in her honest outburst that filled Duke with warm pleasure. "You're a nice girl," he said with sincerity. "I hope you get everything you want and that when you do get it, it turns out to be the way you thought it would be."

She looked at him gratefully and peered into the living room, the vague smile returning and illuminating her expression with a subdued, beatific charm. He took her elbow and turned her.

"Isn't there someplace else you'd like to go? How about a night club or something similar?"

"All right. A night club. Could we go to the Stork Club?"

"Of course."

"I don't mean the bar. Could we get into the Cub Room?"

"Certainly. Let's go."

She hesitated. "Is it all right to leave a party so early?"

"Usually it's wrong to come at all."

"All right," she said, smiling. "Let's say good-bye."

"It isn't necessary. Get your coat."

"Are you sure? I don't want to anger Mr. Cooper."

"Mr. Cooper will be grateful. I'll meet you at the door."

When he returned with his own coat she was already waiting, looking most attractive in a fur jacket and a tiny hat that peeked up over her eye. He commented on the hat, and they were both laughing as they entered the elevator. He remembered the man in the trench coat and, as they passed through the lobby to the street, he asked about him. She reminded him quickly of his promise, and when he agreed, she asked how much money she would make from her book.

"That all depends," he informed her. "Cooper is very confident. And with the book-club sales you should do very well."

"That's wonderful!" she exclaimed with delight. "I know I must sound terribly selfish, but it's just that I've never had anything and now I'll have it all."

She had been in New York only three days. Cooper was her host, and he had been entertaining her regally, providing her with a luxurious apartment and extending her a sizable advance on future royalties. All her dreams had suddenly come true, and the rare pleasure was still entrancing.

The grey day was fading into twilight, but the noon freshness remained, and they decided to walk. When they were stopped by traffic, Duke drew out a cigarette. He turned to light it and, as he cupped the match in his hands, he saw the man in the trench coat standing near the side of a building in the middle of the block. He was standing motionless, even as they were, watching them. The light changed and they continued.

"Is everything all right now?" he asked when they had crossed, watching her closely.

"Everything is wonderful," she exclaimed. "Everything is just wonderful."

"That's good," he said.

As they neared the next corner, he turned again. The man was walking behind them, maintaining the same even pace, keeping the distance between them unchanged. He took the girl's arm as they crossed the next street.

"What's wrong?" he asked.

"Wrong?" Her fade wrinkled in a puzzled frown. "What do you mean?"

"I mean trouble. Are you in any trouble?"

"No. Of course not. Why?"

"How about that man in the trench coat?"

"You promised not to ask."

"But if you're in any trouble," he said, "I want to help."

"Well, I'm not."

"All right," he said. They walked on in silence for a few moments. He looked at her and saw she was waiting for an explanation. "He's following us."

"Who?"

"That man. Don't turn," he warned quickly. "Not until you know what you want to do."

She didn't speak.

"There's a cab on the corner," he said. "It's empty. We can get in if you want to elude him."

"No," she answered slowly. "I don't want to elude him."

"All right," he said. "We'll just keep walking."

Curiosity overcame her finally and she turned to look. Immediately her fingers closed on his arm. "He saw me," she said with alarm. "He saw me and he's coming."

"What do you want to do?"

"I don't know." Her pace quickened. "Keep walking. Walk fast."

When they came to the next corner he turned her down the side street. Then he heard the footsteps rushing up from behind, and in one abrupt moment they were torn apart and the man stepped between them, his back turning to Duke as he faced the girl.

"I have to talk to you," he said.

"Go away," the girl said. Her face filled with fear as she stepped back from him. "Please go away."

"Not until I talk to you. Tell him to go."

Duke measured him carefully, feeling the anger bubble inside. The man reached out for the girl's arm. Duke caught his wrist and stepped before him.

"She said she didn't want to talk to you," he said quietly.

"Go away," the man ordered in a trenchant voice. "It's none of your business. Why don't you go away?"

"She doesn't want to talk to you and neither do I," Duke said. "So beat it."

The man swung quickly before he could get his hands up and hit him on the side of his face. Duke swung wildly at his head and missed. His foot slipped and he fell to his knees. He waited there until the raging fury cleared and he could focus his eyes on the man, who was backing away, his hands raised girlishly before him as though he were trying to fend off the tide of avengeance.

"Don't get angry!" he was shouting. "For God sakes, don't get angry! I don't want to fight!"

Duke's face was numb with pain, and he remembered the girl from Greenwich who was standing somewhere outside the frame of his vision, and he rose slowly, his anger pointed into sharp, clear channels of revenge. He moved forward with grim, methodical determination, his hands coming up before him in a fighter's position and shifting craftily with his shoulders as he advanced on the man with a wary, plotting hatred. He feinted with his left and brought his right into the body. His hand tangled in the loose folds of the trench coat, harmlessly, and he swung at the man's head and felt his fist smash against solid bone, and he swung again and again.

He felt himself grow strong and stronger and his opponent grow weak, and when his vision cleared he saw the man's face before him, marked with blood and raw bruises, and lolling helplessly with the blows as he stood unresisting, and then Duke saw he was crying. Tears were streaming down his cheeks and he was sobbing aloud, and he seemed unaware of Duke's hands pounding his face.

Duke dropped his hands quickly, horrified by the picture, the clean exultancy that had come with that one clear moment vanishing and he realized once again that nothing is so disappointing as victory.

There was a lot of confusion, a lot of people, and then there was a large, angry policeman and an indignant woman shrieking at him that she had seen the whole thing. Duke stepped between them.

"It's nothing, Officer," he said. "Couldn't you forget it?"

"No," was the brusque retort. "I couldn't. What's it all about?"

"It's a personal matter, that's all. And it's over."

"There's nothing personal about a fight on Fifth Avenue."

"Please, Officer." It was Arlene, detaching herself from the confusion and looking most appealing as she smiled at him and explained that it was all a misunderstanding.

The policeman relented finally and set about dispersing the crowd while Duke collected himself, straightening his clothes and smoothing his hair. When he looked up, the man in the trench coat had slipped through the ring of bystanders and was turning the corner. After a period of discomfort that seemed interminable they were able to resume their walking.

"Are you all right?" Arlene asked, when they had passed beyond the curious stares and were again walking alone.

"Yes," he said. "I'm all right."

"You're not hurt?"

"No, I'm not hurt. I'm banged up a little, but it's all right."

"That's good." She took his arm admiringly. "You were marvelous," she said. "You really were."

"That's very nice. Now I'd like to know what it's all about."

"All right. I suppose you have a right to know."

"I think so. First, I'd like to know how you got tangled up with a character like that in three days."

"It isn't three days," she explained. "I know him from home. He lives in Greenwich."

"Go on."

"And he's not the kind of person you probably think he is. He's a respectable shoe salesman."

"Don't tell me he followed you here to collect a bill."

"Don't be silly," she said, pressing his arm as she laughed. "He's my husband."

Duke stopped with amazement and looked at her.

"He wants me to go back to him," she continued. "To live in Greenwich. Can you imagine that?"

She said it so simply that Duke didn't realize immediately. It hit him suddenly with a sickening jolt, and he whirled upon her with surprise. All the pieces fell together in a horrible pattern, and in the center he could see the man's pale face reeling with the punches as the tears streamed down his cheeks.

Duke turned from her with anger and disgust and walked to a cab that was parked near the corner. She followed after him, clutching at his arm with surprise.

"Where are you going?"

"I have another appointment," he said. He shook his arm free and entered the cab. "I suddenly remember that I have another appointment."

"But what about me?" she asked in bewilderment.

"Go back to the party," Duke said, closing the door. "Go back to the party and drink some more martinis."

A MAN NAMED FLUTE

Two policemen, one of them a sergeant, entered the stationery store and tramped heavily to the back where Dave Murdock ran his business. Murdock was a bookmaker. He had arrived shortly before, and he and the two men he employed were still busily tabulating the previous day's results. When the two men entered, Murdock looked up at them with surprise, his dark eyes taking them in without welcome. An angry scowl appeared on his heavy face. "What do you want?" he said.

The policemen hung back several steps before him. "I've got bad news for you, Dave," the sergeant said regretfully. "We have to close you up for a while."

Murdock studied him a moment and then leaned back. He bit the tip from a fresh cigar and spat it out with savage annoyance. "Don't bother me," he said. "I'm busy."

"I'm not fooling, Dave," the sergeant said. "You have about four hours."

Murdock moved forward over the desk, his big shoulders bunching up menacingly, and glared at him with frank belligerence. "What the hell's the idea?" he demanded.

"We have to clean up for a while, Dave. You know that."

"I know that," Murdock said. "But why me?"

"It's not just you, Dave. We're closing every shop in the dis-

Atlantic Monthly, vol. 172, August 1948, pp. 66–70.

trict. I'll make it an easy complaint and you get someone to take the pinch for you. All right?"

Murdock stopped arguing when he saw there was nothing he could do. He collected what papers he thought he would need and went out, leaving his two assistants to make the necessary arrangements, among them the usual task of locating someone to be arrested in Murdock's place. He spent the rest of the afternoon visiting as many of his customers as he was able to, giving the favored ones his home number and taking what business he could get on the way. In the late afternoon he called Nat Baker and got a ride home.

Nat was also a bookmaker, and when they were in the neighborhood, they stopped at a small luncheonette where the counterman took bets for him. They had coffee, and Murdock decided to wait in the car when Nat and his man huddled in a corner of the room. It was already dark when he stood up and walked to the door. When he stepped outside, he was greeted with a thick, rich, weedy smell. A group of boys stood clustered together in the darkened doorway of a hardware store, all smoking with a strangely surreptitious guilt. Murdock sniffed curiously at the air, recognizing the odor with surprise. The furtive manner of the group immediately confirmed his suspicion. They were smoking marijuana. Murdock remained where he was, glancing at the doorway secretly until Nat came out. Nat caught the smell as he came briskly through the door. He looked briefly over Murdock's shoulder as he started toward the car.

"Is that what I think it is?" he asked.

"Probably," Murdock said, with a nod. "Reefers, isn't it?"

"Yeah," Nat said. "It's getting to be quite the thing around here."

Murdock entered the car slowly, glancing at the boys with an interest mingled with regret. Nat began moving the car out. Murdock turned a last commiserating glance on the group, and his eyes came to a sudden stop. His son Dick was among them, smoking, standing far back in the recess of the dark doorway where the shadows were heaviest, but unmistakably his son, Dick, sixteen years old. Murdock gasped with surprise. He reached out and held Nat's arm in a strong grip.

"Nat, who sells it to them?"

"Why?" Nat asked, slightly puzzled. He looked at the group for a moment and then seemed to understand. "I can find out," he said. "Do you want me to find out?"

"Yeah," Murdock said, grimly. "Go find out."

Nat left the car and returned to the luncheonette. Murdock sat motionless, smoldering, feeling his anger boil as he glanced at his boy from time to time. He had a murderous temper and he fought to keep it subdued, because Dick was a good boy and he knew that everything could be settled by a serious talk. As he watched, the boy raised his hand to his face and inhaled deeply. Murdock watched the glowing spark brighten and turned away. He didn't look there again until Nat had returned and pulled the car out.

"They get it from a fellow called Flute," Nat said. "You can find him in the poolroom."

Murdock nodded his thanks and remained silent. When Nat dropped him off, he stood before the house for several minutes, trying to calm himself before he went inside. Claire was surprised to see him so early.

"They closed the place up again," he explained, answering her question. He studied her intently for several moments, trying to guess what she was thinking. She stood before him in silence, watching him with a sad expression. "What's troubling you, Claire?" he asked, feeling a bit guilty.

"Nothing's troubling me," she answered slowly. "I just wish you'd get into a respectable business."

"It's only for a few days," Murdock said. "It doesn't mean anything."

"That isn't what I mean," Claire said.

Murdock well knew what she did mean. He had been a book-maker for almost sixteen years, and in all that time Claire had never stopped disapproving. With an almost puritanical obstinacy, she still refused to regard his income as an honest living.

"Look, Claire," he said, with a slight trace of annoyance. "Stop blaming all the gambling in the world on me. The city is crawling with bookmakers, and if I didn't take the bets I handle, someone else would. Can't you see that?"

"I can see it," Claire said. "But I just wish it wasn't you." She regarded him regretfully for another moment and then turned to the stove.

Murdock left the kitchen and went to the bedroom, where he removed his clothes until he was bare to the waist. He was a big man in his early forties, and his large, heavy frame still had a definite expression of solid, masculine strength. In the bathroom he washed slowly and combed his hair. He put on a fresh shirt, leaving the collar unbuttoned, and returned to the kitchen, where Claire was peering into a simmering pot.

"Where's Dick?" he asked casually.

"He went out."

"Where?"

Claire turned from the stove to look at him. "I don't know," she said. "Why?"

"How is he doing in school this term?" Murdock asked.

"The new term just began. He always does well in school. What's the matter?"

"When does he do his homework?"

"You know when he does his homework. After school and at night. Will you please tell me what's wrong?"

"There's nothing wrong," Murdock said. "I just don't like the idea of my kid running all over the streets and getting into trouble."

Claire moved toward him with alarm. "What kind of trouble? What's he done?"

Murdock smiled and patted her arm with clumsy assurance. "There's nothing wrong," he said. "I guess the police put me in a bad mood." He smiled again and stood up. "I have some work to do," he said, and walked out without waiting to see if she believed him.

2

In the bedroom he sat down and waited. Dick was a good boy, he told himself, and everything would be all right. There had always been a cheerful friendship between them. He knew that Dick gambled occasionally and shot pool frequently, that an imbecile woman had willingly taken his virginity, and that he probably smoked cigarettes regularly even though he had promised to hold off for another year. They had discussed all that with comfortable honesty, and Murdock had always prided himself on the open relationship. This new deed incensed him, because of its evil suggestions and because it had been done secretly, and as he sat waiting he was filled with a fierce resentment.

He heard the boy come in and waited until he settled himself in the living room. Then he rose and went in to him. Dick was sitting in a chair near the window, holding a magazine he had just opened. He was a well-built boy with clear, probing eyes in a handsome face that looked a year or two older than his actual age. Claire came from the kitchen and stood in the doorway, looking on in nervous anticipation.

"Hello, Dad," Dick said, when Murdock entered.

Murdock had decided to let it ride until after dinner, but when the boy spoke, all resolve gave way to an overwhelming indignation. "Where the hell have you been?" he demanded.

The boy looked at him with surprise. "I was outside," he said. "Why?"

"I'll ask the questions," Murdock said. "You answer them."

"I was only gone a couple of hours," Dick said. "Ask Mom."

"I don't have to ask anybody," Murdock said. "I'm sending you away to school."

Dick stared at him with amazement. "What's that?" he asked.

"I said I'm sending you away to school. What's the matter? Can't you hear?"

"What are you talking about?" Claire said.

"I know what I'm doing," Murdock answered.

"It doesn't sound like it," Claire said.

"What kind of school?" Dick asked.

"Military school."

"Military school! Gee, Pop, what's got into you anyway?"

"I'll show you what's got into me," Murdock said. "Stand up." Dick looked at him incredulously and began to rise. Murdock strode up to him and pulled him to his feet. Before the boy realized it, Murdock was going through his pockets, gathering the contents in his large hands. When he had emptied them all, he pushed the boy down roughly into the chair. "Wait in here," he ordered, and walked out.

He went to the boy's room and examined the articles in his hands, doing it quickly and throwing each one on the bed after a brief inspection. He couldn't find what he wanted and turned to the jacket the boy had been wearing. In the breast pocket he found a small packet. He opened the tissue wrapping and saw two thin, wrinkled cigarettes. He split one with his fingernail and examined the seeds to his satisfaction. Now that he was sure, he felt surprisingly calm. He closed the cigarettes in his hand and returned to the living room. Neither Claire nor the boy had moved.

"Come inside, Dick," he said. "I want to talk to you."

The boy followed him back into the room. Murdock closed the door and turned the lock. He let several seconds go by before speaking.

"Dick," he said. "Are you doing anything you wouldn't want me to know about?"

The boy hesitated, watching him cautiously, and then shook his head.

"Or anything you know I'd really object to?"

The boy replied uncertainly. "I can't think of anything."

Murdock took a step forward, feeling the hot anger flame within him. "Are you sure?" The boy nodded, and Murdock came forward another step. He watched Dick's face closely as he raised his arm and held up one of the thin cigarettes. "What's this?" he asked.

A conclusive look of guilt flooded the boy's face. His frightened eyes caught Murdock's for a moment and then dropped to the floor. "A cigarette," he answered.

"What kind of cigarette?"

"A regular cigarette," the boy said. "I've been rolling my own."

Murdock hit him with his open hand. Dick fell back, stumbled to his knees, scampered up again quickly, and retreated in hurried steps. Murdock moved toward him, enraged. He had never struck him in anger before, and the great shame that swept over him he immediately blamed on the boy.

"What kind of cigarette?" Murdock demanded.

"A reefer," Dick said, in a low voice that was filled with shame.

Murdock stepped back, breathing hoarsely, feeling with relief that another point had been won. "Who sells it to you?"

The boy looked down at the floor without answering. A small trickle of blood appeared at the corner of his mouth.

"You don't have to tell me," Murdock said. "I know."

"Who?" Dick asked.

"A fellow named Flute," Murdock said. "Is that right?" Dick nodded slowly. "Can I find him in the poolroom now?" Murdock asked. The boy nodded again. Murdock studied him silently for several seconds. "You're bleeding," he said, in a lower voice.

Dick touched his finger to his mouth and looked at it without emotion. "It isn't anything," he said.

"I'm going out," Murdock said. "You wait in here until I get back. I don't want Mother to know. If she asks you, tell her you've been cutting school. All right?"

The boy nodded and Murdock walked out. Claire blocked his way in the foyer.

"He's all right," Murdock said. "Let him stay there until I get back."

"Where are you going?"

"Out for some air," Murdock said.

3

It was a six-block walk to the poolroom. When he was inside, he stopped by the door and scanned the long, crowded interior. All the tables were in use, each with its small, chattering audience, and in the back a small crowd stood around the ticker that was bringing in the sporting results. Murdock was looking for Marty Bell, the owner, and he spied him coming forward with a greeting smile.

"Hello, Dave," he said. "What brings you here?"

"I want to talk to you," Murdock said. "Is there a fellow named Flute here?"

Marty looked toward the back and nodded. "That's him at the fourth table," he said, pointing. "What do you want him for?"

"I'm going to beat his brains out," Murdock said, and started away.

Marty came after him nervously and caught his arm. He had a soft, owlish face with a peculiarly mournful twist to his mouth that had earned him the nickname Tearful. He looked unusually troubled now. "Be careful, Dave," he said. "He's a strong boy."

Murdock shook him away impatiently and walked back to the fourth table, his eyes fixed on the man but not noticing that Flute was as big as he himself was, with broad, level shoulders and thick forearms. Flute was bending over to make a shot when Murdock came up to him. Murdock tapped him sharply.

"I want to talk to you," he said.

Flute straightened up slowly and studied him with a careless interest, a slight, mocking smile coming to his strong face. "What about?"

"I'll tell you outside," Murdock said.

Flute thought about it a moment and then nodded. He put his cue down and followed Murdock out through the side door. Murdock walked until they were out of the light before he turned.

"You've been selling marijuana to my kid," he said.

Flute showed no emotion. "Who's your kid?" he said calmly. "I sell tea to a lot of people."

"That doesn't matter," Murdock said. "It takes a pretty low bastard to sell it to anyone."

"All right," Flute said. "Talk nice."

Four men came out of the darkness behind Flute, two on either side, and moved forward until they were around Murdock. As soon as Murdock saw them, he swung at Flute. Flute caught his wrist and held it, and before Murdock could move, he had his other arm, and in an instant Murdock was pinned back against the wall, unable to move. He kicked out viciously at the man's groin and struck his thigh. Then the leg moved and Murdock could no longer hit anything. The four men watched without moving. Flute held Murdock powerless with his arms and shoulder, making no attempt to hurt him. Murdock struggled feverishly to break free from the younger man, putting all his strength behind the effort. It was no use, and after a few minutes he sagged in helpless exhaustion. The anger went out of him, leaving him limp with defeat.

"All right?" Flute asked.

Murdock nodded weakly. Flute released him and stepped back. Murdock moved from the wall, his eyes on the ground.

"It's all up to your kid," Flute said. "He comes to me. Tell me who he is and I won't sell it to him."

Murdock was silent. He rubbed his arms slowly, trying to shake the soreness from them. Flute watched him steadily, waiting.

"All right," he said, with a shrug. "Don't tell me. But don't make trouble for me. All right?"

Murdock still didn't speak. His eyes flickered to Flute's square face every few seconds. He was still gasping for breath, still trembling slightly in defeat, but on his face there was a look of stubborn determination which Flute eyed apprehensively. He watched Murdock a moment longer and then stepped back reluctantly, shrugging again. Murdock moved between two of the men and walked away. He left them in a rapid stride, but as soon as he turned a corner his step slowed to a tired pace. He continued home in a weary walk. When he was before the house, he stopped to comb his hair and straighten his clothes. Claire was waiting for him by the door.

"Where have you been?" she asked anxiously.

"Out for some air," Murdock said.

Claire studied him with a puzzled expression. "Have you been fighting?"

"Do I look like I've been fighting?" Murdock said. Claire shook her head slowly and Murdock had to smile. "Get dinner ready," he said. "We'll be right out."

4

He hesitated outside Dick's room and then continued into his own. He closed the door and sat down on the bed, truly feeling his age for the first time. He was humbled by the shameful memory of being handled by Flute as though he possessed only the puny power of an infant. He sat motionless for a while and gazed down blankly at his hands, listening aimlessly to the noise of his breath passing through his nostrils. He didn't hear the doorbell ring and he looked up with surprise when Claire came into the room.

"Marty is here," she said. Murdock looked at her quizzically. "Marty Bell," she explained.

"What does he want?" Murdock said, without looking at her.

"He wants to see you."

"All right," Murdock said.

Claire turned from the door and returned a moment later with Marty. Marty came into the room gingerly, his sad face filled with a troubled gloom. He glanced significantly at Claire, and she left with an anxious glance at Murdock. Marty closed the door and faced Murdock. He didn't speak.

"What do you want, Marty?" Murdock said.

"I was talking to Flute," Marty said. "He asked me to come to see you." Marty stepped forward hopefully. "Do me a favor, Dave. Let him alone, will you?"

"Why?" Murdock demanded brusquely. "Why should I let him alone?"

"Because he's a good boy, Dave. You don't know him, Dave, but he's a good boy."

"Yeah," Murdock said scornfully. "Some good boy. He sells dope to my kid."

Marty shrugged with acute discomfort. "He just looks to make a buck," he explained. "You know how it is, Dave. You knocked around a lot yourself."

"I never sold dope," Murdock said.

"That doesn't mean anything," Marty said, with another deprecating shrug. He stepped close to Murdock and cocked his face forward in an intimate gesture. "He just tries to get by. You know how it is, Dave. There are a dozen guys in the neighborhood who would sell tea to your kid if he wants it. If Flute didn't do it, somebody else would. It's just like your own business."

Murdock's jaw dropped. Marty stopped speaking and looked at him with amazement. He took a cautious step back.

"Beat it, Marty," Murdock said.

"Sure, Dave," Marty said quickly. "But think it over, will you?"

"Get out, Marty," Murdock said. "I won't bother him."

Marty smiled at him gratefully and left. Murdock sat alone for a few minutes and then rose slowly, as a man exhausted, and went to Dick's room. Dick looked up at him quickly when he entered, and then dropped his eyes to the floor. Murdock stared down at his hands for several minutes, breathing slowly and heavily, feeling a strong sense of shame as he stood before his son. After a while he looked up.

"I'm sorry I hit you, Dick," he said.

Dick looked at him with surprise for a moment, and then his face broke into a wide, bashful grin. "That's all right, Pop," he said happily.

"Here," Murdock said. He picked up the small packet containing the two reefers and handed them to him. "We'll talk about it tomorrow. All right?"

"Sure, Pop," Dick said. He hesitated a moment and then replaced the packet on the table. "Anything you say."

Murdock smiled at him and the two of them went in to dinner. As he sat down it occurred to him that Claire must not know. The food was good, but he ate slowly, without appetite, and through the whole meal he never once met her eyes.

NOTHING TO BE DONE

Carl entered the room, placed his raincoat on the back of a chair, and began taking off his clothes. He was a fat little man in his late forties, and the greying hairs on his chest were peculiarly ugly against the pasty folds of his flesh. When he was bare to the waist he sat down on the edge of the bed and began untying his shoelaces. The bed was near the window, and he sat for several minutes gazing out into the street. It wasn't yet noon, but the air was already grey with a shadow that promised rain. With a tired grunt he raised his legs and stretched out on the bed. He lay on his back a long time, staring up at the ceiling, and finally, without moving, he fell asleep.

The sound of footsteps mounting the stairs woke him a short time later. The footsteps stopped outside his door, and there was a light knock. "Come in," he said.

The door opened and Huck entered. Huck was a boy of about twenty who worked for Carl in the poolroom downstairs, and he had come up for the keys. He was fairly good-looking, with a firm, rugged face, and his wide body filled the seams of the leather jacket he was wearing. He smiled when he came in. "Hello, Carl," he said.

"Hello, Huck." Carl watched him as he moved into the room and sat down on a chair facing the bed. Carl didn't speak for awhile, and Huck waited patiently, resting his elbows on his

Esquire, vol. 30, August 1948, pp. 73, 129–30.

thighs. "It's going to rain," Carl said mournfully, turning slowly to look out the window. "It's going to rain like hell."

Huck didn't answer. He held out a pack of cigarettes. Carl shook his head, and Huck lit one for himself. "What are you doing in bed?" he asked. "Don't you feel well?"

"I feel all right," Carl said. He let several seconds go by in silence as he watched the smoke rise from Huck's cigarette and turn blue as it hit the frame of light in the window. "It doesn't pay to open up," he said. "It's going to be a bad day."

Huck shrugged indifferently.

"Till when were you here yesterday afternoon?" Carl asked.

"About two or three, I guess," Huck said. "I hung around for a while after Nat took over."

"Did you take any bets?"

"Some small stuff. Why?"

"Did you phone them in yourself?"

"No," Huck said. "I gave them to Nat. What's the matter?"

"A bet got lost," Carl said.

Huck looked grave. "Who lost it?"

"Nat did," Carl said. He paused a moment. "It was a hundred bucks. The pay-off is twelve hundred."

Huck sat up sharply, his lips repeating the figure with amazement. "Nat wouldn't pocket a bet," he said after a moment. "You know that."

"I know he wouldn't," Carl said. "But Nick London won't care about that. It was London's bet."

"Are you sure London made it?"

"He made it all right," Carl said. "Nat remembers taking it. He got the hundred bucks in a white envelope. But he doesn't remember phoning it in, and he didn't give it to me."

"What's going to happen?" Huck asked.

Carl looked out the window at the building across the street and at the small portion of sky that he could see without moving. "It's going to rain," he said. "It's going to rain like hell."

"Do you want me to open up?" Huck asked.

"You might as well." Carl reached into his pocket and gave Huck a set of keys. "But there won't be any business."

Huck walked to the door, tinkling the keys softly in the palm of his hand. He turned and stared down at Carl thoughtfully. "Nat wouldn't steal anything," he said.

"I know," Carl said. "But it doesn't matter."

"What are you going to do?"

"There's nothing I can do," Carl said. "I don't have twelve hundred dollars. If I had that much dough, I'd be able to cover the bets myself instead of just collecting them for the syndicate."

"Maybe it's someone up there," Huck said. "Maybe someone at the syndicate is fooling around."

"No," Carl said. "He didn't phone it in."

"Who has to make good?"

"Nat," Carl said. "I never saw the bet."

"Does London know that?"

Carl nodded. "He came to collect last night," he said.

Huck shrugged sadly and walked out, closing the door slowly behind him. Carl lay motionless for a while, running his eyes from the ceiling to the window and then back again to the ceiling. Finally he sat up. Sitting on the bed, he could reach out and open the drawers of the bureau. He opened the top one and took out a pint bottle. It was cheap whiskey, and he made an unpleasant face when he swallowed. He stood up, sighing, and padded across the floor to the bathroom where he had a long drink of water. The water was warm and he grimaced again. Watching himself in the mirror, he scraped the heel of his hand against the dark bristle along his jawbone. He ran some hot water into the basin and shaved. Then he went back to the bed. He was just dozing off when Huck came back with Nat.

"Hello, Nat," Carl said.

Nat was a tall boy, much taller than Huck, but thinner. He went to college in the mornings and worked for Carl in the afternoons. As Carl watched him cross the room, he wished there was something he could do. But there wasn't. He had been thinking about it all night, and there wasn't anything he could do.

"Carl," Nat said. "What am I going to do?"

"I don't know," Carl said. "Maybe you'd better go somewhere for a while."

Nat shook his head. He looked tired, and his dark eyes were filled with a baffled look of misery.

"Are you sure you took the bet?" Huck asked.

"I took it," Nat answered. "He gave me the money in a white envelope. I remember that, but I can't remember what I did with it." He shook his head in bewilderment and turned to Carl. "Carl, I didn't give it to you did I?" he asked hopefully.

"No," Carl said. "I remember the ones you gave me. His bet wasn't among them. You don't think I'd pocket it, do you?"

"I didn't mean that," Nat said, and paused despondently. "I wish I could remember. It got busy suddenly and I don't know what I did with the envelope. I must have lost it or given it away by mistake."

"Carl," Huck said, "call up the syndicate. I bet it's up there somewhere."

"No," Nat said. "I didn't phone it in."

"Call them anyway," Huck insisted.

"All right," Carl said.

"Call up London for me," Nat said. "Try and explain it to him."

"It won't do any good," Carl said.

"Do it anyway, will you?"

"All right," Carl said.

The two boys left, and Carl stood up and began dressing. When his shirt was buttoned, he rolled up his sleeves and walked out. The long room downstairs was empty. Huck sat on a corner of one of the tables in the back, talking to Nat, who was hunched up furtively on a bench against the wall.

"I'm going to call," Carl said.

"Thanks, Carl," Nat said. "And talk to London for me."

Carl nodded and started for the door. "Don't sit on the tables," he said to Huck as he walked by.

When he was outside, Carl stopped briefly to look up at the sky. For some reason he didn't know, he wanted it to rain. Next door to the poolroom was a small luncheonette. Carl nodded to the counterman as he walked back to the telephone. He closed the door of the booth carefully, looked out to the front of the store for a moment and then stared at the phone. After awhile he left the booth.

Two young boys were using the first table when Carl returned to the poolroom. He eyed them closely as he walked to the back where Huck and Nat were waiting.

"I called the syndicate," he said. "They never got the bet."

"How about London?" Nat asked. "Did you talk to him?"

"I couldn't get him," Carl said. He stared down into the boy's eyes.

"He's on his way over here, I guess," he said slowly. "He'll bring some friends."

Nat didn't speak and in the silence the noise of the ticker bringing in a rehash of the previous day's results grew very loud. Carl turned and looked down at the boys playing on the first table. He asked Huck, "School kids?"

"I don't know," Huck said.

"Better get them out," Carl said. "The law might be around."

Huck walked slowly toward the front. Carl watched him move away, waiting until he was out of earshot before turning back to Nat.

"You'd better beat it, Nat," he said.

Nat shook his head. "No. I don't want to run away."

"They can get pretty rough," Carl said.

"I'll talk to them," Nat said. "I'll try to explain."

"They won't listen," Carl said.

Nat looked down at the floor without answering. He made no move to go. Carl studied him for a moment. "My brother has a farm in Jersey," he said. "You could go there. He'll treat you right."

Nat didn't move.

"Nat," Carl said, his voice growing sharp. "You'd better go. I've seen them work. They could kill you easy. I've seen them do it."

Nat's face grew white and he shifted nervously.

"They worked someone over right outside," Carl said. "They beat him bloody. I've seen them do it, Nat."

Nat looked up at him quickly. For a moment, Carl thought he might decide to go. Then Nat shook his head vehemently. "All right, Nat," Carl said unhappily. He squeezed Nat's shoulder and then went up to his room. When he got there, he removed his shirt and shoes and lay down on the bed.

A long time passed before he heard footsteps rushing up the stairs, and Huck burst into the room. "They're outside," he said. "They just drove up."

Carl didn't move. "Where's Nat?" he asked slowly.

"He's downstairs." Huck looked at Carl. "Aren't you going down?"

"There's nothing I can do."

"But they'll beat him up."

"Sit down, Huck," Carl said.

Huck sat down. He watched Carl steadily.

"Just relax," Carl said. "Smoke a cigarette and relax."

There was a long, intense silence. Then they heard a door close downstairs. There was the barely audible sound of footsteps. They stopped, and for several minutes all that could be heard was the faint chatter of the ticker in the poolroom. Then, suddenly, there was a cry that broke off abruptly, followed immediately by a loud scramble of footsteps that slowed gradually and disappeared. The silence that followed was complete. Even the ticker was dead.

Huck was sweating profusely. Streams of perspiration flowed freely down his face, and the neck of his shirt was soaked with a dark, spreading stain. "I can't hear anything," he said to Carl in a hoarse whisper.

"I can," Carl said. "I can hear you sweating."

Huck ran his hand over his forehead and looked at the hand with surprise. He pulled out a handkerchief and mopped his face and neck thoroughly. When he was through, he held the handkerchief between his hands in a crumpled ball.

Minutes passed. The door downstairs opened and closed. Huck rose quickly and moved to the side of the window. A car door slammed, and seconds later an automobile started up and drove off. Huck turned from the window. "They're gone," he whispered hoarsely.

"All right," Carl said. He sat up and reached for his shirt. "We'll go down now."

Huck moved across the room slowly, scarcely breathing, and started downstairs. Carl stood up and walked to the door. He stopped there and listened to Huck's footsteps going down cautiously. Then he closed the door and turned the latch. He bent down to the floor, reached under the rug, and withdrew a small white envelope.

He had found it buried in his pocket the night before. Somehow it had got separated from the other bets that Nat had given him, and when he had discovered it, it was already too late. He had been thinking about it all night and all morning, trying to figure out if there was anything that could be done and realizing all the time that there wasn't. Twelve hundred dollars was due, and someone had to pay for the mistake. It was best the way it had happened, he kept telling himself, because he was a soft, middle-aged man, and Nat was young and in good health. He felt sad about it, because Nat was a good, honest kid, and Carl liked him a lot.

Standing by the door, he opened the envelope and looked at the money inside. It contained a hundred dollars, and Carl stared at it for a moment, deliberating. Then he walked slowly into the bathroom and tore it up, money and all. He watched the pieces carefully as they fell into the bowl, but when he came back into the other room he felt no better. He unlatched the door and went downstairs.

WORLD FULL OF GREAT CITIES

The boy left his last telegram with the receptionist in the lawyer's office and walked down Beekman Place to the apartment house. He rode the elevator to the sixth floor, found the door he wanted, rang the bell, and waited. After a few seconds, the door opened, and a blonde woman looked out at him. She opened the door wide when she saw him, and she remained motionless in the doorway, studying him coldly from head to foot. She was a beautiful woman and the boy felt his face color as he lowered his eyes and waited for her to speak.

"Where'd you park your bicycle?" she asked finally.

"We don't have bicycles," the boy said. "I had to walk."

"Is that why you got here so fast?"

"I came as soon as I could," the boy said. "I had to make four stops before I came here."

"I wasn't being sarcastic. You came sooner than we expected. Can you wait a few minutes? My husband is busy."

"I can wait," the boy said.

"Come inside then." The woman stepped back and he followed her into the apartment. As he moved inside, he noted immediately how expensively decorated the room was, and he detected faintly, as if it were far away, a sharp sweet scent that

In *Great Tales of City Dwellers*, ed. Alex Austin (New York: Lion Library Editions, 1955).

lingered in the air. He stared about him with wondrous respect at the large room and at the rich furnishings that met his gaze wherever he looked. There were several photographs about the room and behind her, he noticed a cigarette burning in a silver ash tray.

"How do you like it?" the woman asked caustically.

"I'm sorry," the boy said. "I was just looking around."

"Don't be sorry. You can look around all you want. It's a privilege we extend to the proletariat."

She walked across the room, picked up the cigarette, and crushed it out. She turned slowly and looked at him.

"I bet it's just like your own home."

The boy remained silent. He stood in the center of the room, feeling warm and uncomfortable, and moved his cap slowly in his hands.

"Isn't it?" the woman persisted.

"No," the boy answered softly.

"Why isn't it? I suppose your home is nicer."

The boy didn't speak.

"Is it?"

"My home isn't as nice as this," the boy said.

The woman turned from him and picked a cigarette from an ivory box. On the table, there were some glasses, a bottle of whiskey, and a bottle of soda. She lighted her cigarette and turned, exhaling smoke through the side of her mouth.

"It's a beautiful place, isn't it?" she asked.

"Yes," he said. "It's very beautiful."

"I suppose you think anybody can be happy living here." When he didn't answer, she asked, "Don't you?"

"I don't know." The boy looked down at the floor.

"Don't rationalize. You know damn well they can. Don't you realize the power of money?"

The boy looked up and met her eyes. "Why are you picking on me?" he asked. "I didn't do anything to you."

The woman raised her hand and rubbed it across her cheek, leaving a pallid mark that disappeared instantly, and she pursed her lips together in a nervous expression of regret. "I'm sorry. I didn't mean to pick on you. I'm upset. I have to talk to you until my husband comes and I don't know what to say."

The boy smiled, realizing she was under some strain. She was very beautiful and he was sorry for her.

"What's your name?" she asked.

"Sidney."

A man called from another room, "Who is it?"

"It's the messenger," the woman answered.

"How does he look?"

The woman looked at the boy. He stood without moving, turning his cap slowly in his hands and wondering what they wanted him for.

"He's pretty," the woman said. "But he's very young."

There was the sound of footsteps on tile, and a thin, middle-aged man entered the room, wearing a deep blue dressing gown with a towel around his neck and holding an razor in his hands. He nodded coldly to the boy as he studied him. The woman sat down in a corner of the sofa. She kicked off her shoes and tucked her legs up behind her.

The man frowned. "He looks effeminate."

"That would be just my luck," the woman said bitterly.

"I'll send him back." The man stepped toward the boy and smiled. "Look, go back to the office and tell them to send an older boy. We have a special errand and we need an older boy. Do you understand?"

The boy nodded and turned to go.

"Let him stay," the woman said. "I think it will be better with him."

"Do you really think so?"

The woman nodded.

"All right." He turned to the boy. "I'll be with you in a few minutes. Sit down and wait. Give him a drink, Skelly," he said to the woman and left the room.

"Sit down, Sidney." The boy walked across the room and sat down in a chair facing her. "And don't look so uncomfortable. No one is going to hurt you."

He placed his cap on a table near the chair and looked about the room curiously, disturbed because the woman was watching him. There was a photograph of a good-looking boy in a football uniform, and he wondered if he was her son. She looked too young to be his mother. The sweet smell in the room was growing fainter, and he sniffed for it unconsciously.

"What's the matter?" the woman asked.

"Nothing," the boy said.

"Don't be afraid of me. What were you smelling?"

"There's something sweet in the air," the boy said. "Like perfume."

"Incense. I was burning it before you came in. Do you want a drink?"

He shook his head.

"I didn't think so. You're too young to drink."

"I drink," the boy said.

"Whiskey?"

"Sometimes," he lied. "I like beer, though."

"I have some in the kitchen. Do you want a bottle?"

"No, thanks. We're not allowed to drink when we're working."

"Do you smoke?"

"We're not allowed to smoke either."

"You go ahead and smoke," the woman said. "I'll keep your secret. Do they pay you well?"

"Pretty well."

"How much do you make a week?"

"I don't make so much," the boy explained. "I only work after school. The ones that work all week make a lot."

"You're going to make a lot today," the woman said, sitting up as she crushed her cigarette out. She poured some whiskey into a glass and added some soda. She stared soberly into the glass for a few seconds as she swirled it around in quick circles. Then she raised the glass and emptied it. The boy watched her face. She swallowed without expression.

"Sidney," she said, setting the glass down. "You're a very pretty boy. I'll bet the girls in school go wild over you."

The boy turned away, flushing with embarrassment.

"Do you go with girls?"

He nodded.

"I'll bet you have a lot of them."

"I have a few," the boy answered. He felt good because she thought so.

"Do you get much?"

The boy thought he had misunderstood her and turned to her questioningly.

"You know what I mean. Are you still virginal?"

The boy's face burned with shame and he stared down at a patch of rug between the legs of a round table that stood before the large window.

"You don't have to answer if you don't want to."

"I don't want to."

"All right, don't. If you are, it's your own fault. The girls in school are wild about you."

"No, they aren't," the boy said, smiling shyly.

"Yes, they are. You look around and you'll see. You're a very pretty boy, Sidney. I'd like to see you on a cold day. I bet your lips and cheeks turn crimson when it's cold."

Sidney smiled with guilt. He had already noticed how red his lips and cheeks became on a cold day and how fair and clean-looking he was compared to other boys his age. He had been kept close to home while his father was alive, and it was only recently that he had been allowed the freedom of observation. The world about him was beginning to unfold slowly in a vast and puzzling panorama, delighting him with each new revelation. He pointed to the picture of the boy in the football uniform.

"Is that your son?" he asked.

"No," the woman said. "It's Mr. Ingall's son." When he looked puzzled, she explained, "I'm his second wife."

"Oh."

"He used to stay here six months during the year, but now he's away at college. He hasn't been here for almost six years."

She reached forward and took another cigarette, tapping it nervously against the back of her hand. She picked up the lighter and turned to him, hesitating, and her face became really soft for the first time.

"You're a nice boy, Sidney," she said slowly. "The girls are crazy about you. I was your age once and I know. Get as many as you can before it's too late. That's what they're here for. Take them while you can and you'll never regret it." She stopped speaking when she saw how uncomfortable he looked. "What's the matter?"

"I don't know," he mumbled.

"Are you always afraid to talk to girls?"

"No," he answered.

"Then what is it? Don't you ever discuss such things with them?"

"It isn't that. We talk dirty."

"Then what is it? I'm a girl."

"I don't know."

"Is it because I'm older than you, or because I'm so nice looking?"

"That's probably what it is."

"Don't be vague. Which is it? Age or appearance."

"Both, I guess."

She lighted her cigarette and leaned back. "Do you think I'm nice looking?"

He nodded, blushing.

"Beautiful?"

He nodded again. He looked towards the foyer, wondering when the man would return.

"What do you like about me?"

"Everything, I guess. You're a beautiful girl."

"There must be something special you like. Is it my face, or my breasts, or the way you imagine my thighs are shaped?"

The boy felt himself perspiring and looked at a table in the corner, staring at it with intense interest to relieve the shame and embarrassment that rose within him. He noticed an object on the table with a small rubber tube and a glass water container attached and he wondered what it was.

"Well? Which is it?"

"I wish you wouldn't talk like that," he said.

"All right," the woman said. "I won't talk like that. How would you like to go to bed with me?"

He turned to her with surprise, angry now and afraid. Her husband was in the next room and he suspected some trick. "I have to go," he said, and stood up. "I have to get back to the office."

"All right, Sidney," she said, with a shrug. "Sit down. I won't bother you." He sat down slowly, watching her with suspicious concern. "What's the matter?" she asked. "Don't I appeal to you?"

"Not that way," the boy answered, in a low voice.

"Why not? If you saw me walking on the street I'd appeal to you. Wouldn't I?"

He turned away. She was the most beautiful woman he had ever spoken to, and he knew that if he ever did see her walking on the street, he would stop and stare after her until she disappeared from sight.

"I guess I just don't interest you," the woman said wearily. "What interests you on that table?"

"That thing," he said, pointing. "What is it? A pipe?"

She put her shoes on and walked to the table, motioning for him to follow. He walked after her and stood beside her, trying not to stare at the curves of her body as he looked at the object.

"It's a pipe," she said, picking it up and showing it to him.

"What's the water for?"

"To cool the smoke. We smoke strong tobacco. Hashish. Do you know what hashish is?"

"It's a drug, isn't it?"

"Yes," she said. "It's a drug. Do you want some?"

He stepped back quickly and shook his head. The man entered the room and joined them at the table.

"What are you doing?" he asked.

"I'm offering junior some of our tobacco. With boys who know tobacco best, it's hashish two to one."

The man took the pipe from her and set it down. "Are you crazy?" he said quietly. "He's a minor."

"He'll still be a minor when we put him to work," the woman said.

"All right, Skelly. Please shut up. Go inside. And hurry up. We can't keep him here all day."

She handed him her cigarette and walked from the room. The man turned to Sidney and smiled. He was somewhere in his late forties, with deep, serious eyes, and his face, clean shaven with a tiny blood spot behind his jaw bone, was marked with deep lines running down from the sides of his nostrils to the corners of his mouth. His voice was soft and smooth, calm and serious. He led Sidney to the center of the room and they sat down facing each other.

"Do they mind if you stay out long?" he asked.

"I can't stay too long," Sidney said.

"Can you fix it up someway if we keep you?"

"I don't know," the boy answered.

The man reached into the pocket of his dressing gown and removed two bills. He held one out. Sidney took it, smiling shyly, and put it away, noting, as he folded it, that it was a ten-dollar bill.

"That's for waiting so long," the man said. "I'll give you the other one when you do what we want."

"What do you want me to do?" the boy asked suspiciously.

"Didn't Skelly tell you?"

"No."

"Well, don't worry about it. It isn't anything much." He poured a drink. "Do you want one?"

"No, thanks," the boy said. "What do you want me to do?"

"We'll tell when she comes in." He swallowed the whiskey, making a wry face, and set the glass down. "What do you think of her?"

"She's very attractive," the boy answered.

"She's beautiful," the man said. "Do you like her?"

The boy nodded cautiously. "She's very pretty."

"She's beautiful," the man repeated. He seemed very distressed, very tired. He started to pour another drink, stopped himself, and set the bottle down. "She's an actress," he said.

The boy was pleased. It was a new experience talking to an actress and he was appropriately thrilled. "Are you an actor?"

"I'm on the radio," the man said. He stared thoughtfully before him for several moments. "She's very unhappy," he said, slowly, looking up. "We're both very unhappy."

The boy listened with interest.

"That's why we called you. It's an experiment. Would you want to help us?"

"I'd like to if I can," the boy said.

"All right. Maybe you can. How old are you?"

"I was just seventeen."

"Just a kid. A happy, oblivious kid. You're a good-looking boy. I'll bet you make out all right with the girls."

The boy didn't answer.

"You can talk to me," the man said. "I'm not a woman. Have you had much experience with girls?"

"I go with them a lot," the boy admitted.

"Are they fast?"

"Some of them are," Sidney answered. "Some aren't."

"Do you like the fast ones?"

Sidney grinned sheepishly. "What do you think?"

"Are they pretty?"

"A few are. Most of them aren't."

"You'll find that all through life. Are any of them as pretty as Skelly?"

"No," the boy said. "None are that pretty."

The man leaned forward. "She's really a beautiful girl, isn't she?" he asked, watching the boy closely.

"Yes," he answered. "She is."

"How would you like to make love to her?" the man asked.

The boy turned away quickly. There was a strong undercurrent of intensity in the man's behavior, the same desperate emotion that stirred beneath the woman's manner. It was a strange, threatening current, and he was afraid because it was new to him and he did not know what it meant. The man's eyes were fixed upon him as he waited for a reply.

"I'd like a girl as pretty as her," the boy admitted, in a low, hesitant voice.

The man watched him silently for a while. Then he leaned back in the chair, drumming his fingers slowly on his knee. "Do you ever get lost when you're working?" he asked.

"I used to at first," Sidney said. "I still do sometimes when they send me uptown."

"It's a hell of a feeling, isn't it?"

"It isn't so bad. The first time I was a little scared. Now I just ask somebody. It sure is a big city."

"It's a hell of a feeling being lost in a great city," the man said slowly. "And the world is full of great cities." His voice was deep and solemn. He spoke slowly, staring straight ahead, and his words seemed to emanate from a trance. "The human mind is a great city in which the individual is always lost. He spends his lifetime groping, trying to locate himself."

The boy listened solemnly, too impressed to reply.

"We're still strangers when we die," the man continued. "Lost in a great big city."

He stood up and walked slowly to the window. He stared out at the lost afternoon without moving, and the boy felt that he had forgotten his presence. The man said quietly:

"It's a horrible picture when you think of it that way. A naked arm in every brain groping its way through a great, black city. Can't you just see a world full of naked, groping arms?"

He turned and looked at the boy. He had his hand to his forehead, running his fingers slowly around his temple. "I can feel the arm in my own head. I get headaches. I can feel the fingers probing through the tissues." He looked at the boy with surprise, as though just discovering he was there. "Do you know what I'm talking about?"

"I think so," the boy said.

"No you don't. You're too young. And it's just as well." He walked into the foyer. "God damn it, Skelly. Hurry up. The kid doesn't have all day."

He walked across the room and seated himself in a chair facing the sofa. He poured some whiskey into a glass and held it between his legs, staring down at the floor. After a few seconds, the woman returned. The boy sat up with surprise when he saw her. She had changed into a blue dressing gown and slippers, and when she walked across the room and sat down on the sofa, he could see the lithe, round lines of her body rippling beneath the film of material.

"Well?" she asked, looking at the man.

"Tell him," he said. "This is your idea."

"I thought you were going to."

"Do you want me to?"

The woman nodded. The man raised the glass to his lips and drained it. The boy watched his face curl into an expression of distaste as he swallowed, waiting expectantly as he felt himself in the center of a strange, elastic puzzle. The man set the glass on a table and turned to the woman.

"You do it," he said.

"All right," the woman said, and turned to Sidney. "Have you ever seen a naked woman?"

The boy looked away sharply. He felt the silence grow in the room and start to tingle and then ring in his ears.

"For chrisakes, don't be coy. Have you or haven't you?"

"No," the boy answered faintly.

"Would you like to?"

Through the corner of his eye, the boy watched the folds of her gown, terrified, not knowing what she was going to do. He felt panic rise within him, and the seconds crawled ominously.

"All right, Skelly," the man said. "I'll do it. You have no tact." He turned and looked at the boy. "Here's what we want you to do. We want you to make believe that Skelly is one of your girl friends."

The boy's breath caught in his throat. "What do you mean?"

"You know what I mean. Sit down and neck with her."

The boy leaped to his feet. His face was hot and damp, his body cold with terror. "No!" he said, blurting the word out. "I won't do it. Here." He groped in his pocket. "Here's your money back."

"Forget the money," the man said. "That's yours. Why won't you do it?"

"Because it isn't right, that's why."

The man shook his head slowly and smiled. "You don't understand. It isn't anything wrong." He pointed to the photograph of the boy in football clothes. "You see that boy?" he asked. Sidney nodded. "That's our son. Mine and Skelly's. He's dead now. Skelly misses him. You know how mothers are. We just want you to kiss her, to sort of take his place."

The boy remembered what the woman had told him, and knew the man was lying, but the fear left him slowly. He remembered how the man had turned from the window with his fingers on his forehead.

"You mean you want me to kiss her like she was my mother?" he asked.

"No. Just make believe she's one of your girl friends, the one you like best. That's all."

Sidney glanced at the woman. She was watching him with a tight, hopeful expression. The man leaned forward, waiting with hopeful impatience for the boy to decide.

"All right," the boy said. "I'll kiss her if she says it's all right."

The woman smiled weakly and nodded. "It's all right."

The man stood up and walked to the liquor tray. The woman rose, beckoning the boy to approach, and he walked to her slowly. Behind him he heard the light splash of whiskey spilling into the glass. He came to a stop before her. She was an inch or two taller, and he looked up at her, trembling with fear and uncertainty. She held up her arms.

The man stood to the side, motionless, watching with rigid attention. "Go ahead," he said, when the boy glanced his way. "It's all right."

The boy swallowed nervously. He leaned forward and kissed her on the mouth. The woman slid her arms around him. The boy raised his hands slowly to her shoulders. As he felt his fingers touch her, he pulled his face away quickly and stepped back with alarm.

"What's the matter?" the man demanded.

"He's afraid," the woman said.

"No wonder. You look like you're gonna scratch his eyes out. Smile at him."

The woman turned to the boy and smiled. Her face grew soft and appealing, and deeply sorrowful. The boy felt touched with tenderness, and he smiled back slowly. He stepped near her. She took his arms and placed them around her. She pulled his face against her own and slid her arms around him in a tight grip. Then she began kissing him about his mouth. The boy was too frightened to move.

"He's not doing anything!" the woman cried, tearing her face away and throwing it back against his neck. Her shoulders shook and the boy knew she was crying. He felt the giant sobs roll through her body beneath his arms.

The man ran up behind him and beat his hands on his back, shouting, "Kiss her! God damn you! Kiss her!"

He pushed him hard with both hands, and they tumbled to the sofa. The woman's sobs were piercing his ears and he opened his eyes. Her face was wracked with despair. Suddenly, she put her hands on his shoulders and pushed him away violently. He fell to the floor on his knees. He rose quickly and scooted across the room, away from the man who was glaring down at the woman with a wild, fiery expression.

"It's no use!" she cried. "He's too young."

The man whirled upon the boy. "Go back to the office," he shouted. "Tell them to send an older boy. Do you understand? An older boy. We want an older boy."

The boy nodded. He ran to the table and grabbed his cap, glancing quickly at the woman, whose loud, hysterical cries were tearing through him in waves of pain. The man caught him when he started to the door.

"Wait a minute. Don't tell anybody anything. Forget what happened. Do you understand?"

"Tell them!" the woman cried. "Tell everybody!"

"Shut up, Skelly. For God's sake, shut up."

The woman rose and ran to the boy, her face haggard with hysteria. "Tell everybody, Sidney," she sobbed. "Tell the whole damned world." Her words stumbled over her sobs and she began to shriek.

"Skelly, shut up," the man pleaded, catching her shoulders. "Please shut up."

The boy watched her, unable to move. Her face was like chalk, shaking and cruelly distorted as she struggled to break away.

The man raised his hand and slapped her across the face, stunning her with surprise. He backed her up slowly and let her collapse in a chair. He looked down at her sadly for a moment. Then he turned to the boy and walked him to the door.

"Don't tell anyone a thing," he said. He pushed the other bill in the boy's hand. "Forget all about it. Do you understand?"

The boy could hear the woman sobbing softly, and behind the man, he could see her shoulders shaking in the chair.

"Remember now. Don't tell anyone. Okay?"

The boy nodded.

The man opened the door. "You'll forget all about it, won't you?"

The boy nodded again and stepped into the hall.

The door slammed shut.

MacADAM'S LOG

The captain's first voyage, the beginning of a long and distinguished career on the high seas, had taken place a number of years earlier when his sister, the last surviving relative of his own generation, had sailed back to Scotland to die. She did not give that as her purpose, of course, substituting instead some obstinate nonsense about a girlhood friend now alone and in failing health; but the Captain, whose recollection of the many vast and shambling decades behind him remained surprisingly acute, remembered clearly that he himself was but nine years old when his father, a burly shipwright with a ringing laugh that sounded frequently now in the Captain's thoughts, had uprooted his mother, his wife, and his seven "bairn" in one gigantic impulse that carried them all swiftly from Glasgow over the ocean to Portland, Maine, and that his sister was little more than an infant at the time and could not possibly have severed any close relationships.

The Captain, saddened by her gray and thin appearance, did not raise this objection. He gazed at her with the kindest of expressions, asked only the most innocent questions, and in secret tried vainly to understand. It was twenty years since they had seen each other, five since they had written, and the occasion of their last contact had been the death by heart failure of a brother

Gentlemen's Quarterly, vol. 29, December 1959, pp. 112; 166–76, 178.

in Tucumcari, New Mexico. She had married early and settled with her husband in Richfield, Minnesota, where a sturdy procession of children had come from her during her fertile years, six sons and three daughters in all, not one of whom, it appeared, was able to free himself even temporarily and insist strongly enough upon accompanying her to New York.

It was the day she sailed that first provided the Captain with the grand inspiration that ultimately sent him to sea. The Captain had not been aboard ship since that eventful time nearly fifty years before, and he was left breathless now by the sudden spectacle of the broad and massive vessel with all its ornate luxury glittering endlessly in every direction and its noble air of dignified and compact strength. He was reluctant to go further when, with Neil and Cynthia, he was at last standing on the pier.

"I don't think she'll come to the rail," Neil said, with a meaningful glance at his watch.

"No," murmured the Captain regretfully, recalling that they were busy people, his daughter and his son-in-law. "I suppose not." Still, he lingered. "You two go on," he advised finally. "I have to stay in the city anyway."

He waited patiently as Cynthia kissed his cheek and straightened his tie with a reproving frown. Then, when they had gone, he moved back to where the guests of the other passengers had collected excitedly against a wooden barrier. A daring humor came over him, and he began waving gently toward the figure of a strange woman he had picked out on the topmost deck. Of course, there was no response. He would have been terrified if there had been. Serene and contented, he remained there, beaming benevolently at his anonymous and unsuspecting friend until the ship began to move.

The people about him were soon dispersing, but the Captain stayed on until it was no longer in sight. Across the river, which glistened in places with filthy slicks of oil, the Jersey bluffs were tranquil and clear in the soft daylight. Above them a noiseless flock of clouds dozed like sleeping swans. Slowly it all dissolved, and he could see the open ocean, its vast, blue grandeur rolling calmly and majestically before him into the timeless deep and distance, and it was with this bright vision in mind that he finally turned away.

After that it was only a matter of time before the Captain went to sea.

In the suburban home he shared with Neil and Cynthia and his two grandchildren, there was little to keep him occupied. The Captain had accepted superannuation gracefully—not without regret, it is true, but submissively and without protest. Twenty-seven unstinting years in the hardware business had bred in him a need for purpose and activity, and his retirement, effected by illness and increasing fatigue, found him unprepared for idleness. He was restless and bored, distressed by things he had never before had time to notice, and he was quick to consider the diversion which his sister's departure had suggested.

Even the children did not claim much of his time. He was there whenever they required him, if only to be the victim of their sometimes painful pranks, but he never imposed his presence, and he would have reacted violently to the mere suggestion of ever trying to extract affection from them. They were both spoiled, Nevil, who had been named in tribute to Neil's father, and little Nan, both given to veering moods and raucous displays of temperament. Nan already suffered from harrowing nightmares and would fill the house regularly with her tortured cries. On these occasions it was the Captain who rose and went to her room and shook her gently awake and soothed and consoled her. She was afraid of the darkness, and what she really wanted was someone to share the room with her; but Nevil was of different sex, and Neil and Cynthia resolutely opposed the Captain's solution of allowing them to dwell together.

Only once did the Captain intervene directly between parent and child, and the mere memory of that affair still filled him with dread. Nevil had unintentionally injured Nan slightly in a game they were playing, and Neil stormed out in a rage and began beating the boy, cursing aloud in a vicious outburst that left no care for the direction or force of his blows. The Captain held back as long as he could and then hooked on to Neil's shoulders and tried to restrain him. Neil whirled, a look of brutal hatred on his face, and for a moment the Captain actually feared for his life.

"You're—hurting him," he managed to cry feebly.

Neil showed no sign of having heard. In another second something disastrous might have occurred, but the situation was brought mercifully to a close by the boy, who collapsed in his father's hands.

When Dr. Berensen arrived he was told that Nevil had fallen down the basement steps. He was with the boy a long time, and he returned with an angry frown. Neil followed and lurked sheepishly about the doorway, but Dr. Berensen ignored him and spoke tersely to the Captain.

"What happened to him, Andrew?"

"Will he be all right?"

"I don't know if he'll be all right. His injuries aren't serious, if that's what you mean. Andrew, what happened to him?"

"He fell down the steps."

"I'd like to see those steps. Andy, why do you call me? I retired seven years ago."

"Cynthia wants you. You're the only doctor she's ever had."

"Tell her to get someone else," Dr. Berensen snapped. "I don't understand cases like these." He ended his agitated pacing and continued in a milder voice. "How have you been, Andrew? Stomach all right?" But before he left, he said: "I mean that, Andrew. Don't call me for anything like this again."

It was Dr. Berensen who had delivered Cynthia into the world, and Dr. Berensen also who two years later was forced to stand by helplessly after an abortive attempt at a caesarean had opened a hemorrhage through which the substance of the Captain's first treasure had emptied remorselessly. The Captain had never married again. For one thing, Cynthia would not have permitted it. Almost from the start she had shown a jealous possessiveness; and now she guarded him with a greedy solicitude which kept him closely at her side and made him account for each moment away from the house. The Captain had some small investments and would have preferred living elsewhere, but he had been moved to a point where only to oblige was an occupation, and he did not quarrel.

It was not until Cynthia went away to college that the Captain really tasted loneliness. They had been close to each other, but one day she returned to him a stranger, nervous in conversation and inflexibly determined to be about affairs of her own. She already knew Neil, and soon she disclosed their plans for an early marriage.

"We'd both really like a small wedding, but Neil is an only child and Mrs. Stevens has always wanted something special. She says she'll take care of all the expenses if you let her manage it."

"Please tell her," said the Captain, "that it doesn't matter to me who pays for it. I do feel, though, that you and Neil should decide what kind of ceremony to have."

The wedding took place under the direction of Mrs. Stevens. It was a truly impressive affair, one by which each guest seemed more than properly awed, and in due time the bills for it all found their way to the Captain's table.

It was the week after his sister sailed that the Captain's future was virtually determined.

He was called into the city one day—as executor of a deceased friend's will, it was his unpleasant role to preside over a quarrel that had broken out among the beneficiaries—and he soon found himself alone with the whole of a beautiful spring day still before him. In his newspaper he saw that the *Washing-*

ton was sailing that very noon, sailing for such distant retreats as Cobh, Le Havre, and Southampton. A moment's hesitation and he was in a cab. Almost miraculously he found himself aboard the ship, with no obligation this time to confine his roaming. A sense of indescribable ease and contentment pervaded him, and as he moved leisurely over the decks and through the passageways he could not help pretending to himself that he really was sailing. Back on the pier, he did not wave to anyone, but he found the experience even more wonderful than before, and his imagination was still more deeply stirred.

A coincidence, though very slight, finally decided him.

He was drawn from his bed several days later for one of the powders Dr. Berensen had provided for his gastric attacks and then—that very same morning—learned from the papers that the *Washington* had been delayed and was tossing in heavy seas outside of Southampton.

It had been a miserable crossing—very miserable, indeed, if even the Captain suffered with seasickness—but the return trip more than atoned for it with a daily treat of quiet waters, gentle winds, and endlessly invigorating showers of clean air and sunshine.

The Captain passed the time in a deckchair on his porch, smiling up placidly at the porcelain sky, or playing shuffleboard with a very young lady whose acquaintance he made his second day at sea. An Austrian girl orphaned by the Anschluss, she was on her way to Atlanta—a city she fervently hoped would not be too unlike Vienna. She spoke English with a fetching inaccuracy and brooded continually over the Captain's inability to remember his muffler.

Two days at home and he was away again, this time on the *Nieuw Amsterdam.* He was not sorry to go.

Neil had begun the Captain's shoreleave by renewing his assault on the management of the Captain's securities, the inducement this time being an oil issue to appear shortly. The amount actually involved was small, but Neil, himself with an investment house, was incessantly annoyed by the matter of the Captain's own broker, and it required consummate tact to resist him. Finally he gave up. Almost immediately the children were at his side.

"What's oil?" Nan demanded.

"Petroleum."

"What's petroleum?"

Neil turned angrily to where Cynthia was busy at the table. Cynthia belonged to a women's organization devoted to the maintenance of a nursing home for children, and she was engaged in estimating the receipts to accumulate from the annual spring luncheon, at which, for the first time, she would be seated on the dais.

"God damn it, Cyn! Can't you keep them away from me on my one day off?"

Cynthia faced him with an icy stare. "Don't swear at me in front of the children. I've told you that before."

The Captain spied the storm warnings, and he quickly guided the children into the study. Once there they waited expectantly. The Captain, remembering something Dr. Berensen had once told him about the childhood of Robert Browning, picked a book from the desk and placed it on the carpet.

"This," he began cautiously, "is oil. A very valuable thing, and very hard to get. Now, the first thing we must do is bring it out of the ground. You two are a bit younger than I am, so you handle the drilling. I'll sit back and try to supervise."

In a moment they were all transported to the plains of Texas, laboring happily for the strike that would soon be theirs. They made phenomenal progress and were already in the refinery—Nevil had just castigated Nan severely for smoking in the plant—when Neil appeared, wearing that boyish indecision which always spelled repentance.

"What's going on?"

"Come on, Daddy," Nan cried. "We're getting the oil out."

Neil relaxed a bit. "What's that book doing on the floor?"

"That's not a book. That's *oil.*"

"Oil is something else," Neil said. "That's only a book."

The children were suddenly embarrassed. They drew away from the Captain accusingly.

"Grandpa said it was oil."

Neil began to understand, and he spoke with a loud buoyancy that echoed strangely in the quiet room. "Well, it isn't really oil, but I guess we can make believe it is. Come on! Let's get it out."

But Nan had had enough, and she marched indignantly through the door. Nevil followed, leaving a strained silence behind.

"I—I guess I spoiled their game."

"It wasn't important."

"I—I hope you understand that I don't mean to speak roughly to the kids or to Cynthia. It's just—just that sometimes they get after me when I'm in a bad mood."

The Captain said nothing.

The next evening Ralph Paterson came there for dinner. Neil drew the Captain aside in the afternoon.

"He's not too nice a person, I guess," he said nervously. "He has some pretty unusual opinions about Hitler and doesn't care who knows it. But he's really not bad when you know him, and anyway, he's a very important client and we have to handle him with kid gloves."

The Captain saw the familiar hint. It was an effort to keep his voice steady. "Truthfully, Neil, I wasn't planning to dine tonight. I'm a bit tired, and I thought I'd have something light and retire early."

"Oh, I didn't mean that I didn't want you there," Neil hastened to explain. "It's just—just that I know how strongly you feel about what's going on over there. He's pretty touchy, and it would sort of make things awkward if you got into a—a discussion."

The Captain was grateful when the chance to sail on the *Nieuw Amsterdam* arrived. The Captain liked the *Nieuw Amsterdam* at first sight, was immediately at home there. He was sorry when the time came to make his way back to the pier, but it was with considerable satisfaction that he saw the gangplanks loosened and, amid the festive blare of horns and a sudden, bright shower of falling streamers, watched himself depart on his second voyage.

Having committed himself to a new career, the Captain now plunged into work with an energy and devotion that would have been exhausting in someone less zealously inclined. Voyage followed voyage, and soon he was at sea almost all the time.

At first Neil and Cynthia treated the whole thing as a joke. The night the Austins, friends of theirs just returned from a trip to Europe, were there, was typical. The Captain liked the Austins, especially Ruth, who called him Andy and teased him blatantly about a young mistress in the city. The Captain rejoiced in this raillery, but it was gall to Cynthia, who would grow tense and resentful and try with stiff perseverance to deflect the conversation. Once she had even fled the room and later had upbraided the Captain fiercely for encouraging Ruth. Neil sided with the Captain and turned on Cynthia angrily, and in the end the Captain was forced to pacify them both. The Captain listened indulgently as the Austins recounted their journey.

"Ah, Cobh," he interrupted at one point. "A lovely harbor."

"Have you been there?"

"Oh, yes. Many times."

"It must have been a long time ago."

"Not so long," smiled the Captain. "In fact, quite recently, you might say."

"That's odd. We didn't even enter the harbor. I thought none of the regular liners ever docked in Ireland."

"It is all a matter of the tides," announced the Captain, recovering from a sudden cough. "As you know, Cobh is a small harbor lined with very dangerous shoals. The tide has to be exactly right before they can bring a large vessel in. It was unfortunate you missed it."

Neil and Cynthia both broke into laughter as soon as the Austins had gone.

"Why, you old faker," Neil cried appreciatively.

"Well," chuckled the Captain. "I have been there."

"When?" demanded Cynthia. "When were you ever there?"

"Oh, a long time ago, my dear. At one time I traveled a great deal."

They were satisfied with that, and once again the Captain prided himself on his navigation. But inwardly he was sober, for he was surprised that Cobh was in Ireland. He had imagined it in one of the Low Countries, in Belgium, Holland, or Norway, and the next day found him guiltily in the town library. It was pleasant there, and he returned often to read about places he was visiting. He would sit by the window and pause for long intervals. He would grow absorbed in the loafers jollying each other across the street or relaxing on the bench in the sunshine, content in their tobacco and quiet talk, men his own age with whom it had been too late to grow familiar.

Actually he learned little from his books, for his fancy would alter each fact to his taste. Italy became a land of festivals and mandolins in which the sole means of conveyance was the gondola. There were no coal mines in Spain; groves of citrus trees covered the countryside, and the women were as fertile as the land and had dark hair and dark eyes and were all lovely and vibrant with a wholesome, passionate, and incorrigibly pagan wantonness.

The Captain's voyages continued, and of all ships he came to prize the *Queen Elizabeth* most, not on merit alone, but also for the historical associations which the name recalled. The Captain had never heard the Elizabethans described as "the giant race before the flood," but it was a judgment in which he would have heartily concurred; and the names Shakespeare, Chaucer, and Milton, Raleigh, Byron, Drake, and Newton all sounded paeans in his thoughts.

The war, of course, changed everything. When duty called, the Captain knew what to do, and he did not hesitate. He enrolled in the merchant marine, and, against the advice of his broker, began converting his securities into defense bonds.

Those were grim years for the Captain, years when the ocean was black and the voyage to Murmansk longer than a trip to Mars. He was torpedoed again and again, eighteen times in all, and once, after floating three days in a blinding gale, was brought to bed with an acute case of indigestion.

"Fried oysters," Dr. Berensen grumbled, in a dour and complaining mood. "Won't you ever grow up?"

"Too much water," declared the Captain.

"What's that?"

The Captain covered a smile, in excellent spirits now that his gravest fears had been dispelled. He was propped up in bed, dapper and gay in a pair of navy blue pajamas, and he pressed a mischievous pinky over his white moustache.

"Too much water," he repeated. "That's what brought it on."

"Water wouldn't bother you. It's what you eat. You have to be careful, Andrew."

"It was the water," the Captain persisted merrily. "You can't expect a man my age not to be affected by icy water."

"Don't drink ice water," Dr. Berensen said. "And don't eat any fried foods. Get some sleep now. I'll be in to see you tomorrow."

"You don't understand," the Captain continued dangerously. "I've been torpedoed."

"We've all been torpedoed," Dr. Berensen said tiredly. He closed his visiting bag and stood up. "Good-bye, Andrew. Please take care of yourself."

Ten days passed before Dr. Berensen grudgingly returned him to duty, but he was proudest of all when the Captain was awarded the D.S.M.O. and his photograph—a poor likeness, everyone admitted—blazoned across the front page of every newspaper in the land.

Shortly after the war ended, a wonderful thing happened to the Captain. He met Mr. Simpson. The Captain had not meant to resume all his activities when peace came, but he was soon at sea again more than ever before. One day as he was peering at the city in a vain attempt to find his bearings, a voice spoke at his side.

"You're an old sailor, I see."

The Captain turned to face a young man in the braided blue uniform of a ship's officer, about Neil's age, with a friendly, uninquisitive smile that stilled the Captain's alarm.

"Yes," he agreed modestly. "How could you tell?"

Mr. Simpson merely smiled. In silence they stared out together past the angulate, green piersheds and the rude juts of land, past the black spouts rising in indolent drifts from the plodding tugboats, at the vanishing sweep of the horizon. The sun was warm and sent channels of sparks shimmering through the water. Only when the stewards appeared did the Captain stir.

"I have to go now. I must—look after my luggage."

"Perhaps I'll see you during the trip."

"Yes," said the Captain. "Yes, of course."

Furtively he made his way ashore, dazed by this truly astonishing encounter, and at home that evening he was unable to resist describing his fortuitous reunion that day with his good friend Mr. Simpson.

"Who?" asked Cynthia.

"Mr. Simpson. Surely you remember my telling you about him. He's the officer I met on one of my voyages."

"Oh," grunted Neil. "One of your voyages."

The Captain fell silent, sulking because he had been prepared to enumerate the many adventures which only a man in Mr. Simpson's profession could enjoy. Impatiently he looked forward to their next meeting. Cynthia detained him that morning with a plea to extend his leave.

"You aren't going into the city again? Please, Daddy, you know how it tires you."

"I'm afraid I must," he lied. "More trouble with the estate."

He found Mr. Simpson in the same place, and the young man could not conceal his amazement when he saw the Captain.

"Hello! Sailing again?"

The Captain nodded and came to a palpitating halt.

"Let's see," Mr. Simpson began musing aloud, and broke off with a look of puzzlement.

The faint, trembling signs of a smile hovered eagerly, hope-fully, about the Captain's mouth. His forehead was burning, and his heart thumped wildly in a desperate prayer. He had taken his umbrella with him. It embarrassed him now as he held it feebly before him. All this while Mr. Simpson was peering at him intently. Finally he seemed to understand, and his face opened with a gentle smile.

"I'm very glad you could make it," he said softly. "I was afraid we'd have to sail without you."

The Captain released a thankful sigh.

"I'm sorry I was unable to see you during the last trip," Mr. Simpson went on. "I spent most of my time below. A lovely voyage, wasn't it?"

"Yes, lovely," said the Captain. "The loveliest voyage," he confided, with a chuckle, "that I have ever made."

Mr. Simpson laughed appreciatively, and from then on the

Captain sailed on only one ship. He did not make every voyage—sometimes the weather was inclement and occasionally a prior commitment to Dr. Berensen confined him to the house—but whenever he did sail it was with Mr. Simpson as his first mate. A close friendship grew between them. Often he thought of inviting him to the house, but Neil, he knew, would dislike him.

"What's so wonderful about him?" Neil had challenged one day. "Oh, go right on talking about him if it makes you happy, but try to remember that he's only a sailor, that's all, a sailor."

Mr. Simpson, on the other hand, was always eager to hear about Neil, or about any other subject of which the Captain spoke. He listened to everything with a smile that was always a bit sad, his brown eyes troubled usually with vague flutters of melancholy.

One day he unexpectedly conducted the Captain to his quarters, an experience which thrilled the Captain so, his legs trembled as they walked there. Small bookcases, their shelves full, were set back in the recesses of the square, compact room. Volumes on navigation and engineering were outnumbered by books of plays and poems and by works of philosophy, history, and psychology. There was a collection of sermons by a man named Donne, and several volumes with such inscrutable titles as *The Meaning of Meaning* and *The Allegory of Love*. Both portholes were open, fastened back by sturdy metal hooks, and twin shafts of light converged diagonally through the room. Mr. Simpson stooped over a foot locker and emerged with glasses and a bottle of good brandy.

"These books," asked the Captain, with a certain, conscious naïveté. "Do you use them all for your work?"

Mr. Simpson smiled and shook his head. "Most of them are things I've held on to. I was going to college when the war came."

"And you never went back?"

"It seemed so pointless," Mr. Simpson said. "So out of date. The noise of machines used to fill the library and distract me."

The Captain nodded sympathetically.

"And it's so senseless to make plans," Mr. Simpson went on, with an abrupt touch of bitterness. "We're in the hands of something big. Something sweeps us along, makes us limp along in step, and we can only wriggle our hips a bit from side to side. I get *furious* as I see my time being wasted. There's nothing I'm incapable of. I can do anything, anything at all, just to prove that I've a will of my own."

Mr. Simpson seemed really incensed now, and the Captain sat before him in wonder and awe. Suddenly the mood was shattered by three deafening blasts from the smokestack overhead. Mr. Simpson glanced at his watch and rose with a harsh, erratic laugh.

"My God! It's late. We'll have to hurry."

The Captain, responding with alarm to the distress signal, rushed out behind him. He attained the gangplank with only a minute to spare, but his relief was only momentary and melted into regret when, safe and breathless on the pier, he yearningly contemplated the many enviable embarrassments which could have been his had he delayed but a few minutes longer.

It was not until after Cynthia's recovery that the Captain saw Mr. Simpson again.

Cynthia came home with Neil one afternoon, tottering weakly against him, her face drawn and bloodless, her eyes dry and burning with a dim, sunken fire. A low moan escaped her.

"She had a fainting spell in my office," Neil explained to the Captain, after he had installed her in the bedroom and returned downstairs.

"We'd better get the doctor."

"I had one come to the office. He says it's nothing to worry about, just—nervous exhaustion." Neil spoke without conviction and produced a grotesque effect when he tried to smile.

There were just the two of them. Nevil was away at military school, and only that very morning Nan had been dispatched unwillingly for a weekend in Connecticut with Neil's parents. Neil went upstairs at regular intervals and returned each time to report that Cynthia was sleeping. A vacant, unearthly stillness filled the house. At dinner there were the tiny bangs of the utensils and the rustling motion of the maid, but the silence was heavier than ever when she had gone, and the place seemed empty and strange, a weird mansion of numberless dark and unapproachable rooms.

Soon Neil journeyed upstairs again. He came stumbling back excitedly.

"She's very sick! She wants Dr. Berensen!"

"You'd better call him."

"I—I wish you would. He'd come quicker if you did."

Dr. Berensen remained with Cynthia a long time. The Captain waited grimly. Neil kept drifting restlessly from room to room, suffering silently in a kind of gloomy and useless desolation. At last Dr. Berensen emerged, moving rapidly with a stern, professional determination.

"How is she, Henry? Is she all right?"

Dr. Berensen brushed by without a word and strode to the telephone. The Captain was incredulous as he arranged for a nurse to be sent immediately.

"Henry, what's wrong? Is she very ill?"

"I have to get back," Dr. Berensen snapped.

For a moment the Captain was stunned. Then he rushed after him and seized his arm. "What is it, Henry? God damn it! Tell me what's wrong!"

Dr. Berensen softened in the Captain's grasp.

"She's very sick, Andrew. She may have to go to the hospital."

"Hospital?" the Captain echoed with dismay. "But what's wrong with her?"

"She has a bad infection," Dr. Berensen said. "A kind of poisoning of the blood."

The Captain turned from him dejectedly and moved into the depths of the living room. A second later Neil drifted from the darkness and paused haltingly in the doorway. The fingers of his large hands worked in salientian spasms.

"Did he tell you?"

The Captain nodded.

Neil took another step forward. "I want you to know," he said, "that it wasn't my fault. I didn't care about it one way or the other."

The Captain gazed at him with dull, unresponsive eyes.

"I can see you don't believe me," Neil went on abjectly. "Well, I guess it doesn't matter. But it was Cynthia's idea. She wanted it." He broke off sharply. "What did Dr. Berensen tell you?" he demanded.

The Captain turned from him and stared down glumly at the red carpet. "He told me that Cynthia is very ill," he said tonelessly, "that she may have to go to the hospital."

"Oh." Neil groaned and murmured something inaudible, then drifted back and slipped soundlessly away.

It was almost midnight when Dr. Berensen, at last ready to depart, told the Captain that Cynthia was waiting to see him.

"Henry!"

"Go on up, Andrew, I'll do all I can."

In Cynthia's room everything was still. The nurse, a woman of Cynthia's years with strong eyes and clear, hardened features, sat soundlessly in a corner. Cynthia gazed upward with a distant stare. The veins of her hands were a vivid, glistening blue, and her brittle fingers lay motionless before her like fallen soldiers.

"Tell her to go out," she said weakly.

The nurse rose, but the Captain restrained her.

"It isn't necessary for you to talk."

"I want to talk. Oh, Daddy, Daddy! I've made you so miserable. I've made such a mess of everything, such a rotten mess!"

The Captain placed his hand over her mouth and forced her gently back to the pillow. "Please try to rest, my dear. You haven't made me miserable, and there is nothing I want you to explain. You must get well, Cynthia. That's all that matters to me now."

Slowly she began to cry. Once before the Captain had watched a woman weep. That was when his own wife had revealed that she must soon undergo surgery. She had carried the knowledge in silence until she could no longer bear it alone, and one evening all her aching fear and misery came gushing out violently. Time had dimmed the vision, but it came back to him now in frightening detail, and he caught a ruthless glimpse of the moment through the yellowed, vacillating shadows of the past. Cynthia cried a long while, without sound or motion, and her face was like a weeping stone beneath the Captain's comforting hand. Finally the tears stopped, and she smiled up at him with a deep and wistful affection.

"My daddy," she murmured, with loving pride. "My daddy."

There were three days of doubt, three days in which the fear of death haunted each trudging moment, and then the fever broke. She wanted the Captain with her always, was unwilling to spare him for even a moment. For Neil she had absolutely no use. When she was well enough, she took the Captain with her to a small farmhouse in Vermont. It was May and they were the only guests, and for a while it was all very pleasant. But she regained strength rapidly and grew restless, and after a week she transferred them both to a livelier and more popular resort nearer New York. This was no haven for the Captain, and he waited only until she was safely settled before he came to her with a lie.

"It's that infernal estate again. I must return at once."

Cynthia made no attempt to dissuade him. "Tell Neil to come up," she said, with a slight whine. "Tell him to come right away. I'm really not well enough to be left alone."

Six weeks on land were more than enough for the Captain, and he was glad to get back to sea.

"Did you enjoy your leave?" was Mr. Simpson's casual greeting when the Captain finally showed himself on deck.

"No, not really," the Captain admitted, as he advanced slowly to the rail. "My daughter was ill."

"She's all right now, I hope."

"Yes," said the Captain cheerlessly. "As good as ever."

Mr. Simpson studied him a moment and turned away. A gray launch cut deftly through the water with a lonely roar. The small waves it raised came billowing in lazily against the pilings and washed back in a greasy froth. It was a dreary, depressing day; a brooding silence filled the air.

"We have some time," Mr. Simpson suggested suddenly. "How would you like to inspect the engine room?"

The Captain whirled disbelievingly.

Mr. Simpson laughed and guided him through a door, and suddenly they were spiraling down through a glittering array of valves and instruments, grotesque metal fittings, and unending planes of giant rivet heads. Men of flowing brawn labored everywhere, and the Captain noted the deference with which they regarded him. Down they went to the very bottom, where a huge, powerful shaft glistened in golden oil amid a queer, clacking battery of gears and pistons. From every side came the resonant harmony of clinking iron and hissing steam. There the Captain was introduced to Mr. Henslowe, another officer.

"I'm very pleased to know you, Captain," Mr. Henslowe said. "I hope you like our ship."

The Captain was far too excited to reply. He did not dare tamper with anything, but every second convinced him that he had never in his life known such intense joy.

That was the grandest of the Captain's adventures, a fitting climax, as it proved, for soon after he was to sail on his last voyage.

It was but a few weeks later that Ralph Paterson came unexpectedly to the house, bringing with him his recent bride, a fair young girl less than half his age. The Captain was caught by their sudden arrival, and he planned to excuse himself after a decent interval, but he noticed how the new Mrs. Paterson was excluded from the group and sat ill at ease. He engaged her gently in conversation, and she responded gratefully. She was soon absorbed in his descriptions of foreign places. They were proceeding splendidly when Ralph Paterson swung his attention upon them.

"What's that?" he asked, in his gruff voice. "What's that about Genoa?"

"I was telling Mrs. Paterson," replied the Captain, "that she must certainly see the Blue Grotto if ever she goes abroad."

"Well, she's not going abroad," Mr. Paterson asserted rather harshly, and then uttered a sharp laugh. "We've only just gotten together and now you're trying to send her away. Anyway, it's not in Genoa. It's on Capri."

"No, no," the Captain disagreed amiably. "I remember it distinctly. There are some lovely places on Capri, but the Blue Grotto is in Genoa."

"I don't care what you remember." Mr. Paterson turned to look him squarely in the face. "It's on Capri whether you remember it or not."

The Captain smiled pleasantly and shook his head. "I really don't think so. Possibly you're—"

His voice trailed away as be took note of Mr. Paterson's belligerent indignation and grew aware suddenly of the tense quiet in the room. Cynthia was glaring at him fiercely, and Neil gaped with pale astonishment. The situation came abruptly into focus, and he hastened to make amends.

"Perhaps you are right. Yes, I must be mistaken."

"I know damn well I'm right," Mr. Paterson said angrily.

"Yes, yes, of course. I was—a bit confused. Will you please excuse me? There are—are some things I must attend to."

There was not the slightest sound as the Captain walked unsteadily from the room and made his way upstairs, where he sat down limply on the edge of his bed. He was still sitting there when Cynthia entered without knocking. She closed the door carefully and confronted him with a face that was all bone and tight skin.

"You fool!" she exclaimed furiously. "You stupid, stupid fool!"

"But I was right, Cynthia. It is in Genoa."

"I don't care where it is! You and your damn lies about your trips to Europe and your precious Mr. Simpson and his engine room. And tonight of all times! Are you insane?"

"They aren't lies," protested the Captain.

"They are lies! How would you know where anything is? You've only taken one trip in your life and that on the dirty old steamer that brought you here. A lot of traveling you've done! That's the truth, isn't it?"

"But it is in Genoa, Cynthia. I swear it is."

"Answer me! They are lies, aren't they?" Her face blazed wildly as she took a menacing step toward him. "Aren't they?"

"Yes," the Captain whispered, and his voice covered a sob. "Yes, they are lies."

Cynthia stepped back and surveyed him with grim scornful satisfaction. "Well, we're sick of hearing them. Do you understand? There's not to be another word about them. Not another word."

The Captain began trembling as soon as she had gone, trembling in every part with an increasing violence that thundered dreadfully through his soul. Only when he remembered his experience in the engine room, the men watching him with respect and Mr. Henslowe asking his opinion, did he begin to grow calm.

In the morning he could not bring himself to move. He gave no reply when a timid knock sounded on the door and was repeated. Finally Cynthia entered. Her eyes were hollow and moist. The Captain stared down at his chest.

"Are you feeling all right, Daddy?" she inquired in a tremulous, low voice.

The Captain nodded.

"You didn't come down for breakfast. I thought maybe you were sick when you didn't come down."

The Captain shook his head.

"Shall I bring you anything?" she offered hopefully. "Some orange juice and cereal? I'll bring it if you want me to."

Again he shook his head.

Cynthia waited yearningly, held back by a last shred of pride that begged only the tiniest payment for submission. The Captain gave no sign.

"Please come down, Daddy," she said, as she sadly prepared to go. "I'll worry about you if you stay up all day."

"All right," said the Captain. "I'll come down."

A dismal mood filled the house during the next few days as the Captain resisted all attempts at a tacit reconciliation. They were ready to forgive, but he was not. He found no pleasure in their unhappiness. He himself was deeply distressed, but some obdurate resolution would not let him yield, and he was sustained only by the thought he would soon be sailing again with Mr. Simpson. The only comfort came from Nan. She approached him one day when he was alone and kissed him softly on the forehead.

"Poor Grandpa," she murmured, as though musing aloud. "You used to come to me when I had nightmares. I still have them, you know."

"I'm afraid there's no longer anything I can do," said the Captain, patting her hand gratefully.

The Captain left for his next voyage in total secrecy and arrived at the ship much too early to find Mr. Simpson. Coming aboard was like stepping from some mephitic cavern into the blowing, warm fragrance of day. Everything seemed unusually beautiful; even the gulls—ugly, avaricious things, he had always thought them—gleamed with an unnaturally white brilliance. The Captain grew bold in his elation, and he strode up to another officer and inquired for Mr. Simpson. His manner must have been abrupt, for the officer regarded him with surprise.

"It's really very important."

The officer smiled. "Of course. Please come this way."

"If you would just tell him I am waiting."

"It's perfectly all right," the officer assured him. "Come right along."

He led the Captain to an empty cabin where he took his name and politely requested him to wait. The Captain was sorry now that he had acted so impulsively. The din of voices drifted from the deck below, distant and unreal, like the beach noises of a sultry summer's day. He grew more uncomfortable as he waited, and suddenly an airy sensation of dizziness came over him and everything began to seem unreal.

At last there were footsteps in the corridor. He stood up with relief when the door opened; then stared stupefied as four men entered the room. There were two officers, the one he had first addressed and another with a flowering opulence of gold braid, and two men in topcoats, one somewhat stout, the other with a sharp, red face. The Captain was alarmed.

"Is anything wrong?"

"Please come with us," the stout man instructed curtly.

"But what is it? Where is Mr. Simpson?"

"We'll explain everything," said the man with the sharp, red face.

"But where is he?"

"He's in jail."

The Captain reeled with amazement. "In jail?" he cried.

"Yes, in jail. He was arrested for smuggling."

The Captain gasped. The light in the room grew dim, the room began to sway, he felt he was slowly falling. One part of his intelligence remained clear and alertly inquired why none of these strange people observed that he was falling and reached out to catch him. It seemed very odd, almost comical, and he thought he might even have laughed were it not for the fact, the indisputable fact, that he was about to fall.

"You'll have to answer some questions," a voice said from a distance.

"Yes, of course," said the Captain, as his vision began to clear. "But—you must forgive me. I'm not well, not well at all. May I—may I sit down? Thank you. Thank you. I will try to answer your questions," he promised weakly. "But you must be patient with me. I'm—I'm really not very well."

The questions came, and he answered as best he could, sinking deeper and deeper into shame as he bared his most personal secrets. He told them everything in a dull, wavering voice that cracked away often into a dry whisper, interrupting his bleak odyssey frequently with appeals for them not to contact his family. He gave references. The man with the sharp, red face wrote them down and left the cabin. The Captain omitted nothing, propelled by the conviction that only by presenting the complete picture could he properly vindicate himself. The others were no longer questioning him, but had fallen silent to listen with motionless attention.

He was still speaking when the man with the sharp, red face returned. There was a whispered conference, and then the Captain was free to go. They were very nice to him now, and the officer with the flowering opulence of gold braid seemed genuinely regretful when he said:

"You mustn't come aboard again unless you are visiting someone who is sailing or you yourself really are. I'm very sorry, but those are regulations."

The Captain nodded rapidly, scarcely understanding. The man with the sharp face accompanied him out into the street and offered to drop him at the station.

"Thank you. Thank you. But I believe I will take a taxi home."

The man hailed a cab for him and held the door open and helped him inside. "Good luck, Captain," he said, and slowly closed the door.

The ride to the house took over an hour. There was time to think, and it was in the cab going home that the Captain reached a decision and began planning his last voyage.

He was normally the earliest in the house to awake, and it was he generally who stepped out to the porch at the beginning of each day and carried the mail inside. That evening he made peace with Neil and Cynthia. He let a full week go by to allay suspicion, and then one morning delivered his solemn announcement.

"I received a letter," he began in a firm voice, when the entire family had assembled for breakfast. "From my sister in Scotland. She has fallen ill."

LOVE, DAD

Second Lieutenant Edward J. Nately III was really a good kid. He was a slender, shy, rather handsome young man with fine brown hair, delicate cheekbones, large, intent eyes and a sharp pain in the small of his back when he woke up alone on a couch in the parlor of a whorehouse in Rome one morning and began wondering who and where he was and how in the world he had ever got there. He had no real difficulty remembering *who* he was. He was Second Lieutenant Edward J. Nately III, a bomber pilot in Italy in World War Two, and he would be twenty years old in January, if he lived.

Nately had always been a good kid from a Philadelphia family that was even better. He was always pleasant, considerate, trustworthy, loyal, helpful, friendly, courteous, kind, obedient, cheerful, not always so thrifty or wise but invariably brave, clean and reverent. He was without envy, malice, anger, hatred or resentment, which puzzled his good friend Yossarian and kept him aware of how eccentric and naïve Nately really was and how much in need of protection by Yossarian against the wicked ways of the world.

Why, Nately had actually enjoyed his childhood—and was not even ashamed to admit it! Nately *liked* all his brothers and

Playboy, vol. 16, December 1969, pp. 181–82, 348; reprinted in *A Catch-22 Casebook*, ed. Frederick Kiley and Walter McDonald (New York: Crowell, 1973).

sisters and always had, and he did not mind going home for vacations and furloughs. He got on well with his uncles and his aunts and with all his first, second and third cousins, whom, of course, he numbered by the dozens, with all the friends of the family and with just about everyone else he ever met, except, possibly, the incredibly and unashamedly depraved old man who was always in the whorehouse when Nately and Yossarian arrived and seemed to have spent his entire life living comfortably and happily there. Nately was well bred, well groomed, well mannered and well off. He was, in fact, immensely wealthy, but no one in his squadron on the island of Pianosa held his good nature or his good family background against him.

Nately had been taught by both parents all through childhood, preadolescence and adolescence to shun and disdain "climbers," "pushers," "*nouveaux*" and "parvenus," but he had never been able to, since no climbers, pushers, *nouveaux* or parvenus had ever been allowed near any of the family homes in Philadelphia, Fifth Avenue, Palm Beach, Bar Harbor, Southampton, Mayfair and Belgravia, the 16th *arrondissement*, the north of France, the south of France and all of the good Greek islands. To the best of his knowledge, the guest lists at all these places had always been composed exclusively of ladies and gentlemen and children of faultless dress and manners and great dignity and aplomb. There were always many bankers, brokers, judges, ambassadors and former ambassadors among them, many sportsmen, cabinet officials, fortune hunters and dividend-collecting widows, divorcées, orphans and spinsters. There were no labor leaders among them and no laborers, and there were never any self-made men. There was one unmarried social worker who toiled among the underprivileged for fun, and several retired generals and admirals who were dedicating the remaining years of their lives to preserving the American Constitution by destroying it and perpetuating the American way of life by bringing it to an end.

The only one in the entire group who worked hard was Nately's mother; but since she did not work hard at anything constructive, her reputation remained good. Nately's mother worked very hard at opening and closing the family homes in Philadelphia, Fifth Avenue, Palm Beach, Bar Harbor, Southampton, Mayfair and Belgravia, the 16th *arrondissement,* the north of France, the south of France and all of the good Greek islands, and at safeguarding the family traditions, of which she had appointed herself austere custodian.

"You must never forget who and what you are"; Nately's mother had begun drumming it into Nately's head about Natelys long before Nately had any idea what a Nately was. "You are not a Guggenheim, who mined copper for a living, nor a Vanderbilt, whose fortune is descended from a common tugboat captain, nor an Armour, whose ancestors peddled putrefying meat to the gallant Union Army during the heroic War between the States, nor a Harriman, who made his money playing with choo-choo trains. Our family," she always declared with pride, "does *nothing* for our money."

"What your mater means, my boy," interjected his father with the genial, rococo wit Nately found so impressive, "is that people who make new fortunes are not nearly as good as the families who've lost old ones. Ha, ha, ha! Isn't that good, my dear?"

"I wish you would mind your own business when I'm talking to the boy," Nately's mother replied sharply to Nately's father.

"Yes, my dear."

Nately's mother was a stiff-necked, straight-backed, autocratic descendant of the old New England Thorntons. The family tree of the New England Thorntons, as she often remarked, extended back far past the Mayflower, almost to Adam himself. It was a matter of historical record that the Thorntons were lineal descendants of the union of John Alden, a climber, to Priscilla Mullins, a pusher. The genealogy of the Natelys was no less impressive, since one of Nately's father's forebears had distinguished himself conspicuously at the battle of Bosworth Field, on the losing side.

"Mother, what is a regano?" Nately inquired innocently one day while on holiday from Andover after an illicit tour through the Italian section of Philadelphia, before reporting to his home for duty. "Is it anything like a Nately?"

"Oregano," replied his mother with matriarchal distaste, "is a revolting vice indulged in by untitled foreigners in Italy. Don't ever mention it again."

Nately's father chuckled superiorly when Nately's mother had gone. "You mustn't take everything your mother says too literally, son," he advised with a wink. "Your mother is a re-markable woman, as you probably know, but when she deals with such matters as oregano, she's usually full of shit. Now, I've eaten oregano many times, if you know what I mean, and I ex-pect that you will, too, before you marry and settle down. The important thing to remember about eating oregano is never to do it with a girl from your own social station. Do it with sales-girls and waitresses, if you can, or with any of our maids, except Lili, of course, who, as you may have noticed, is something of a favorite of mine. I'm not sending you to women of lower social station out of snobbishness, but simply because they're so much better at it than the daughters and wives of our friends. Nurses and schoolteachers enjoy excellent reputations in this respect. Not a word about this to your mother, of course."

Nately's father overflowed with sanguine advice of that kind. He was a dapper, affable man of great polish and experience whom everybody but Nately's mother respected. Nately was proud of his father's wisdom and sophistication; and the elo-quent, brilliant letters he received when away at school were treasured compensation for those bleak and painful separations from his parents. Nately's father, on the other hand, welcomed these separations from his son with ceremonious zeal, for they gave him opportunity to fashion the graceful, aesthetic, meta-physical letters in which he took such epicurean satisfaction.

Dear Son (he wrote when Nately was away at Andover):

Don't be the first person by whom new things are tried and don't be the last one to set old ones aside. If our family were ever to adopt for itself a brief motto, I would want it to be precisely those words, and not merely because I wrote them myself. (Ha, ha, ha!) I would select them for the wisdom they contain. They urge restraint, and restraint is the quintessence of dignity and taste. It is incumbent upon you as a Nately that dignity and taste are always what you show.

Today you are at Andover. Tomorrow you will be elsewhere. There will be times in later life when you will find yourself with people who attended Exeter, Choate, Hotchkiss, Groton and other institutions of like ilk. These people will address you as equals and speak to you familiarly, as though you share with them a common fund of experience. Do not be deceived. Andover is Andover, and Exeter is not, and neither are any of the others anything that they are not.

Throughout life, you must always choose your friends as discriminately as you choose your clothing, and you must bear in mind constantly that all that glitters is not gold.

Love,
Dad

Nately had hoarded these letters from his father loyally and was often tempted to fling their elevated contents into the jaded face of the hedonistic old man who seemed to be in charge of the whorehouse in Rome, in lordly refutation of his pernicious, un-

kempt immorality and as a triumphant illustration of what a cultivated, charming, intelligent and distinguished man of character such as his father was really like. What restrained Nately was a confused and intimidating suspicion that the old man would succeed in degrading his father with the same noxious and convincing trickery with which he had succeeded in degrading everything else Nately deemed holy. Nately had a large number of his father's letters to save. Following Andover, he had moved, of course, to Harvard, and his father had proved equal to the occasion.

Dear Son (his father wrote):

Don't be the first person by whom new things are tried and don't be the last person to set the old things aside. This pregnant couplet came to me right out of the blue only a few moments ago, while I was out on the patio listening to your mother and a Mozart clarinet concerto and spreading Crosse & Blackwell marmalade on my Melba toast, and I am interrupting my breakfast to communicate it to you while it is still fresh in my mind. Write it down on your brain, inscribe it on your heart, engrave it for all time on your memory centers, for the advice it contains is as sound as any I have ever told you.

Today you are at Harvard, the oldest educational institution in the United States of America, and I am not certain if you are as properly impressed with your situation as you should be. Harvard is more than just a good school; Harvard is also a good place at which to get an education, should you decide that you do want an education. Columbia University, New York University and the City College of New York in the city of New York are other good places at which to get an education, but they are not good schools. Universities such as Princeton, Yale, Dartmouth and bungalows in the Amherst-Williams complex are, of course, neither good schools nor good places at which to get an education and are never to be compared with Harvard. I hope that you are being as choosy in your choice of acquaintances there as you know your mother and I would like you to be.

Love,
Dad

P.S. Avoid associating familiarly with Roman Catholics, colored people and Jews, regardless of how accomplished, rich or influential their parents may be, although Chinese, Japanese, Spaniards of royal blood and Moslems of foreign nationality are perfectly all right.

P.P.S. Are you getting much oregano up there? (Ha, ha, ha!)

Nately sampled oregano dutifully his freshman year with a salesgirl, a waitress, a nurse and a schoolteacher, and with three girls in Scranton, Pennsylvania, on two separate occasions, but his appetite for the spice was not hoggish and exposure did not immunize him against falling so unrealistically in love the first moment he laid eyes on the dense, sluggish, yawning, ill-kempt whore lounging stark naked in a room full of enlisted men ignoring her. Apart from these several formal and rather unexciting excursions into sexuality, Nately's first year at Harvard was empty and dull. He made few close friends, restricted, as he was, to associating only with wealthy Episcopalian and Church of England graduates of Andover whose ancestors had either descended lineally from the union of John Alden with Priscilla Mullins or been conspicuous at Bosworth Field, on the losing side. He spent many solitary hours fondling the expensive vellum bindings of the five books sent to him by his father as the indispensable basis of a sound personal library: *Forges and Furnaces of Pennsylvania; The Catalog of the Porcellian Club of*

Harvard University, 1941; Burke's Genealogical and Heraldic History of the Peerage, Baronetage and Knightage; Lord Chesterfield's Letters Written to His Son; and the Francis Palgrave *Golden Treasury* of English verse. The pages themselves did not hold his interest, but the bindings were fascinating. He was often lonely and nagged by vague, incipient longings. He contemplated his sophomore year at Harvard without enthusiasm, without joy. Fortunately, the War broke out in time to save him.

Dear Son (his father wrote, after Nately had volunteered for the Air Corps, to escape being drafted into the Infantry):

You are now embarked upon the highest calling that Providence ever bestows upon man, the privilege to fight for his country. Play up, play up and play the game! I have every confidence that you will not fail your country, your family and yourself in the execution of your most noble responsibility, which is to play up, play up and play the game—and to come out ahead.

The news at home is all good. The market is buoyant and the cost-plus-six-percent type of contract now in vogue is the most salutary invention since the international cartel and provides us with an excellent buffer against the excess-profits tax and the outrageous personal income tax. I have it on excellent authority that Russia cannot possibly hold out for more than a week or two and that after communism has been destroyed, Hitler, Roosevelt, Mussolini, Churchill, Mahatma Gandhi and the Emperor of Japan will make peace and operate the world forever on a sound businesslike basis. However, it remains to be seen whether the wish is just being father to the thought. (Ha, ha, ha!)

My spirit is soaring and my optimism knows no bounds. Hitler has provided precisely the right stimulus needed to restore the American economy to that splendid condition of good health it was enjoying on that glorious Thursday just before Black Friday. War, as you undoubtedly appreciate, presents civilization with a great opportunity and a great challenge. It is in time of war that great fortunes are often made. It is between wars that economic conditions tend to deteriorate. If mankind can just discover some means of increasing the duration of wars and decreasing the intervals between wars, we will have found a permanent solution to this most fundamental of all human ills, the business cycle.

What better advice can a devoted parent give you in this grave period of national crisis than to oppose government interference with all the vigor at your command and to fight to the death to preserve free enterprise—provided, of course, that the enterprise in question is one in which you own a considerable number of shares. (Ha, ha, ha!)

Above all this, to your own self be true. Never be a borrower or a lender of money: Never borrow money at more than two percent and never lend money at less than nine percent.

Love,
Dad

P.S. Your mother and I will not go to Cannes this year.

There had been no caviling in the family over Nately's course once war was declared; it was simply taken for granted that he would continue the splendid family tradition of military service that dated all the way back to the battle of Bosworth Field, on the losing side, particularly since Nately's father had it from the most reliable sources in Washington that Russia could not possibly hold out for more than two or three more weeks and that the War would come to an end before Nately could be sent overseas.

It was Nately's mother and Nately's eldest sister's idea that he become an aviation cadet, since Air Corps officers wore no wires in their dress caps and since he would be sheltered in an elaborate training program while the Russians were defeated and the War was brought to a satisfactory end. Furthermore, as a cadet and an officer, he would associate only with gentlemen and frequent only the best places.

As it turned out, there was a catch. In fact, there was a series of catches, and instead of associating only with gentlemen in only the best places, Nately found himself regularly in a whorehouse in Rome, associating with such people as Yossarian and the satanic and depraved mocking old man and, even worse, sadly and hopelessly in love with an indifferent prostitute there who paid no attention to him and always went off to bed without him, because he stayed up late arguing with the evil old man.

Nately was not quite certain how it had all come about, and neither was his father, who was always so certain about everything else. Nately was struck again and again by the stark contrast the seedy, disreputable old man there made with his own father, whose recurring allusions in his letters to oregano and rhapsodic exclamations about war and business were starting to become intensely disturbing. Nately often was tempted to blot these offending lines out of the letters he saved, but was afraid to; and each time he returned to the whorehouse, he wished earnestly that the sinful and corrupt old man there would put on a clean shirt and tie and act like a cultured gentleman, so that Nately would not have to feel such burning and confusing anger each time he looked at him and was reminded of his father.

Dear Son (wrote his father):
Well, those blasted Communists failed to capitulate as I expected them to, and now you are overseas in combat as an airplane pilot and in danger of being killed.

We have instructed you always to comport yourself with honor and taste and never to be guilty of anything degrading. Death, like hard work, is degrading, and I urge you to do everything possible to remain alive. Resist the temptation to cover yourself with glory, for that would be vanity. Bear in mind that it is one thing to fight for your country and quite another thing to die for it. It is absolutely imperative in this time of national peril that, in the immortal words of Rudyard Kipling, you keep your head while others about you are losing theirs. (Ha, ha, ha! Get it?) In peace, nothing so becomes a man as modest stillness and humility. But, as Shakespeare said, when the blast of war blows loose, then it is time for discretion to be the better part of valor. In short, the times cry out for dignity, balance, caution and restraint.

It is probable that within a few years after we have won, someone like Henry L. Mencken will point out that the number of Americans who suffered from this War were far outnumbered by those who profited by it. We should not like a member of our family to draw attention to himself for being among those relative few who did not profit. I pray daily for your safe return. Could you not feign a liver ailment or something similar and be sent home?

Love,
Dad

P.S. How I envy you your youth, your opportunity and all that sweet Italian pussy! I wish I were with you. (Ha, ha, ha!)

The letter was returned to him, stamped KILLED IN ACTION.

YOSSARIAN SURVIVES

If my memory is correct, no episodes or characters were deleted when the first typed manuscript of Catch-22 *was reduced in the editing from about eight hundred pages to six hundred. My memory is not correct. Shortly after the novel was published in late 1961, a friend who had read the original deplored the omission of a series of letters from Nately to his father. Subsequently, those eight or ten pages were published in* Playboy *under the title "Love, Dad" (December 1969).*

I should state that all of the cutting had been for the sole purpose of obtaining more coherence and effectiveness for the total work.

More recently, on the twenty-fifth anniversary of the publication of the novel, two officers at the U.S. Air Force Academy doing research on the work wanted to know why I had removed an entire small chapter dealing with a physical-education instructor and with the application of calisthenics and other exercises as preparations for combat and survival.

My reactions of surprise were contradictory: I had forgotten I had written it; I was positive I had left it in. "Do you mean it's not there?" I exclaimed. "That line 'Don't just lie there while you're waiting for the ambulance. Do push-ups'?"

They assured me that the entire chapter had been excluded, that they felt it was good, still timely, and that it ought to be published.

Playboy, vol. 34, December 1987, pp. 144–46, 184, 186.

*Checking on my own, I find them correct on all points. That
chapter is not in the novel; I think it ought to be published.
Here it is.*

—JOSEPH HELLER

Actually, Yossarian owed his good health to clean living—to
plenty of fresh air, exercise, teamwork and good sportsmanship.
It was to get away from all of them that he had gone on sick call
the first time and had discovered the hospital.

At Lowry Field, where he had gone through armament
school before applying for cadet training, the enlisted men were
conditioned for survival in combat by a program of calisthenics
that was administered six days a week by Rogoff, a conscientious
physical-education instructor. Rogoff was a staff sergeant in his
mid-thirties. He was a spare, wiry, obsequious man with flat
bones and a face like tomato juice who was devoted to his work
and always seemed to arrive several minutes late to perform it.

In reality, he always arrived several minutes early and concealed himself in some convenient hiding place nearby until
everyone else had arrived, so that he could come bounding up in
a hurry, as though he were a very busy man, and launch right
into his exercises without any awkward preliminaries. Rogoff
found conversation difficult. He would conceal himself behind a
motor vehicle if one were parked in the vicinity or hide near the
window in the boiler room of one of the barracks buildings or
underneath the landing of the entrance to the orderly room. One
afternoon, he jumped down into one of ex-Pfc. Wintergreen's
holes to hide and was cracked right across the side of the head
with a shovel by ex-Pfc. Wintergreen, who poured a stream of
scalding abuse after him as he stumbled away in apologetic hu-
miliation toward the men waiting for him to arrive and put
them through his exercises.

Rogoff conducted his exercises from a high wooden platform

between two privates on the ground he called his sergeants, who shared the same unquestioning faith in the efficacy of exercise and assisted him by performing each calisthenic up front after he himself had stopped to rest his voice, which was reedy and unpredictable to begin with. Rogoff abhorred idleness. Whenever he had nothing better to do on his platform, he strode about resolutely, clapped his hands in spasmodic outbursts of zeal and said, "Hubba, hubba." Each time he said "Hubba, hubba" to the columns of men in green fatigues on the ground before him, they would say "Hubba, hubba, hubba, hubba" right back to him and begin scuffing their feet and shaking their elbows against their sides until Rogoff made them stop by unctuously raising his hand high in an approving kind of benediction and saying, as though deeply moved, "That's the way, men. That's the way."

Hubba, hubba, he had explained, was the noise made by an eager beaver, and then he had laughed, as though at an extraordinary witticism.

Rogoff conducted them through a wide variety of obscene physical experiences. There were bending, stretching and jumping exercises, all executed in unison to a masculine, musical cadence of "One, two, three, four, one, two, three, four." The men assumed a prone position and did push-ups or assumed a supine position and did sit-ups. The men learned a lot from calisthenics. They learned the difference between prone and supine.

Rogoff named, then demonstrated, each exercise he wanted done and exercised right along with them until he had counted one, two, three, four five times, as loudly as he could, at the top of his frail voice. The two privates he had promoted to be his sergeants continued doing the same exercise after he had stopped to rest his voice and was pacing spryly about on the platform or clapping his hands with spirit.

Occasionally, he would jump down to the ground without any warning, as though the platform were on fire, and dart inside one of the two-story barracks buildings behind him to make certain that no one who was supposed to be outside doing calisthenics was inside not doing them. The men on the athletic field would still be bending, stretching or jumping when he darted back out. To bring them to a halt, he would begin bending, stretching or jumping right along with them, counting one, two, three, four twice, his voice soaring upward almost perpendicularly into another octave the first time and squeezing out the second set of numbers in an agonized, shredded falsetto that made the veins and tendons bulge out gruesomely on his neck and forehead and brought an even greater flood of color to his flat red face. Every time Rogoff brought an exercise to an end, he would say "Hubba, hubba" to them, and they would say "Hubba, hubba, hubba, hubba" right back, like the bunch of eager beavers he hoped from the bottom of his heart they would all turn out to be.

When the men were not bending, stretching, jumping or pushing up, they were taught tap dancing, because tap dancing would endow them with the rhythm and coordination necessary to do the bending, stretching, jumping and push-ups that would develop the rhythm and coordination necessary to be proficient at judo and survive in combat.

Rogoff emoted the same ardor for judo as he did for calisthenics and spent about ten minutes of each session rehearsing them in the fundamentals in slow motion. Judo was the best natural weapon an unarmed fighting man had for coping with one or more enemy soldiers in a desert or jungle, provided he was unarmed. If he had a loaded carbine or submachine gun, he would be at a distinct disadvantage, since he would have to shoot it out with them. But if he was lucky enough to be trapped by them without a gun, then he would be able to use judo.

"Judo is the best natural weapon a fighting man has," Rogoff would remind them each day from his pinnacle in his high and constricted voice, spilling the words out with haste and embarrassment, as though he could not wait to be rid of them.

The men faced one another in rows and went through the movements slowly, without making contact, since judo was so destructive a natural weapon that it could not even be practiced long enough to be learned without annihilating its students. Judo was the best natural weapon a fighting man had until the day the popular boxing champ showed up as a guest calisthenics instructor to improve their morale and introduced them to the left jab.

"The left jab," said the champ without any hesitation from Rogoff's platform, "is the best natural defensive weapon a fighting man has. And since the best defensive weapon is an offensive weapon, the left jab is also the best natural offensive weapon a fighting man has."

Rogoff's face went white as a sheet.

The champ had the men face one another in rows and counted cadence while they learned and practiced the left jab in slow motion to a dignified four-beat rhythm, without making contact.

"One, two, three, four," he counted. "One, two, jab, four. Now the other column. Remember, no contact with the left jab. Ready? Jab, two, three, four, jab, two, jab, four, one, jab, three, jab, jab, two, three, jab. That's the way. Now we'll rest a few seconds and practice it some more. You can't practice the left jab too much."

The champ had been escorted to the athletic field in his commissioned-officer's uniform by an adulating retinue of colonels and generals, who stared up at him raptly from the ground in lambent idolatry. Rogoff had been bumped aside off his platform and was completely forgotten. Even the honor of introducing the champ to the men had been denied him. An embarrassed little smile tortured his lips as he stood off by himself on the ground, ignored by everyone, including the two privates he had made his sergeants. It was one of these sergeants who asked the champ what he thought of judo.

"Judo is no good," the champ declared. "Judo is Japanese. The left jab is American. We're at war with Japan. You figure it out from there. Are there any more questions?"

There were none. It was time for the champ and his distinguished flotilla to go.

"Hubba, hubba," he said.

"Hubba, hubba, hubba, hubba," the men replied.

There was an awkward hush after the champ had gone and Rogoff had returned to his desecrated platform. Rogoff gulped in abasement, failing abysmally in his attempt to pass off with casual indifference the shattering loss of status he had just suffered.

"Men," he explained weakly in a choked and apologetic voice, "the champ is a great man and we've all got to keep in mind everything he told us. But he's been traveling around a lot in connection with the war effort, and maybe he hasn't been able to keep up to date on the latest methods of warfare. That's why he said those things he did about the left jab and about judo. For some people, I guess, the left jab is the best natural weapon a fighting man has. For others, judo is the best. We'll continue concentrating on judo here, because we have to concentrate on something and we can't concentrate on both. Once you get overseas to the jungle or desert and find yourselves attacked by one or more enemy soldiers when you're unarmed, I'll let you use the left jab if you want to instead of judo. The choice is optional. Is that fair? Now, I think we'll skip our judo session for today and go right to our game period instead. Will that be okay?"

As far as Yossarian was concerned, there was little in either the left jab or judo to justify optimism when confronted by one or more enemy soldiers in the jungle or desert. He tried to conjure up visions of regiments of Allied soldiers jabbing, judoing and tap dancing their way through the enemy lines into Tokyo and Berlin to a stately four-beat count, and the picture was not very convincing.

Yossarian had no need of Rogoff or the champ to tell him what to do if he ever found himself cornered without a gun by two or more enemy soldiers in a jungle or desert. He knew exactly what to do: throw himself on his knees and beg for mercy. Surrender was the best natural weapon he could think of for an unarmed soldier when confronted by one or more armed enemy soldiers. It wasn't much of a weapon, but it made more sense than left jabbing, tap dancing or judoing.

And he had even less confidence in calisthenics. The whole physical-exercise program was supposed to toughen him for survival and save lives, but it couldn't have been working very well, Yossarian concluded, because there were so many lives that were being lost.

In addition to exercising, tap dancing, judo and left jabs, they played games. They played games like baseball and basketball for about an hour every day.

Baseball was a game that was called the great American pastime and was played on a square infield that was called a diamond. Baseball was a very patriotic and moral game that was played with a bat, a ball, four bases and seventeen men and Yossarian, divided up into one team of nine players and one team of eight players and Yossarian. The object of the game was to hit the ball with a bat and run around the square of bases more often than the players on the opposing team did. It all seemed kind of silly to Yossarian, since all they played for was the thrill of winning.

And all they won when they did win was the thrill of winning.

And all that winning meant was that they had run around the square of bases more times than a bunch of other people had. If there was more point to all the massive exertions involved than this, Yossarian missed it. When he raised the question with his teammates, they replied that winning proved that you were better. When he raised the question "Better at what?" it turned out that all you were better at was running around a bunch of bases. Yossarian just couldn't understand it, and Yossarian's team-mates just couldn't understand Yossarian.

Once he had grown reasonably familiar with the odd game of baseball, he elected to play right field every time, since he soon observed that the right fielder was generally the player with the least amount of work.

He never left his position. When his own team was at bat, he lay down on the ground in right field with a dandelion stem in his mouth and attempted to establish rapport with the right fielder on the opposing team, who kept edging farther and farther away, until he was almost in center field, as he tried to convince himself that Yossarian was not really there in right field with a dandelion stem in his mouth, saying heretical things about baseball that he had never heard anyone say before.

Yossarian refused to take his turn at bat. In the first game, he had taken a turn at bat and hit a triple. If he hit another triple, he would just have to run around a bunch of bases again, and running was no fun.

One day, the opposing right fielder decided that baseball it-self was no fun and refused to play altogether. Instead of run-ning after a ball that had come rolling out to him between two infielders, he threw his leather baseball glove as far away from him as he could and went running in toward the pitcher's mound with his whole body quaking.

"I don't want to play anymore," he said, gesticulating wildly toward Yossarian and bursting into tears. "Unless he goes away. He makes me feel like an imbecile very time I go running after that stupid baseball."

Sometimes Yossarian would sneak away from the baseball games at the earliest opportunity, leaving his team one man short.

Yossarian enjoyed playing basketball much more than he en-joyed playing baseball.

Basketball was a game played with a very large inflated ball by nine players and Yossarian, divided up into one team of five players and one team of four players and Yossarian. It was not as patriotic as baseball, but it seemed to make a lot more sense. Basketball consisted of throwing the large inflated ball through a metal hoop horizontally fastened to a wooden backboard hung vertically high above their heads. The team that threw the ball through the hoop more often was the team that won.

All the team won, though, was the same old thrill of winning, and that didn't make so much sense. Playing basketball made a lot more sense than playing baseball, because throwing the ball through the hoop was not quite as indecorous as running around a bunch of bases and required much less teamwork.

Yossarian enjoyed playing basketball because it was so easy to stop. He was able to stop the game every time simply by throwing the ball as far away as he could every time he got his hands on it and then standing around doing nothing while somebody else ran to get it.

One day, Rogoff sprinted up to Yossarian's basketball court during the game and wanted to know why nine men were standing around doing nothing. Yossarian pointed toward the tenth man, who was chasing the ball over the horizon. He had just thrown it away.

"Well, don't just stand there while he gets it," Rogoff urged. "Do push-ups."

Finally, Yossarian had had enough, as much exercise, judo, left jabs, baseball and basketball as he could stand. Maybe it all did save lives, he concluded, but at what exorbitant cost? At the cost of reducing human life to the level of a despicable animal— of an eager beaver.

Yossarian made his decision in the morning, and when the rest of the men fell out for calisthenics in the afternoon, he took his clothes off and lay down on his bed on the second floor of his barrack.

He basked in a glow of superior accomplishment as he lay in a supine position in his undershorts and T-shirt and relaxed to the rousing, strenuous tempo of Rogoff's overburdened voice putting the others through their paces just outside the building. Suddenly, Rogoff's voice ceased and those of his two assistants took over, and Yossarian heard his footsteps race into the building and up the stairs. When Rogoff charged in from the landing on the second floor and found him in bed, Yossarian stopped smirking and began to moan. Rogoff slowed abruptly with a look of chastened solicitude and resumed his approach on tiptoe.

"Why aren't you out doing calisthenics?" he asked curiously when he stood respectfully by Yossarian's bed.

"I'm sick."

"Why don't you go on sick call if you're sick?"

"I'm too sick to go on sick call. I think it's my appendix."

"Should I phone for an ambulance?"

"No, I don't think so."

"Maybe I'd better phone for an ambulance. They'll put you in bed in the hospital and let you rest there all day long."

That prospect had not occurred to Yossarian. "Please phone for an ambulance."

"I'll do it this very minute. I'll—oh, my goodness, I forgot!"

Rogoff whirled himself around with a bleat of horror and flew at top speed down the long boards of the echoing floor to the door at the end of the barrack and out onto the tiny wooden balcony there.

Yossarian was intrigued and sat up over the foot of his bed to observe what was going on.

Rogoff jumped up and down on the small porch, clapping his hands over his head.

"One, two, three, four," he began yelling downward toward the men on the ground, his voice struggling upward dauntlessly into his tortured and perilous falsetto. "One, two, three, four. Hubba, hubba."

"Hubba, hubba, hubba, hubba," came back a sympathetic mass murmur from his invisible audience below that lasted until Rogoff raised his hand high in a formal caricature of a traffic cop and choked it off.

"That's the way, men," he shouted down to them, with a clipped nod of approbation. "Now we'll try some deep knee bends. Ready? Hands on hips . . . place!" Rogoff jammed his own hands down on his hips and, with his back and neck rigid, sank down vigorously into the first movement of a deep knee bend. "One, two, three, four, one, two, three, four."

Then Rogoff sprang up, whirled himself around again and flew back inside the building toward Yossarian and zipped right past him with a chin-up wave of encouragement and pounded down the stairs. About ten minutes later, he came pounding back up the stairs, his corrugated red face redder than a beet, zipped right past him with a chin-up wave of encouragement and flew down the full length of the building again and out onto the balcony, where he yanked the men out of their deep knee bends, hubba-hubbaed them a few seconds and flung them back into straddle jumping. He was showing signs of the heavy strain when he returned to Yossarian. His spare, ropy chest was pumping up and down convulsively in starving panic, and fat, round drops of sweat were shivering on his forehead.

"It will take—I ain't getting any air! It will take the ambulance a little while to get here," he puffed. "They have to drive from all the way across the field. I still ain't getting any air!"

"I guess I'll just have to wait," Yossarian responded bravely.

Rogoff caught his breath finally. "Don't just lie there while you're waiting for the ambulance," he advised. "Do push-ups."

"If he's strong enough to do push-ups," said one of the stretcher-bearers, when the ambulance was there, "he's strong enough to walk."

"It's the push-ups that make him strong enough to walk," Rogoff explained with professional acumen.

"I'm not strong enough to do push-ups," Yossarian said, "and I'm not strong enough to walk."

A strange, regretful silence fell over Rogoff after Yossarian had been lifted onto the stretcher and the time had come to say farewell. There was no mistaking his sincere compassion. He was genuinely sorry for Yossarian; when Yossarian realized that, he was genuinely sorry for Rogoff.

"Well," Rogoff said with a gentle wave and finally found the tactful words. "Hubba, hubba."

"Hubba, hubba to you," Yossarian answered.

"Beat it," said the doctor at the hospital to Yossarian.

"Huh?" said Yossarian.

"I said, 'Beat it.'"

"Huh?"

"Stop saying 'Huh?' so much."

"Stop telling me to beat it."

"You can't tell him to beat it," a corporal there said. "There's a new order out."

"Huh?" said the doctor.

"We have to keep every abdominal complaint under observation five days, because so many of the men have been dying after we make them beat it."

"All right," grumbled the doctor. "Put him under observation five days and then throw him out."

"Don't you want to examine him first?" asked the corporal.

"No."

They took Yossarian's clothes away, gave him pajamas and put him to bed in a ward, where he was very happy when the snorers were quiet, and he began to think he might like to spend the rest of his military career there. It seemed as sensible a way to survive the war as any.

"Hubba, hubba," he said to himself.

CATCH-23
Yossarian Lives

When we last saw Yossarian, it was 1945 and he was preparing to save his life—and his sanity—by running away from the Twenty-seventh Air Force in the Mediterranean and heading for Sweden, though he did not think he would be able to get there. Forty-odd years later...

1

Yossarian began dreaming of his mother, and he knew he was going to die. The doctors were upset when he gave them the news.

"We can't find anything wrong with you," they kept insisting with unanimity.

"Keep looking," he instructed them.

"You're in perfect health."

"Just wait."

Yossarian was back in the hospital, having retreated there again under another one of those neurotic barrages of confusing physical symptoms to which he had been increasingly vulnera-

Smart, no. 9, May 1990, pp. 81–96.

ble since finding himself dwelling alone for the first time in his life, had, so to speak, gone bolting back in after just four months out at the shocking announcement that George Bush was indeed determined to resign from the presidency, no matter *who* would succeed him, and at the startling intelligence, inadvertently come by, that Milo Minderbinder, with whom Yossarian was by now indefinably, uncomfortably, and indissolubly united, was expanding beyond surplus commodities like old chocolate, old Egyptian cotton, secondhand uranium fuel rods, and reconditioned nuclear reactors into the area of military equipment with plans for a warplane of his own advanced design, armed with atomic weapons, that he intended to sell to somebody.

These two were reasons enough to be fearful, and he had a fresh tide of others. Another oil tanker had broken up. This was not mere hysteria. There was venality in government. Responsible industrialists in West Germany were selling the technology to manufacture poison gas to belligerent militarists in the Middle East who would surely employ those same poison gases against the industrialists and their countrymen in the great war between East and West that was someday certain to break out, the war to end wars. In California a boyish young adult named Mike Milken had reputedly earned $550 million in one calendar year by providing not one product or service of any social value to anyone in the national community other than those who happily made possible his extraordinary compensation and doubtless felt he was worth at least as much as he received, while in Iran the leading religious leader had posted a reward of $1 million for the murder of a novelist living in London who had written a novel irreligiously. China, a developing nation with by far the largest population on earth, was developing into a major weapons supplier. The United States was financing an anti-Soviet revolutionary movement in Afghanistan, the Soviet Union was financing one anti-American regime in Cuba and another in Nicaragua and selling the latest in sophisticated warplanes to the warmongering leader of Libya; India had nuclear power; Pakistan was testing a long-range missile. There was nerve gas in Iran, low-enriched uranium in South Africa, heavy water in Argentina and India, and uranium- and tritium-processing plants sprouting up all over the Near East and the Far East. There was discord in Israel. Winston Churchill was gone, as were Mussolini and Fred Astaire, and Joe DiMaggio was going. Yossarian's mother and father were dead, and so by now were all of his uncles and aunts, and it wasn't funny. And if that wasn't funny, there were other things that weren't even funnier. Everywhere Yossarian looked was another nut, and it was all that a reasonable and eminent senior citizen like himself could do to maintain his own benevolent mental stability amid so much madness and moral and physical danger. His health was in jeopardy, and he knew he needed help.

At least once each morning the doctors came bursting in without an appointment, breezing right in upon Yossarian in a peremptory, brisk, and serious tutorial group, his doctor Leon Shumacher with his brisk and serious entourage of brisk and serious burgeoning physicians with efficient faces and inefficient eyes, accompanied by Melissa Wedenmuller, the lively, attractive floor nurse with the pretty face and the magnificent ass who was openly drawn to Yossarian, despite his years, and whom he was slyly enticing to develop a benign crush on him, despite her youthfulness. She was a tall woman with impressive hips who remembered Pearl Bailey but not Pearl Harbor, which put her age, he had calculated, somewhere between thirty-five and sixty, the best stage, he believed, for a woman. He had no idea what she was really like. He unscrupulously embraced with enormous selfishness every chance he spied to help pass the time enjoyably for the several peaceful weeks he was resolved to remain in the hospital to rest up and put his outlook together. Like the inept navigator he'd been for a few months of operational training in the army air corps in Columbia, South Carolina, during the Second World War and on the flight overseas from there to Brazil and Africa and finally on to Pianosa in the Mediterranean, he mostly did not know where he was or what direction to take. When he confessed this to intimates, they did not believe him.

It was a good room this time, with pleasant neighbors who were not critically or offensively ill and an expansive view of the park, and it was Melissa, laughing modestly and with a flounce of hauteur, who had made the pronouncement that the ass she had was magnificent.

Magnificent the ass or not, by the middle of his first week Yossarian was flirting with all his might with this approachable and responsive woman upon whom he now depended for his well-being and for most of his occasional, brief good times. Dr. Leon Shumacher did not look kindly upon this salacious frivolity.

"It's bad enough I let you in here. I suppose we both ought to feel ashamed, you in this room when you aren't sick—"

"Who says I'm not?"

"—and so many homeless people outside on the streets."

"Will you let one in here if I agree to leave?"

"Will you pay the bills?"

Yossarian preferred not to.

Some mornings when Leon came breezing in with his deferential bunch, he would have in tow some distinguished medical peer or two from areas of professional dedication remote from his own who had signed up for the excursion that day simply to gaze in wonderment at this notorious and jittery patient who had come back into the hospital again for his thorough annual checkup just four months after his last one because he'd had a brief vision of a morbid vision and because he felt more at home in the hospital with them than he did at home with whomever he lived with and because he felt very much safer inside a private room with a good view of a very risky park than he did outside in the world of business, where he was now in semi-retirement as something of a semiconsulting semiexecutive after serving as a consulting executive with Milo Minderbinder and his M&M Enterprises & Associates for something like twenty-five consecutive years.

A great man with angiograms confirmed to Yossarian soberly that he did not need one, and a neurologist reported with equal gloom that there was nothing the matter with his brain. Leon Shumacher himself was recognized locally as a foremost national authority on stones in the gallbladder and myasthenia gravis, subjects without connection to each other. Leon himself was susceptible to chronic spastic colitis and feverish jealousy of people like his children who were not doctors or entertainers and yet made very much more money than he did. Yossarian did not have myasthenia gravis and had no stones in his gallbladder, and Leon again was using him pridefully with his pupils as an exemplary model of a patient entirely free of all of the symptoms—every single one—normally associated with myasthenia gravis or any irregularity in the functioning of the gallbladder. He was a rare specimen that doctors would not have the opportunity to come upon often in their medical careers, and they must study him closely, a man without symptoms of any disease, not even hypochondria.

There was no blood in his stool, but they examined him inside anyway, up and down, with instruments of simple appearance and glints of light that pumped in air to inflate his own inner tubes for simplified viewing. His auditory and spinal apparatus had been CAT scanned. The physicians found nothing. Even his sinuses were always clear, and there was no evidence anywhere of arthritis, bursitis, angina, or neuritis. His blood pressure and breathing capabilities were the envy of every doctor who saw him. He gave urine and they took it. He had demanded a urologist and they had delivered one for discussion and clarification of the sample, as well as for some illuminating commentaries on his reproductive organs: during the last thirty or forty years, he admitted bashfully, his procreative urges, his *libido,* so to speak, had flagged considerably from a peak in late adolescence and early manhood.

"So has mine," said Leon Shumacher in grumpy consolation when they were discussing the test results. He was grumpy because Yossarian seemed much more blithe about that waning in virility than Shumacher could be about his. "And my prostate is just as enlarged as yours is."

"And what difference does that make?" asked Yossarian impatiently. "Leon, do you think I care what's happening to you? There was a time I felt I could bludgeon down doors with my hard-ons. Now look at my poor thing."

"Never mind. Put it back in, John. Where do you think you are? You're not going to live forever, you know."

"Yes, I am," Yossarian shot back. "Or I'll at least die trying. And I am still counting on you people in the medical world to make that possible, but with less and less confidence. What's the matter with you people? Why can't you move?"

There'd been a lymphologist for his lymph, a dermatologist for his derma, an endocrinologist for his endocrines, a physiatrist for his physique, a cystologist for his cysts, and an articulate orthopedist for his orthopedic articulation. His hematologist had twice given his blood a clean bill of health: his cholesterol was low, his hemoglobin was high, and even his blood nitrogen was ideal. The experts found no polyps or fissures, not a single hemorrhoid, no problems with elimination or respiration. They found him phenomenal. And they pronounced him a perfect human being.

Yossarian did not believe it.

Biologically, they said, he was a credit to the human race. Yossarian did not believe that one either. He thought his wife, from whom he had now been separated a full year, might have some demurrers as well.

There was a champion cardiologist for his electrocardiograms and thoracic fluoroscopes, who found no fault with them; a pathologist for his pathos, who found no cause for concern either; an enterprising gastroenterologist, who ran back to the room for a second opinion from Yossarian on some creative investment strategies he was considering in Arizona real estate; a cryptographer for his handwriting; and a psychologist for his psyche, upon whom Yossarian was left in the end with no recourse but to rely, as the last resort.

"I think I can confide in you," he said to the psychologist. "I have to know if it's psychogenic or not. Do I really feel this good and healthy now, or am I just imagining I do? It has me worried. I even have this full head of hair."

"I think the head of hair is remarkable."

"And what about these periodic periods of boredom and fatigue and disinterest and depression?" Yossarian rushed on in a whirlwind of whispers. "I find myself detached from listening to things that other people take quite seriously. I'm tired of information I can't use. I wish the daily newspapers were smaller and came out weekly. I'm not interested anymore in all that's going on in the world. Comedians don't make me laugh, and long stories drive me wild. Nothing moves me the way it used to. Is it me, or has the world grown boring? If I were younger, I might want to save myself and maybe even most of humanity. If my children were younger, I would feel some responsibility to save them. If I were closer to my grandchildren and found them endearing, I would tremble for their safety and want to cry. But I don't feel these things and am tired of trying to convince myself I maybe ought to. My enthusiasms are exhausted. Tell me straight, Doc. I've got to have the truth. Is my depression mental?"

"It isn't depression, and you aren't exhausted," the psychologist told him bluntly, with a glance at his wristwatch, and then went away abruptly to take his lithium.

In due course, the psychologist conferred with the chief of

psychiatry, who consulted with Shumacher and most of the rest of the medical men, and they concluded with one voice that there was nothing psychosomatic about the excellent health he was enjoying and that the hair on his head was real, too.

"The way it looks to us now, Mr. Yossarian," said the chief medical director, speaking for the whole institution, with Leon Shumacher's head, three-quarters bald, hanging over his shoulder and moving up and down, "you might live forever."

Toward the end of Yossarian's second week in the hospital, the doctors hatched the plot that drove him out. They drove him out with the man from Belgium in the room adjacent to his. The man from Belgium was a very sick man and spoke no English, which did not matter much because he had just had his larynx removed and could not speak at all, understood no English either, which mattered greatly to the nurses and several doctors, who were unable to address him in meaningful ways. All day and much of the night he had at his bedside his waxen and diminutive Belgian wife in unpressed fashionable clothes, who smoked cigarettes continually while she spoke and understood no English either and jabbered away at the nurses ceaselessly and hysterically, flying into alarms of shrieking fright each time he groaned or choked or slept or awoke or tried to twist away out of bed from all the overwhelming miseries afflicting him and the tangled and inhuman maze of apparatus supporting and restraining him. He had come to this country only to be made well medically, and the doctors had taken out his larynx because he certainly would have died had they left it in. Now it was not so certain he would live. He had a chest tube and a belly tube and required constant vigilance. Christ, thought Yossarian, how can the guy stand it?

Yossarian worried about the man from Belgium more than he wanted to. His sympathies were overburdened. He was moving into a state of stress and knew that stress was not healthy. He worried about that also and began to feel sorry for himself too.

A few times a day Yossarian would venture from his own bed into the hallway to look into the other room just to see what was going on. Each time, he came reeling back to his own bed after a few seconds and collapsed there in a woozy faint, moaning soundlessly to himself with an arm thrown over his face to block out his persistence of vision. When he looked up again, the most mysterious of the several private detectives who had shadowed him into the hospital would be peering in at him quizzically. This secret agent was spare and short, with a sallow complexion and small, dark eyes in a thin, long, oval face that looked vaguely Asian and reminded him of a nut, a shelled almond.

"Who the fuck are you?" Yossarian wanted to shout at him.

"Who speaks French?" the people taking care of the Belgian cried out a dozen times a day.

Yossarian spoke a little bit of French very poorly, but after the first few torturous attempts at being of some assistance to the staff and the overwrought Belgian woman with the bodice of her dress always mottled palely with streaks of cigarette ash, he decided to mind his own business and pretend he knew none. He was nervous about malpractice. Who could tell? Conceivably, an error in translation might very well render him liable to a charge of practicing medicine without a license. Yossarian could tell: he could tell about himself and the man from Belgium that if he ever had to go through all of that at his age for four or fourteen days just to be able to go on living with or without a voice box for God knew how little longer, he thought he would prefer not to. In the end it came down to elementals. He could not stand the Belgian's pain and the nearness of his imminent death.

Yossarian was symptom suggestible and knew it. Within half a day of the arrival of the Belgian, his voice turned husky. He had no fever or physical discomfort, and there was no visible evidence of inflammation anywhere in his ears, nose, or throat, said the ear, nose, and throat man who had been summoned.

The next day, though, his throat did feel sore. He felt a lump back there too that seemed to be growing by the minute, and he had difficulty swallowing his food, although there was still not a sign of infection or obstruction, and he knew as absolutely as he knew anything else on earth that he too would soon lose his larynx to a malignancy if he hung around there any longer and did not get the hell away from that hospital room fast.

2

Outside the hospital it was still going on. A draft dodger named Dan Quayle was about to be president and was disliked by many for having given to the ancient tradition of draft dodging a very bad name. Now even he on public occasions told modest jokes about himself immodestly. Even newspapermen laughed.

There were still plenty of poor people.

Yossarian looked askance at a few living on the sidewalk outside the hospital as he strode from the entranceway to the car and driver he had reserved to transport him across town to the luxury high-rise apartment building in which he now made his home. It was called a luxury building because the costs of living there were large. The rooms were small, the ceilings were low, there were no windows in his two bathrooms, and there was no room in the kitchen area for a table or chair.

Fewer than ten blocks away was the notorious and often scandalous bus terminal of the Port of New York Authority, as it was known lawfully, with its police desk and three holding cells in use, which overflowed several times each day with new prisoners and into which his youngest son, Michael Yossarian, had once been conducted on charges of emerging from a subway exit while carrying a pipe without tobacco and attempting to step back in without paying an additional fare upon realizing he had got off one stop too soon on his way downtown to the architectural firm for which he was doing drawings.

"That was the day," Michael still needed to recall, "you saved my life and broke my spirit."

"Did you want me to let them lock you up with those others and take you downtown to be booked?"

"I would have died if they had. But it wasn't easy seeing you blow up at all those cops and get away with it. And knowing I wasn't able to do the same."

"We get angry in the way we have to, Michael. I don't think I had much choice."

"I get depressed."

"You don't have much choice, do you? You had an older brother who bullied you," Yossarian ventured, alluding to Adrian, the firstborn son. "Maybe that's why."

"Why didn't you stop him?"

"We didn't know how," confessed Yossarian. "We didn't want to bully him."

"He would bully me still if I gave him the chance. You were something to watch. You had a whole crowd. There was even clapping."

They were both drained afterward. There was no sense of triumph. Michael was one of only three whites among the four dozen prisoners arrested and squeezed into the detention cells or shackled to the wall chains outside, and the other two were crack addicts who had by error jumped a plainclothesman for money.

People lived in the bus terminal now, a resident population of men and women and wayward boys and girls, and, under the safeguards of the U.S. Constitution, could not be forced out from a public facility unrestricted to others.

There was hot and cold running water in the lavatories on the different levels of the terminal, along with an abundance of whores and homosexuals for every appetite imaginable, and plentiful shops close at hand for such basic daily necessities as chewing gum, cigarettes, newspapers, and jelly doughnuts. Toilet tissue was free. Fertile mothers in flight from idyllic hometowns arrived regularly with small children and took up lodgings there immediately as the safest place in the world they could find for refuge and drugs. The terminal was a good home base for streetwalking. Thousands of business commuters, along with hundreds of visitors to the metropolis as well, paid them little mind as they passed through each morning on their way to employment and went back to their homes at the conclusion of each working day.

From the lofty picture windows of the bedroom and living room in his high-rise apartment, Yossarian commanded an excellent view of another luxury apartment building just across the way with an even higher rise than his own, and between these overtowering structures ran the broad thoroughfare below, which teemed more and more monstrously now with growing clans of bellicose and repulsive panhandlers, prostitutes, addicts, dealers, pimps, robbers, pornographers, perverts, and disoriented psychopaths, all of them plying their criminal specialties outdoors amid multiplying strands of degraded and bedraggled people who were *living* outdoors. Among the homeless there were whites now too, and they also pissed against the wall and defecated in the alleyways that others in their circle eventually located as accommodating sites to bed down in. Here and there one occasionally spotted elderly white-haired couples clinging to their remaining shreds of respectability, sitting clean and upright side by side in the recessed entrance to some locked-up store they had found for the night, sometimes on chairs and sometimes on the ground, swaddled neatly to the lips and eyes in scarves and in colored sheets and blankets in defense against the swirls of wind and dust that spun and skipped along the pavement, their savings of a lifetime stored up in bundles at their feet and in bundles, wrappings, and paper-bag packages stacked neatly in grocery shopping carts curiously purloined. Even in the better neighborhood along Park Avenue, Yossarian knew, women could be seen squatting to relieve themselves in the tended flower beds of the traffic islands in the center.

It was hard not to hate them all.

"They don't vote," said the mayor, "because they don't have a voting address, and they don't turn out their friends for elections because they have no friends."

"The way to eliminate crime in the streets," said the cardinal, "is to eliminate streets."

"The way to eliminate poverty," said Olivia Maxon, a socialite woman prominent most of all for her prominent attendance at philanthropic social events, "is to eliminate poor people."

"You must listen to my wife when she tells you that, Mr. Yossarian," instructed her husband, Christopher, who managed money.

"You can believe my husband when he tells you that," said his wife, "for he did not get where he is by being stupid."

"You can believe my wife when she tells you that."

This was New York, the Big Apple, the Empire City in the Empire State, the financial heart, brains and sinews of the country, and the city that was greatest, barring London, perhaps, in cultural actions in the whole world.

Nowhere in his lifetime, Yossarian was bound often to remember, not in wartime Rome or on the island of Pianosa or even in blasted Naples or Sicily, when he was there as a captain in the air force during World War II, had he been spectator to such atrocious, blatant squalor as he saw crowding in around him now. Nor observed such joyless sexual and other social and occupational transactions as, merely by looking, he could witness negotiated in the street scores of times an hour between prostitute and purchaser, dealer and user, policeman and quarry, buyer of stolen property and seller of stolen property. Not even—he had commented once in his cynicism to his youngest son, once in the hospital to his new woman friend, Melissa Wedenmuller, and more than once to an old lady friend from the past—at the lusterless gala fund-raising luncheons and black-tie dinners he attended more times than he wanted to as a kind of goodwill ambassador for his company and to which he was routinely invited as the only presentable official of the Double-M E&A concern.

It was nobody's fault. Landlords were blamed. Banks were helpless. "It's not our business," said people in the federal government.

"My God, what's that?" cried Frances Beach, Yossarian's friend from the past, as they rode in her rented limousine with her rented chauffeur from still another tepid daytime party at the New York Public Library.

"The bus terminal."

"What's it for?"

"What do you think?"

"I've never seen anything so seedy."

"Yes, you have. You might consider sponsoring your next fashion show inside. That would really make the news."

"What are you talking about?"

"I've made some friends there since my son was busted. I've got good contacts. Why not a wedding? A real big wedding?"

"Please stop joking. A society wedding in the bus terminal?"

"Sounds good to me. You've had them in the museum and the opera house. The terminal's more picturesque."

"You must be mad. Although it sounds like fun. My God!" She sat up suddenly as the car cruised onward. "Look at those people! Are they men or women? And why must they do those things right out in the street? Why can't they wait till they're home?"

"Many don't have homes, Frances dear," said Yossarian, smiling at her. "And the lines for the toilets at the bus terminal are too long. Reservations must be made in the peak hours. No one can be seated without them. The lavatories in the restaurants and hotels, say the signs, are for the convenience of patrons only. Have you ever noticed, Frances, that men who take leaks in the street usually take long ones?"

No, she had not noticed, she informed him frostily.

"You sound so bitter now," she added. "You used to be funnier."

"They flow into Times Square. Would you like to see more?"

"I don't want to talk about Times Square."

"I insist," he muttered.

"And so cynical."

Years back, before either was married, they had luxuriated together in what would today be termed an affair, although neither then would have thought of applying a title so decorous to the things they were doing with each other so incessantly and passionately.

"You used to be more sympathetic," he reminded her now.

"You too."

"And radical."

"So were you. And now you're so negative," she observed without much feeling. "And always sarcastic, aren't you?"

"I didn't realize that," he answered soberly.

"No wonder our men are not always comfortable with you. They don't know what you really think. And you're always flirting."

"I am not!"

"Yes, you are," Frances Beach insisted, without even turning her head to give emphasis to her argument. "With just about everyone but me. You know very well who flirts and who doesn't. Patrick and Christopher don't. You do. You always did."

"Well, I don't ever mean it. It's the way I joke."

"Our women don't know that, John. They imagine you have one young mistress a day."

"Mistress?" Yossarian turned the sound of the word into a snorting guffaw. "I don't want even one."

"A companion, a girlfriend? What would you like to call her?"

"Only one would be too many."

Frances Beach laughed, and the suggestion of strain with which she had been sitting for several minutes seemed to vanish. They were both past sixty-five. He had known her when her name was Franny. She remembered when they called him Yo-Yo. They had not toyed with each other since, not even after she'd learned from others that he was now living alone.

"There seem to be more and more of these poor and awful people everywhere," she murmured wearily, with a despair she made clear would be easily controlled, "every hour, doing everything imaginable right out on all of the streets. Patrick's pocket was picked a month ago just in front of our house, and there are whores on the corners day and night. John, you used to know everything. What can be done about them?"

"Nothing," he obliged her helpfully in reply.

For things were good, he reminded her: this time only the poor were very poor, and the need for new prison cells was more pressing than the needs of the homeless. He did not add that by now he was one more in the solid middle class who was not keen to have his taxes raised to ameliorate the miseries of those who paid none. He preferred more prisons.

His second wife was still divorcing him. All of his children came from his first. In that marriage, six or seven years after he had discontinued all extramarital dalliances, his wife began to accuse him of starting them, and when he finally tired of hearing her tell him to move out, he finally did.

His daughter, Gillian, a bossy overachiever, was divorcing her husband, who was not achieving as much.

His oldest son, Adrian, was another overachiever, a minor major hotshot on Wall Street, and he and his wife were now living in separate quarters of their obsolete suburban mansion while their respective lawyers made ready to sue and countersue for divorce while attempting, impossibly, to arrive at a division of property and children that would supply total satisfaction to both.

Yossarian sensed trouble brewing in the marriage between his second son, Julian, a chemist without a graduate degree who worked for a cosmetics manufacturer in New Jersey, and his wife: she had taken to enrolling in adult-education courses.

Michael, unmarried and still without steady employment, had once joked to Yossarian that he was going to put money away for his divorce before starting to save for his marriage, and Yossarian resisted wisecracking back that his joke was not a joke.

Women, especially women who had been married one time before, liked Michael and lived with him because he was peaceful, understanding, and undemanding, and then they tired of living with him and moved out because he was peaceful, understanding, and undemanding—and unexciting. Yossarian had a respectful suspicion about Michael that in his quiet way, with women as with work, he knew what he was doing.

When needing money, Michael did free-lance artwork for agencies and magazines or for art studios doing contract assignments, or with clear conscience accepted what he needed from Yossarian.

And Yossarian was still under surveillance. He could tell from the small white Fiat parked in the no-parking area downstairs outside his building whose driver pulled away after Yossarian met his eye and from the red compact Toyota that arrived about half an hour later in the no-parking area across the avenue about half a block away from the trim, vaguely Asian-looking secret agent from the hospital who was hiding behind a fashion magazine most of the time and was perhaps in cahoots with a French assistant who kept his distance while nibbling croissants and sipping coffee alone at one of the dainty white wrought-iron tables in the green coffee-and-fresh-pasta café at the corner. After a day, there was another newcomer, a husky, raw-boned American with carrot hair and a close-cropped cut that exposed him on first sight as an American foreigner to the city or as one of those undercover operatives got up deliberately to be marked immediately by the sharp-eyed as a plainclothesman for one of the government law enforcement agencies. Then there came a brooding Orthodox Jew who either resided in the neighborhood and went out slowly on long and solitary walks about every two hours with his head low and hands clasped behind him or was also on duty as a secret agent with some kind of ulterior motive that Yossarian could not make head or tail of. By the end of the week, there was a second gangling red-headed detective taking turns with the first and a call on his machine from Melissa with the news that the Belgian patient whose presence in the room next to his had driven him from the hospital was alive but still in pain and that his temperature was back to normal.

Yossarian would have bet his life that the Belgian would now be dead.

Of all those tailing him, he could account for only a couple—the ones retained by the lawyer of his estranged wife and those retained by the estranged, impulsive husband of a woman he'd bantered with suggestively once or twice and hoped to see again privately who had detectives shadow every man she knew in his frothing effort to obtain evidence of adultery to balance the evidence of adultery she had earlier obtained against him.

The idea of the others was annoying, and after another few days of rising embitterment Yossarian took the bull by the horns and telephoned the office.

"Anything new?" he began with the underling who was also his superior.

"Not as far as I know."

"Are you telling me the truth?"

"To the best of my ability."

"You're not holding anything back?"

"Not as far as I can tell."

"Would you tell me if you were?"

"I would tell you if I could."

"When your father calls in today, M2," he said to Milo Minderbinder II, "tell him I need the name of a good private detective. It's for something personal."

"He's already phoned," said the junior Milo. "He recommends a man named Jerry Gaffney at an agency called the Gaffney Agency. Under no circumstances mention that my father suggested him."

"He told you that already?" Yossarian was enchanted. "How in the world did he know I was going to ask?"

"That's impossible for me to say."

"Okay. How are you feeling, M2?"

"It's hard to be sure."

"I mean personally. Are things all right?"

"Wouldn't I want to tell you if they were?"

"But would you tell me?"

"That would depend."

"On what?"

"If I could tell you the truth."

"Would you tell me the truth?"

"Do I know what it is?"

"Could you tell me a lie?"

"Only if I knew the truth."

"Thanks for being honest with me."

"My father wants me to be."

"Mr. Minderbinder mentioned you were going to call," said the peppy voice belonging to the man named Jerry Gaffney when Yossarian telephoned him.

"That's funny," said Yossarian. "Which Mr. Minderbinder?"

"Mr. Minderbinder senior."

"That's very funny then," said Yossarian in a harder manner. "Because Minderbinder senior insisted I not mention his name to you when I phoned."

"It was a test to see if you could keep things secret," Mr. Gaffney said lightly.

"You gave me no chance to pass it, did you?" said Yossarian.

"I trust my clients, and I want all of them to know they can always trust me. Without trust, what else is there? I put everything out front. I'll give you good proof of that right now, so you'll know what I mean. You should know, if you don't know, that this telephone line is tapped. Is that news?"

Yossarian caught his breath in a gasp of anger. "Tapped? It is? How the hell did you find that out so fast?"

"It's my telephone line, and I want it tapped," Mr. Gaffney answered in his very low voice. "There, see? You can trust me. It's only me who's recording it."

"Is *my* line tapped?" Yossarian thought he should ask. "I make many business calls."

"Let me look it up. Yes, your business is tapping it. Your apartment may be bugged, too."

"Mr. Gaffney, how do you know all this?"

"Call me Jerry, Mr. Yossarian."

"How do you know all this, Mr. Gaffney?"

"Because I'm the one who tapped it, and I'm the one who may have bugged it, Mr. Yossarian. Let me give you a tip. All of the walls may have ears. Talk only in the presence of running water if you want to talk privately. Have sex only in the bathroom or kitchen if you want to make love or under the air conditioner with the fan setting turned up to—that's it!" he cheered after Yossarian had walked into the kitchen with his portable phone and turned on both faucets full pressure in order to talk secretly. "We're picking up nothing. I can barely hear you."

"I'm not saying anything."

"Learn to read lips."

"Mr. Gaffney—"

"Call me Jerry."

"Mr. Gaffney, you tapped my telephone and you bugged my apartment?"

"I *may* have bugged it. I'll have one of my staff investigators check. I keep nothing back. That's the only way to work confidentially. Now you know you can trust me. I thought you knew that your telephone was tapped and that your apartment might be bugged and your mail, travel, and bank accounts monitored."

"Holy shit, I don't know what I know." Yossarian soaked up all this disagreeable intelligence with a prolonged groan.

"Look on the bright side, Mr. Yossarian, if you can find one. Always do that. You'll soon be party to a matrimonial action, I believe, won't you? You can pretty much always take all of that for granted even before the suit begins if the principals have the wherewithal to pay us."

"You do that too?"

"I do a lot of that too. But this is only the company. Why should you care what the company hears if you never say anything you wouldn't want the company to know? It's beneficial for M&M E&A to know everything, isn't it? You believe that much, don't you?"

"No."

"No? You said no? Keep in mind, Mr. Yossarian, that I'm getting all of this down, although I'll be pleased to erase any of it you wish if that will make you feel better. How can you have any reservations about M&M E&A? You have a share in its progress, don't you? Doesn't everybody have a share?"

"I have never gone on record with that, Mr. Gaffney, and I'm not going to do that now. When can you and I meet to begin?"

"I've already begun, Mr. Yossarian. Grass doesn't grow under Signor Gaffney's feet. I don't waste time. You'll soon find that out. I've sent for all your government files under the Freedom of Information Act, and I'm getting your credit record from one of the best private consumer-credit bureaus. Like it so far?"

"I am not hiring you to investigate me!"

"I want to find out what they know about you before I try to find out who all of them are. How many did you say there were?"

"I count at least six, but two or four may be working in pairs. I notice they seem to drive cheap cars."

"Economy cars," Gaffney corrected and explained punctiliously, "to escape being noticed." He seemed to Yossarian to be extremely exact. "Six, you say? Six is a good number to start with," Gaffney continued happily. "Yes, a very good number. Forget about meeting me yet—I'm often followed, too. I wouldn't want any of them to pick up my scent yet and figure out that I'm working for you unless it turns out that they're working for me. I like to get the solutions before I find out the problems. Please turn off that water now if you can bring yourself to do that, will you? It doesn't make it easy for me. I'm making myself hoarse trying to shout above it, and I can hardly hear you. You really don't need it when you're talking to me. Your friends call you Yo-Yo? Some call you John?"

"Only my close ones, Mr. Gaffney."

"Mine call me Jerry."

"I must tell you, Mr. Gaffney, that I find talking to you exasperating."

"I hope that will change, Mr. Yossarian. If you'll pardon my saying so, it was good to get that report from your nurse."

"What nurse?" said Yossarian. "I have no nurse."

"Miss Melissa Wedenmuller, sir," corrected Gaffney courteously, dropping his voice and clearing his throat softly with a sound that was reproving.

"You heard that too?"

"We monitor them all. The patient is surviving. There's no sign of infection."

"I think it's phenomenal."

"We're happy you're pleased."

And the chaplain was still out of sight: in detention somewhere secret for examination and interrogation by persons unknown after tracking Yossarian down in his hospital four months before through the Freedom of Information Act and popping back into his life with a problem he could not grapple with and had nobody else in the world to whom he felt he could bring it in confidence. Without warning—Yossarian had attempted to alert him by telephone but was half a day late—the chaplain had been apprehended at his home in Kenosha, Wisconsin, and snatched away into custody by agents on a matter of such sensitivity and national importance that these agents said they could not even say who they were without compromising their secrecy or the security of the agency of high national importance for which they said they worked. They were nicely dressed and seemed like upstanding men who would not lie. They were big, they were several, they spoke and moved with commanding authority.

The local police of Kenosha would be lame in contention against them, and they had taken the chaplain away.

The day the chaplain came, Yossarian was lying on his back with the rear section of his hospital bed raised, and he waited with a look of outraged hostility as the door to his room inched open after he'd given no response to the timid tapping he'd heard. He saw an equine, bland face with a knobby forehead and thinning strands of hay-colored hair come leaning in shyly to peer at him. It was a slender, angular face with high and delicate cheekbones and pink-lidded eyes that flared with brightness the instant they alighted upon him and widened enormously into an ecstasy of amazement.

"I knew it!" the man bearing that face burst right out with joy. "I wanted to see you again anyway! I knew I would recognize you anywhere the minute I saw you!"

"Who the fuck are you?" Yossarian demanded austerely, without altering in the least his rigid stare.

The response to his question was instantaneous.

"Chaplain, Tappman, Tappman, Chaplain Tappman, Albert Tappman," chattered Chaplain Tappman. "Chaplain Albert Tappman. Pianosa. Pianosa? The air force? World War II? Remember?"

Yossarian, responding slowly, at last let out an exclamation of recognition and afterward bestowed on him cautiously a good-natured smile. "Who the hell would have thought it? Come in, come on in. Sit down, for God's sake. How are you?"

The chaplain sat down submissively and looked worried suddenly and answered softly. "Not good, I'm beginning to think, no, maybe not so good."

"Not good? That's bad then," said Yossarian, who felt grateful that the time to come right to the point was already at hand. "Well, then, tell me, Chaplain, what brings you here?"

"Trouble," the chaplain said simply.

"That's a much better reason than I usually get from my visitors."

"I think it may be serious. I don't understand it."

When none in the continuing stream of intimidating newcomers materializing in Kenosha on official missions to question him about his problem seemed inclined to help him understand what the problem was, he'd remembered Yossarian and thought of the Freedom of Information Act. With Yossarian's personal history, Social Security number, and address in his possession, he had come from Wisconsin to the home in Manhattan with the cleaning woman from Haiti who informed him that Yossarian was no longer living there and directed him to the high-rise apartment building on the West Side of Manhattan with the uniformed doorman who referred him to the hospital on the East Side into which Yossarian had earlier committed himself with insomnia, intestinal cramps, tremors, nausea, chills, and diarrhea at the disquieting news that President Bush intended to resign and that Quayle would succeed him.

Arriving outside Yossarian's room, the chaplain was stunned for a minute by the notice on the door stating without waste of words that no visitors were allowed and that violators would be shot.

"Go right in," urged the blond heavyset nurse who had guided him there. "It's his idea of a joke."

He was back in Wisconsin no more than one day or two when the detachment of sturdy secret agents in dark suits, white shirts with midget collars, and low-key solid neckties descended upon him without notice to spirit him away. They had no arrest warrant. They said they did not need one. They had no search warrant either but proceeded to search the house anyway, and they had been back many times since to search it some more from ridgepole to foundation, turning up on occasion with crews of technicians with badges and white robes, gloves, and surgical masks, who took away samples of soil, paint, wood, and water. The neighborhood wondered.

The chaplain's problem was heavy water. He was passing it.

"I'm afraid it's true," Leon Shumacher confided to Yossarian one week later, when he had the full urinalysis report from the hospital laboratory. "Where did you get that specimen?"

"From that friend who was here last week. You saw him once when you dropped by."

"Where did he get it?"

"From his bladder, I guess. Why?"

"Are you sure?"

"How sure can I be?" said Yossarian. "He closed the door when he went into the bathroom. I didn't watch him. Where the hell else would he get it?"

"Grenoble. Georgia or South Carolina, I think. That's where most of it is made."

"Most of what?"

"Heavy water."

"What the hell does all of this mean, Leon?" Yossarian wanted to know. "Are they absolutely sure downstairs? There's no mistake?"

"Not from what I'm reading here. They could tell it was heavy almost immediately. It took two people to lift the eye-dropper. Of course they're sure. There's an extra atom of hydrogen in each molecule of water. Do you know how many molecules there are in just a few ounces? That friend of yours must weigh fifty pounds more than he looks."

"Listen, Leon," Yossarian said, bending close and speaking in a voice lowered warily. "You'll keep this secret, won't you?"

"Of course we will. This is a hospital. We'll tell no one but the federal government."

"The government? They're the ones that've been bothering him! They're the ones he's most afraid of!"

"We have to, John," Leon Shumacher intoned with practiced penitence in a faultless bedside manner. "The lab sent it to radiology to make sure that it's safe, and radiology had to notify the Nuclear Regulatory Commission and the Department of Energy. John, there's not a country in the whole world that allows anyone to manufacture heavy water without a license, and this guy is producing it by the quart several times a day. This deuterium is dynamite, John."

"Is it dangerous?"

"Medically? Who knows? I tell you I never heard of anything like this before. But he ought to find out. He might be turning into an atom bomb. You ought to alert him immediately."

By the time Yossarian telephoned Chaplain Albert O. Tappman, USAF, Retired, to warn him, there was only Mrs. Tappman at home, in hysteria and in tears. The chaplain had been disappeared only hours before, and he was in the custody still of some undisclosed authority in some undisclosed location. She had not heard from him since, although punctually each week Mrs. Karen Tappman was assured he was well and given cash approximating on the generous side the amount he would have brought in weekly were he still at liberty.

"I'll keep trying to find out what I can, Mrs. Tappman," Yossarian promised every time they spoke. The lawyers she'd consulted did not believe her. The police in Kenosha filed a missing-persons report and were skeptical also. She had three grown children and they were doubtful, too, although they could give no currency to the hypothesis of the police that the chaplain had eloped with another woman. "But I don't think I'll be able to find out much."

"Thank you again, Mr. Yossarian. Please call me Karen. I feel I know you so well."

"Call me Yo-Yo."

"Thank you, Yo-Yo."

All that Yo-Yo Yossarian had been able to find out since was that whatever significance the chaplain represented to whoever were his official captors was only monetary, military, scientific, industrial, diplomatic, and international.

He learned this from Milo Minderbinder.

"Heavy water?" said Milo, when Yossarian, for the second

time in his life, went to him in desperation for illicit assistance on a matter of government business. "How much is heavy water selling for?"

"It fluctuates, Milo. A lot. And there's a gas that comes from it that costs even more. About $30,000 a gram, right now. But that's not the point."

"How much is a gram?"

"About one-thirtieth of an ounce. But that's not the point."

"Thirty thousand dollars for one-thirtieth of an ounce? That sounds almost as good as drugs, doesn't it?" Milo spoke with his eyes fixed on a distance speculatively, each brown iris pointing off in a different direction, and with his mustache twitching in a cadence of attentiveness. "Is there much of a demand for heavy water?"

"Every country wants it. But that's not the point."

"What's it used for?"

"Nuclear energy, mainly. And atomic warheads."

"That sounds much better than drugs," Milo went on as though fascinated. "Would you say that heavy water is as good a growth industry as illegal drugs?"

"I would not call heavy water a growth industry," Yossarian answered wryly. "But all of this is not what I'm talking about. Milo, I want to find out where he is."

"Where who is?"

"Tappman. The one I'm talking to you about. He was the chaplain in the army with us."

"I was in the army with a lot of people."

"He gave you a character reference when you nearly got in trouble for bombing your own air base."

"I get a lot of character references. Heavy water? Yes? That's what it's called? What is the gas?"

"Tritium. But that's not the point."

"Yes. I think I can get interested in that. What makes heavy water?"

"Chaplain Tappman does, for one. Milo, I want to find him and get him back before anything happens to him."

"And I want to help you find him," promised Milo, who had already succeeded in placing one of his M&M E&A marketing directors on the team carrying out the covert examinations and interrogation of the chaplain.

"How'd you manage that?" Yossarian asked in wonderment.

"That wasn't hard," said Milo. "I simply said it was in the national interest."

"Is it in the national interest?"

"What's good for M&M E&A is good for the nation, isn't it?" answered Milo, who had just gone off again to Washington with Eugene Wintergreen for a second presentation of the new secret bomber he had in mind that went faster than sound and made no noise and could not be seen.

3

"You can't hear it and you can't see it. It makes no noise and is invisible. It will go faster than sound and slower than sound."

"Is that why you call it sub-supersonic, Mr. Minderbinder?"

"Yes."

"When would you want it to go slower than sound?"

"When it's landing and when it's taking off, for example."

"And sometimes to conserve fuel, when that's preferable."

"Thank you, Mr. Wintergreen."

"Will it go faster than light?" asked a general of lowest standing with rimless bifocals who was one in the uniformed half-circle of twelve military officials who sat on the far side of the curving walnut table divided perfectly into two lines of six on both sides of the figure with highest rank, who sat in the center like a monarch, a high priest, or a chief executive officer.

"Almost as fast."

"Just about as fast."

"We could even probably make it go faster than light if that's what you believe you'd like us to do."

"With just a few simple modifications, if that's what you believe you think best."

"There would be, possibly, a slight increase in fuel consumption, but that wouldn't matter."

"Faster than the speed of light? I like the ring of that, Mr. Minderbinder. I like the ring of that."

"So do we, sir. So do we."

"Wait a minute, please wait just one minute, Mr. Minderbinder. Let me ask something," slowly cut in a puzzled colonel with a professional demeanor who just one month before had been awarded an honorary doctorate in physics by a leading technological university after steering a research grant of meaningful substance that way which he was now certified by the degree from that university to be qualified to oversee. "There's something I don't get. Why would your bomber be noiseless? We have supersonic planes flying now, don't we, and we can hear the sonic booms, can't we?"

"It would be noiseless to the crew, Colonel Pickering," Milo Minderbinder explained carefully.

"Unless they slowed down and allowed the noise to catch up," added ex-PFC Wintergreen.

"Why would that be important to the enemy, whether the men in our plane could hear the noise of their own plane or not?"

"It might not be important to the enemy, but it could be important to the crew. Some of them may be aloft a long time, for months and months with the procedures for aerial refueling I recommend."

"Even for years if that's strategic, with the refueling planes we'll develop that go just as fast and have a longer range."

"Will they be invisible too?"

"Of course."

"If you want them to be."

"And make no noise?"

"The crew won't hear them."

"Unless they go slow."

"I see, Mr. Wintergreen. It's all very clever."

"Thank you, Colonel Pickering."

"How large is the crew of your second-strike defensive attack bomber?" asked a major on the other end.

"Just two."

"That's good. I mean I think it's good. Maybe it's not so good. We may have to think it through."

"Two are cheaper to train than four."

"I think that may be right, Mr. Minderbinder."

The man in the center, who was ensconced on a chair half a foot higher than the rest, brought a halt to this dialogue by clearing his throat as a proclamation of intent, and he seemed at last to be ready to say something. The room fell still. For more than twenty minutes he had looked lost, all alone unsmilingly in cumbersome rumination, his muscled jaws working away tirelessly and methodically as though chewing on some tough food for thought. His complexion was tan, his face and torso were lean, and of all those who were in the room he looked the most fit physically.

"Does light move?" he asked finally.

"Oh, yes, certainly light moves, General Binger," Milo Minderbinder answered promptly.

"Faster than anything," ex-PFC Wintergreen added helpfully. "Light is just about the fastest thing there is."

"And one of the brightest too."

Binger turned in doubt to the six men on his left, and four of them nodded in corroboration.

"Are you sure?" he asked, frowning, and swiveled his sober mien to the six subordinates on his right.

Two of them nodded, and one shrugged his shoulders.

"That's funny," Binger said slowly, with a flat smile and a brief sniffle of humorless laughter. "I am looking at that light over there on the small table, and it seems to me that it is standing perfectly still."

"That's because it's moving so fast," offered Milo quickly.

"It's moving faster than light," said Wintergreen.

"You can't see light when it's moving," one of his officers explained to him fearfully, as though putting his life on the line.

"That's right, Major, thank you," Milo said, nodding rapidly.

"That's quite all right, Mr. Minderbinder."

"It's like a bullet from a gun," said Wintergreen.

"You can't see the bullet when it's traveling, but you certainly know it's been there when it strikes the target."

"Unless you're the target."

"You can see light only when it isn't there," said Milo.

"Let me show you," said Wintergreen, surging to his feet as though losing patience. He stepped to the table and switched off the lamp, putting that corner of the room into shadow. "See that?"

"Now I see what you mean, Gene," Binger said, and all in the room seemed at length in accord. "Yes, I'm beginning to see the light, eh? Get it? Wouldn't it be a coup," he went on wistfully when the loud, perfunctory laughter died down, "if we could train our men to march at the speed of light when we have our parades? That would really be a beautiful sight for the Joint Chiefs to see, wouldn't it?"

"Except," corrected a thin, young lieutenant colonel impertinently at the very end of one side of the table before he gave himself a chance to think twice, speaking while all of the others were still bobbing their heads, "we wouldn't be able to see them, would we?"

"I'm afraid we couldn't, if they went at the speed of light."

"Here's an idea to consider," said Milo usefully. "You could just tell the Joint Chiefs and everyone else watching that they were marching that fast and no one would be able to contradict you. You would get all the credit without doing the work. They would never even have to practice, would they?"

"Would they have to be there?"

"No, they would be invisible, the whole parade. You wouldn't even need any men if they were going to march that fast."

"Milo, that's a good idea to consider, an invisible parade, without any men marching. We could have had one at the inauguration." With this speculation, General Binger relaxed his military bearing and slumped sideways along the arm of his chair. "Put simply, Milo, what does your plane look like?"

"On radar? It won't be seen. Not even when fully armed with all its nuclear weapons."

"To us. In photographs and drawings. When we want to show off."

"Put simply, General, our plane is a flying wing with a heavy arsenal of nuclear weapons, shaped on the order of the B-2 Stealth. Please keep that quiet."

"The B-2 Stealth?" cried Binger, sitting up with a shock.

"But better than the Stealth," Milo put in hastily.

"Very much better, oh, very much better than the Stealth indeed!" Wintergreen added in support.

Binger pondered a moment while the whole crowd was tense, then loosened and slanted back again on his armrest, grinning. "Milo, I think all of us like what I'm hearing from you today. Better than the Stealth? I should hope so. It would certainly be a big feather in my cap if we can put your planes through while those others are still trying to salvage something from the wreckage of their Stealth. And a black eye for them."

Milo spoke boldly. "I have to tell you, sir, that I have considered the alternatives and definitely think it would be in the best interests of the nation if you gave us all the money we want to go ahead with my plane."

"I don't disagree. And I also think it would be in the best interests of the nation if we went ahead with your plane and I was promoted to the Joint Chiefs of Staff."

"Hear, hear!" chorused the men on both sides of Binger, who beamed as though shy, and there went through the room for several seconds the low, subsiding vibration of the soles of men's shoes being scuffled against the floor.

"Hubba-hubba," said Binger, cutting off this unrehearsed display of devotion with another smile and a nod. "Milo, what do you call your airplane? We'll have to know when we want to discuss it."

"The M&M E&A Sub-Supersonic Invisible and Noiseless Defensive Second-Strike Offensive Attack Bomber."

"That's a good name for a second-strike attack bomber. It will look good in a proposal."

"It sort of suggested itself, sir."

"It seemed obvious," said Wintergreen.

"I agree, Gene. Milo," Binger went on, while the rest of the room was still, "please put something down on paper for me while we work this over a little more. Just a few glowing paragraphs. Sooner or later, I'm afraid, we will have to ask for more details. But I already know I'm going to want to run for the gold with this one and pass it right along."

"To the little prick?" Milo burst out with hope.

"Oh, no, it's still a little too soon for Little Prick," Binger replied with humoring jollity. "Although I sure do wish I could go directly to him now. No, there are channels we must go through, above us and below us, and there are those civilians in the Department of Defense. In the end Rosenblatt will have to approve, I guess. I want to sell this concept and start building support for you. You're not the only one after this, you realize."

"Who are the others?"

"I'm not sure I know. Strangelove is one. I don't know all the rest."

"Strangelove?" said Milo.

"That German?" sneered Wintergreen.

"He was pushing the Stealth."

"What's *he* up to now?"

"I'm not all that sure," Binger confessed. "But he has this Strangelove All-Purpose Do-It-Yourself Defensive First Second or Third Strike Indestructible Fantastic State-of-the-Art B-Ware Offensive Attack Bomber he wants to sell. Take a look at his new business card. One of the security agents in our unit stole it from one of the security agents in another unit in procurement with which we are in mortal competition and just about ready to go to war. Your bomber will help."

The business card passed down was of best quality, it appeared, with the double eagle of the Austro-Hungarian empire imprinted in black and with raised lettering of auburn gold that read: Elliott Strangelove Associates. Fine Contacts and Advice. Secondhand Influence Bought and Sold. Bombast on Demand. Notice: The Information on This Card Is Classified.

Milo was downcast.

"May I make a copy?"

"Please take it," pressed Binger. "I brought it for you. It would pretty much be the end of our chances in this affair if one of someone else's security agents found in our possession a business card stolen from one of someone else's security agents. Milo, we're all in a race to deliver a defense weapon that could lead to the end of the world and bring victory to the winner who uses it first. Whoever sponsors that baby could be elevated to a Joint Chief of Staff."

"Then I hope you'll move fast," said Wintergreen churlishly, speaking his mind with a sulking and irascible disgruntlement he did not try to disguise. "We don't like to just keep sitting around with a hot product like this one."

"Just give me that page or two on what you've been telling us today so we'll know what we are talking about when we talk to people about what you've been talking about to us today. And we will move right along as fast as we can. As fast as light, eh? Get it? And oh, Milo, there's one thing more we forgot to ask you, and I suppose we should. It's touchy, so I'm sorry. Will these planes of yours work?"

"Will they work?"

"Will they do the job you say they will? The future of the world may depend on it."

"Would I lie to you?" said Milo Minderbinder.

"When the future of the world may depend on it?" said ex-PFC Wintergreen.

"I would sooner lie to my wife, sir."

"Thank you, Milo. Thank you, Gene. I know I can count on that promise."

"General Binger," said Wintergreen, with the pained solemnity of a man taking umbrage, "I understand what war is like. With all due respect, I think there is no one on earth who knows it better than I do. In the big war I served overseas as a PFC. I dug ditches in Colorado. I sorted mail in a small mail room in the Mediterranean when the Normandy invasion was planned and executed. I was there on D day, in my mail room, I mean, and it was not much bigger than this room we're in today. I stuck my neck out in the Rome-Arno campaign with stolen Zippo lighters for our fighting men in the Italian theater of operations."

"I did that with eggs," said Milo.

"We don't have to be reminded of all that's at stake. I understand the enemy, and I know what all of us are up against. No one in this room has a stronger understanding than I have of my responsibilities in this matter or a deeper commitment to my duty to fulfill them."

"I'm sorry, sir," said General Binger to him humbly.

"Unless it's you, General, or Mr. Minderbinder here. Or any of your colleagues at the table with you, sir.

"I knew those bastards were going to ask for something," he said with a growl to Milo as soon as the two of them had left the room and were together outside.

"Wintergreen," whispered Milo, as they moved away from the august building from which they had just made their exit, "will these planes of ours work?"

"How the fuck should I know?"

"If the future of the world is going to depend on it, I think the future of M&M E&A may be affected, too. I think we ought to have something put down on paper pretty fast so they can move right along, shouldn't we? We'll need some punchy sales copy for a booklet or leaflet. Who can we get who's good at that?"

"Yossarian?"

"No."

"Why not?"

"He might object."

"Fuck him," said Wintergreen. "We can ignore him again."

"I wish you wouldn't swear so much in the nation's capital."

"No one but you can hear me."

Milo looked apprehensive, shaking his head, and the uneven halves of his russet-gray mustache flickered unevenly, as though the two were not attached to the same upper lip. "No, not Yossarian. He's been objecting a lot lately. I really don't think I want him to know any more about what we're doing than he's already found out."

"How come?"

Milo continued shaking his head. "I'm not sure I trust him. I think he's still honest."

4

Nearby in the White House, the president was just finishing up his packing on the final day of final decision.

"Aren't you going to dress?"

George Bush said no to his friend as he completed his last preparations before departing officially. "That's another one of the great retirement benefits of being just plain George," he stated jauntily. He was attired casually in khaki chino trousers, a box-plaid flannel shirt of red and black, and a sleeveless shooting jacket with game pouches, into which he had set carefully a number of the citations and awards he'd been packing. He gazed quizzically at another one of the paper emblems of office he was on the verge of folding away. "Say, Charlie," he inquired pensively, "what do you know about heavy water?"

"Nothing. Why? It's got something to do with nuclear reactions, doesn't it?"

"We've got a guy who's producing it, an American. A chaplain, no less. A retired chaplain from the old army air force back in World War II."

"Make him stop. What's the problem?"

"He can't stop. He's producing it sort of, if you know what I mean, biologically."

"Biologically? No, I don't know what you mean."

"That's what it says in this memo, code name Tap Water. He eats and drinks like the rest of us, but what comes out of him is, I guess, heavy water."

"Well, I'll be damned. That so?"

"That's what they tell me is so. It seems he was researched and developed by Milo Minderbinder of the Double-M E&A company, who claims to have an option on him."

"I know about Milo Minderbinder. I've known about Milo Minderbinder for a long time."

"And our intelligence agencies tell us this chaplain was in close contact with another M&M man named Yossarian before we took him into custody. Another former air-corps man, a captain."

"Yossarian?"

"Yes, he talks to the chaplain's wife regularly. Nothing dirty between them yet. He talks to a registered nurse too, and she may also be involved. There may be a Belgian connection. 'The Belgian is swallowing,' she said to Yossarian the last time they spoke."

"Yossarian?" repeated Charlie Stubbs. "You're saying Yossarian?"

"You know him? You want his first name?"

"How many Yossarians could there be? I knew about Yossarian when I was back in Pianosa during the war, before they transferred me to the Pacific. He was a bombardier, right? He was a little bit crazy then."

"Crazy?"

"That's what everybody thought. I remember saying to someone during a very bad time there that I thought that crazy son of a gun Yossarian was the only sane one of us left."

"Dangerous?"

"I wouldn't think so. Not normally. Where've you got this chaplain? I may know him too."

"In a cellar. With lead-lined walls."

"What can you do about him?"

"Oh, any one of our counterterrorist intelligence units can kill him easily, if it ever comes to that. But he may be valuable. We're having a problem with our heavy water, you know. And with our tritium too."

"What's tritium?"

"The gas we get from it, it says here. And we need that for our nuclear warheads. We might want a lot more like him, if he can teach others to pass heavy water too. We don't know what to do. We've got Yossarian under round-the-clock surveillance forty-eight hours a day now, it says here. I suppose that means by two men twenty-four hours a day."

"Or four men twelve hours a day."

"Yes, that could be true, too. Would that be round-the-clock?"

"No, George."

"He and the chaplain's wife talk in code on the phone and pretend they don't know much about it."

"How about a public-opinion poll?"

"That would be the intelligent way to decide. The problem, though, is that we still want to keep him secret, in case we do have to disappear him."

"Are you sure you want to take that report with you as a citation, George? It sounds like a complicated problem. Why not let your successor cope with it?"

"Quayle? Of course. He's just the one."

THE DAY BUSH LEFT

"Politics, they're saying, stops at the water's edge."

"What's it mean, George?"

"I'm not sure I know. Charlie?"

"Maybe it has something to do with our borders, that we try to pretend we are unified in outlook and won't tolerate disagreement when it comes to foreign affairs."

"That's a funny thought," said the President, who was persisting to the end in his determination to resign. "But why water? Our borders north and south aren't water, are they? You see, Charlie, I've been learning my history."

"That's geography, George."

The three men sat flopped comfortably about the White House office, each looking and feeling looser than at any time since Election Eve. There were the President himself, his Secretary of State, and his trusted friend Charlie Stubbs.

"Well, it doesn't really matter now that I'm leaving. Right? How many are there waiting to see me?"

"About a dozen. The leaders from both political parties in the House and the Senate, the chairmen and a few others from both national committees."

The Nation, vol. 250, 4 June 1990, pp. 779–85; originally published as "The Day Bush Left the White House" in *The Guardian* (Manchester), 12–13 May 1990, pp. 4–6.

"My goodness, I didn't realize they all liked me that much," said President Bush.

"They don't like you at all, George. It's the idea of Quayle that appalls them. We think you should see them."

"Aaaaw, shoot. Jim, you talk to them first and prepare them for disappointment. Well, Charlie, what do you think?" George Bush asked when alone with Stubbs. "I have to stick to my decision, don't I?"

"Only if you're sick of the job and truly want to leave it. You've proved your point. You made it to the top and you are your own man. You're not much of a man, we know, but at least you're your own. So go ahead and resign if that's what you want."

"That's the only advice I've been given since I took office that seems to add up."

"And it's the only thing you've done that seems to make sense."

The President laughed like the good sport he was widely acknowledged to be. "I still have all this packing to finish. Give me a hand with some of these trophies and citations. Golly, there's a mess of them."

"You're taking them all?"

"I wouldn't want to leave a dirty White House."

"You didn't mind conducting a dirty campaign, did you?"

"Wasn't that a beauty, Charlie?"

"Certainly the filthiest presidential campaign in my recollection, George."

"I doubt it will ever be surpassed. I think history will celebrate that as my highest achievement."

"What confounds me still, George, is that you could be the standard-bearer of the vilest, dirtiest, most ugly presidential campaign in modern history and still come out of it looking so squeaky clean. How can it be, George, that people still think you're basically decent, kind, and gentle?"

"I have a thousand points of light."

"And you did such a magical job between the day you were elected and the day you took office."

"I was good then, wasn't I?"

"You've never been better. Between the election and your inauguration you were dazzling, inspiring, charismatic, irreproachable. Your approval rating hit the top before you even took the oath."

"I should never have taken the oath."

"You'd be remembered as the most popular President in history if you'd never become one."

"I have to admit that's true," George Bush admitted. "Charlie, it's hard work, and tedious too. All that posing around for photographers every day. There are thousands of people who can do the job as well as I can. As far as I can tell, there's not much to it."

"But Dan Quayle isn't one of them. George, there's just no way in the world you're going to get anyone sensible to like him, not even if he turns into Willie Mays."

"It's funny you should say that," George Bush said and laughed. "Because for a time we were thinking of picking Willie Mays as my running mate."

"I can guess why you didn't." Stubbs nodded sagely. "It would have been hard to run that antiblack hate campaign if you had Willie Mays on the ticket."

"We didn't really run an antiblack hate campaign, Charlie," the President protested. "All we set out to do was reach those white people in the country who hate blacks. We figured if we could get our message to voters who are antiblack, we would get close to a hundred percent of the white vote. Willie Horton is the one we decided to concentrate on, not Willie Mays."

"And that's what dumbfounds me, George, how you were able to be up to your eyeballs in that cesspool of a campaign and still come out of it smelling like a rose. No one held you to blame."

"That was neat, wasn't it? It *was* rather low, yes?"

"The lowest. You were spineless and shameless and you still are. You're a perfect hypocrite, George."

"Thank you, Charlie. I know you wouldn't say that just to flatter me."

"It comes from the heart."

"That's why I treasure it. It's easy to explain, Charlie. The American people love a winner."

"The press too?"

"Oh, they're the easiest. They don't really mind, even when they criticize. They love to be invited to anything official, even press conferences. Owners never get angry. They're very rich and can't afford to."

"Your managers must love you. You never say no to them, do you?"

"Only when they tell me to."

"I was amazed when——"

"I know. When even Willie Horton conceded on Election Night and sent me that telegram of congratulation."

"That was a nice gesture you made, George, granting him a presidential pardon."

"I felt I owed him that much. Especially since he hated that photograph we used. The way we designed it, Charlie, was to give the public the impression that other people in the background were making those dirty campaign decisions and I was just an innocent wimp doing and saying whatever they ordered me to, like some kind of dumb dodo."

"But isn't that pretty much the way it happened?"

"The Willie Horton thing was my idea."

"To focus on him?"

"To pardon him, and then to take him into the State Department as an Under Secretary for Latin American affairs. That's a very good post for a person who doesn't mind crime, Charlie. Latin America is just about the best place left where we can still get away with murder. You see, I've learned my geography too."

"That's history, George. George, what is there about you that convinces people you're not actually as bad and mean as the person who says and does all those bad and mean things you continually say and do? At times you're as bad as the worst, and you're always transparent."

"Thanks, Charlie. I think it's that daffy preppy style I have. And of course, there's my background at Yale."

"William Buckley has that."

"And I play dumb. That's where I'm smart. That's pretty easy for me."

"I didn't think it would be hard. So tell me, George. Now that we're nearing the end and you can speak freely." Stubbs paused. "Why did you pick him?"

"Don't ask me that again!" cried President George Bush, with a terrible wince that would have wrung with remorse the heart of a weaker man than his close friend Charlie Stubbs. "If I hear that question one more time I think I'll scream!"

"You are screaming," answered Charlie Stubbs. "George, today is your last full day in office, and God dammit, I want to know. You barely knew him. You didn't even know he'd been dodging the draft. What was the gimmick? Where was the catch?"

"There was none, darn it. There was no gimmick, no need for any kind of deal. How can I make you believe me?"

"I have trouble believing there is even such a person as this J. Danforth Quayle, even one."

"I liked the idea. I thought he'd be good. So there."

"Why didn't you ask someone?"

"I did, by God. Do you think I'm an idiot? I consulted with the best minds around me. They all said no."

"Then why did you do it?"

"To show those smart alecks I was my own man. By then I was sick and tired of living in Reagan's shadow."

"Don't take offense, George, but I believe I speak for the majority of mankind when I say you looked better in Reagan's shadow than you've looked since. Should I go?"

"No, stay. When those Congressmen come traipsing in to beg me to reconsider, I want you right up here beside me. The second you see me waver, speak out and stop me so they will see that I'm not so easily swayed once I'm reminded I shouldn't be. Bring them on. I feel like kicking some ass again."

"Oh, George, for Christ sakes!"

Stubbs was still wearing the wince of his own when the door was opened by the Secretary of State to admit the gentlemen in the delegation of supplicants from the Congress and from both national political parties, who filed in singly, silently, and somberly. They numbered ten in all. The greeting with which their President welcomed them was cordial.

"Come in, guys, come on in. Isn't this gorgeous weather we're having neat? What are you all looking so glum about? It's always darkest before the dawn, isn't it?"

"George," Charlie Stubbs admonished cautiously.

"Sorry, Charlie."

"Well, if I may begin," said the Secretary of State, "these gentlemen all respectfully recognize that your mind is made up, Mr. President, but they've come with pages of petitions signed by just about every member of both parties in both houses of Congress begging you to reconsider your decision to leave. And by now, I have received messages, some stained with tears, from leaders in just about every developed nation in the free world and in the communist world, and from most in the Third World too."

"Imagine that." George Bush beamed. "The Soviets too?"

"Of course. The message from the Soviet ambassador is one of those that is stained with tears. They no sooner want a nuclear war than we do."

"Well, fellas," said George Bush, in his nicest nice-guy mode,

"I have to tell you candidly what I have already said in public. What I am doing is right, and while I am still the President, I am still the best person to tell other people what is right. Right? It is right because I have grown to realize—I have grown in office—that being President is something I'm really not cut out for."

"You will get no argument on that point, Mr. President," said a Congressional member from his own party.

"Call me George, Bob. I'm glad I've succeeded in convincing you."

"My name is John, George."

"My name is Bob," spoke up a tall man.

"So is mine," said a small one.

"It's good to get to know you all again," said George Bush. "I thought you didn't like what I was doing with my Administration, Bob."

"My name is Tom, George."

"I'm Bob, George, and I don't like what you've been doing, either. But politics must stop at the water's edge."

"What does that mean, Tom?"

"It means that in times of great crisis, Mr. President, we lay aside our partisan bickering and forget about the lousy job you've been doing while we think, for a change, of the public good."

"But why the water's edge?"

"I'm not sure. But that doesn't matter right now, any more than does the question of whether your lousy Administration has been lousier than Reagan's or not."

"Lousier than Reagan's?" Here the President perked up alertly. "Oh, no, we can't let that one pass. Let me make one thing clear. With me it's been mainly a matter of reserved presidential style, and you may not have noticed all of the good improvements we've been making steadily, along with many of the bad improvements."

"George," Stubbs said.

"In a minute, Charlie. We've been making many of these good and bad changes for the better so gradually that they just as well might not have been made at all for any difference they made, and we would have been much better off just leaving things as they were instead of wasting all that time and money making them. Now my agenda is complete, and the time has come for me to pass the torch and fade away."

"George," Stubbs admonished.

"Sorry, Charlie."

"What about Quayle, Mr. President? Will you tell us once and for all why you picked him?"

"If you ask him that he'll scream."

"Thank you, Charlie."

"You're leaving all of us in a lurch. What about the S.D.I.?"

"What's that?"

"Star Wars. Should we go ahead or shouldn't we? By the way, Mr. President, is this room bugged? Are you secretly recording everything for some future book you have in mind?"

"That suggestion is offensive," the President replied with asperity. "But let me give you the assurance you want." With long steps he strode to his desk and buzzed his secretary. "Primrose, please turn off all the recording equipment. And see that everything we've got is erased."

"Yes, Mr. President," a woman responded immediately. "Does that mean you want it left on?"

"No, I want it turned off."

"Now I understand, sir. But I think I've forgotten the code. You want it on?"

"I want it off. Just ask the sound engineer. Tell him I really want it off."

"Yes, Mr. President. But he's not sure of the code either. He's filling in."

"Oh, Primrose, just forget it, please forget I even asked." The President turned back with an exaggerated shrug. "And you

guys are asking *me* about the S.D.I.? That thing is all too technical for the White House to decide, and we won't know what to do
until we read the latest public opinion polls."

"Does he know that?"

"Who?"

"Quayle. Your Vice President. God dammit, Mr. President,
where the hell did you find that guy anyway?"

"Please call me George. Look, you guys control the Congress.
If you're all so worried, why don't you just stop him from doing
anything? And then impeach him."

"For what?"

"For not doing anything."

"Couldn't you at least persuade him to resign before you do?"

"Resign? Of course. I could do that in a minute. But who
would replace me if he resigns first?"

"Does it matter?"

"Politics stops at the water's edge."

"Consider it accomplished." Nobly, and with a condescend-
ing air of self-satisfaction, he moved to his desk and flipped the
switch on his intercom. "Primrose?"

"Yes, Mr. President?"

"Get me Little Prince. I want to talk to him."

"On the telephone, sir?"

"Of course on the telephone! Do you think I want him here?
I'll take it inside. Excuse me, fellas. He'll be gone before you
know it." With the wave and the over-the-shoulder smile familiar to news photographers, he exited, closing the door behind
him on a room relaxed into silence.

"See, Jim? I promised he'd do the right thing, didn't I?"

"Thanks, Jim. He's a real George, isn't he?"

"In England they would call him a Charlie," said the Secretary of State, who by then had been there.

"It's one of the reasons he remains so popular."

"Give me another."

"No one dislikes him."

"No one disliked Reagan either."

"Except George."

"What about Quayle, Jim? You're the one who checked him out, weren't you?"

"Don't ask me that."

"He'll scream too."

"Thank you, Charlie. He swore to me on everything holy to him, and there seems to be a lot, that there was not a single thing in his entire background that could ever prove embarrassing. That should have made me suspicious. When that National Guard draft-dodging scam unraveled I hit the ceiling. By then George had to keep him, but he almost dumped me."

"Why won't he tell us why he picked him?"

"He doesn't know."

"Do you?"

"He wanted a running mate who'd look worse than he does. Quayle was the only name the computer would give."

"I miss Richard Nixon."

"So do we."

They froze at the turn of the doorknob and all turned with expectation to face in that direction. The man who had sauntered away confidently came ambling back in with an appearance of amused bewilderment, moving his head moderately from side to side and chuckling to himself rhythmically.

"Well, guys, guess what—I think you're all out of luck," he announced, laughing, as though releasing good news. "The Little Prince refuses to resign. He says he's very happy where he is right now."

"There's nothing funny about that."

"I think there is. I may have caught him at a bad time. I think he was playing a video game. 'Varoom, varoom, varoom' was the first thing he said. He tells me he can't imagine a better spot than the one he's got right now. He also tells me he's just a heartbeat away from the presidency."

"What the hell does that mean?"

"Does he mean your heartbeat or his?"

"I forgot to ask. The way he puts it, if he wasn't the Vice President he might have to go back to welding or writing press releases, and he fears he may have lost his magic. He doesn't know if there's anything else he could be much good at but leading the free world and being head of the greatest industrial nation on earth. I didn't think we were still the greatest industrial nation, but he might know more than I do. And as Vice President, he says, he would be first in line to succeed me when I leave tomorrow."

"How the hell did he find that out?"

"Somebody must have told him!"

"Maybe he read my lips."

"He doesn't like to read."

"I knew it was a mistake, I told you it was a mistake!" howled the Secretary of State in a wail of piercing anguish. "We should never have given him that money for a tutor!"

The President's last official act in public was to wrap himself in the flag once more and pledge allegiance to it.

"That was disgraceful, George," said Charlie Stubbs frankly. "You degraded yourself and you desecrated the flag."

"Thank you, Charlie."

TO LAUGH IN THE MORNING

In New York they sometimes gave you the cold turkey treatment, that is they locked you in a cell with your panic and left you to suffer alone, not caring if you tore your eyes out in the cry for sleep or went insane in that awful, aching misery of slowly coming awake and realizing where you were and what it was you wanted. They brought you your meals and if you made too much noise they gave you a sedative that didn't do much good, but nobody really cared, and when they let you out it wasn't a doctor who examined you but a burly, beef-eating sergeant who looked at you with contempt and didn't care if you fell dead before him the minute after he had signed you out. That was why he had gone to Kentucky. At least there they tapered you off so that the dry agony was minimized and delayed and, if nothing else, there were the free shots every day that insured the trip against being completely abortive. Someone from the neighborhood was always going to Kentucky. One or two actually hoped to be cured, but most went for the laughs—it was like going away on vacation—or because they were broke and there were always the free shots.

He had gone to be cured.

Coming back there was a three-hour wait in Washington. He stood uncertainly in the bus terminal, made uncomfortable by all the activity there and by the fact that he was alone. He car-

Previously unpublished; written between 1946 and 1949.

ried his belongings in a barracks bag and he wore the green flying jacket he had brought home with him from the army. He had been a gunner. He eyed himself furtively in the mirror over a vending machine. His skin was poor and his wide face was tired and without flesh. He turned from the mirror quickly, embarrassed by the thought that someone might observe him studying himself. He checked his bag and left the terminal.

Outside he began to sweat. It was winter and the air was cold with a frosty wind, but the perspiration poured from his face. He had been wondering about that for a long time, this sweating on the coldest days, but each time he thought about it he felt that it had always been happening, that he had always been this way. In his pocket was a list of doctors who would usually give you a prescription for the price of a visit. The inmates exchanged this information, and there was a sour irony in the fact that twelve names were listed within fifty miles of the hospital itself. He had three hours to spend, and he decided to check one of the names on the list, not because he needed or wanted anything but only because it would kill time. He didn't like being alone in a strange city, even in New York he didn't like being alone. It was most painful in restaurants. Sometimes he could barely eat.

The doctor's offices were on the first floor of an old brownstone building. There were lemon curtains in the windows and a card with his name and office hours. As soon as the nurse appeared Nat was sorry that he had come. He had composed a conversation, but it was all suddenly forgotten in the feeling of guilt and shame that came when she looked at him.

"I—I'd like to see the doctor," he murmured.

The nurse led him inside. She was a thin, middle-aged woman with coarse, graying hair and a desiccated expression that seemed incapable of joy or sympathy. She sat down at her desk and turned to him.

"Do you have an appointment?"

He shook his head.

"Are you a regular patient of his?"

He shook his head again. The nurse reached for a card and asked his name.

"Nathan Scholl," he said, and then realized that she would ask more questions. He stepped forward nervously. "I—I don't live in Washington. I was passing by and saw his sign. Can't I talk to him about it? It—it's kind of personal."

The nurse rose and went inside. As soon as she was gone he wanted to leave. He took a step toward the door, then stopped abruptly with the fear that she might return as he was going and call him back. He waited helplessly. The nurse returned finally and sent him inside.

The inner office was filled with a musty gloom. The heavy chairs were upholstered in brown leather, the cabinets were of brown wood. The doctor wore a brown suit. He was a short, balding man with very sharp, dark eyes. He studied Nat piercingly as he waited for him to speak.

"I," Nat began uncertainly, "I've just come from Kentucky. They told me that if I needed anything I could come to you for a prescription."

The doctor grew suspicious. "I'm afraid I don't understand you."

"I was taking the cure there," Nat said. He knew that the doctor wanted time to analyze him. "Someone gave me your name. They said you'd take care of me if I—if I needed a shot."

The doctor studied him carefully, trying to determine if there was any subterfuge. He saw an asthenic, self-conscious boy of about twenty-five with sallow skin and a wide frame that should have packed a great deal of weight but didn't, a boy of obviously impecunious means who had forgotten most of what education he had ever received. He reached for a prescription pad and began writing.

"What's your name?"

"Nathan Scholl."

The doctor had him spell it.

"What do you want?"

"Heroin."

The doctor wrote rapidly. When he finished he tore the slip from the pad and pushed it forward. Nat reached for it slowly.

"How much is that?"

"Ten dollars."

"I—I don't have ten dollars," Nat confessed shamefully.

"How much do you have?"

Nat put his hand in his pocket. He knew exactly what he had, but he pretended to be counting. His bus ticket was paid for, and he had a five and two singles and about a dollar in change. That was all the money he had in the world and he didn't want to part with any of it. He had not meant to take the prescription. At this point he had intended laughing aloud and strolling from the office, but his resolution faded beneath the steady scrutiny of the doctor. He had always felt uncomfortable with doctors.

"I've got six dollars," he said.

"Let me have it."

Nat gave him the money. The doctor straightened the two bills on his desk and stared at them intently. He put the five in his pocket and pushed the single toward Nat.

"Take this," he said dryly. "You'll need it for the prescription. It will cost more than a dollar, but I'm quite certain you have the rest in your pocket."

Nat hesitated, feeling his face turn red. He snatched the dollar and fled from the office. Outside he tore up the prescription, doing it very deliberately so that the pieces were tiny. When that was done he felt better.

He reached New York in the afternoon and took the subway to the last stop and then a bus to the street on which he lived. The day was damp and dreary. A few strangers moved along the sidewalks. He did not know many people there, although he had lived in the same house all his life. It was not the kind of neighborhood where people generally remained long. Families came, stayed a few months, and then moved on. Only his family had taken root there. He felt a quiet conflict of emotions as he entered the house. He was glad to be home, yet it was with a sense of depression that he mounted the steps.

He found his sister in the kitchen. He liked May. She was almost thirty, a pleasant-faced girl, and she was astonished when he appeared.

"My God!" she said excitedly, as they moved into the front room. "We weren't expecting you for months. Why didn't you tell us you were coming?"

Nat shrugged, still grinning at her. He moved awkwardly to a chair and sat down, placing the barracks bag between his legs. "Where's Mom?"

"Out shopping. Why didn't you ever write? She's been worried sick about you."

Nat shrugged again, smiling at her uneasily. "I sent you a card from Kentucky on the way down. Didn't you get it?"

"Yes, but—" May laughed. "Well you weren't really gone long. Didn't you like Florida?"

Nat looked down at the flowering pattern of the linoleum. "It was all right," he said.

"You must have worked hard. Look how pale you are."

"Yeah," he said, grateful for the lead she had supplied. "I was inside all day. It wasn't much of a job, just knocking around. That's why I came back. I'd like to find something steady." The palms of his hands were wet and he wiped them on his thighs. "Where's the kid?"

"Dick? Don't tell me you missed him."

"I guess I did," Nat said grudgingly. May had two children, an infant of less than a year and Dick, who was about nine. "I brought him a present."

He searched inside the barracks bag until he found a package. Inside was a pair of learner's skates that he had purchased on the way down. The knot was tight and he tore the string impatiently. "Learner's skates," he said, displaying them with bashful pride.

May smiled sadly. "Nat, he's too old for them," she said softly. "He's been using regular skates for a few weeks now."

Nat was silent. The skates were suddenly very heavy in his hand. "Well," he said uncomfortably, "it seemed like a good idea."

"It was," May answered quickly. "Why, the princess will soon be ready for them. She's probably calling for them now."

The baby had started crying. May stood up and left the room. Nat toyed with the skates for a minute and then placed them carefully back in the box. He was still staring at them when May returned.

"Nat," she said. "Did you really mean that about finding something steady?"

He nodded, looking at her dejectedly and speaking in an unhappy voice. "I don't like to knock around, May, you know that. It's just that there isn't anything I can do."

"What would you like to do?"

"I'd like to learn a trade, something steady, maybe even go to college." He sat up suddenly. The idea excited him and he went on eagerly. "You know, I could go to college. The government would pay for it. I used to write pretty good compositions in school. Maybe I could do something there, newspaper work or something like that." There was a silence when he stopped, and he looked down at the floor as his unnatural optimism gave way to a conviction of futility. "H—how is Fred?" he asked, in a lower voice.

"He's fine. Did I tell you we found an apartment?"

Nat shook his head. He was very happy for her. "When will you be moving?"

"I don't know if we're going to take it," May said. Her face filled with distress. "I don't feel right about leaving Mom here alone."

"She won't be alone," said Nat. "I'll be here."

"Yes, but you're never home. Oh, nobody's blaming you, Nat. We don't expect you to stay home much at your age. But there's still Mom. We haven't even told her. She'd make us take it if she knew."

Nat sat perfectly still, feeling hideous with a dreadful sense of shame. He rose after a moment and crossed the room slowly until he stood above her. "Take the apartment, May," he said. "I'll look after Mom."

May was silent.

"I mean it," he said.

"I know you do." May smiled into his eyes for a moment and then reached for a cigarette. "We'll talk about it when Fred comes home. Do you want to shower? The baby's things are there, but I can get them out in a moment."

"No. I think I'll go out for a while."

May walked with him to the door. "Nat," she said. "Be home early. Mom will want to see you."

"Sure, May, of course."

She caught his elbow as he was leaving. "Do you need any money?" she asked gently.

Nat hesitated awkwardly. He felt that same degraded uncertainty he had experienced in the doctor's office. He didn't want to take money from her, but he only had a few dollars and there was no telling how long that would last. "Can you spare a buck or two?" he asked, without looking at her.

May nodded and went for her purse. She came back with a five dollar bill. He thanked her and turned to go. Once more she stopped him. Her manner was anxious.

"Nat, you'll be home for dinner, won't you?"

He assured her that he would.

Outside he paused to look back at the house. It was one of a long row, all crammed together without an inch of daylight between them and identical in appearance with a drab monotony that extended to the last, dusty, old yellow brick and the black ash cans outside spinning their cinders into the air. Some boys were playing association, a game of passing that was played with a football. He remembered how he had been good at association. He had been good at other sports too, punchball, hockey, football, but all that was at a time when being good at sports was all that was necessary. Then he had gone to high school where he suddenly found himself among people with different interests and personalities, and into his confusion had come the creeping realization that his own neighborhood was a bad one, that his family was poor, that he was clumsy, uncouth, and something of a roughneck. He had been good at sports but not good enough to make the school teams, and suddenly he was lost in a swarm of familiar faces with nothing to do and no place to turn.

He walked to the avenue and looked around. Two blocks to his left was the luncheonette which served as a gathering place for everyone he knew. Past that was the poolroom. He did not want to go there, either to the luncheonette or the poolroom, but there was nothing to turn him elsewhere.

A number of people moved around in the cold outside the luncheonette, a bookmaker, some gamblers, two hoodlums, and, in a group of their own, some kids who had grown up too fast. Nat went inside and ordered a sandwich and coffee. He ate very slowly. Each time the door opened he looked up, hoping to see someone he knew, yet feeling an inner relief when the person was a stranger. He finished eating and walked outside. He paused a moment and then went to the poolroom.

Several people were there, some of them familiar, but no one he wanted to talk to. Carl, the owner, spotted him and came forward. Nat didn't like him. Carl was a Rabelaisian vulgarity, a very short, round, very hairy man with a coated tongue he displayed frequently to whomever he thought it would annoy. He spoke in his high, taunting voice.

"Well, look who's here."

"Hello, Carl," Nat said.

Carl was capable of anything, and he waited fearfully.

"Where the hell have you been?"

"Out of town," Nat said. "I was down in Florida for a while."

Carl studied him, cocking his head slightly and smiling mockingly. "Florida," he said, with contempt. "Florida, my ass. Don't hand me that. You weren't in Florida. Do you know where you were? You were down in Kentucky taking the cure with the other junkies. Some Florida. Who you trying to kid?"

Nat looked down guiltily, then managed to smile as he raised his eyes. "How the hell did you know?" he asked, with a weak attempt at bravado.

"How did I know?" Carl asked incredulously, as though amazed by the question. "Carl knows everything. Didn't you know that?"

Carl laughed triumphantly and then moved off to a table in the rear. Nat was almost afraid to move, certain that everyone had heard, but when he looked up finally he saw that no one was watching him. Carl returned in a few minutes, approaching very deliberately. His face was fat and his swollen cheeks made wicked slits of his eyes. He spoke as though he had planned every word.

"Business is bad. Business is lousy. And do you know why? Carl will tell you why. Because it's cold and you can't heat this place. Everyone comes in and complains to Carl about the cold. Everyone but you. You come in and you sweat like a pig. How can you sweat like that when it's so cold?"

Nat walked outside.

It was colder now and soon it would be dark. Winter was like that, dark in the afternoon. In the summer the air was nice and people came from all over to use the beach. There was noise in the night and it was easy to get a girl, but in the winter people seemed silent and alone and everything grew still in a bleak reminder of despair.

Nat mopped his face viciously, cursing himself for his strange affliction. He walked several yards and hid himself in the doorway of a vacant shop. The small enclosure afforded a tenuous security, allowing him to watch the entrance to the poolroom without being readily observed. Several people passed, and then a figure appeared who made him start and step forward.

"Sol!" he called. "Sol!"

Sol was surprised to see him. He smiled and shook Nat's hand warmly.

"Hello, Nat," he said.

"Hello, Sol. How've you been?"

Sol nodded. He was a few inches taller than Nat, fairly good-looking with nice eyes and very fine black hair. For a moment he was puzzled by the doorway. Then he looked at the poolroom and seemed to understand.

"Have you got some time?" he asked casually. "I want to get a bet down, but I'll be right out."

Nat nodded. He was glad to see Sol. Sol was very intelligent; he had been to college for three years. They had once been very close, but for a while now Sol had been keeping to himself. Nat's friends didn't like him, resenting what they took to be an air of superiority, and they often joked about him. It always bothered Nat when they did, but he had never defended him.

Sol returned in a few minutes. "Where've you been, Nat? I haven't seen you around."

Nat paused a moment. "I was down in Florida for a while."

"Make out all right?"

"Pretty good," Nat said.

They began walking slowly, moving past the poolroom and across the street to the next block, seating themselves finally on some steps before a house. Sol gave him a cigarette and they smoked in silence for a while.

"Sol," Nat said. He looked away awkwardly. "I wasn't down in Florida. I was in Kentucky."

Sol laughed quietly. "I know you were," he said. "Did you go for the cure?"

Nat nodded. "They fixed me up too. I guess I wasn't hooked so bad. I didn't even have to stay the full time."

"Was it bad, Nat?" Sol asked.

"Yeah. For a while it was pretty bad." Nat laughed nervously, feeling painfully self-conscious. "Sol, do you still pick up? You can get on if you want to."

"It won't bother you?"

Nat shook his head. Sol found a reefer, and in a few seconds the sweet, rich smell of marijuana was very strong. In the side street a boy and girl were talking in a doorway. The boy looked somewhat familiar, but it was the girl Nat watched. She seemed very pretty from the distance, very pretty and very happy, and Nat envied the boy for being with her and for being able to make her happy. Sol made sucking noises as he smoked the reefer and Nat eyed him greedily. Tea was all right, he told himself. It gave you a lift and it wasn't too bad if you didn't have any, not like The Horse and Big C, but tea was all right. He asked for the reefer and Sol hesitated doubtfully as he gave it to him. Nat felt steadier immediately. He kept it a while and then passed it back, exhaling comfortably.

"It's funny how tea acts when you're hopped," he said. "One stick can whack you out."

"Yeah," Sol said. "So I've heard."

"Sol, how come you never got hooked?" Nat asked seriously.

Sol shook his head slowly. "Junk is bad, Nat," he said with conviction. "I guess you know that now. You were there when they first brought it around. Do you remember what happened?"

Nat remembered perfectly. A sailor had skipped with money given him to buy a pound of marijuana. He was seen some time later and two of the fellows went to wait outside the house in which he roomed. When he didn't show they broke into the room and went through everything he had, finding only a bag of capsules that had been carefully concealed. Some instinctive voice had told them of its value, and they returned with it to the neighborhood. An older person there recognized the contents and knew what to do with it.

There were about twenty in the crowd that moved from the avenue to the darkened side street, some, like Nat and Sol, merely going to watch. They borrowed a spoon from the luncheonette, and there were enough cigarette lighters in the group to boil the capsules down. They didn't have a hypodermic syringe so they had each of them taken a skin pop. With an open safety pin they punctured the skin over the forearm and jabbed the grains beneath. Some were clumsy and there was a lot of blood. It was a slow process, and even before the last one had finished the first one was throwing up. In a few minutes they were all vomiting into the street, every single one who was taking it for the first time. The picture was vivid in Nat's memory and he chuckled nostalgically.

"Yeah," he said. "That was quite a sight."

"It was awful," Sol said, with strong feeling. "The most sickening thing I've ever seen. Nat, how come you got hooked after that?"

It was a question Nat had pondered over many times before, and he took a long time answering. "I don't know," he said, in a very low voice. "It was just something to do, I guess."

"Yeah," Sol said. "I guess that's it."

They were silent and Nat looked down the block at the couple talking in the doorway. They weren't touching, but he noticed how they swayed deliciously toward each other and then apart in the subtle, unconscious game of temptation, promise, and denial that underran their conversation.

The girl had light hair, and he would have loved to touch its soft strands and breathe its sweet, fresh fragrance. That was what he needed, he decided, a girl, not a whore but a nice girl, someone to laugh in the morning. But he couldn't talk to a nice girl. He did pretty well with the tramps, not meeting them but moving in after someone else had found them, but he never knew what to say to a nice girl. Then you needed money with a nice girl. You couldn't sit in a hallway or take her to the park, and even when he had the money to take her to the city he could never find anyplace to go but a movie, and all night long he would be petrified with the agonizing awareness that she wasn't having a good time and that he was helpless and had failed pathetically.

All this went through Nat's mind, and he turned to Sol with a sudden motion. "Sol, where's Berry? Have you seen him around?"

Sol looked surprised. "I thought you were cured," he said.

"I was. At least I thought I was. I don't know, Sol." Nat shook his head miserably. He clasped and unclasped his fingers, staring down past them at the hard sidewalk. "I've been jittery ever since I hit New York. It was all right while I was away, but I've been shaking inside ever since I got home. I don't know what'll happen when I see him. It isn't that I want a shot, but I want something, and I don't know what'll happen when I see him."

"Nat, why don't you go away?" Sol clasped his arm and peered earnestly into his eyes. "To another city. There's nothing here for you."

"I've thought about that, Sol. But I could only go to Florida or California, someplace where I knew someone, and then it would be the same thing all over again."

"Go someplace where you don't know anyone."

Nat laughed bitterly. "I'd never make it, Sol. It's pretty bad being alone in a strange city."

"Yeah," Sol said gravely. "I guess it is."

They were both silent. Nat was sweating again, and inside he was filled with a cold, penetrating uncertainty. He looked up from the sidewalk toward the doorway in which the boy and girl had been standing. The girl had disappeared and the boy was walking slowly toward the avenue. Nat watched him approach the corner, his eyes widening with amazement. It was Berry, and he was seized with a horrible disappointment when he recognized him.

"There's your man," Sol said quietly.

Nat nodded glumly. He looked back at the empty doorway, trying to remember what the girl had looked like, but he could recall nothing of her appearance, not even the color of her hair. Berry was walking on the other side of the avenue. Nat called him.

Berry crossed slowly. He was tall and thin with a face that was very pale and a wide, self-satisfied grin. He nodded to Sol and spoke to Nat. "I thought you were away at camp," he said.

"I just got back."

"You weren't gone long." There was a trace of contempt in Berry's voice. "You didn't go for the cure by any chance, did you?"

"Cure, hell!" Nat said. He could feel Sol's eyes upon him, but it was easier to talk to Berry. "I checked out as soon as they cut me off."

"Yeah?" Berry drawled suspiciously. "Nick and Charley left before you did and they're still getting fed."

"They were luckier. Where you going now?"

"Home for dinner. Why?"

"Have you got anything there?"

"Can you pay for it?"

"I've got five dollars."

"Then I've got something there," Berry laughed.

Nat rose with weary resignation and stepped to the sidewalk. He met Sol's eyes for a moment and then looked away uncomfortably. "So long, Sol. It was nice seeing you."

"Yeah," was all Sol said.

Nat started to leave with Berry. They got as far as the corner and then Nat asked him to wait and walked back to the stoop. Sol was still sitting there. Nat bent close to him and spoke with an anguished intensity.

"Sol, what I told him just now, it wasn't like that at all. I went for the cure. I went for the cure and I suffered like hell getting it but I guess it just wasn't any good."

"That's all right," Sol said. "You don't have to explain."

"I just wanted you to know, Sol."

"Sure, Nat. I understand."

Nat straightened and moved away regretfully.

"Well, so long, Sol. I'll see you around."

"Yeah," Sol said. "Take it easy."

A DAY IN THE COUNTRY

The poolroom was almost empty. A few high school kids were playing a noisy game of rotation at one of the front tables, their books littering the wooden benches that ran, one against each of the soiled yellow walls, the full, gloomy length of the long and narrow room. Nat glanced quickly at each of them. He frowned immediately with disappointment and continued toward the rear where Carl sat. The tip of his tongue ran anxiously over his lips. He passed Crazy George, who sat off by himself and stared blankly ahead, tranquil and self-amused, nibbling placidly at a sandwich and drinking chocolate pop from a bottle. There was the odor of dust in the air. The poolroom was old, older than Nat, who was twenty-six. He could recall loitering about the entrance as a boy, asking everyone who came out for the baseball scores. Once a man had been killed inside, shot down years before, during prohibition, it was said, as he stood chalking up his cue and plotting the table angles for a difficult shot. No one knew why. Old timers like Crazy George were fond of repeating the story. "For Christ's sake!" Nat had snapped irritably at Crazy George one time. "Is that the high spot of your life?" He remembered clearly now the hurt look in the old man's eyes.

"Carl, I need some money."

Carl was perched motionless behind the glass-faced cabinet in which he stored the cue balls and the tiny cubes of chalk. His

Previously unpublished; written between 1950 and 1952.

expression was blank and bored. He was short and fat and had a hard, broad forehead and sagging cheeks with deceptively mirthful lines curling down around them toward a small, bloodless mouth. He said nothing.

"Not much, Carl."

Carl gazed at him without interest. After a few seconds he shrugged and shook his head.

"Why not?" Nat demanded, in a rising voice.

There was a sudden burst of laughter from the front as one of the players sent a ball rocketing over the cushions to the floor, where it struck with a bang and went thudding hollowly against the wall.

"Damn kids," Carl murmured.

"Christ, Carl!"

"It's your habit," Carl said calmly. "Not mine."

"I never hung you up. I never beat you for a dime."

"What will you do tomorrow?" Carl asked, speaking slowly with the same toneless detachment.

Nat stared at him a moment longer, his fingers flexing themselves rhythmically, and then turned bitterly away. He knew Carl, and it was useless to argue further. He left through the door close by that led into the side street. The cold, damp air made him pause. *Jesus, Jesus Christ,* he moaned inwardly. *There isn't much time!* As if summoned by the thought, the fear boiled up inside him with thundering force, and he began walking rapidly. At the avenue he stopped and glanced about. He could find no place to go, and he began drifting back uncertainly, moving backwards as though retreating until he stood in the recess formed by the front entrance to the poolroom.

What discouraged him most was the waste. The time, the money spent for carfare, the whole grisly struggle, with all its incredible pain and horror and yearning despair, had been good for only three days (the fact that he was counting should have told him), and all it took was the sight of Cookie. On Monday he was standing on that same corner with Solly Harris, telling him, with a laughing, irrepressible overflow of happiness and pride, of how he had won what he had humorously chosen to call the Battle of Lexington. Then Cookie was there, standing silently on the other side of the avenue, his face sallow and shrunken, his thin, shrivelled form pitiably clothed in rags, Cookie was there, appearing soundlessly like some grim and inexorable spectre, and suddenly it was all over. The Battle of Lexington was over, and he had lost.

"Don't go, Nat," Solly Harris had warned gravely.

"Just to say hello."

"You'll regret it, Nat."

"You're crazy, Solly," Nat had laughed. "I'll be back in a minute."

"No, you won't, Nat. You won't *ever* be back."

Nat threw his cigarette away and looked up desperately at the pale, cheerless sky. It was a gray, blustery December afternoon. A few tattered clouds were chased darkly through the sky, driven by a severe, rattling wind that rose every few minutes like a tyrant's rage and lashed vengefully about. He glanced with brief antici-pation at everyone who passed. There was a solemn, ominous, straggling procession of strangers, of women, small children, and old men, packed to clumsiness in warm clothing, walking in heavy silence with heads thrust stiffly against the wind, all of them drab, even the children, with a musty, spiritless pallor. He had been everywhere, had hammered on doors and rung bells; no one was home, no one was expected until evening. Already the tickle was in his cheek, malicious, sharp, and prodding. He set his teeth grimly and began walking.

He met no one on the way home. A quick flaring of hope came when he first spied Dr. Weiner's house, a familiar, gray two-story building set back from the corner behind a handful of scrawny bushes and a few paces of lawn, but he lost courage instantly and even crossed to the other side to avoid a chance meeting with the slim, white-haired physician who had ministered to his family for almost thirty years and with whom he had once been so friendly. Mrs. Cooperman, Nat's mother, still saw him regularly for her varicose veins and her dangerously high blood pressure that made the hot summer months a hell for her, paying him with what she managed to save from the money given her by her daughter and older son, both of whom were married and lived in homes of their own. Only Nat lived with his mother. Mrs. Cooperman was a proud, obstinate, emotional woman who imposed an inflexible limit on the amounts she would accept from her children and brooded in stern silence over the fact that Nat and his brother did not speak to each other.

She was out when Nat arrived at the house. His room had been made up, cleaned, dusted; his clothes, even his moccasins, which he liked to have remain beneath the bed, had been placed carefully in the wardrobe. He waited a moment to make certain he was alone and then began opening drawers. He went through one after the other, moved with frantic determination from cabinet to cabinet, through every closet, searching the flat rapidly with a sly, calculating thoroughness. His hands shook uncontrollably. At times his excitement rose and he began scattering things about, but these panics passed, and in the end he made an excruciating effort to rearrange everything. Through it all, his face showed a strange lack of enthusiasm, as though he were resigned in advance to defeat. Suddenly his energy waned, bringing him to a stop, and he was left standing helplessly in his mother's bedroom. There would be nothing of value, he knew. In the whole house there was only one thing, his mother's winter coat, and she had that with her.

He moved despondently to his own room and lay down on the bed, one arm cast heavily over his face. There was no pain yet, but the first signs were there. From the kitchen came the tap, tap, tap of a dripping faucet. The fear brought a pain of its own, and he began to groan aloud.

His mother found him that way, stretched out flat on the bed, emitting weird, tortured noises and staring up at the ceiling with such rigid intensity that he seemed to be in a trance. Her startled cry surprised him, and when he spun around his gaze fell on her thick, shapeless legs with their elastic bandages that he could never bring himself to look at without grief and which always filled him with shame because other people could see them too. He met her eyes guiltily, nervously flicking his tongue, and then raised himself to one arm.

"Ma," he gasped quickly. "I need some money."

Mrs. Cooperman was watching him with a tearful, incredulous horror. For a few moments she was unable to speak. "Again, Nathan?" she cried finally, with sharp anger and despair. "Again? You said it was over. You told me. You told me it was over."

"It isn't, Ma. I tried, but it isn't."

She shook her head feebly and passed a hand red with cold across her face. "Go to Dr. Weiner, Nathan," she urged earnestly, her voice shaking with emotion. "Please, Nathan. Go to him. He'll know what to do."

"I've been to doctors!" he barked furiously, enraged by the time it was all taking. "God damn it, what the hell do you think they have there?"

Her eyes widened with further shock, and her lips began to tremble. All at once she gave way. A low, wailing sound rose from her and she began rocking sideways, hugging the paper bag she carried to her bosom as though it were a dying child.

"Ma!" he shouted fiercely, with impatience. "Ma!"

"Where will I get?" she cried defensively. "Where will I get to give you?" She regarded him with wild indignation for a moment; then her mood changed again and she took a quick step toward him, her eyes flashing and her face turning red. "I have money," she exclaimed, through tight, quivering lips. "Wait. I have money for you." She plunged a hand inside her coat and emerged with a tiny leather purse which she flung scornfully to the bed. "There! There's money for you!"

He seized the purse greedily. There were only a few small coins inside, and he gazed up at her with imploring bewilderment, the purse slipping from his fingers to the floor.

"Forty-three cents," she announced with the same passionate sarcasm, after she had watched him count. "Forty-three cents. I have more for you if you need it. Wait! If that isn't enough I have more. I can save you the trouble of looking. Here! Here's more for you!" She took another step toward him and held out the bag. "Here! Sixty cents chopmeat. Take it. Go ahead. Take it. Go with it to the butcher. Here's your money! Sixty cents chopmeat for supper tonight!"

He whirled away from her, rolling himself over violently and smacking hard against the wall. His eyes filled with tears. He closed them and pressed them shut savagely with a punishing strength that made the blood roar in his ears. Mrs. Cooperman had stopped talking and there was a silence, but he was not aware of it until a gentle hand fell on his arm.

"Where will I get, Nathan?" Mrs. Cooperman said again, but this time softly, with tender and pathetic regret. "Where will I get to give you?"

Slowly he grew calm, comforted by her light touch and by the soothing, consoling misery in her voice. He turned and looked at her. She was standing above him, nodding her head slightly and gazing down at him with moist, loving eyes, smiling at him sadly in tragic and eternal apology.

"Have I got to give you, Nathan? Go to Dr. Weiner, *kindt*. Go, Nathan, please. You'll see, he'll help you. *Geh, kindt, geh.*"

There was time now for nothing else. He could already feel the regions going numb inside him, dead, ashy areas of tissue that would hang like rocks for a while and then come alive suddenly with a ripping, stabbing pain that would tumble him screaming to the ground and lead him finally, mercifully, into unconsciousness.

"Can I see him, Ma? Is he in now?"

Mrs. Cooperman nodded and held his coat for him, hurrying him along with hasty phrases of encouragement and nervously reassuring pats, her eyes sparking brighter with a mounting anxiety.

"Should I go with you, Nathan? Wait, I'll go with you."

He shook his head vehemently and walked out.

It was five blocks from his house to Dr. Weiner's office, a very long one to the avenue and four others after that to the corner on which the gray house stood, and he felt from the beginning that he would not make it. In his jaw again was that throbbing, wicked, delicious itch, sharper now than before and even more tantalizing in its urgings, and he knew it was a matter of minutes. He was still two blocks away when the first pangs came. Immediately he began to run, but stopped instantly as a blazing agony tore through him. His gait grew lopsided as he struggled on, his hands in the pockets of his coat spread wide against his sides, his fingers digging in. A hard pounding rang against his temples, and he found it difficult to breathe. At last the building was before him. He tripped going up the steps and fell against the door, where he clung for a few moments, gasping hysterically for air and praying for strength to stand. The rush had left him exhausted, and his head was swimming as he reeled into the waiting room. There was the dancing tinkle of a bell in the distance and a very fat woman with a coarse, red face and a fiery sty in her left eye who gave him a hostile look when he entered and went round and round with the sombre walls of the room. A chair came sweeping by, and he crumpled toward it.

He awoke inside the examining room. A biting odor lingered in his nostrils, and he began squinting with distress from the dim light that came through the tan curtains on the two windows.

"What is it, Nat? Tell me quickly."

Dr. Weiner was watching him steadily with a penetrating expression of concern. Nat warmed with a peaceful flow of relief when he saw the fine strands of white hair before him and recognized the thin, sensitive face with its tired gray eyes and its delicate, pale skin that was still shining like a baby's. He began to smile gratefully, but then came awake a bit more and felt the pain. It was all through him now, cutting inside like a knife, in his kidney, his liver, in the pit of his stomach, twisting, tearing, and plunging about in the naked, raw depths of his organs.

"I need a fix!" he cried out sharply.

"What kind of fix, Nat?"

Nat started to reply. The imp jumped to his cheek before he could get a word out, and his jaw shot violently to the side, the sudden spasm distorting his face horribly, filling his ears with the noise of crunching cartilage and wrenching the muscles in his neck. Dr. Weiner recoiled in amazement, and his look darkened with understanding.

"This is awful, Nat, awful!" he said, in a hushed voice.

Nat waited, gritting his teeth and watching him beseechingly.

Dr. Weiner shook his head with a dazed unhappiness as he moved around slowly to the other side of the desk. "I can't believe it," he went on glumly, spacing his words evenly with the meticulous care of habit. "I really can't believe it."

"Dr. Weiner!" Nat pleaded.

"You must get treatment," Dr. Weiner continued perseveringly. "That's all there is to it. You must get treatment. I'll give you what money it takes."

Nat sprang forward in desperation and seized his arm. He tried to speak, to beg, but his mouth would not respond, and he began pulling at him roughly in a frenzied effort to make him understand. He started around to him and was knocked off balance when his hip struck the sharp corner of the desk. He just did reach a chair before the blackness hit him again.

When he came awake this time, he was aware with the first glimmer of consciousness of a pleasant, healing sensation seeping all through him. There was something tiny and very cold in the bend of his elbow; he felt the spot keenly; the effect was titillating, and he smiled with hidden delight. It was several minutes before he could recover completely, and even while still laboring in darkness he formed a plan. The ice was already broken, and once that happened, it no longer mattered. There was tomorrow to think about (Carl had hit it on the head, by God!), and the day after, and the day after that, but he had to act quickly, before the full force of the shot burst inside him and carried him up into the hazy unreality that would make him forget about everything.

"Better, Nat?"

Dr. Weiner was standing beside him, still holding the hypodermic syringe. Nat nodded. Dr. Weiner inspected the old puncture marks for infection and then moved listlessly toward a corner to deposit the syringe in a jar of antiseptic solution. Nat's eyes grew busy the moment he turned. He had already noticed the small glass container on the desk, and he glanced quickly at each of the many cabinets in the room, trying to identify others like it inside them on the shelves. He felt fine now, really fine, but he kept a dejected look on his face, purposely acting.

"There's a federal hospital in Lexington, Kentucky," Dr. Weiner said, seating himself wearily and working a neat crease with his thumbnail into the top page of a calendar pad. "I suppose you know about it."

"I've been there, Dr. Weiner." Nat put a note of pathos into his voice and cautiously edged his chair forward a bit, watching him cagily and waiting. "It was no good."

"Go there again," Dr. Weiner said. "And this time don't come back. This is a bad neighborhood for it. I get someone like you in here at least once a week. Generally I put them to sleep and call the police."

"It's no good, I tell you," Nat protested, flaring up suddenly with a real and quarrelsome annoyance. "I tried and suffered and it's no good. There are people there for the ninth and tenth time. There are people who spent most of their life there. I can't kick it. Some can and some can't. I tried and I can't."

"You won't go back, Nat?" Dr. Weiner asked softly.

Nat shook his head bitterly.

"But what else is there, Nat? What else can you do? You can't let yourself go to hell like this."

"There's this," Nat said, touching the cotton swab on his arm and looking him fully in the face.

"Is there, Nat?" Dr. Weiner smiled with a faintly mocking sympathy. He lowered his eyes and continued in a tone of irony. "Your mother hasn't been in to see me for nearly two months now. Did you know that? She should be in to see me regularly. It's dangerous for her to stay away that long and she knows it, but she won't come. She won't come because she hasn't any money to bring me."

Nat listened to him restlessly. He decided to give him one more minute.

"Where will you get it, Nat? Dope is expensive and you won't be able to hold a job. Where are you going to get it?"

"You get it, Dr. Weiner," Nat said, and waited tensely.

"No, Nat. Not a chance. You can get rid of that idea right now."

Nat hesitated a moment longer. There was one way left. He came forward like a shot and grabbed the bottle from the desk, then jumped back quickly, half expecting an attack of some sort, and when it did not come, he held his prize up triumphantly and laughed aloud. Dr. Weiner observed the whole action with a cold and curious surprise.

"You've just insulted me," he said quietly, with cool and unhurried dislike. "I should have expected it, I suppose."

Nat laughed again, gloating. He kept rolling the container between the palms of his hands. He was feeling a bit woozy now, and he squeezed it to convince himself that he really did have it. He laughed once more.

"You won't laugh much longer if you fool with that," Dr. Weiner said soberly. "It will only put you to sleep, and if you take too much it will kill you."

Nat stiffened immediately, and his body quivered with rage. "Is that what you gave me?"

"I was going to," Dr. Weiner said, with a sour expression, "but I changed my mind. I thought it might do some good to talk to you."

Nat stared at him a moment, breathing hard, and then came around the desk like an animal and bent over him with a ferocious glare. "Where is it?" he cried furiously. "God damn it, where is it?"

"You're crazy, Nat!" Dr. Weiner said, and his voice rose to a shout with an anger of his own. "Do you hear me? You're crazy like all the rest of them!"

Nat seized him by the lapels and lifted him from the chair, and all at once the whole scene hurtled over him and he was trapped like an innocent stranger inside the grotesque and demonic blur that flashed by him on every side and which he was now no longer able to control and powerless to understand. There was his own voice shouting from somewhere off in the corner and he had Dr. Weiner in his hands and was shaking him up and down, up and down, again and again, and there was the funny white head bouncing all around like the ping-pong ball in a popcorn machine. A hand beat weakly against his chest and opened to offer a small glass jar which he took and rammed into his pants pocket. Then he was shaking again and the white head was tossing all about once more, and there was his own voice hollering "More! More!" right into his ear, paining him with its bellowing force, and then, suddenly, he exploded inside with a golden, warm radiance that filled his chest and rolled with a wonderful, shivering ecstasy up the muscles of his sides and down the length of his legs, soaking through his bones and oozing into the very tips of his fingers like a sinuous, serpentine, naked creature, leaving him warm and numb and happy, without strength and without care.

He turned slowly, smiling dreamily, and looked about the office. Everything seemed to doze beneath a shimmering blanket of tranquillity. He could see perfectly, but he stood staring at the door a few seconds before he realized it was what he was looking for. It was taking him so long to reach it. He could hear someone retching behind him and the choking voice trying to speak.

"—call the police. If—you come again—I'll call—the police."

He began giggling, sniggering to himself furtively over the prankish secret of the weight in his pocket.

A woman spoke as he passed through the waiting room, and he turned politely and made (or thought he made—he couldn't quite be sure) some gracious reply. He would go home now and lie in bed. He had the bottle from Dr. Weiner and he would show it to his mother and say it was medicine and that Dr. Weiner said he should lie in bed and not be disturbed. He could stay in bed then and she wouldn't bother him.

Outside, the same muffled peace prevailed, and it was like those pleasant June days when he was a child and his father used to take the family to the Palisades for a day in the country, or like those frosty, clear mornings after a snowfall when he awoke early and found everything in the street so clean and calm and white. The sun was warm on his face. It was more like a day in the country with the sun so warm, and he walked along the avenue with the satisfying knowledge that it was never going to set.

FROM DAWN TO DUSK

They walked through the park leisurely and after a while the road turned and guided them down toward the lake.

"I'm sorry I'm like this today," she said finally, with a regretful smile.

Andy smiled but didn't speak. In a few minutes, they came to the lake, and they walked in silence, following the rippling edge of the water. The spell of a warm autumn afternoon covered the entire scene, muffling the noises and slowing all motion so that everything about them seemed distant and unreal. The sky was a clean blue and the sun was bare, but it was chilly, and Andy knew it would be cold in the evening. Esther stopped by the side of the path and snapped a long branch from a shrub. When they continued, she dragged it lazily against the trees and shrubs and benches that stood beside the road.

Andy studied her small, round face as she stared out over the lake where scattered rowboats moved slowly in an aimless network. She was exactly the same. Carelessly dressed, she was appealing in her very casualness, a small, winsome girl, her face still a little pale from bad hours and poor food eaten in late cafeterias. In a frail way she was pretty, with clean blonde hair and breasts surprisingly full for so thin a figure, and there was something eternally beautiful in her unstudied gait and spontaneous manner. It wasn't even three months, and he wanted her back already.

Previously unpublished; written between 1946 and 1949.

A group on bicycles came wheeling around the bend in the road. They stepped aside and waited until the noise of the tires passed behind them and faded into the rustle of leaves.

"You look like a man with a purpose," she had said, when they were across Columbus Circle and entering the park.

He told her then, and she took the news without surprise. A long silence followed, and when she finally did speak, it was about Debussy's music. He had been waiting so eagerly, he didn't understand at first. When he did, he wanted to laugh out loud because she was still the same, and because he was confident that everything would be all right.

"Are you back at the office?" she asked now.

He nodded.

"Same job?"

"Yes," he said. "Same job."

That was it, he knew, the damn job. You went along doing the best you could, and one day you realized that you were wasting time and not doing anything at all. There were so many things you had wanted to do, so many you still wanted, and you saw clearly that you weren't doing any of them and never would, and you grew so frantic thinking about it, you could feel the panic forming inside you. You saw how immense the world was, and you realized that you were so limited it was all going to waste around you, and you felt that you had to do something quick before it was too late. There was the job and the girl. It was the job, of course, writing copy when you should be writing plays, but you couldn't get rid of the job because the job was bread and alcohol, so you got rid of the girl instead. When you added it up later you saw that you had gained nothing but had lost a great deal instead.

"Look," Esther said. She tapped his arm lightly with the branch and pointed it toward the water. "They're fishing."

A large rock formation stood on the water's edge, and behind it, a small, flat peninsula jutted out into the lake. Some young boys stood above the water, dangling makeshift poles out expectantly. Behind them, a mother or two watched with benign surveillance, and on the other side, a young couple in love laughed as they snapped pictures with a cheap camera.

"Do you want to go down and watch?"

She nodded and they left the road and moved down until they were standing behind the boys. A young boy in a sailor suit, the smallest boy there, pulled up a tiny fish. He fought it with his small hands, removing it from the hook. It jerked from his fingers and fell to the ground, flapping in the dirt with wet, whipping noises. The boy pounced on it, scooped it up, and dropped it into a tin can. The other boys watched admiringly, and he was proud and very precise as he baited his hook and returned it to the water. In the can, the fish continued its wild flailing.

"Let's go," Esther said. She turned and started up the path. "I feel sorry for the fish. I feel sorry for everything today."

Andy took her arm and helped her up to the road. "Do you want to take a boat out?"

She shook her head. "I'm not much good today, I guess. It hasn't anything to do with seeing you again. You know I get this way every now and then."

They walked until the boys dropped from sight behind some trees and then seated themselves on a bench. Esther was silent, staring pensively out at the water. Andy watched her from the side, studying the planes of her face and the melancholy in her dark eyes. It was nice being with her again, and he forgot for the moment that he was awaiting an answer.

She turned from the water slowly. "How long were you in the country?"

"About a week," he said.

"I thought you'd stay longer."

"I was going to. I got bored after a week and came back. I

knew it wouldn't take you that long to move. Did you have any trouble finding a place?"

"No trouble," she said. "I was out in two days." Her hand was moving the branch in the dust beneath the bench and she stared down intently at the crude patterns it made. "I cleaned the whole apartment just before I left," she said proudly. "It was clean, wasn't it?"

"Yes," he said. "It was very clean."

"And I didn't leave anything. I went over the whole place like a vacuum cleaner, picking up everything that belonged to me, even my toothpaste. I didn't leave anything, did I?"

"No. There wasn't a thing."

The apartment was spotless when he returned. Some dust had gathered in the few days, but everything was neatly in place. The linoleum in the foyer and the tile in the bathroom and the sink, basin, and bathtub had all been scrubbed clean, but when he got into bed that night and moved the pillows he found one of the small combs she was always losing. He didn't tell her about the comb now. She was so pleased for having done everything just right, and the comb wasn't important.

Esther turned her face slowly. "It's a stupid world, isn't it?" she said unhappily.

"Yes," Andy said. "It's very stupid."

They sat without talking for several minutes. She stood up unexpectedly and looked around with displeasure. "Fresh air is over-rated," she said. "Let's go someplace else."

"All right," Andy said. He stood up, buttoning his topcoat. The sun was paling as it moved in the sky, and the late hours were bringing in a brisk wind. "Where do you want to go?"

"I don't know. Let's find a bar and drink wine."

Andy nodded, frowning. They both drank a lot, but never excessively, and only in the evening. He took her arm and they walked to the exit. "Do you drink in the daytime now?"

"Not usually. I just feel like drinking now. The mood demands it. It's all right, isn't it?"

"Sure," he said. "It's all right."

They found a bar on Columbus Avenue. It was empty except for the bartender, a small, wizened man who sat on a high stool behind the bar reading a newspaper. He looked up when they entered and watched them move into the room and seat themselves in a booth against the wall. He rose reluctantly and came to them. He waited without a word, his face determinedly vacant as his sharp eyes scrutinized them closely.

"What do you want?" Esther asked Andy. "Is wine all right?"

"Sure," he said. "Wine is all right."

"Sweet or dry?"

"Anything you say."

"How about port? Is port all right?"

He nodded and she turned to the bartender. "Port for both," she told him. "And forget the small glasses. Pour it into a big glass. Fill up a highball glass, and bring mixers so we can play with them instead of smoking."

The bartender waited a moment when she stopped. When he was sure she was through he turned away. Esther leaned back and sighed. She shook her coat from her back, and her small shoulders fitted nicely into the corner formed by the wall. Her thin fingers had already discovered the matchbook in the ashtray, and they were busily picking it apart. Andy lit two cigarettes and held one out. She shook her head and he placed it on the ashtray. A moment later she picked it up.

"Well?" he said, after a few minutes. He had the matchbook now, and he stared at his thumbnail as it shredded the paper.

"Did you have any trouble finding me?"

He shook his head. "I just asked some people."

She regarded him sadly. "Things certainly get confused, don't they?" she said.

"Yes. They get very confused."

"I mean simple things, things that are clear and obvious and have no right getting confused. They get themselves all tangled up like a ball of yarn, don't they?"

"Yes," he said. "They do."

"And now you want me back." She waited until he nodded. "Why did you want me to go?"

He leaned back and shrugged with embarrassment. "You know me," he said. "You know why, don't you?"

"I know. But I want you to tell me."

He shrugged again and shifted uncomfortably. "Futility, I guess," he said. "Shame, futility, disillusion, despair. The whole Thesaurus. They all keep piling up until they get too big. You want to get involved with something important. You want to reach out and grab a piece of something permanent. Instead, there's nothing, nothing at all. It's too much, and you feel you have to do something."

"So you got rid of me," she said. "I'm not blaming you," she added quickly.

"I know you're not," he said. "You never blame anyone for anything."

She smiled again, and she seemed paler and more forlorn. She seemed tiny and lost, and he wanted to lean forward and throw his arms around her and assure her that everything was all right. Instead he played with the matches and waited.

"What a rotten world," she said. "What a rotten, stinking world."

He nodded understandingly.

"We get so tangled up, don't we?"

"Like a ball of yarn."

"Just like a ball of yarn," she agreed. "And for no reason. For no reason at all we make ourselves miserable."

He nodded again.

"And besides," she said. "I'm in love."

Andy straightened with surprise. "With who?"

"You don't know him. He paints. He does a lot of magazine work. He's very successful, very intelligent, and very unhappy. He wants me to live with him."

"Are you going to?"

"I don't know, Andy," she said. She shook her head with distress. "I don't know what to do."

Neither of them spoke. To escape the uncomfortable silence, they turned to the bartender. He had been very slow with the drinks, and he was just getting them on a tray. He returned to the table slowly, a dogged look on his thin face, and set the drinks before them. He placed the tray beneath his arm and waited defiantly. The wine had been delivered in small glasses. Esther looked at them with surprise. Puzzled, she turned to him. The bartender maintained a stubborn silence, forcing her to speak first.

"We asked for big glasses," she said. "Don't you remember?"

"We don't serve wine in big glasses here," he said, making each word solid and distinct so that his small speech sounded prearranged.

"You could have told us that when we ordered," Esther said.

"I could do a lot of things," the bartender said. "But I don't. If you don't like it you can leave. Nobody asked you to come here."

Andy studied him closely, without anger, but searchingly, and he thought he knew, but Esther was completely baffled and looked from one to the other with bewilderment.

"We don't want your kind here," the bartender continued.

Esther raised her hands in exasperation. "So that's it," she exclaimed, looking despairingly at Andy. "There it is again. Everytime you forget about it, someone comes along to remind you."

The bartender, very content now, smiled with satisfaction. "If you don't like it you can go," he said again.

"It's too much," Esther said. "On top of everything else, you. All in the same day. I wish to hell you'd go."

"This is my place," the bartender said. "You go."

Andy sat up straight, bunching his shoulders, and seated, he was almost as tall as the man. "All right," he said. "That's enough. You made your point and we understand. I'm twice your size, and if you say one more word, I'll pick you up in both hands and snap you in two."

He spoke slowly in a grim, careful voice, and there was no mistaking the sincerity behind his threat. The bartender stepped back, frightened. His face paled and his eyes shifted wildly as though hoping to discover strength in some unexpected corner of the room. Andy watched the fear come, and he felt sorry for the man.

"Let's get out of here," Esther said.

"No," Andy said. "You wanted to drink and you're going to." He turned to face her, dismissing the bartender. The bartender left resentfully with a last sullen glance. He returned to his stool, turned a page, and resumed reading without another look at them.

"I'm miserable now," Esther said. "Now I'm really miserable."

"Forget about it," Andy said. "It isn't anything new. What's his name?"

"Whose?"

"This man you're in love with."

"His name is Proust." She anticipated his question and laughed. "No, it's Harry. Harry Proust. Do you know him?"

"I don't think so. Are you sure about this?"

"I don't know," she said. "I really don't know. It wouldn't solve anything if I came back. Everything would still be the same. You'd want me to leave again. Then you'd want me back, and it would go on and on and on, and all the time I'd be getting older and less pretty until even you would stop wanting me, and then I would be old and all alone."

She continued looking at him as though she might go on, and he waited, watching her. Then, as if realizing with surprise that she was through, she smiled weakly and turned away.

"It doesn't have to be that way," Andy said. "We could get married this time."

"That wouldn't help anything. It would only make everything worse, wouldn't it?"

"Yes," he said. "I guess it would."

"It's a rotten world, Andy. Whatever is, isn't right. It's wrong, completely wrong. Don't you feel that way?"

He nodded soberly. He felt like crying.

"It isn't our fault," she continued. "It's the world. It's bigger than we are and there's nothing we can do. That's right, isn't it?"

"Yes," he said. "I guess it is."

She touched his hand gently. "I'm sorry, Andy."

"It's all right."

"I'm really sorry. I want you to know I'm sorry."

"I know," he said. "There's no need to be."

"Let's get out of here," she said abruptly. "I don't like it. It's dark and gloomy and the host doesn't like us."

"Do you want the rest of your drink?"

She said no. He left a dollar bill on the table and they walked to the door, walking slowly and silently and ignoring the wary glance of the bartender. Outside, it had gotten colder. A derelict wind swooped down suddenly and chased a tumbling cloud of leaves and papers down the street before them. It whipped the refuse up into a swirling circle by the curb and then spilled it out into the gutter beneath the wheels of a sudden surge of traffic. Unconsciously, they walked back toward the park.

They both saw the pigeons in the street near the end of the block, but neither of them mentioned it. Neither of them spoke at all. When they came to the pigeons they stopped to watch. A large mob of them waddled in the street, picking at crumbs that had been scattered for them and wading in the grimy puddles that lay in the gutter against the sidewalk, filling the air with their quiet, croaking noises.

"I could never decide if they're pretty," Esther said. "Are pigeons pretty?"

"I wouldn't say so. They remind me of pregnant women."

"And they're very stupid. All they do is perch on the rooftops and come down to eat. You'd think they'd find something better to do with their freedom, wouldn't you?"

"There's no such thing as freedom," Andy said. "Freedom is an illusion."

"Proust doesn't think so. He's an existentialist."

"I don't care what he is. You tell him that I said there's no such thing as freedom. Tell him he's being tricked. Tell him if he doesn't believe me he can come here and watch the pigeons and see for himself."

"A canary would know what to do," Esther said. "Set a canary free and he'd know what to do." She stopped abruptly as if struck with a sudden thought. She hesitated, her lips pursed in an expression of deliberation, and clutched his arm excitedly. "Andy, let's do it. It's a fine idea."

He was puzzled and he smiled at her unexpected burst of eagerness. "Do what?"

"Set a canary free. It isn't much and it would make me feel good. Please, Andy. It wouldn't cost much. We passed a pet shop near Columbus Circle."

"Sure," he said, watching her with surprise. She was almost feverish with the idea, and he laughed at her intense manner. He took her arm and hurried her to the avenue.

In the cab going downtown, she chatted unceasingly about the canary. She was no longer sad. The world, like herself, had suddenly become beautiful. She was unable to sit still but shifted animatedly with the impulsive delight of a little girl, clasping and unclasping her hands with ecstatic joy.

"I'll wait here," she said, when they had left the cab and were standing across from the pet shop. "You get it, Andy. And hurry."

She pushed him forward impatiently. He nodded and started away. She ran after him and pulled him to a stop, her face suddenly grave. "I just remembered, Andy. It's very important. Should we get an old one or a young one?"

"A young one," he said immediately. "A very young one."

"No, an old one. The oldest one they have." She pushed him forward again. He stepped from the curb and started across the street. "Remember," she called after him. "The oldest one they have."

He nodded without turning and hurried to the door of the shop. A man approached to greet him when he entered, watching him with a questioning smile.

"I want a canary," he said. The man nodded and invited him to the rear. Andy shook his head. "You pick it out for me. I want a young one, the youngest one you have."

The man eyed him with surprise. He shrugged indulgently and went to the back. He returned, carrying a green cage, and moved behind the counter to wrap it.

"Never mind," Andy said. "I'll take it that way. How much?"

He paid the man, seized the cage, and strode to the door, holding it carefully before him and watching the small, yellow bird inside. He stopped by the door and turned slowly. He hesitated and walked back to the man.

"This bird," he said, in a sober tone. "What would happen to it if it had to live by itself in this weather?"

The man thought for a moment. "It wouldn't last long," he decided. "It would probably die from the cold."

Andy nodded and walked out. Esther was waiting impatiently, and she rushed forward to meet him. She took the cage from his hands and held it up before her. A few passersby stopped to watch, but she didn't notice them.

"It's very small," she said. "It doesn't look old."

"That's the way they are," he lied. "It's very old for a canary."

"Well," she said solemnly. "This is a very important moment."

She opened the door of the cage. The bird remained on its perch for a moment, jerking its small head about nervously. It hopped down to the floor of the cage and approached the opening. It paused, staring out suspiciously. After a moment it leaped up and stood in the opening, facing its freedom with concern. It looked for a second as though the bird would return to the interior, but then, with surprising swiftness, it flew into the air above their heads. It stopped there as if stunned by the miracle of space, fluttering its wings rapidly. It seemed to hesitate fearfully, and then it rose gloriously, shooting upward in erratic lunges until it was above the rooftops. It disappeared over a building while they craned their necks upward watching. It returned in a moment, flying toward the opposite side of the street, and vanished over the tops of the buildings there. Andy continued staring after it until he was sure it would not return. When he looked down, Esther was smiling at him happily. She took his arm.

"Let's go," she said.

"Where?"

"Come with me," she said. "I want you to help me pack."

He squeezed her arm joyously and they began walking quickly. He felt as though a great burden had been lifted and he wanted to laugh out loud. But then, when the first flair of exhilaration passed, he was saddened by an immovable thought that stood like a dark sentinel beneath his feelings. He remembered what the man in the pet shop had told him, and he kept thinking of the young, little bird that would soon die in the cold.

THE DEATH OF
THE DYING SWAN

Before he was married Sidney Cooper gambled excessively. Louise often reproached him, but secretly she was intrigued. After they were married, she proceeded with grinding persistency to cure him of this habit and to purge him of all others which she found displeasing, and after eighteen years of marriage, she had succeeded in making him the type of man she had always wanted for her husband, a man who was successful and proper and showed it in his appearance. Cooper had rebelled at first, but through the years he had learned that submission ultimately yielded the best results. By remaining passive, he at least achieved the domestic tranquility which soon became his outstanding pleasure. He did not enjoy the life she laid out for him, but, as a rule, he did not mind it. This evening, however, he was finding it unbearable.

He looked at Ed Chandler and shook his head slowly with mild disgust. Chandler was the most successful of the lot. Before the war he had been a cattle buyer for a packing house, and during the ensuing confusion he had somehow contrived two packing plants of his own, a tanning business, and an undisclosed fortune in cold cash. He reminded Cooper of a perverted Buddha as he sat back in expansive comfort and showered his compla-

Previously unpublished; written between 1946 and 1949.

cency upon those around him, a large diamond glittering on the little finger of his left hand. Cooper smiled wryly and shook his head.

"What a waste," he thought sadly. "What a shameful waste." His lips formed the toneless words. "Sidney Cooper, the intellect, the sybarite. If the walls of this room could talk, they wouldn't have a thing to say."

The party was obviously a success. A woman had already thrown up on the bathroom floor and he had been assigned the task of cleaning up. When he finished, he closed the windows vindictively so the odor would remain, and he returned to the living room for a strong drink. Everyone was drinking and talking a lot, so he imagined the party was successful. Louise had already cautioned him.

"I wouldn't mind so much if it was someone else's party," she had said, "but it doesn't look right for the host to pass out."

"All right," he replied. "I won't get drunk."

"I know you won't, darling," she had concluded, flashing him her party smile. "Now have a good time."

He sat in a corner by himself now, glad in being ignored by the others. The house was cluttered with Ed Chandlers and Louises, and he was completely alone. He was just about fed up. He was fed up with all the tedious routines required by his artificial existence, with all the dull people he met at all the dull parties, with being nice to people he secretly despised.

He longed for people who were real, people who lived with honest passions and found vigorous pleasure in the mere event of existing, people for whom death came too soon. Occasionally, he came in contact with them. Some evenings he would see the couples making love in shadowed corners or come across people quarreling in the street. He would often hear careless laughter roll out to him through open bar room doors. On buses he would listen to young people discussing Huxley or Schoenberg in eager voices, and he had many times noted the students walking near the library with sad, serious faces, blind to everything but the hideous enchantment of some hopeless dream. And in France, near the Spanish border, what remained of the Loyalists, a ragged group of men, were dying daily from tuberculosis, neglected and forgotten, a fading handful of forgotten heroes, and in his living room there were men with diamond rings on their pinkies and women who never read an editorial page.

"Oh, *here* you are." He looked up, startled, and saw Louise smiling at him. "What are you doing all by yourself?"

"I'm resting," he replied. "Everyone seems happy."

"And drinking, I see. Please don't get drunk."

"I won't get drunk," he said. He found it difficult to mouth his words and he knew that he was getting drunk. "I wouldn't dream of getting drunk at our party. It wouldn't look right."

Louise studied him for a moment. Then, as she always did when she saw he was annoyed, she smiled gaily to indicate that nothing was really wrong. "But that isn't what I want," she continued. "Darling, something terrible has happened. I'm all ready to serve cold cuts and there's no mustard." She waited expectantly.

"Do you want me to go for some?" he asked.

"Would you?"

"Of course," he said. "You know there's nothing I like better than running down for mustard."

"Please, darling," she pleaded. "I wouldn't ask you if it wasn't necessary."

"Before I met you it was my favorite pastime."

She glared at him with her eyes, keeping her face calm. "You've been drinking too much," she said, in a stern, low voice. "I warned you against drinking too much. Now please be reasonable. I can't serve without mustard, can I?"

"No," he said. "You can't serve without mustard." He rose slowly and handed her his glass.

"And please hurry, darling. We can't keep them waiting."

"That's right," he said. "We can't keep them waiting."

He made his way to the foyer and walked slowly to the bathroom. He washed his face with cold water and combed his hair. As he came back, a woman turned from the living room, walking unsteadily, and stopped before him. It was Marcia Chandler, Ed's wife.

"I've been looking everywhere for you," she said, smiling up at him. "And now I've found you."

He smiled at her dutifully and stood patiently as she put her hands on his shoulders and kissed his cheek.

"You always look so beautiful," she giggled. She was tall and thin, with a sharp face and large teeth. "So clean and sweatless. I bet you never sweat, not even in the summertime." She looked at him provocatively, and when he didn't speak, she said, "I wish you worked for me. God, how I wish you were my chauffeur."

"Why?" he asked.

"Because I could kiss you as much as I wanted to."

He bent his head toward her. "Do you want to kiss me?"

"It could be fun," she answered softly. She ran her hand up the side of his face, closing her eyes and raising her face. He placed his hand flat on her chest and pushed her back hard against the wall. He heard her gasp with surprise as he strode away.

The night air kindled with the liquor and set him aflame with a surging sensation of youth and vigor. He crossed the street in the middle of the block so that he could pass the cabaret near the corner, walking comfortably in a slow, aimless stride, delighting in the silent rippling of the crisp, clean air and in the happy glow of being alone and content and feeling young and in good health. He was sorry now that he had pushed Marcia. Maybe he should have an affair with her, he thought, just for an apology. He had always meant to have an affair with another woman, but an affair required so much preparation. It was the same way with divorce; at the last moment there would come a deceiving rush of affection—and later, regret.

Outside the cabaret, a man stood near the curb talking to someone in a cab. The car moved away and the man stepped back, bumping into him.

"I beg your pardon," Cooper murmured, smiling.

The man stepped back and studied him. "*Quo vadimus,* friend?" he demanded loudly.

Cooper stopped with surprise. The man was big, and his florid face shone with alcoholic vitality. Cooper liked his frank good-humor and he thought back through the years and re-membered. "*Ubinam gentium sumus?*" he answered.

"A scholar!" the man exclaimed with delight. "Scratch the man on the street and you find a scholar. Come inside, friend, and have a drink."

Cooper hesitated, tempted. It was a long time since he last spent an evening in a bar, a long time since he had gambled. "I don't know," he said. "I'm on an errand."

"An errand? Forget it." The man took his elbow and led him toward the door of the cabaret. "Schwoll's the name. Harry Schwoll, the brassiere king. I make brassieres. I make more brassieres than any man in the country, which probably means I make more brassieres than any man in the world. It may not mean anything to you but it means a hell of a lot to the institu-tion of marriage."

Cooper laughed and he let himself be guided through the door to the bar. Schwoll disdained a seat, pushing it aside with his hip and raising his foot to the rail as he set his arms on the bar and leaned toward him. "Money, money, money," he said loudly. "What's the good? What's your name, friend?"

"Cooper," he said. "Sidney Cooper. I publish books, books about brassieres. You may not realize it, but your product is the hero of every story that pleases the American public."

"What's the good?" Schwoll said. He pulled a chair to him and sat down, his face growing serious. "Despite all intelligent reports, money is a great potentiality. When I was a kid selling newspapers a man once gave me a dime and brought the happiest moment of my life. So much happiness for a dime. It still amazes me. Now I have a wife and two daughters, God bless them, and not one of them can appreciate anything under a hundred dollar bill. So what's the good? What'll it be?"

"Scotch. With water."

Schwoll turned to the bartender, who was waiting patiently for the order. "Make it two, Frank," he said. The bartender smiled and turned away. "His name is Frank Costello," Schwoll said confidentially. "No relation to the gambler."

"That's too bad," Cooper said.

"It keeps him awake nights."

Costello returned with the drinks and set them on the bar.

"I forgot to ask you," Schwoll said to him. "How'd I do today?"

"You did fine," Costello said. "One of your horses was scratched, so you saved some money. Gregg is in the back. He wants his money."

"Okay," Schwoll said. "I'll go see him." He raised his glass to Cooper. "To you, friend."

Cooper swallowed the shot straight and smiled as the glow burned in his belly and flared through his veins. Schwoll was good company and he was able to relax. "Ready for another?" he asked.

"Order them. I'll be back." He stood up and made his way through the people around the bar, disappearing behind the partition that led to the dance floor.

Cooper ordered another round. He poured the scotch into the water and took a long swallow. The room was crowded with people milling about in loud, laughing groups and mingling easily with a wanton lack of restraint. It was the free atmosphere he had always enjoyed, but he was now consciously a stranger to it. In one booth, a boy and girl were facing each other, and the girl was going to cry. The boy's words were lost in the noise, but he gestured with finality while the girl watched him sadly, her face moulded weakly into melting lines as she lost her struggle with composure. She looked up suddenly and their eyes met. Cooper turned quickly, flushing with shame, degraded because he had been caught spying on an intimate scene.

A woman sat at the curve of the bar, smoking, a drink before her, and her face stared straight ahead with a stone expression of sorrow. He studied her closely, noting each detail of her head and shoulders and the slender slope of her neck. There were lines of torment in her face. Her lips formed a thin, red line that glared morosely against her white face. In the darkness of her eyes there was deep melancholy. She sat motionless, like a carven image. He wanted her. It was academic, he knew, but he needed her because she was a sad woman. He watched the people around her, trying to determine if she was alone. A hand dropped on his shoulder and he looked up with surprise.

"You don't want her," Schwoll said. He was surprisingly sober. "Her teeth are bad and she talks too much about her husband."

For a moment Cooper was embarrassed. "Where's her husband?" he asked.

"He's dead. Knocked off in the war. It makes you feel bad afterward when she starts talking about him."

Cooper nodded, watching her through the corner of his eye.

"You a stranger in town?" Schwoll asked.

"Yes," Cooper said. "Just about."

"Know anybody here?"

Cooper signalled to Costello for another round. He looked into the mirror behind the bar and shook his head slowly. "Not a soul."

"Where you from?"

"Here."

"All alone?"

"Just about."

"Don't you know anybody?"

"I know a lot of people."

"But no friends. Is that it?"

"That's it," Cooper said. "No friends."

"Married?"

"She's upstairs. I live down the block. There's a big party in my house. People I don't like. She sent me down for a jar of mustard. She can't very well serve without mustard."

"I figured you something like that. It's very odd. There's a party in my house also, but my wife doesn't even bother inviting me anymore. You look unhappy—what was your name again? I never remember names the first time."

"Cooper. Sidney Cooper."

"That's right. You look unhappy, Cooper. I don't like despondent people around me." A slight smile played with his mouth. "Let me have men about me who are fat and happy. You'll never be fat, but maybe I can make you happy. You wait here and I'll bring you some interesting company." He stood up and left.

"That girl," Cooper said to Costello, when he arrived. "Who is she?"

"A tramp," Costello said, grimly. "Through and through."

"She lost her husband in the war, didn't she?"

Costello nodded. "She talks about him all the time. All of a sudden it's love. She was a tramp before and she's a tramp now. A guy gets killed and all of a sudden she loves him. Yours was water, wasn't it?"

He nodded. The girl was watching him and their eyes locked in a tight stare. He waited for some flicker to shake the calm of sorrow and show him he was welcome. She turned away, her face immutable, and he knew she had not seen him. He did not want her now. She was too clean to touch, a trollop in a bar with black hair blending into the gloom of night and cigarette smoke and a white, bony face that was cast in despondency, and she was too clean for him to touch.

And upstairs, smug men with diamond rings on fat pinkies talked about sex and success, and wanting women discussed clothing designers and women with more money. A man had died in the war and a slut was filled with grief. They were dropping like flies near the border in France. They needed artificial limbs also, he remembered. There had been pictures of them in the paper, pictures of bearded men staring with dull apathy in gaunt faces, faces sapped dry of the will to live, empty of hope, sallow-faced, living skulls, sculptured skulls gleaming beneath dirty skin, like that woman there, beaten numb with sorrow. They needed dentists also, he remembered, and now they needed doctors, and iron lungs, and good food, but most of all, they needed a place to go, a home, a homeland, the leaf, the stone, the unfound door, a forgotten race growing extinct on a barren strip of barren ground awarded them for a burial ground, dropping like flies from the silent gnaw of T.B. The reward for courage against tyranny was a rotten molar and a capsuled coccus; and upstairs there was Ed Chandler and Louise, and Marcia, with large teeth and a thin, cold body made warm by the cry against age and mediocrity, and in the limbo of doubt and discouragement was a man named Sidney Cooper who once rolled a ten spot up to eighteen hundred dollars and lost it all the next day on a pitcher named Rube Marquard who before then had won eighteen or nineteen consecutive games. He had looked up at the sky that night, and in the sparkling myriads he had discovered the Big Dipper, and he had burned with the knowledge that the air was his to breathe, that the world spun and the minutes passed for him alone, and he had curled his toes around the equator. Byron had already died in Greece, but there was a man named Hemingway who wrote a book he understood and a man named Wagner who wrote music that almost made him cry, and a man named Cooper who stared up at the sky and drank the air like wine as though it held some anodyne, and a man named Oscar Wilde who wrote some fairy tales and was thrown in jail, and then, suddenly, Sidney Cooper no longer owned the world but was biding his time patiently as he waited to die, like the men near the border in France, but for a different, a much different reason.

When he looked up, a man who reminded him instantly of Ed Chandler was talking to the woman, and the young girl in the booth was crying at last while the boy tried ineffectually to console her, and the happy stranger who had called him in the street was leading a young girl toward him. The melancholy woman had not yet moved and the boy in the booth had not yielded to the girl's tears and there was still hope.

"Here she is," Schwoll said. "Sit down, honey, and have a drink with my friend."

The girl looked at Cooper and turned to Schwoll. "I'll bet he thinks I'm a prostitute," she said.

"No, he doesn't. Why should he think you're a prostitute?"

"I don't know why, but every time you introduce me to a man he thinks I'm a prostitute."

"Not Cooper," Schwoll said. "He's an expert on frustrations." He turned to Cooper. "How does she look?"

Cooper smiled self-consciously. "She looks frustrated." The girl was young and small and her wide, round face was lax with disinterest.

"Sit down, honey," Schwoll said. "This is Esther Gordon. Honey, my lonely friend, Sidney Cooper."

She gave him a small smile and sat down. "Any friend of Harry's," she announced, "is degenerate."

Cooper hesitated and said, "I won't decide until I know you better." She threw back her head and laughed and he felt better. Schwoll winked and walked away.

"Has Cupid gone?" the girl asked.

"Yes," Cooper said. "He's gone."

"What's bothering you?" she asked, turning to him. "Is it your libido?"

"I have no libido." He spoke carefully because he wanted to impress her. "I think I am being haunted by childhood dreams."

"That's not unusual," she said. "That's life. It stinks. Call him, please. I want a drink."

He beckoned to Costello.

"Calvados," she said, when he approached.

Costello blinked. "What was that?"

"I want a glass of calvados. Or a bottle. I don't know how they drink it."

"What is it?" Costello asked.

"I don't know what it is. I read about it in a book."

"Try something else," Costello said. "We don't read books here."

"All right," the girl said. "Bring me some gentian violet."

Cooper was about to laugh when Costello turned to him for an explanation. "I'll have another scotch," he said, evenly.

Costello turned back to her. "Lady," he appealed. "Why can't you order something simple, like beer?"

"All right," she said. "Bring beer."

Costello left, satisfied, and she looked at Cooper and smiled, and at that moment, he fell in love with her. They were silent until the drinks came, and then, he was unable to speak. He felt the silence grow between them, and when she turned back, her face had lapsed back into lines of indifference.

"What do you do?" she asked.

"I publish books," he said. "What do you do?"

"I dance," she said. "I dance like hell."

"A dancer?" he asked with surprise.

"No," she said, and a forlorn note crept into her voice. "Not a dancer. I'm a dancer who doesn't dance. I plug switchboards. But I can dance. I'm good too."

"Then why don't you dance?"

"I don't want to."

"What do you want?"

"I want to dance on the stage of the Metropolitan," she said softly, her face growing wistful as she stared at a point over his shoulder. "I want to glide before the eyes of the populace. I want to posture before the king and queen of England. And I could too if I wasn't so damn lazy."

"Are you really good?"

"I studied it all my life. I know what's good and I know what isn't, and I know I'm good."

"Then why don't you?" he asked, noticing how intense she had become. "Why don't you dance?"

She shrugged and turned to her drink. "What's the good? I'm dying."

He sat up with shock. "What's the matter?"

She looked at him and laughed. "Nothing's the matter. I'm just dying. We're all dying. From the day we're born, we begin to die. They get cradles and coffins from the same tree." She reached out and touched his hand. "Don't look so sad, Sidney Cooper. It's all the way you look at it. Either life is beautiful, but it stinks, or life stinks, but it's beautiful. Don't feel sorry for me. I'm really very happy, I'm the happiest person I know."

"Can you really dance?"

"I swear to God I can. I'm so good that sometimes it frightens me. Have you ever seen the swan?"

"What swan?"

"In the *Swan Lake* ballet. She turns thirty-two times. Thirty-two fouettés. It isn't easy. You have to turn thirty-two times on one foot and the idea is not to move your foot. The less it moves the better you are. I can do it on a dime."

"Can you really?"

"I can," she said. "I swear to God I can."

"Do it."

"Here?"

"Yes. Here."

She paused a moment, considering, and he noticed the corners of her mouth trembling. "All right," she said. "All right, Sidney Cooper. I'll dance for you. I'll do it right here."

She rose from the chair and bent to the floor. "Here's the circle," she said, drawing an imaginary circle with her finger. "Now you watch and see if my foot leaves it." She straightened up and flexed her leg muscles, rising up and down on her toes and bending her knees. The people around them pressed forward curiously. "Move back," she pleaded. "Please. Please move back." She put her hands on a man's arm and pushed him back gently, moving about with a frantic determination. She stopped suddenly and turned to him. "Oh, God, I forgot. I don't have shoes."

"What's the matter with those you're wearing?"

"I can't get on my toes. I'll do it on the ball of my foot. All right?"

"All right. On the ball of your foot."

"You watch now," she said, extending her arms and turning to assure herself of enough room. "You count for me."

"Go ahead. I'll count for you."

Costello ran up excitedly. "What's going on?"

"Remember," she said. "Thirty-two. And watch my foot."

"For God sakes, lady," Costello shouted. "What are you gonna do?"

"I'm going to dance," she said. "I'm going to dance like a son of a bitch."

"Dance? You can't dance here."

"Let her alone," Cooper said.

"It's not allowed. There's a dance floor inside."

"For Christ sakes, shut up!" Cooper snapped. He turned to the girl and smiled. "Go ahead, honey," he said. "Go ahead and dance."

"All right," she said. She smiled at him weakly. Her face was pale and her fingers plucked nervously at the sides of her skirt. "I'll dance for you."

She raised her leg and began turning. The room grew silent and even Costello stared with sober curiosity. Cooper watched her foot, counting. She turned seven . . . eight . . . nine times without wavering. She was dancing on a dime! At fifteen, he raised his eyes, and when she came around, he smiled. Her face was grim. When he looked down, her foot was shaking. The muscles in her calf and thigh were quivering in sharp spasms and her foot was beginning to wobble within the circle. At twenty-five, he looked up. Her face was contorted in a grimace of terrible pain. Her lips were pulled back into her face and her gums gleamed like wet blood around her teeth. The only sound was the asthmatic gasp of her breath. She reached thirty . . . thirty-one . . . and then thirty-two and spun dizzily into his arms, crying:

"I did it! My God! I did it!" over and over again.

She was laughing and her face was shining and she looked like a happy little girl. She broke from his arms and rushed around excitedly.

"I did it! My God, I did it!"

Cooper felt her joy well up within him, and he was filled with a warm flood of affection, a sad and tragic affection. When she was calm, she sat down beside him, her eyes still sparkling with joy. They looked at each other for a long while without speaking, and his love for her grew until he felt sweetly that he was going to cry, and then—he remembered Louise and the jar of mustard.

He looked up quickly to the end of the bar. The woman was talking to the man who reminded him of Ed Chandler. His hand was on her arm, his fingers nipping the flesh beneath her sleeve, and she was smiling at him with interest. In the booth, the young boy was sitting beside the girl with his arm around her. She had stopped crying and she was smiling with satisfaction. It was no use. He was sad now because the men were dying in France. The Spanish countryside was covered with dirt from the mines in Asturias and he was a book publisher who was giving a party for some people who were waiting upstairs for a jar of mustard. He stood up slowly. She looked at him with surprise and he avoided her eyes.

"Where are you going?" she asked.

"I'm sorry." He tried to smile but it wouldn't come. "I have to go."

"Why? Why do you have to go?"

"I'll see you again," he said quickly. "I can't explain, but I'll see you again."

"When?"

"I'll see you here. I don't know when, but I'll see you here. You'll be here, won't you?"

"Yes," she said. "I'll be here. When?"

"I don't know when, but you be here."

He turned abruptly and walked away without looking back. When he was outside, he walked quickly to the avenue. The store was about to close. He bought the mustard and walked back down the street to the house, walking as fast as he could, because he had been gone a long time and they were waiting upstairs for the jar of mustard. Before he was there he looked at his watch, and he began to run.

THE SOUND OF ASTHMA

It was a warm, humid night, and Peter was sweating as he sat ponderously in a chair that was too narrow for his soft bulk. He was tired and a little depressed as he felt the perspiration ooze warmly from his pores and turn cold as it dried on his underclothes. He leaned forward over his desk, scratching aimlessly at the worn surface with wide, jaundiced fingernails. The hollow knock of a ping-pong ball came faintly from the recreation room of the Youth Organization across the hall. Alex was talking but Peter's mind kept wandering and it was difficult to listen to him.

"I don't know," Alex said. "Sometimes I don't know." His old, bent frame was perched on a high, wooden stool against the wall. "Sometimes I'm not so sure anymore."

Peter grunted because he didn't feel like answering. It was hot and moist and he was sweating and tired. They were playing ping-pong across the hall and Alex was talking, and he was depressed because he felt that it had all dropped dead some time ago and he had been living with a corpse without knowing it. What should have been a vibrant, vigorous organization had somehow turned sluggish and feeble. It was all different now and it was sad and depressing.

".................... faith," Alex said.

Previously unpublished; written between 1946 and 1949. The typescript for this story has been heavily edited, presumably by Heller's instructor. The story is printed here, without the edits, as Heller wrote it.

"That's the way it is," Peter said slowly, having no idea what Alex had said. "That's always the way it is."

Alex turned silent, and for a while his labored breath joined with the sound of the ping-pong ball to form the only noise. It had all changed somehow. You lived intimately with something for a long time, certain you knew what it was, and then one day you looked and it turned out to be something altogether different. He was older now and Max and a good many of the others were gone now, and in their places there were tired, puzzled old men like Alex, and sneering pedants like Crawford, and young, unhappy people with red pimples and sex frustrations. Traumatic idealism, he thought, and smiled because he liked the phrase.

"Even the philosophers aren't sure," Alex said sadly. "They grope."

Peter didn't reply. Doubles, he thought, listening to the faint staccato of the ping-pong ball, they are playing doubles. He toyed whimsically with the idea of rising and going across the hall to see if they really were playing doubles, whimsically, because he knew he would not exert the energy for so trivial a purpose. He turned and stared out the window at the irregular pattern of lights that hung like tiny patches over the soft, deep cloak of night, listening to Alex breathing behind him. There were the lights on the lampposts along the avenue, and there were the square, yellow lights in the windows, and there were the spatulate beams from the headlights in automobiles that reached out like long, white fingers and squashed themselves against the pavement. There were a lot of lights, and if you included the stars, there were too many lights to count.

The door opened and Crawford entered, chewing on a toothpick, his stooped shoulders draped in an old tweed suit. He nodded and Peter looked at him without expression. Ira Crawford was a slim, swarthy-faced man who could prove or disprove anything with a set of statistics he always kept in memory and whose jeering, contemptuous manner never seemed to vary. He closed the door behind him and sat down on a corner of the desk. He removed the toothpick from his mouth and applied it to his fingernails. After a few minutes, he looked at Peter.

"I saw your friend today," he said, his dark face filling with slow amusement.

"I have no friends," Peter said. His fingers plucked at the surface of the desk. "Which friend?"

"Max."

Peter sat up. "Max Hirsch?"

Ira nodded. "Max Hirsch."

"Where?"

"I saw him in a bar on the west side," Ira said. He turned to Alex and spoke to him directly with slow, painstaking nonchalance. Peter listened impatiently. "I was there with an amazingly flat-bellied young lady, trying to dispel her moral trepidations with a new technique. I was trying to seduce her with dialectics and alcohol. We were on our fifth beer and she was getting gay when the door opened and Max came in." He turned back to Peter. "Max Hirsch."

"You talk a lot, Ira," Peter said with annoyance. "Was he in uniform?"

"He was in civilian clothes," Ira said.

"What was he doing there? Did you speak to him?"

"He was buying a pitcher of beer. I did not speak to him."

"Did you follow him?"

"I knew you would want his address so I followed him." Ira turned to Alex. "Reluctantly, very reluctantly, I followed him. I bought another drink for the young lady, told her I would return presently, and went after him. Here's his address." He drew a folded envelope from his pocket and gave it to Peter. "When I returned," he continued to Alex, "she was with a big marine who was continuing from where I had stopped. From the position of his hands when I left, I would say he was successful. My beer and dialectics—the marine wins the prize. That's the way it goes, eh Peter?"

Peter looked up at him. "You talk too much," he said.

"Do I?" Ira asked with amusement.

"Yes," Peter said. "You do. And please get the hell off my desk."

"The chair has to be fixed," Ira said. He made no motion to rise.

"I don't care about that," Peter said, his voice rising with anger. "You can sit there or you can stand, but get the hell off this desk."

Their eyes met, and then Ira looked away. The smile on his face fidgeted and disappeared. He rose slowly, walked across the room, and sat down on the arm of the chair.

"You talk too much, Ira," Peter said slowly, in a soft, menacing voice. "You talk too damn much."

Ira avoided his eyes, his assurance gone. "I was only joking, Peter," he said.

"You joke too much," Peter said. He listened for several moments to the asthmatic breathing of Alex, thinking about what he would say to Max when he saw him. Then he stood up and walked down the office without a word. He walked across the hall to the recreation room to see if they were playing doubles.

The smell of wasting wood, dust, and dry heat grated in his nostrils and throat as he climbed the first flight to Max's apartment. He held the bannister with his wet hand, cursing Max because he lived on the top floor and there were eight flights to climb. At the first floor, his fat body was hot with sweat and he paused there, sucking loudly at the dry air for breath. He rested a few moments and continued. He arrived at the fourth floor with grateful relief, feeling the heavy drag of exhaustion and the damp warmth beneath his chin.

The house was quiet. The door to the flat was open and he peered inside. Seeing no one, he stepped through the doorway and moved inside. As he approached the kitchen, he heard voices, and he stopped abruptly and listened. One of the voices was a woman's. Peter smiled without amusement and retreated to the door.

"Max?" he called.

The voices stopped. A chair scraped, and Max came to the kitchen entrance, a worried look on his thin face. He stopped with surprise when he saw Peter, his face turning solemn and hostile. Peter was disappointed.

"Hello, Max," he said wryly.

Max continued to stare at him. A woman came up behind him and peered over his shoulder. Max caught her arm and stopped her. "Go back in the kitchen," he said. He stopped her protest with a gesture. "Go inside, Sarah," he said gently. She looked curiously at Peter, then disappeared. Max moved into the room slowly. "What is it, Peter?" he asked quietly.

Peter studied him for a moment. "I'm sorry I'm not welcome, Max," he said. "I came as a friend."

Max hesitated. "I'm sorry," he said. "Sit down."

Peter sat down wearily. "It's good to see you again, Max."

Max smiled doubtfully.

"How've you been?" Peter asked.

"Pretty good."

"I was afraid you were dead when you stopped writing. Were you wounded?"

"No," Max said. "I wasn't wounded."

"Were you where the fighting was?"

"For a little while. Air raids, that's all."

"That's good," Peter said. Max was watching him with suspicion and Peter grew resentful. "You haven't changed much, Max," he said, teasingly. "Who's the woman?"

"My wife," Max replied.

"Your wife?" Peter said, concealing his surprise. "How long have you been married?"

"Seven months."

"That's very nice, Max. Call her in. I want to meet her."

"I'd rather not," Max said. "What do you want, Peter?"

"Don't joke, Max. You know why I'm here. Call her in please."

"It doesn't concern her."

"I want to meet her. Now call her."

Max looked at him, thinking. Then he turned slowly. "Sarah!" he called. The woman entered quickly. "Sarah, this is Peter Winkler."

The woman looked at Peter and nodded blankly.

"How do you do," Peter said, making no effort to rise. "I heard Max was married and I wanted to meet his wife."

The woman didn't answer and there was a short silence.

"Go finish your dinner," Max said to her.

She walked back to the kitchen and turned in the doorway. "Come finish yours," she said.

"I'll be in later. I have to talk to Peter."

"It'll get cold."

"I don't want anymore," Max said.

"Go finish your dinner, Max," Peter said. "I'll wait."

Max paused doubtfully. Then he followed her out. Peter heard them whispering and he was pleased. He slumped on the divan, thinking. Max looked better. He had gained weight and he actually looked younger. There was nothing he could say for the woman. She was plain, spinsterish. He guessed from the ink stains on Max's arms that he was working. And he knew what he himself must do. He must force Max to return.

He thumbed slowly through a magazine, studying the advertisements with contempt, until Max returned. Max came in slowly. He walked to the side of a chair and waited. Peter remained silent. He held a pack of cigarettes out. Max shook his head. Peter took one and replaced the pack. He brushed the tobacco crumbs from the end and sighed. He lit the cigarette and smoked. Finally, Max spoke.

"Let's get to the point, Peter," he said.

"All right, Max," Peter said. "We'll get to the point. Sit down." Max sat down. "Why did you stop writing?"

Max answered slowly, choosing his words with care. "A lot of things happened while I was gone. I had a chance to look around and think. I had a lot of time to think. I changed my whole outlook, Peter, and I realized that you belonged to the past."

He stopped and Peter pursed his lips and pretended he was thinking. It was exactly what he had expected. "What are you doing now?" he asked.

"I'm working," Max replied. "I have a job with a printing firm."

"A union shop, I hope," Peter said, joking. He waited until Max smiled, then, quickly, he said, "You know what you've done, Max? You've quit cold."

Max shifted uncomfortably.

"You've become a simple proletariat, that's what."

"I thought you liked the proletariat," Max said defiantly.

"I do. But I don't like a coward."

"Coward? Why do you say that?"

"Because you are. You're leaving the fight. Your beliefs haven't changed that much."

"They really haven't changed at all," Max said. "I'm tired of fighting, that's all. I've done it all my life and now I want to rest. I want to take a little time off to enjoy life. I want to enjoy it as much as I can."

"That's very nice," Peter said, derisively. "That's really very nice. How much enjoyment do you think you'd have if everyone felt that way?"

"Everyone doesn't feel that way."

"That's another fine argument. You're full of fine arguments, Max. You couldn't live this way for long and you know it. You're too intelligent to be satisfied. Now listen to me. Things are very bad and we need an experienced man like you. There's a meeting this Monday. I'll expect you."

"Leave me alone, Peter. Why can't you leave me alone?"

"It's for your own good, Max. You'd better come back."

"I'm not coming back," Max said. His thin, sharp face was determined.

"Yes you are," Peter said. "Max, I don't want to have to threaten you."

"Then don't."

"You're not satisfied here. The neighborhood is dirty. You smell garbage in the hall. You don't have so much."

"I have enough to be happy."

"Happy!" Peter exclaimed, with indignant anger. "Why the hell should you be happy? The whole world is miserable and you want to be happy. I'm not happy. Why the hell should you be?"

"Yes, you are," Max said. "You all are. Nobody forces you into what you're doing. It makes you happy. You enjoy it."

Peter stood up quickly. "All right, Max," he said quietly. "I tried to be nice but you wouldn't let me. You can't see. You're blinded by a woman's body and home-cooked meals and you can't see. Well, I'm telling you what to do. You be at that meeting. If you're not there, you'd better get the hell out of this place and go somewhere where I can't find you, because I'm going to annoy the hell out of you."

"Peter, why don't you leave me alone?"

"I'm not going to. Now are you going to be there or not?"

Max's face sagged, and in a moment he looked old and tired, and very much defeated. "All right," he said slowly. "I'll be there."

"That's good, Max," Peter said. His heavy face broke into a smile. Now that it was over, he was glad. He felt that everything was all right, that Max was back and they would be good friends again, that everything would be different now.

Unnoticed by either of them, the woman came from the kitchen and moved toward the door. "Don't do it, Max," she said.

The two men turned with surprise. The woman stopped before the door, her empty arms limp at her sides, her face fluid with emotion.

"Sarah, go back in the kitchen," Max said.

"No," she said, in a low, brittle voice. "I won't let him do it."

Her tense face frightened Peter. She stood before him, pathetic and helpless, a small, unhappy woman about to cry, and suddenly, as he looked at her, he grew afraid. "Max, get her out of here."

Max looked at her for a few seconds. Then he turned back to Peter. "There's your answer," he said quietly. "I'm not coming back."

"All right," Peter said. "You know what I'm gonna do."

Peter looked at the woman, then at Max. "All right," he said. "You know what I'm gonna do."

"I know," Max said. "There's nothing I can do to stop you."

"No there isn't." Peter stepped toward the door and stopped. The woman barred his way.

"I can stop you," she said, and began crying.

Peter stepped back, watching the tears grow in her eyes and tumble down her cheeks, the thin, shaking shoulders. "Max! Get her out of here." She sobbed aloud and he retreated another step. "Get her out, Max."

"Go back in the kitchen," Max said.

"Don't let him do it, Max," she pleaded. She straightened, and for a moment she faced Peter defiantly, then, as though realizing how futile it was, her body sagged and she moved slowly to the kitchen. In the doorway, she turned to speak. A loud sob choked her voice, and she fled into the kitchen. Peter stared after her, listening to her muffled sobs.

"You made her cry," Max said.

Peter shifted his great weight with guilt. "I'm sorry," he said, his eyes fixed on the doorway. "Does she always cry like that?"

"I don't know," Max said. "I never saw her cry before." He stepped to the side and faced Peter. "You can go now," he said. "There's no one in your way."

Peter kept looking toward the kitchen. The sobbing stopped, but he continued to stare, thinking. Then he turned slowly. "I won't bother you, Max," he said. Max didn't move. "Do you understand, Max? I won't bother you."

Relief came to Max's face, and he smiled. "You mean that?"

"Yes," Peter said. "I mean that." He moved to the door. "I'll go now. I'm sorry I disturbed you. I don't suppose we'll see each other again. Good-bye, Max."

"Good-bye, Peter," Max said. He waited impatiently, unsure of himself as long as Peter remained.

Peter turned to go. He could see that Max wanted him to leave. In the doorway, he stopped, hesitated, and turned again.

"Max," he said. He spoke quickly, in a strange humble voice. "Do you think that maybe some night you could ask me over for dinner?"

Max looked at him with surprise.

"I could dress up," Peter continued quickly. "I have a new suit and I would wear it, and we could be like old friends."

Max came forward, beaming with joy. "Of course, Peter. Why don't you stay tonight?"

Peter was about to agree. Then he looked at the kitchen and shook his head. "Not tonight, Max," he said. "I have to keep an appointment. Sometime next week maybe."

"Any time at all," Max said.

"You call me up and invite me, eh Max?"

"Sure, Peter. I'll call you."

They shook hands without pressure, and Peter walked out and moved around to the top of the steps. His hand found the bannister and he started down slowly, feeling tired and perspiring already, and knowing sadly that he would never see Max again. He thought of the woman. He was sorry that he had made her cry. She was a plain woman and a complete stranger to him, but he knew he could very easily fall in love with just such a woman.

CLEVINGER'S TRIAL
A Play in One Act

*About the process of adapting the novel to a stage play, Mr.
Heller has stated: "It was clear from the outset that large changes
would have to be made. Much of the book would be eliminated or
compressed. Many well-known episodes were excluded simply
because they could not fit closely enough with the chosen themes
of war, death, persecution, and repression. Some were discarded
with relief; others were abandoned with reluctance. The trial
of Clevinger was written and then taken out with regret for
reasons of length rather than substance. The scene ran nearly
twenty pages, too many for a secondary character whose basic
function in the play is to come on stage as a trusting, idealistic
young man and be slaughtered. As countless acting classes have
discovered from the time the book was published, the chapter
'plays beautifully,' and I knew I would probably offer it soon as a
one-act play, since most of the work of dramatizing it was already
done."*

What follows is the one-act play Clevinger's Trial, *published
here for the first time, based upon Chapter 8 of Joseph Heller's
novel* Catch-22 *and upon Section 8 of Official Army Regulations,
which deals with lunacy.*

◆

Crawdaddy, August 1973, pp. 45–54.

A table, some chairs, a small bench. A rifle rack, with one rifle standing, and one shovel.

Clevinger enters from one side, carrying a cumbersome, antiquated rifle on his shoulder, pacing slowly as though on sentry duty. Yossarian enters from the other side.

Yossarian

What are you doing on sentry duty?

Clevinger

I'm not on sentry duty.

(Clevinger turns and paces in the other direction. Yossarian walks along with him.)

Yossarian

Why are you walking back and forth with that rifle?

Clevinger

It's a penalty tour. I got a hundred and fifty-seven hours of them.

Yossarian

For *what?*

Clevinger

I'm not sure.

Yossarian

Clevinger, I told you you'd get in trouble some-day, always obeying orders.

Clevinger

It wasn't that, Yossarian. One day I stumbled in formation, while we were practicing parading, and the next thing I knew I was up on trial.

Yossarian

For stumbling? That's a serious crime.

Clevinger

I know I must deserve what I got, or they wouldn't have punished me. I couldn't be innocent, could I?

Yossarian

Clevinger, you're a dope.

Clevinger

That's when it began. When you called me a dope.

Yossarian

I'm always calling you a dope.

Clevinger

I mean the time Lieutenant Scheisskopf called all the men together because we were all so unhappy with him. Remember?

Yossarian

Sure, I remember.

(They move to the bench and sit down.)

Clevinger

I'm going to tell him, Yossarian. If he asks—

Yossarian

Clevinger, don't be a dope.

(Lieutenant Scheisskopf enters, wild and distraught, and speaks as though addressing a multitude of seated soldiers. He carries a sheet of paper to which he occasionally refers.)

Scheisskopf

Why me? *(He paces about like a tragic actor.)*

Yossarian

(Sotto voce) Why not?

Scheisskopf

Why must it be me, Lieutenant Scheisskopf, who has to have the unhappiest squadron of cadets on the whole air base? Do you know how it makes me feel to see you all so miserable? Do you know what other officers call me?

Yossarian

Shithead.

Scheisskopf

Is it any of my fault?

Yossarian

Yes.

Clevinger

I think it's our duty to tell him.

Yossarian

I think it's our duty to keep our mouths shut.

Scheisskopf

Do you know what the problem is? I know what the problem is. It's your morale. You've got bad morale . . . very bad. I've been in the army a long time, fourteen months, and I have seen some bad morale in my time, but your morale is really terrible. You have the worst morale I have ever seen.

Yossarian

That's true.

Scheisskopf

You've got no . . . *(consults his paper)* . . . *esprit de corps.*

Clevinger

That is true.

Scheisskopf

Don't I do everything I can for you?

Yossarian

No.

Scheisskopf

Don't I make you practice marching more than any other squadron so you'll look better in the Sunday parades? And what happens?

Yossarian

We look worse.

Scheisskopf

You look worse. If you meet me halfway, don't I always meet you more than halfway?

Yossarian

That may be why we never meet at all.

Scheisskopf

I can tell you this. How sharper than . . . *(glances at paper)* . . . a serpent's tooth it is to have a thankless group of men like you in my command.

Yossarian

Not bad.

Clevinger

It will make it easier if we tell him.

Yossarian

Don't be stupid, stupid.

Scheisskopf

Let's bring it all out into the open, man to man. Isn't there one person in the whole lot of you with the guts to speak the . . . *(glances at paper)* . . . truth?

(Clevinger puts his arm up. Yossarian jerks it down.)

Clevinger

I'm going to tell him.

Yossarian

Keep still, idiot.

Clevinger

You don't know what you're talking about.

Yossarian

I know enough to keep still, idiot.

Scheisskopf

I *want* someone to tell me. If any of it is my fault, I *want* to be told.

Clevinger

He wants someone to tell him.

(Clevinger puts his arm up. Yossarian jerks it down.)

Yossarian

He wants everyone to keep still, idiot.

Clevinger

Didn't you just hear him?

Yossarian

I heard him. I heard him say very loudly and very distinctly that he wants every one of us to keep our mouths shut if we know what's good for us.

Scheisskopf

I won't punish you.

Clevinger

He says he won't punish me.

Yossarian

He'll castrate you.

Scheisskopf

I swear I won't punish you. I'll be grateful to the man who tells me the truth.

Yossarian

He'll hate you. To his dying day he'll hate you.

Clevinger

You're wrong.

Yossarian

You're a dope.

Scheisskopf

My office door is always open. *(He exits.)*

Clevinger

I'm going to tell him.

(Clevinger hurries out after him. He stumbles on the way. Yossarian exits in the opposite direction. Clevinger is brought back in immediately, a prisoner of Scheisskopf and Major Metcalf. The colonel and a stenographer enter from the other side and take places behind the desk.)

Colonel

Okay, let's move it along. Major Metcalf? Who's next?

Metcalf

Clevinger, sir.

Colonel

What's the charge against him?

Metcalf

Guilty.

Colonel

Good. What's the verdict?

Metcalf

Telling the truth.

Colonel

That's terrible. Any evidence?

Metcalf

He went to college, listens to classical music, likes foreign movies, asks questions, disagrees—

Colonel

I know the type. Bring the insubordinate son-of-a-bitch in.

Metcalf

He's here.

Colonel

Good. We can save valuable time when there's a war going on. Which one of you two insubordinate son-of-a-bitches is the criminal?

Scheisskopf

(*Quickly*) He is, sir. I'm Scheisskopf.

Clevinger

That's not entirely true, sir.

Colonel

That he's Scheisskopf?

Clevinger

That I'm a criminal. I've only been accused, sir, and I'm innocent until proven guilty. All I did was stumble in formation and . . .

Colonel

Who says so?

Clevinger

Everyone, sir. The Bill of Rights, the Declaration of Independence, the common law, the Military Code of Justice, the——

Colonel

You believe all that crap?

Clevinger

Yes, sir. I'm a free citizen in a free country, and I have certain rights guaranteed to me by——

Colonel

You're nothing of the kind. You're a prisoner in my dock. So go stand there in my dock and keep your stupid, young, insolent mouth shut.

Clevinger

Where's the dock?

Colonel

Metcalf, where's my dock?

Metcalf

I'm not sure, sir. What's a dock?

Scheisskopf

It's where a ship comes in.

Metcalf

What ship?

Colonel

The ship that's going to carry one of you people away to the Solomon Islands to bury bodies if we don't get moving fast enough. In sixty days you've got to be rough enough and tough enough to fight Billy Petrolle, and you think it's a big, fat joke, don't you?

Clevinger

No, sir. I don't think it's a big, fat joke.

Metcalf

Neither do I, sir.

Colonel

Metcalf, shut your mouth and keep out of this.

Metcalf

Yes, sir.

Colonel

Do you know what I mean when I tell you to keep your mouth shut?

Metcalf

Yes, sir.

Colonel

Then why do you answer "Yes, sir" when I tell you to keep your mouth shut?

Metcalf

I don't know, sir.

Colonel

Do you call that keeping your mouth shut?

Metcalf

No, sir.

Colonel

Good. Then keep your mouth shut from now on when I tell you to keep your mouth shut.

Metcalf

Yes, sir.

Colonel

That's better. *(To Scheisskopf)* Cadet Clevinger—

Scheisskopf

He's Clevinger, sir. I'm Scheisskopf.

Clevinger

I'm Clevinger, sir. All I did was stumble—

Colonel

Do you understand the charges against you?

Clevinger

No, sir. I don't know the charges against me. All I did was—

Colonel

Will you please stop saying that? In sixty days you'll be fighting Billy Petrolle and you keep wasting time telling me you stumbled. Just answer my question. Do you or don't you?

Clevinger

What?

Colonel

I forgot.

Metcalf

And it's your fault.

Colonel

Is there anything you want to say in your own defense, before I pass sentence?

Clevinger

Yes, sir! First you have to find me guilty.

Colonel

We can do that in a second. I find you guilty. There.

Clevinger

Of what? I have a right to face my accuser, sir, and to have an officer defending me.

Colonel

Does he?

Scheisskopf

I have no objections to letting him face me.

Colonel

You can face him if you want to. Now let's get on with it. Face him. Good. Who's handling the prosecution?

Scheisskopf

I am, sir.

Colonel

Okay, Shithead, then—

Scheisskopf

Scheisskopf.

Colonel

What?

Scheisskopf

Scheisskopf, sir. That's my name.

Colonel

Scheisskopf? What kind of a name is Scheisskopf? I thought your name was Shi—

Scheisskopf

Scheisskopf. It's *my* name, sir. It's German.

Colonel

Aren't we at war with Germany?

Scheisskopf

It's just my name that's German, sir. Not me. It isn't even *my* name, sir. I got it from my father. I'll give it back if you want me to.

Colonel

Oh, that's not necessary. I have no quarrel with Adolf Hitler. In fact, I kind of like the job he's doing of stamping out un-American activities in Germany. Let's hope we can do as well with this punk when we've all got to be sharp enough to cut the mustard and rough enough and tough enough to fight Billy Petrolle. Are we ready to begin?

Clevinger

Who's defending me?

Colonel

Who's defending him?

Scheisskopf

I am.

Colonel

That's good. We'll need one more judge, just in case Major Metcalf and I—ha, ha—should disagree.

Scheisskopf

I could be a judge too, sir. As long as I'm prosecuting him and defending him, I would be able to see both sides of the question and probably have an unprejudiced view.

Colonel

That makes sense to me. Then we're ready to begin. Now, on the basis of the evidence I've seen, the case against Clevinger is open and shut. All we need is something to charge him with.

Scheisskopf

I believe I have that, sir. In anticipation of the possibility that such a contingency was likely to arise. I took the liberty, in my capacity of prosecutor, of drawing up—

Colonel

—Shi—

Scheisskopf

Scheisskopf.

Colonel

Get to the God damned point.

Scheisskopf

Yes, sir.

Colonel

What did the little son-of-a-bitch do?

Scheisskopf

I charge the prisoner Clevinger—

Clevinger

I'm not a prisoner. Under the terms of—

Colonel

Order in the God damned court!

Scheisskopf

I charge the convict Clevinger with . . . *(reading)*
"Stumbling without authority, breaking formation while in formation, felonious assault, indiscriminate behavior, going to school, mopery—"

Stenographer

Sir?

Metcalf

Mopery?

Scheisskopf

M-O-P-E-R-Y.

Metcalf

That's a very serious charge.

Colonel

What is it?

Scheisskopf

No one seems to know, sir. I couldn't find it anywhere.

Colonel

Then he'll certainly have a hard time disproving it, won't he?

Metcalf

That's what makes it so serious.

Colonel

Metcalf, you have a brother in the Pentagon, I believe?

Metcalf

Yes, sir.

Colonel

But he's without much influence there, is that right?

Metcalf

He has none at all, sir.

Colonel

And unlikely to acquire any?

Metcalf

His prospects are poor, sir. He's a buck private.

Colonel

In that case you'd better be God damned careful how you act here now or I'll put *you* on trial for mopery and ship this snotty son-of-a-bitch to the Solomon Islands to bury corpses. Please continue—

Scheisskopf

Scheisskopf.

Colonel

Scheisskopf, with the reading of the charges against this smart-assed, wise-assed, half-assed, son-of-a-bitchin' bastard of a son-of-a-bitch.

Scheisskopf

Yes, sir. ". . . going to school—"

Clevinger

He said that once.

Colonel

Didn't we have that one already?

Scheisskopf

Yes, sir. But he went to more than one school. ". . . very high treason, provoking, being a smart guy, listening to classical music, and . . . *so on.*"

(The Colonel and Metcalf whistle gravely when the reading of the last charge is concluded.)

Colonel

Well, Clevinger. Now you've heard the charges against you. Do you understand them?

Clevinger

I'm not sure, sir. There was stumbling without something and . . .

Stenographer

"Stumbling without authority."

Colone

Stumbling without authority, breaking formation while in formation, felonious something . . .

Scheisskopf

Assault, indiscriminate behavior, going to school twice—

Metcalf

Mopery.

Scheisskopf

Mopery, very high treason . . . er . . .

Stenographer

"Provoking, being a smart guy, listening to classical music, and *so on.*"

(The officers let out solemn whistles again.)

Colonel

You've already admitted to stumbling. As to the rest of these charges, are you guilty or innocent?

Clevinger

Innocent.

Colonel

And what makes you think we care? Do you know why you're here? Guilt or innocence has nothing to do with it. You're here because you're trouble—that's what you are, trouble—and nobody likes trouble. Do you? Don't contradict me! That's more trouble.

Metcalf

Kill him, sir! Kill him!

Colonel

Metcalf, you shut your mouth and keep out of this. Clevinger, in sixty days you'll be fighting Billy Petrolle. And you still think it's a big fat joke.

Clevinger

I don't think it's a joke at all, sir.

Colonel

Don't interrupt.

Clevinger

Yes, sir.

Metcalf

And say "sir" when you do.

Clevinger

Yes, sir.

Metcalf

Weren't you just ordered not to interrupt?

Clevinger

But I didn't interrupt, sir.

Metcalf

No. And you didn't say "sir" either. Add that to the charges against him. Failure to say "sir" to superior officers when not interrupting them.

Colonel

Metcalf, you're a goddamn fool. Do you know that?

Metcalf

(Swallowing with difficulty) Yes, sir.

Colonel

Then keep your goddamn mouth shut. You don't make sense. Clevinger, how would you like to be washed out as a cadet and shipped to the Solomon Islands to bury bodies?

Clevinger

I wouldn't, sir.

Colonel

That's strange. Would you rather be a corpse or bury one?

Clevinger

I don't think I'd mind going into combat, sir.

Colonel

You might not be good enough! Just what *did* you mean when you said we couldn't punish you?

Clevinger

When, sir?

Colonel

I'm asking the questions. You're answering them.

Clevinger

Yes, sir. I——

Colonel

Did you think we brought you here to ask questions and for me to answer them?

Clevinger

No, sir. I——

Colonel

What *did* we bring you here for?

Clevinger

To answer questions.

Colonel

You're goddamn right. Now suppose you start answering some before I break your goddamn head.

Just what the hell did you mean, you bastard, when you said we couldn't punish you?

Clevinger

I don't think I ever made that statement, sir.

Colonel

Will you speak up, please? I couldn't hear you.

Metcalf

Will you speak up, please? He couldn't hear you.

Clevinger

Yes, sir. I—

Colonel

Metcalf?

Metcalf

Sir?

Colonel

Didn't I tell you to keep your stupid mouth shut?

Metcalf

Yes, sir.

Colonel

Then keep your stupid mouth shut when I tell you to keep your stupid mouth shut. *(To Clevinger)* Will you speak up, please? I couldn't hear you.

Clevinger

Yes, sir. I—

Colonel

Metcalf, is that your foot I'm stepping on?

Metcalf

No, sir. It must be Lieutenant Scheisskopf's foot.

Scheisskopf

It isn't my foot.

Metcalf

Then maybe it is my foot after all.

Colonel

Move it.

Metcalf

Yes, sir. You'll have to move your foot first, Colonel. It's on top of mine.

Colonel

Are you telling me to move my foot?

Metcalf

No, sir. Oh, no, sir.

Colonel

Then move your foot and keep your stupid mouth shut. *(To Clevinger)* Will you speak up, please? I still couldn't hear you.

Clevinger

Yes, sir. I said that I didn't say that you couldn't punish me.

Colonel

Just what the hell are you talking about?

Clevinger

I'm answering your question, sir.

Colonel

What question?

Stenographer

"Just what the hell did you mean, you bastard, when you said we couldn't punish you?"

Colonel

All right. Just what the hell *did* you mean, you bastard?

Clevinger

I didn't say you couldn't punish me, sir.

Colonel

When?

Clevinger

When what, sir?

Colonel

Now you're asking me questions again.

Clevinger

I'm sorry, sir. I'm afraid I don't understand your question.

Colonel

When didn't you say we couldn't punish you? Don't you understand my question?

Clevinger

No, sir. I don't understand.

Colonel

You've just told us that. Now suppose you answer my question.

Clevinger

But how can I answer it?

Colonel

That's another question you're asking me.

Clevinger

I'm sorry, sir. But I don't know how to answer it. I never said you couldn't punish me.

Colonel

Now you're telling us when you did say it. I'm asking you to tell us when you didn't say it.

Clevinger

(Taking a deep breath as he finally understands) I *always* didn't say you couldn't punish me, sir.

Colonel

That's much better, Mr. Clevinger, even though it is a barefaced lie. Last night in the latrine. When you thought you were alone and none of us were eavesdropping. Didn't you whisper that we couldn't punish you to that other dirty son-of-a-bitch we don't like? What's his name?

Scheisskopf

Yossarian, sir.

Colonel

Yes, Yossarian. That's right, Yossarian. Yossarian? What the hell kind of a name is Yossarian?

Scheisskopf

It's Yossarian's name, sir.

Colonel

Yes, I suppose it is. Didn't you whisper to Yossarian that we couldn't punish you?

Clevinger

Oh, no, sir. I whispered to him that you couldn't find me guilty—

Colonel

I may be stupid, but the distinction escapes me. I guess I am pretty stupid, because the distinction escapes me.

Clevinger

W—

Colonel

You're a windy son-of-a-bitch, aren't you? Nobody asked you for clarification and you're giving me clarification. I was making a statement, not asking for clarification. You are a windy son-of-a-bitch, aren't you?

Clevinger

No, sir.

Colonel

No, sir? Are you calling me a goddamn liar?

Clevinger

Oh, no, sir.

Colonel

Then you're a windy son-of-a-bitch, aren't you?

Clevinger

No, sir.

Colonel

Are you trying to pick a fight with me?

Clevinger

No, sir.

Colonel

Are you a windy son-of-a-bitch?

Clevinger

No, sir.

Colonel

Goddammit, you are trying to pick a fight with me. For two stinking cents I'd jump over this big fat table and rip your stinking, cowardly body apart limb from limb.

Metcalf

Do it! Do it!

Colonel

Metcalf, you stinking son-of-a-bitch. Didn't I tell you to keep your stinking, cowardly, stupid mouth shut?

Metcalf

Yes, sir. I'm sorry, sir.

Colonel

Then suppose *you* do it.

Metcalf

I was only trying to learn, sir. The only way a person can learn is by trying.

Colonel

Who says so?

Metcalf

Everybody says so, sir. Even Lieutenant Scheisskopf says so.

Colonel

Do you say so?

Scheisskopf

Yes, sir. But everybody says so.

Colonel

Well, Metcalf, suppose you try keeping that stupid mouth of yours shut, and maybe that's the way you'll learn how. Now, where were we? Read me back the last line.

Stenographer

"Read me back the last line."

Colonel

Not *my* last line, stupid! Somebody else's.

Stenographer

"Read me back the last line."

Colonel

That's *my* last line again!

Stenographer

Oh, no, sir. That's *my* last line. I read it to you just a moment ago. Don't you remember, sir? It was only a moment ago.

Colonel

Oh, my God! Read me back *his* last line, stupid. Say, what the hell's your name, anyway?

Stenographer

Popinjay, sir.

Colonel

Well, you're next, Popinjay. As soon as his trial ends, your trial begins. Get it?

Stenographer

Yes, sir. What will I be charged with?

Colonel

What the hell difference does that make? Did you hear what he asked me? You're going to learn, Popinjay—the minute we finish with Clevinger you're going to learn. Cadet Clevinger, what did— you *are* Cadet Clevinger, aren't you, and not Popinjay.

Clevinger

Yes, sir.

Colonel

Good. What did—

Stenographer

I'm Popinjay, sir.

Colonel

Popinjay, is your father a millionaire, or a member of the Senate?

Stenographer

No, sir.

Colonel

Then you're up shit creek, Popinjay, without a paddle. He's not a general or a high-ranking member of the Administration, is he?

Stenographer

No, sir.

Colonel

That's good. What does your father do?

Stenographer

He's dead, sir.

Colonel

That's *very* good. You really are up the creek, Popinjay. Is Popinjay really your name? Just what the hell kind of name is Popinjay, anyway? I don't like it.

Scheisskopf

It's Popinjay's name, sir.

Colonel

Well, I don't like it, Popinjay, and I just can't wait to rip your stinking, cowardly body apart limb from limb. Cadet Clevinger, will you please repeat what the hell it was you did or did not whisper to your friend late last night in the latrine?

Clevinger

Yes, sir. I said that you couldn't find me guilty—

Colonel

We'll take it from there. Precisely what did you mean, Cadet Clevinger, when you said we couldn't find you guilty?

Clevinger

I didn't say you couldn't find me guilty, sir.

Colonel

When?

Clevinger

When what, sir?

Colonel

Goddammit, are you going to start pumping me again?

Clevinger

No, sir. I'm sorry, sir.

Colonel

Then answer the question. When didn't you say we couldn't find you guilty?

Clevinger

Late last night in the latrine, sir.

Colonel

Is that the only time you didn't say it?

Clevinger

No, sir. I always didn't say you couldn't find me guilty, sir. What I did say was—

Colonel

Nobody asked you what you did say. We asked you what you didn't say. We're not at all interested in what you did say. Is that clear?

Clevinger

Yes, sir.

Colonel

Then we'll go on. What did you say?

Clevinger

I said, sir, that you couldn't find me guilty of the offense with which I am charged and still be faithful to the cause of . . .

Colonel

Of what? You're mumbling.

Metcalf

Stop mumbling.

Clevinger

Yes, sir.

Metcalf

And mumble "sir" when you do.

Colonel

Metcalf, you bastard!

Clevinger

Yes, sir. Of justice, sir. That you couldn't find—

Colonel

Justice? What is justice?

Clevinger

Justice, sir, is—

Colonel

That's not what justice is. That's what Karl Marx is. I'll tell you what justice is. Justice is a knee in the gut from the floor on the chin at night sneaky with a knife brought up down on the magazine of a battleship sandbagged underhanded in the dark without a word of warning. Garroting. That's what justice is when we've all got to be tough enough and rough enough to fight Billy Petrolle. From the hip. Get it?

Clevinger

No, sir.

Colonel

Don't "sir" me.

Clevinger

Yes, sir.

Metcalf

And say "sir" when you don't.

Colonel

You're guilty, Clevinger, or you would not have been accused. And since the only way we can prove it is to find you guilty, it's our patriotic duty to do so. Clevinger, by a unanimous vote of the three judges, I find you guilty of all charges and sentence you to walk fifty-six punishment tours.

Clevinger

What's a punishment tour?

Colonel

Make that fifty-seven. A punishment tour is sixty minutes of pacing back and forth in the hot sun with an unloaded, heavy World War I rifle on your shoulder. Is there anything you wish to say before I pass sentence?

Clevinger

You just did!

Colonel

That? That was nothing.

Clevinger

Sir, I believe I have the right of appeal.

Colonel

I just took it away from you. Make that a hundred and fifty-seven. First you want to face your accuser, next you want to appeal. Have you anything else to say in a bid for clemency? If you do,

I'll double your punishment. *(Clevinger shakes his head.)* Then grab a rifle and start walking. Faster, faster. I want you to try to cut those sixty minutes of each hour down as much as you can.

Clevinger
(Pacing with the rifle again) I don't understand.

Colonel
I can see that. In sixty days you'll be fighting Billy Petrolle, and you've got nothing better to do than stand there walking back and forth, back and forth, with a useless rifle on your shoulder. Well, justice is done? Are we all through?

Metcalf
Sir? Who is Billy Petrolle?

Colonel
I'm glad you asked that.

Scheisskopf
I was going to ask that too, sir.

Colonel
I'm sure you were, Sh—

Scheisskopf
Scheisskopf.

Colonel
Scheisskopf. Billy Petrolle was a professional boxer who was born in Berwick, Pennsylvania in 1905. He fought a hundred and fifty-seven bouts and won eighty-nine of them, sixty-three by knockouts. On November fourth, 1932, he fought for the world lightweight championship in New York against Tony Canzoneri and lost the deci-

sion in a fight that went fifteen rounds. He was also known as the Fargo Express. Fargo is in North Dakota. I'm glad you've all learned something from this experience. This court is adjourned.

Stenographer

What about me?

Colonel

You? Who's you?

Scheisskopf

Popinjay, sir. You said you'd punish him, too.

Colonel

That's right, I did—

Scheisskopf

Scheisskopf.

Colonel

Scheisskopf. Lock him up to teach him a lesson. That's quick thinking, Captain. I think you'll go far.

Scheisskopf

I'm a lieutenant, sir.

Colonel

I'm promoting you, Captain. I'm promoting you to major.

Scheisskopf

Gee—I am going far! Move along, Popinjay. Get your toothbrush and a clean handkerchief, and report to the stockade.

(Scheisskopf takes Popinjay's arm and points him offstage.)

Colonel

See how right I was about him, Metcalf? I said he'd go far, and he has.

Metcalf

If he's a major, what does that make me?

Colonel

Metcalf, it makes you the guy that will have to go to the Solomon Islands to bury bodies.

Metcalf

Me?

Colonel

There *are* bodies. Would you rather be a corpse or bury one?

(Metcalf shakes his head. He takes up the shovel, shoulders it as he would a rifle, and paces offstage, passing Clevinger, who paces in the opposite direction. Scheisskopf rejoins the colonel as Yossarian re-enters. Clevinger turns and paces back.)

Clevinger

(To Yossarian) I still can't understand it.

Yossarian

What?

Colonel

(As Clevinger's pacing brings him near) I hate you.

(Clevinger's pacing takes him back toward Yossarian.)

Scheisskopf

So do I.

Clevinger

They hate me.

Colonel

I hated you before you came, hated you while you were here.

Scheisskopf

Me too.

Colonel

And we're going to keep on hating you after we go.

Scheisskopf

I would have lynched him if I could.

Clevinger

They were three grown men, and I was a boy, and they hated me.

Colonel

And wish you dead.

Clevinger

They speak the same language I do and wear the same uniform, but nowhere in the whole world are there people who hate me more.

Colonel

And wish you dead.

Scheisskopf

Me too.

Colonel

I like to see justice done.

Yossarian

(Pacing along with Clevinger) I tried to warn you, kid. They hate Jews.

Clevinger

I'm not Jewish.

Yossarian

It will make no difference to them.

Colonel

We're after everybody.

Yossarian

You see?

Colonel

And do you know why I like to see justice done, Shi—

Scheisskopf

Scheisskopf.

Colonel

. . . Scheisskopf? Because—*(as Yossarian paces near)* I said *everybody.*

(Yossarian halts, ponders, and gets the message. He goes to the rifle rack, shoulders the other rifle, and begins walking penalty tours behind Clevinger.)

Colonel

. . . Because *I'm* the one that does it.

(The colonel exits laughing with Scheisskopf in one direction, as Clevinger and then Yossarian pace offstage in the other.)

CURTAIN

CATCH-22 REVISITED

Bastia, the largest city in Corsica, was empty, hot and still when we arrived. It was almost one o'clock, and the people in Corsica, like those in Italy, duck for cover at lunchtime and do not emerge until very late in the afternoon, when the harsh and suffocating summer heat has begun to abate. The hotel in Île Rousse, on the other side of the island, had sent a taxi for us. And driving the taxi was François, a sporty, jaunty, chunky, barrel-chested, agreeable ex-cop. He was in his forties, and he wore a white mesh sport shirt, neat slacks and new leather sandals.

There were two roads from Bastia to Île Rousse, a high road and a low road. "Take the low road," said my wife, who has a fear of dying.

"D'accord," François agreed, and began driving straight up. In a minute or two the city of Bastia lay directly below us.

"Is this the low road?" asked my wife.

It was the high road, François informed us. He had decided, for our own good, that we should take the scenic high road to Île Rousse and then, if we still insisted, the low road coming back. François was indeed an agreeable person; he agreed to everything we proposed and then did what he thought best.

I had remembered from my military service that there were

Holiday, vol. 41, April 1967, pp. 44–60, 120, 141–42, 145. Reprinted in *A Catch-22 Casebook,* ed. Frederick T. Kiley and Walter McDonald (New York: Crowell), 1973.

mountains in Corsica, but I had never appreciated how many there were or how high they rose. For the record, there is one peak nine thousand feet high and eight more than eight thousand. It was one of these eight-thousand-foot mountains we were now crossing. The higher we drove, the more the land began to resemble the American West. We soon saw cactus growing beside the road, and then eagles wheeling in the sky—down below us!

After about two hours we had crossed the island and came to the other coast, still riding high above it. We drove southward now, passing, on a small beach, some German pillboxes no one had bothered to remove. Soon we saw Île Rousse resting in a haze below us between the mountains and the shore. The road descended slowly. We continued through the town and out to the hotel, which stood almost at the end of a narrow spit.

My main purpose in coming to Corsica again was to visit the site of our air base, to tramp the ground where our tents had stood and see what changes had occurred to the airstrip on which our planes had taken off and landed so many times. This was not in Île Rousse but back on the other side of the island, about fifty miles south of Bastia. I had come to Île Rousse now because it's a summer resort and because the Air Force had a rest camp there during the war. I was disappointed in what I found now. The Napoléon Bonaparte, the large luxury hotel that had accommodated the officers, was not open. The hotel in which enlisted men had stayed was dilapidated. There was not, of course, any of the wartime noise, energy and excitement. With the exception of Rome and Naples, almost all the towns and cities I was to visit that were associated with my war experiences brought me the same disappointment. They no longer had any genuine connection with the war, but it was only through the war that I was acquainted with them.

We went swimming that afternoon. A jukebox at the beach played records by Bob Dylan, the Beatles, the Rolling Stones and

Nancy Sinatra. At the tables were a number of teen-age girls and boys, good-looking and ultra cool, down for the season from Nice, Marseilles and even Paris. They were inert and blasé, determinedly paying no more attention to us than they did to each other.

That evening I was taken to dinner by a man who had been an important public official in Île Rousse for eighteen years and would be one still if he had not grown weary of the honor. We drove down the coast several miles to the village of Algajola, where we had dinner in a small new hotel perched on a hill overlooking the water. He introduced me to an old man who had worked at the Hotel Napoléon Bonaparte as a bartender when it was an American rest camp. The old man had nothing unpredictable to offer in the way of recollections. There was much liquor and few women, except for occasions when Army nurses were brought in for dances from other parts of Corsica.

More interesting than the rest camp was my host himself, a stout, generous, dark-complexioned man in his fifties who had been in his youth an authentic *bon vivant*. He had gone to school in Paris and had planned to spend the rest of his life there in pleasure and idleness. Then, in a short period, he had lost his father, uncles and grandfather, and it was necessary for him to return to Corsica to take charge of the family's business affairs. He had lived in Corsica ever since. He really loved Corsica, he told me without conviction, although he missed the opera, the ballet, the theater, literature, good food and wine, and the chance to talk about these things with others who enjoyed them as much as he did. He smiled frequently as he spoke, but his geniality was clouded with a tremendous regret. He had a grown son who was supposed to return for us with the car at ten o'clock. He would arrive here on time, I was assured. And precisely at ten his son appeared.

"He is always on time," my host remarked sorrowfully as we rose to go. "He does not even have enough imagination to come late once in a while." Here, in a small village in Corsica, I had found Ethan Frome, for this was truly a tale of blasted hopes and wasted years that he had related.

Early the next day we headed back across the island in search of the old air base. François made us listen as he sounded the horn of the car. It was a Klaxon. He had installed it for the journey back over the low road, so that we all might be more at ease. Each time we whizzed into a blind curve, I instructed François, *"Sonnez le Klaxon,"* and he was delighted to oblige.

The low road from Île Rousse was very high for part of the way. But the land soon leveled out, and we found ourselves whizzing along comfortably on flat ground. Jokingly, I remarked to François that I might bring him back with me to New York, where I knew he would excel in the Manhattan traffic. François pounced so readily on this chance at the big time that I had to discourage him quickly. A New York taxi driver, I told him, works for other people, makes little money and *n'est pas content, jamais content,* and only someone very rich, like Alan Arkin, could afford his own car and chauffeur. While François was still pondering this information solemnly, the fan belt snapped, and a wild clatter sounded from the front of the car. François eased the car softly to a stop at the side of the road, in back of a small truck already parked there. Two men lifted grease-stained faces from beneath the truck's open hood and looked at us questioningly. It turned out that we had been forced to come to a stop, purely by chance, directly in front of the only garage in miles.

In minutes we were ready to proceed. François, while asking directions to the old American air base, chanced to mention that I was one of the officers who had been stationed there. Both mechanics turned to me with huge grins, and one of them called for his wife to come out of the house to see me. To François this reaction was electrifying; it had not occurred to him that he was driving a potential dignitary whose presence could enlarge his own importance. Chest out, the cop in authority again, he pushed his way between me and this welcoming crowd of three, keeping them back as he screened their questions. After a minute he declared abruptly, to us as well as to them, that it was necessary for us to go. They waved after us as we went driving away.

I was unable to spy anything more familiar than the Mediterranean. Instead of the ageless landmarks I recalled, I saw Fire Island cottages that I *know* had not been there during the war. We did, however, find the crossroad to Cervione, another mountain village to which we used to drive in a jeep every now and then for a glass of wine in a cool, darkened bar. The bar was still there. It was larger now, and much brighter. Coca-Cola was advertised, and a refrigerated case offered *gelati allemagne,* German ice cream, direct from Leghorn, in Italy. The several patrons inside were a generation or two younger than the silent, brown, old men in work clothes I remembered. These wore summer sport shirts and wash-and-wear trousers.

François entered first and announced to all in the room that he had brought them an American officer who had been stationed at the airfield below and had returned for a visit after so many years because he loved Corsica and loved the people of Cervione. The response was tumultuous. Ice cream and cold soda appeared for my wife and children; beer, wine and other flavorful alcoholic drinks appeared for me. I was, it turned out, the only American from the air base who had ever returned, which helped account for the exuberant celebration. My wife asked through the noise whether we could have lunch in Cervione. A meal was ordered by telephone, and we walked to the restaurant ten minutes later, following François, who swaggered ahead with such inflated self-importance that I was certain he had exaggerated enormously the part I had played in beating Hitler and vanquishing Japan.

The only restaurant in Cervione was on the second floor of the only hotel, and it seemed to be part of the living quarters of the family who ran it. A large table had been made ready for us in the center. Food began arriving the moment we sat down, and some of the things looked pretty strange.

"Don't drink the water," my wife warned the children, who ignored her, since they were thirsty, and no other suitable beverage was available.

"Don't drink the water," François said to me, and popped open a bottle of wine.

My wife and children got by on cooked ham, bread and cheese. I ate everything set before me and asked for more. The main dish was a slice of what seemed like pan-broiled veal, which was probably goat, since kid is a specialty of the island.

Back at the bar we had coffee, and then a strange and unexpected ceremony took place. The entire room fell silent while a shy, soft-spoken young man stepped toward us hesitantly and begged permission to give us a *cadeau*, a gift, a large, beautiful earthenware vase from the small pottery shop from which he gained his livelihood. It was touching, sobering; I was sorry I had nothing with which to reciprocate.

After Cervione, the airfield, when we finally found it, was a great disappointment. A lighthouse that had served as a landmark for returning planes left no doubt we had the right place, but there was nothing there now but reeds and wild bushes. And standing among them in the blazing sunlight was no more meaningful, and no less eccentric, than standing reverently in a Canarsie lot. I felt neither glad nor sorry I had come; I felt only foolish that I was there.

"Is this what we came to see?" grumbled my son.

"The airfield was right here," I explained. "The bombers used to come back from Italy and France and land right out that way."

"I'm thirsty," said my daughter.

"It's hot," said my wife.

"I want to go back," said my son.

"We aren't going back to Île Rousse," I said. "We're spending the night in Bastia."

"I mean back to New York!" he exclaimed angrily. "I'm not interested in your stupid airfield. The only airfield I want to see is John F. Kennedy."

"Be nice to Daddy," my daughter said to him, with a malicious twinkle. "He's trying to recapture his youth."

I gave my daughter a warning scowl and looked about again, searching for a propeller, a wing, an airplane wheel, for some dramatic marker to set this neglected stretch of wasteland apart from all the others along the shore. I saw none; and it would have made no difference if I had. I was a man in search of a war, and I had come to the wrong place. My war was over and gone, and even my ten-year-old son was smart enough to realize that. What the grouchy kid didn't realize, though, was that *his* military service was still ahead; and I could have clasped him in my arms to protect him as he stood there, hanging half outside the car with his look of sour irritation.

"Can't we go?" he pleaded.

"Sure, let's go," I said, and told François to take us straight to Bastia.

François shot away down the road like a rocket and screeched to a stop at the first bar he came to. He had, he mumbled quickly, to go see his aunt, and he bounded outside the car before we could protest. He was back in thirty seconds, licking his upper lip and looking greatly refreshed. He stopped three more times at bars on the way in, to see his mother-in-law, his best friend and his old police captain, returning with a larger smile and a livelier step from each brief visit.

François was whistling, and we were limp with exhaustion, by the time we arrived in the city, where the heat was unbearable. Add humidity to Hell, and you have the climate of Bastia in early July.

François and I went to the nearest bar for a farewell drink.

He was jaunty and confident again. "New York?" he asked hopefully.

I shook my head. He shrugged philosophically and lifted his glass in a toast.

"Tchin-tchin," he said, and insisted on paying for the drinks.

The first time I came to Corsica was in May, 1944, when I joined the bomb group as a combat replacement. After four days I was assigned to my first mission, as a wing bombardier. The target was the railroad bridge at Poggibonsi.

Poor little Poggibonsi. Its only crime was that it happened to lie outside Florence along one of the few passageways running south through the Apennine Mountains to Rome, which was still held by the Germans. And because of this small circumstance, I had been brought all the way across the ocean to help kill its railroad bridge.

The mission to Poggibonsi was described to us in the briefing room as a milk run—that is, a mission on which we were not likely to encounter flak or enemy planes. I was not pleased to hear this. I wanted action, not security. I wanted a sky full of dogfights, daredevils and billowing parachutes. I was twenty-one years old. I was dumb. I tried to console myself with the hope that someone, somewhere along the way, would have the good grace to open fire at us. No one did.

As a wing bombardier, my job was to keep my eyes on the first plane in our formation, which contained the lead bombardier. When I saw his bomb-bay doors open, I was to open mine. The instant I saw his bombs begin to fall, I would press a button to release my own. It was as simple as that—or should have been.

I guess I got bored. Since there was no flak at Poggibonsi, the lead bombardier opened his bomb-bay doors early and took a long, steady approach. A lot of time seemed to pass. I looked down to see how far we were from the target. When I looked back up, the bombs from the other planes were already falling. I froze with alarm for another second or two. Then I squeezed my button. I closed the bomb-bay doors and bent forward to see where the bombs would strike, pleading silently for the laws of gravitational acceleration to relax just enough to allow my bombs to catch up with the others.

The bombs from the other planes fell in an accurate, concentrated pattern that blasted a wide hole in the bridge. The bombs from my plane blasted a hole in the mountains several miles beyond.

It was my naïve hope that no one would notice my misdemeanor; but in the truck taking us from the planes a guy in a parachute harness demanded:

"Who was the bombardier in the number two plane?"

"I was," I answered sheepishly.

"You dropped late," he told me, as though it could have escaped my attention. "But we hit the bridge."

Yeah, I thought, but *I* hit the mountain.

A few days after I returned to Italy from Corsica with my family, we rode through Poggibonsi on our way south to Siena to see an event there called the Palio. The railroad bridge at Poggibonsi has been repaired and is now better than ever. The hole in the mountains is still there.

As soon as we checked in at our busy hotel in Siena, a flushed, animated woman in charge smiled and said, "Watch out for pickpockets! They'll steal your money, your checks, your jewelry and your cameras! Last year we had three guests who were robbed!"

She uttered this last statistic in a triumphant whoop, as though in rivalry with another hotel that could boast only two victims. The woman cradled an infant in her arms, her grandchild; her daughter, a tall, taciturn girl in her twenties, worked at a small tabulating machine. Our own children, in one of those miraculous flashes of intuition, decided not to attend the Palio but to remain at the hotel.

Something like forty thousand people packed their way into the standing-room section of the public square to watch the climax of this traditional competition between the city's seventeen *contrade*, or wards. Soon many began collapsing from heat exhaustion and were carried beneath the stands by running teams of first-aid workers. Then, up behind the last row of seats in our section, there appeared without warning a big, fat, bellowing, intoxicated, two-hundred-pound goose with crumbs in his mouth and a frog in his throat. He was not really a goose but an obese and obnoxious drunk who wore the green and white colors of his own *contrada,* which was, I believe, that of the goose or duck or some other bird. He had bullied his way past the ticket taker to this higher vantage point, from which to cheer his *contrada* as it paraded past and to spray hoarse obscenities at the others. Immediately in back of us, and immediately in front of him, was a row of high-school girls from North Carolina, touring Europe under the protection of a slender young American gentleman who soon began to look as though he wished he were somewhere else. One of the girls complained steadily to him in her southern accent.

"How do you say 'policeman' in Italian? I want you to call that policeman, do you hear? That Italian is spitting on me every time he yells something. And he smells. I don't want that smelly Italian standing up here behind me."

With us at the Palio were Prof. Frederick Karl, the Conrad authority from City College in New York, and his beautiful wife, the Countess D'Orestiglio, who is an Italian from Caserta. The countess, who has a blistering temper, was ready to speak out imperiously, but could not decide to whom. She found both principals in this situation equally offensive. Before she could say anything, the horse race started, and a great roar went up from the crowd that closed off conversation.

We did not see who won, and we did not particularly care. But the outcome apparently made a very big difference to other people, for as soon as the race was over three men seized one of the losing jockeys and began to punch him severely. Suddenly fist fights were breaking out all over, and thousands of shouting people were charging wildly in every direction. Here was the atmosphere of a riot, and none of us in the reserved seats dared descend. As we sat aghast, as exposed and helpless on our benches as stuffed dolls in a carnival gallery, a quick shriek sounded behind me, and then I was struck by a massive weight.

It was the drunken goose, who had decided to join his comrades below by the most direct route. He had simply lunged forward through the row of girls, almost knocking the nearest ones over, and tumbled down on us. With instinctive revulsion, Professor Karl and I rolled him away onto the people in the row ahead of us, who spilled him farther down, on the people below them. In this fashion our drunken goose finally landed sprawling at the bottom. He staggered to his feet with clenched fists, looking for a moment as though he would charge into us, but then allowed himself to be swept along by the torrents of people.

Somehow, after ten or twenty minutes, all the fighting resolved itself into a collective revelry in which people from different *contrade* embraced each other, joined in song and pushed ahead to take part in a procession through the city behind the victorious horse. The sense of danger faded. In a little while we went down and moved toward the exit, passing pasty-faced people lying on stretchers and an occasional Peeping Tom staring up solemnly at the legs of women who were still in the stands. Once outside, we kept near the walls of the buildings, clutching our money, jewelry and cameras, and returned to the hotel, where our two bored and rested children told us they wanted to return to Florence that same night and where the woman in charge was exclaiming rapturously about the race and the three men who had beaten up a jockey.

While my wife went upstairs to pack, I drew the woman aside to talk to her about the war. Tell me about it, I asked; you were here. No, she wasn't. She was in Bologna during the war, which was even better; she was at the railroad station there with her little girl the day American bombers came to destroy it in a saturation attack. She ran from the station and took shelter on the ground somewhere beside a low wall. When the attack was over and she returned to the station, she could not find it. She could not distinguish the rubble of the railroad station from the rubble of the other buildings that had stood nearby. Only then did she grow frightened. And the thought that terrified her— she remembered this still—was that now she would miss her train, for she did not know when it would leave, or from where.

But all that was so far in the past. There was her little girl, now grown up, tall and taciturn at the adding machine, and the woman would much sooner talk about the Palio or about Siena, which at the request of the Pope had been spared by both sides during the war—for Siena is the birthplace of Saint Catherine, patron saint of Italy. So the Germans made their stand a bit farther north, at Poggibonsi, which was almost completely leveled.

Poor Poggibonsi. During those first few weeks we flew missions to rail and highway bridges at Perugia, Arezzo, Orvieto, Cortona, Tivoli and Ferrara. Most of us had never heard of any of these places. We were very young, and few of us had been to college. For the most part, the missions were short—about three hours—and relatively safe. It was not until June 3, for example, that our squadron lost a plane, on a mission to Ferrara. It was not until August 3, over Avignon, in France, that I finally saw a plane shot down in flames, and it was not until August 15, again over Avignon, that a gunner in my plane was wounded and a copilot went a little berserk at the controls and I came to the startling realization—*Good God! They're trying to kill* me, *too!* And after that it wasn't much fun.

When we weren't flying missions, we went swimming or

played baseball or basketball. The food was good—better, in fact, than most of us had ever eaten before—and we were getting a lot of money for a bunch of kids twenty-one years old. Like good soldiers everywhere, we did as we were told. Had we been given an orphanage to destroy (we weren't), our only question would have been, "How much flak?" In vehicles borrowed from the motor pool we would drive to Cervione for a glass of wine or to Bastia to kill an afternoon or evening. It was, for a while, a pretty good life. We had rest camps at Capri and Île Rousse. And soon we had Rome.

On June 4, 1944, the first American soldiers entered Rome. And no more than half a step behind them, I think, must have come our own squadron's resourceful executive officer, for we received both important news flashes simultaneously: the Allies had taken Rome, and our squadron had leased two large apartments there, one with five rooms for the officers and one with about fifteen rooms for the enlisted men. Both were staffed with maids, and the enlisted men, who brought their food rations with them, had women to cook their meals.

Within less than a week friends were returning with fantastic tales of pleasure in a big, exciting city that had girls, cabarets, food, drinking, entertainment and dancing. When my turn came to go, I found that every delicious story was true. I don't think the Colosseum was there then, because no one ever mentioned it.

Rome was a functioning city when the Germans moved out and the Allies moved in. People had jobs and homes, and there were shops, restaurants, buses, even movie theaters. Conditions, of course, were far from prosperous; food, cigarettes and candy were in short supply, and so was money. Clothing was scarce, although most girls succeeded in keeping their dresses looking pretty. Electric power was rationed, limiting elevator service, and there was a curfew that drove Italian families off the street—men, women, children and tenors—just as they were beginning to enjoy the cool Roman evenings.

Then, as now, the busiest part was the area of the Via Veneto. What surprised me very strongly was that Rome today is pretty much the same as it was then. The biggest difference was that in the summer of 1944 the people in uniform were mainly American and the civilians all Italian, while now the people in uniform were Italian and the civilians mainly American. The ambience there was one of pleasure, and it still is. This was vastly different from Naples, where it was impossible to avoid squalor, poverty and human misery, about which we could do nothing except give a little money. In this respect, Naples too is unchanged.

On the Via Veneto today the same buildings stand and still serve pretty much the same purpose. The American Red Cross building, at which we would meet for breakfast and shoeshines, was in the Bernini-Bristol Hotel, at the bottom of the Via Veneto; American rest camps were established in the Eden, the Ambasciatori and, I think, the Majestic. The Hotel Quirinale on Via Nazionale was taken over by New Zealanders, and a man at the desk still neatly preserves a letter of praise he received from their commander. The men who now work in the motor pool at the American embassy are the same men who worked as civilian chauffeurs for the American military command then, and they are eager to relate their war experiences as automobile drivers during the liberation. They could not agree on the location of the Allied Officers Club, a huge nightclub and dance hall whose name, I think, was Broadway Bill's. For the war itself, one must go outside the center of the city, to the Fosse Ardeatine, where more than three hundred Italian hostages were massacred by German soldiers.

During the war we came from Corsica by plane and stayed five or six days each time. Often we would take short walks during the day in search of curiosities and new experiences. One time on a narrow street, a sultry, dark-eyed girl beckoned seductively to me and a buddy from behind a beaded curtain covering the entrance to a store. We followed her inside and got haircuts.

Another time we were seized by a rather beefy and aggressive young man, who pushed and pulled us off the sidewalk into his shop, where he swiftly drew caricatures of our heads on printed cartoon torsos. He asked our names and titled the pictures *Hollywood Joe I* and *Hollywood Joe II*. Then he took our money, and then he threw us out. The name of the place was the Funny Face Shop, and the name of the artist was Federico Fellini. He has made better pictures since.

Only once in all the times I came there as a soldier did I attempt any serious sight-seeing; then I found myself on a bus with gray-haired majors and with Army nurses who were all at least twenty years older. The stop at the catacombs was only the second on the schedule, but by the time we moved inside, I knew I'd already had enough. As the rest of the group continued deeper into the darkness, I eased myself secretly back toward the entrance and was never heard from again.

Today, of course, it's a different matter in Rome, for the great presence there, I think, is Michelangelo. He complained a lot, but he knew what he was doing. His *Moses* is breathtaking, particularly if you can see it before the groups of guided tourists come swarming up and the people in charge give the same apocryphal explanations of the horns on the head and the narrow scar in the marble of the leg. The story about the latter is that Michelangelo, overwhelmed by the lifelike quality of his statue, hurled his ax at it and cried, "Speak! Why won't you speak?"

The story isn't true. I have seen that statue, and I know that if Michelangelo ever hurled an ax at it, Moses would have picked up the ax and hurled it right back.

With the ceiling of the Sistine Chapel, however, I have recurring trouble. The gigantic fresco has been called the greatest work ever undertaken by a single artist. No summer tourist will ever be able to tell, for no summer tourist will ever be able to see it, his view obstructed by hundreds of others around him. The lines outside are as long as at Radio City Music Hall, and the price of admission is high. Once inside, you walk a mile to get there. And once you arrive, you find yourself in a milling crush of people who raise a deafening babble. Women faint and are stretched out to recover on the benches along the side. Attendants shout at you to keep quiet or keep moving. Jehovah stretches a hand out to Adam and pokes his finger into the head of the Korean in front of you. If you do look up, you soon discover it's a pain in the neck. The ideal way to study the ceiling would be to lie down in the center of the floor. Even then the distance is probably too great for much sense to be made of that swirling maelstrom above. E. M. Forster defined a work of art as being greater than the sum of its parts: I suspect that just the reverse may be true of the Sistine ceiling, that it is much greater in its details than in total.

However, Michelangelo's fresco of the Last Judgment, on a wall in the same chapel, is another matter entirely. The wall is forty-four feet wide and forty-eight feet high, and the painting is the most powerful I know. It is the best motion picture ever made. There is perpetual movement in its violent rising and falling, and perpetual drama in its agony and wrath. To be with Michelangelo's *Last Judgment* is to be with Oedipus and King Lear. I want that wall. I would like to have enough money and time someday to fly to Rome just to look at it whenever I felt a yearning to. I know it would always be worth the trip. Better still, I would like to put that wall in my own apartment, where it would always be just a few steps away. But my landlord won't let me.

After Rome was captured by my squadron executive officer, the fighting rapidly moved northward. By the middle of June French forces captured Leghorn, where broken blocks of stone from the battle still lie near the docks and will probably remain forever. On August 13 the Americans were in Florence. Before the Germans evacuated the city and moved up into the mountains beyond, they blew up the bridges across the Arno River; they hesitated about the Ponte Vecchio and then blew the approaches instead, leaving the old bridge standing. The damage at both ends of the Ponte Vecchio has been restored with buildings of stone and design similar to those around them, and only a searching eye can detect that the destruction of the war ever touched there.

Perugia, Arezzo, Orvieto, Siena and Poggibonsi were all on our side of the action now. Pisa was captured on September 2, and the Germans pulled back along the flat coastal land to take positions in the mountains past Carrara. This was the Gothic Line now, extending clear across the country to the Adriatic; they were able to hold it all through the winter and far into the following spring. It was not until the middle of April that the Allies were able to push through to Bologna, and by then the war in Europe was all but over.

Rome, Siena and Florence had all been given over by the Germans in fairly good condition. In the tiny village of Saint Anna, high up in the mountains, past the marble quarries of Carrara, some seven hundred inhabitants, the entire population, were massacred by the German army in reprisal for the killing of two soldiers. When the deadline came and the town did not produce the guilty partisans, every house was set on fire, and the people were gunned down as they fled into the streets. One can only wonder why people so indifferent to the lives of other human beings would be so sparing of their cities. Perhaps it's because they expected to come back.

Every spring now they do come back, as German tourists thirsting for the sun. Unmarried girls, I have heard, descend in great, aggressive crowds on Rimini and other spots along the Adriatic shore in a determined quest for sunburns, sex and sleep, in that order. On the western coast, where we stayed for several weeks on a fourteen-mile stretch of sand beach known as the

Versilian Riviera, menus, signs, notices and price lists are printed in four languages—Italian, English, French and German. This area includes Viareggio, Camaiore, Pietrasanta, Forte dei Marmi. There was no doubt in June that German families were the main visiting group. By the beginning of July, they had all but vanished. Every year, we were told, they come early and depart before July. The Tuscans, who dislike the Germans with well-guarded propriety, sometimes hint that the Germans leave so soon because the high season starts and rates go up. I suspect there is something more. By July Italy turns hot; there is warm weather closer to home.

The Hotel Byron in Forte dei Marmi is an inexpensive jewel of a family hotel. The rooms are comfortable, the food is meticulously prepared, and the setting is beautiful; but more delightful than any of these are the owner, the manager, the concierge and the entire staff of maids and waiters, who are all exquisitely sweet, polite, accommodating and sympathetic. They would fall to brooding if I snapped at my daughter or my son looked unhappy. A brief compliment to any one member of the staff was enough to bring us grateful smiles from all the rest. This was true in almost every restaurant and hotel in Italy. In Italy a word of praise, particularly for an endeavor of personal service, goes a very long way toward creating happiness.

The owner of the hotel had served in Africa with the Italian army and could tell me nothing from his own experience about the war in Italy. I did not tell anyone at the hotel about mine, for we had flown many missions to targets in this area. We bombed the bridges at Viareggio at least once, those at Pietrasanta at least four times.

I was soon very curious to visit Pietrasanta because of a strange war memorial near the road bridge there. The bridge was new and smooth and spanned a shallow river no wider than a city street, which helped explain why it had been bombed so frequently—it was so easy to repair. The war memorial was a bombed-out house that the people of Pietrasanta had decided to leave standing as an eternal reminder of the German occupation. I almost smiled at the incongruity, for the building stood so close to the bridge that it must certainly have been destroyed by bombs from American planes. On the new bridge was a memorial of another kind, which I found more moving—a small tablet for a girl named Rosa who had been killed there by an automobile not long before.

One day my wife thought she recognized Henry Moore, the famous English sculptor, having lunch at the hotel. The manager confirmed it. It was indeed Henry Moore. He owned property in Forte dei Marmi and had many acquaintances around Viareggio and Pietrasanta. Shortly after that we met Stanley Bleifeld, a sculptor from Weston, Connecticut, and his wife. That made two sculptors we had come upon here in a short period of time, and Bleifeld told us about others—Jacques Lipchitz, who owns a spectacular mountain villa on the way to Lucca, and Bruno Lucchesi, who sells, it is said with envy, everything he produces, and many more sculptors who come to this part of Italy every summer to work and play. They work in bronze, which is cast in Pietrasanta in the foundry of Luigi Tommasi, who thinks they are crazy.

He thinks they are crazy because of the work they do and the money they pay him to have it finished. Tommasi is a smiling, handsome man of about forty in blue Bermuda shorts and dust. His basic source of income is religious objects and, I suppose, leaning towers of Pisa—good, durable items of established appeal. But he is happy to set this work aside every summer when his artists arrive. Neither he nor his workers can convince themselves that the clay models they receive are deliberate; he has, however, given up trying to correct the errors he sees, for he has found in the past that such good intentions have not been appreciated. His foundry is a striking treasure house of works in various stages of progress. As we walked through, Bleifeld could not restrain himself from flicking out nervously with his thumbnail at a piece of residue on a casting of one of his own works, while a young laborer regarded him coolly. In the yard stood a tall and swarming statue by Lipchitz, a fecund and suggestive work of overpowering force and beauty that will soon stand before a building in California.

Florence is the nearest large city to Forte dei Marmi, and we went there often to revisit the masterpieces of Michelangelo and Botticelli and to buy earrings for my daughter. Florence is the best city in the world in which to have nothing to do, for it offers so much that *is* worth doing. Except to my son; he had nothing to do but review all the uncomfortable places he had visited. One evening in Florence we all went to the race track to watch the trotters. Children are admitted, and many play politely on the grass in back of the grandstand or sit on the benches with their parents and watch the horses run. The minimum bet is small. The race track is a family affair, social and safe. My son picked four straight winners and came out eight dollars ahead. The next day he no longer wanted to go home. He wanted to go back to the race track. There were no races that night, so I took him to the opera instead. After that he wanted to go home.

Soon he was a step nearer, for we were leaving Italy by train, on our way to Avignon. We arrived in a debilitating heat wave that settled for days over all of southern Europe. My family had never heard of Avignon before from anyone but me, just as most of us in Corsica had never heard of Avignon before the day we were sent there to bomb the bridge spanning the River Rhône. One exception was a lead navigator from New England who had been a history teacher before the war and was overjoyed in combat whenever he found himself in proximity to places that had figured importantly in his studies. As our planes drew abreast of

Orange and started to turn south to the target, he announced on the intercom:

"On our right is the city of Orange, ancestral home of the kings of Holland and of William III, who ruled England from 1688 to 1702."

"And on our left," came back the disgusted voice of a worried radio gunner from Chicago, "is flak."

We had known from the beginning that the mission was likely to be dangerous, for three planes had been assigned to precede the main formations over the target, spilling out scraps of metallic paper through a back window in order to cloud the radar of the anti-aircraft guns. As a bombardier in one of those planes, I had nothing to do but hide under my flak helmet until the flak stopped coming at us and then look back at the other planes to see what was happening. One of them was on fire, heading downward in a gliding spiral that soon tightened into an uncontrolled spin. I finally saw some billowing parachutes. Three men got out. Three others didn't and were killed. One of those who parachuted was found and hidden by some people in Avignon and was eventually brought safely back through the lines by the French underground. On August 15, the day of the invasion of southern France, we flew to Avignon again. This time three planes went down, and no men got out. A gunner in my plane got a big wound in his thigh. I took care of him. I went to visit him in the hospital the next day. He looked fine. They had given him blood, and he was going to be all right. But *I* was in terrible shape; and I had twenty-three more missions to fly.

There was the war, in Avignon, not in Rome or Île Rousse or Poggibonsi or even Ferrara, when I was too new to be frightened; but now no one in Avignon wanted to talk about anything but the successful summer arts festival that was just ending.

JOSEPH HELLER

More people had come than ever before, and the elated officials in charge of this annual tourist promotion were already making plans for doing still better the following year.

Avignon subsists largely on tourism, I was told, and this surprised me, for the city is small. It is so small that the windows of our bedrooms, at the rear of the building, were right across a narrow street from what I took to be a saloon and what the people at the hotel hinted was a house of ill repute. A woman with a coarse, loud voice laughed and shouted and sang until four in the morning. When she finally shut up, a baker next door to her began chopping dough. The following day I asked to have our rooms changed, and the man at the desk understood and advised me not to visit the place across the street from the back of the hotel.

"It is a very bad place," he observed regretfully, as though he was wishing to himself that it were a much better one. He transferred us to rooms in the front of the hotel, overlooking a lovely dining patio with an enormous tree in the center that shaded the tables and chairs.

A day later we were traveling by train again, my tour of battlefields over. It had brought me only to scenes of peace and to people untroubled by the threat of any new war. Oddly, it was in neutral little Switzerland, after I had given up and almost lost interest, that I finally found, unexpectedly, my war. It came to me right out of the blue from a portly, amiable middle-aged Frenchman whom we met during our trip on one of those toy-like Swiss trains that ply dependably over and through the mountains between Montreux and Interlaken.

He spoke no English and smoked cigarettes incessantly, and he stopped us at one station from making a wrong change of trains. He was going to Interlaken, too, to spend his vacation with a friend who owned a small chalet in a village nearby. That morning he had parted from his wife and son in Montreux; they

296

had boarded the train to Milan to visit Italy, where his son wanted to go.

He volunteered this information about his family so freely that I did not hesitate to inquire when he would be rejoined by his wife.

Then it came, in French, in a choked and muffled torrent of words, the answer to the questions I hadn't asked. He began telling us about his son, and his large eyes turned shiny and filled with tears.

His only boy, adopted, had been wounded in the head in the war in Indochina and would never be able to take care of himself. He could go nowhere alone. He was only thirty-four years old now and had lain in a hospital for seven years. "It is bad," the man said, referring to the wound, the world, the weather, the present, the future. Then, for some reason, he said to me, "You will find out, you will find out." His voice shook. The tears were starting to roll out now through the corners of his eyes, and he was deeply embarrassed. The boy was too young, he concluded lamely, by way of apologizing to us for the emotion he was showing, to have been hurt so badly for the rest of his life.

With that, he turned away and walked to the other end of the car. My wife was silent. The children were subdued and curious.

"Why was he crying?" asked my boy.

"What did he say?" my daughter asked me.

What can you tell your children today that will not leave them frightened and sad?

"Nothing," I answered.

JOSEPH HELLER TALKS ABOUT
CATCH-22

For me, turning *Catch-22* into a film was quite easy since I had nothing to do with it. I solved the problem very quickly back in 1962 by stepping out. I really didn't give a damn what happened to it once I sold it to Columbia Pictures and the first check cleared.

That may sound surprising, and maybe even corrupt, but I don't really think there are so many good movies made that I could have realistically expected a good one to be made out of my book. So I didn't care if they never made it at all, or if they put the Three Stooges in it.

Of course, I had to do a great job of acting during the next four or five years because most people I met were desperately concerned that "they" not spoil my book, or that "they do justice to it," and I had to pretend I was equally concerned. But I really wasn't. I was so little concerned, in fact, that even though I had the right to do the first script—the studio didn't have to use it, just pay me for it—I very early waived that right. I didn't want to do a movie script of *Catch-22* because then I would have to be concerned with what came out. And I knew that the script writer has very little control over a movie.

When the novel was published in 1961, inquiries about stage rights and movie rights began to come in. There would be calls

Audience, vol. 2, July–August 1972, pp. 48–55.

from producers and directors to my agent asking, "Are the movie rights available?" and she would say, "Yes" and they'd say, "I'll get back to you" and then she'd never hear from them again.

The truth was that nobody at any of the studios really wanted the movie rights to *Catch-22* because the people who read for studios really don't read. They just read the best-seller lists, and what they like to buy are best-selling books or hit plays. Well, *Catch-22*, which never did make the *New York Times* best-seller list, was like a blight to all these studio executives, a plague, a swarm of gnats, because actors and directors began calling up in growing numbers and insisting that the studio buy *Catch-22* and that they be allowed to make it. But the studios didn't want to have anything to do with it. In the first place, as I said, it was not a best seller. Secondly, these people at the top couldn't figure out what sort of book it really was. If any of them did try to read it, I'm sure they stopped at about page eight and said, "There's no love story here. What's missing from this plot is a girl who dies from leukemia in her early twenties and makes millions of dollars for us."

So when I would meet with executives of movie companies I could detect an active dislike on their part even before I revealed that unpleasant side of my personality which might have stimulated it. I was a problem with which they didn't want to contend.

On the other hand, there were a few people who really did want the book and did see it as a motion picture. Orson Welles, for example. In 1962 or 1963 I was in London and Welles called me up on the phone. It had been a strange week for me because the phone had rung the day before, too, and it had been Bertrand Russell calling to say *he'd* like to meet *me*. I did go to Wales to meet him and it was one of the more thrilling experiences I have had.

And now here was Orson Welles saying *he* liked the book and would do anything, would *give* anything, to be allowed to make the movie. He asked me to talk with Mr. Mike Frankovich, who at the time was with Columbia Pictures, and to tell him that he would come to London and get down on his knees because he would do anything he could to make *Catch-22* into a movie. So I did talk with Frankovich about allowing Orson Welles to make the movie, and before I had hardly begun Mike was shaking his head saying, "He goes over budget and he goes over schedule and he changes his mind in the middle of a movie. There's no chance of Orson Welles making this movie for us." Then, when I got back to the States, I read two interviews with Orson Welles by John Crosby in the New York *Herald Tribune,* which was still being published then, and in both of them Welles spoke about his need, his craving, to be the one to make *Catch-22* into a movie. It was his feeling, he said, that *Catch-22* was the book that could be turned into *the* movie of the mid-century.

So it was a real irony that Orson Welles wound up being in the movie, in a bit part that anyone could have played.

Well, my lawyer at that time—he's a kind of Svengali—finally managed to lure two studios into a reluctant auction for *Catch-22.* I didn't *need* money particularly, because I had a very good job as an advertising man, but I *wanted* money desperately, for good as this very good job was, I hated it. Then, just as things were heating up in the bidding, the man negotiating for one of the companies dropped dead. So there was only one studio left and that was Columbia and Columbia did eventually buy the movie rights.

But it wasn't that easy. Negotiations over movies are endless. Just when you're shaking hands and think you've reached an agreement, each side tries to sneak in certain things that nobody, until that moment, had even thought of. I know that my contract with Columbia eventually covered everything. It even covers sweatshirt rights and breakfast cereal rights. They own them. But I did retain TV and stage rights and am already in the process of exercising them.

What happened from then on was one of those dreams come true—the kind that, when they do come true, are inevitably disappointing. I began to meet very famous and important people—actors from Hollywood, who would call me up or arrange through mutual friends to meet me, and would then whisper in my ear that they were the only ones in the whole world who could play a certain role in *Catch-22*, usually the leading role.

I remember the first of these calls. It was from a person named Sam Shaw, who knows lots of Hollywood people, and Sam said, "Tony Quinn's in town. He's leaving for Yugoslavia right away and before he does he wants to talk with you. He's got to see you right now." So I said, "Okay, where do we meet?" And he said, "The Stage Delicatessen." And I said, "What the hell is Anthony Quinn doing at the Stage Delicatessen?" And he said, "Interviewing a secretary." So I went to the Stage Delicatessen, and as soon as Quinn had hired the secretary and sent her off to Yugoslavia, we sat down at a small table and began to talk about *Catch-22*. It turned out that his only reservation about playing Yossarian was that perhaps he was too old. And he asked me, "Do you think I'm too old?" And I said, "Of course not. You're just the guy I had in mind when I wrote it."

That was a reply I was to use twenty or thirty times in reference to actors ranging all the way from Wally Cox to Jack Lemmon and Mel Brooks. And I really believed it each time I was saying it. I really believed that any actor in the world could play Yossarian effectively with only a few slight changes. I don't know whether it's because I genuinely felt that *Catch-22* was so adaptable and indestructible that any good actor could play in it, or whether I was just corrupt.

One reason Columbia didn't get started on the film right away was because of what I like to think of as the year of the double war. The poor company found itself in the unfortunate position of sponsoring two antiwar movies in one year, and the Pentagon doesn't like that. Apparently each studio is allowed to make one antiwar movie a year. But not two. What had happened is that Columbia had financed Stanley Kubrick's *Dr.*

Strangelove and an independent organization had financed *Fail-Safe*. Because there were certain similarities between the two films, lawsuits were starting, and the simplest way to resolve things was for Columbia to buy *Fail-Safe*. So they already had two antiwar movies and they didn't want to embark on another one.

And all this time my reputation continued to suffer because the rumor kept spreading that *Catch-22* was proving hard to adapt for the screen. Someone like Harold Robbins or Irving Wallace sells the movie rights to his novel the moment he thinks of writing one. It's been proven by experience that their books lend themselves to screen adaptation. But I was getting stigmatized. People were saying, "Heller's books don't make good screenplays." I was not invited to parties. My credit was cut off at Brooks Brothers and Arthur Murray Dance Studios. The story was that it was impossible to adapt *Catch-22* to the screen. I knew all this time, of course, that no effort at all was being made.

Then, Columbia lured Richard Brooks away from another studio. Brooks had made two successful pictures, *Elmer Gantry* and *Cat on a Hot Tin Roof,* I believe, and he said he'd make movies for Columbia only if he could make two of his favorite works of literature, *Lord Jim* and *Catch-22*. Fine, Columbia said, for Columbia Pictures had long been known for its weakness for Joseph Conrad. So Brooks started on *Lord Jim.* Brooks is the kind of director who is very painstaking about details. He does everything himself. So, during a lull in the shooting of *Lord Jim* he came to New York and we spent about a week together. Brooks said he wanted to understand *Catch-22* thoroughly. Then he mentioned that he'd like to have all my outlines and my notes and the various versions, and he asked if I'd mind getting them together for him. I said, "Well, it's going to be an effort." And he said, "We'll pay you." And I said, "Well, it's going to be a very *big* effort." Actually, I already had all the stuff catalogued and organized because I was donating it to the Brandeis University library. But there were more negotiations and I got twenty or twenty-five thousand dollars for giving Columbia Pictures copies of the material I had already given to Brandeis University.

I know it's vulgar to talk about money, but in motion pictures money and art are the same thing, and in talking about money I am really talking about art. I hope you don't think I'm rich now, for all of this goes back over ten years, and I'm not. I've wasted all that money and art. I wish I had it now.

At any rate, Richard Brooks went off to make *Lord Jim.* He spent two or three years doing that, and he came back exhausted from exotic places like Bangkok and London and Beverly Hills. When the movie came out, it got disappointing reviews and Brooks was so discouraged that he told Columbia he didn't want to take on another tough movie just then.

So now Columbia had *Catch-22* back and nobody wanted to make it. Nobody at Columbia, anyhow.

At about this time, Mike Nichols had begun to establish himself as a director. I admired Nichols. As a matter of fact, when I went to see *Luv*—Murray Schisgal's play that Mike Nichols directed and Alan Arkin starred in—I called up Mike Frankovich at Columbia Pictures in New York and left word that I had seen this play the night before and that I thought he could do much worse than consider Alan Arkin for the role of Yossarian and Mike Nichols for director. I never heard from Mike Frankovich again. And then Nichols went on to direct other things, *Who's Afraid of Virginia Woolf?* among them.

Also about this time there appeared on the scene a producer named Marty Ransohoff, who, according to some people, is possibly the most disliked person in an industry that includes Joe Levine, which is quite an achievement. Anyhow, Ransohoff wanted to make *Catch-22*. He spoke to Mike Nichols and said he'd like Mike to direct a movie for him. Nichols said he would agree to do it only under one condition: if the movie were *Catch-22*. So Ransohoff bought the rights from Columbia.

The first I learned that Nichols was involved was through a press announcement that he was going to direct *Catch-22* and Alan Arkin was going to play the part of Yossarian. Now this was at a time when not many people west of Jersey City knew who Alan Arkin was; he hadn't yet made *The Russians Are Coming, The Russians Are Coming*. But Nichols' contract gave him full casting control and he wanted Arkin, so that was that, and an excellent choice it was.

When the announcement that Nichols was going to direct *Catch-22* was made, people for some reason began to congratulate *me*. They had some curious ideas about me in relation to the movie. When the movie went into production and the publicity began, people began acting so much nicer to me. The elevator man. The landlord. And then, as reports began circulating about the high cost of the movie, people assumed that the more money the movie cost, the richer I was becoming. My wife would go into a shop to have a fur coat shortened and the man would say, "Look at you! Wearing a coat two years old, and with a husband whose movie has just gone over budget again." And then, when the rumors spread that the movie was costing twenty or thirty million dollars the feeling took hold—it's totally irrational, I know—that I was getting it all. But I didn't deny this, because I've discovered that when people think you're rich, they'll do anything for you. It's those poor people who really *need* help who have trouble getting it.

Meanwhile, more years passed. And all this time, there was poor Buck Henry somewhere working away. He's the writer who had the job of turning *Catch-22* into a script. One day the phone rang and my daughter answered it. She turned to me and said, "It's another one of your friends." And I said, "Which friend?" And she said, "I don't know but he's giving me false names. He says he's Mike Nichols." So I got on the phone and sure enough it *was* Mike Nichols. He was very polite and charming and said he felt it might be a good idea to consult the author before the picture was made, and he wondered if I'd meet with him. I said sure and he said, "Okay, I'll get back to you."

Fourteen months passed. Then one day one summer, I was out at the beach and the phone rang again and it was Mike Nichols getting back to me. The reason he hadn't gotten back to me sooner, he said, was that he wanted to get a script close to a final version before they showed it to me. I kept saying, "You know, you don't have to show it to me. I might just raise questions that would complicate it for you." And I really meant it. I've never felt that anyone had any obligation to remain faithful to the book or to me, or even to make a good movie. I don't have much sympathy with novelists who go on television and complain about the bad movies that are made from their books, which are usually not much better to begin with.

Anyway, Nichols said, "No, we want you to see it. Buck Henry's rewriting and the script is being mimeographed and we're ready to meet with you." So I said all right and he said, "Okay, I'll get back to you."

Fourteen *more* months passed. Then I got another call from Nichols, who told me that the mimeographing was finished and a copy of the script was being sent to my house for me to read. There was a lot in it that I didn't like and a lot more that I did. But I know this much about movie scripts: on paper, they all look terrible to anyone who reads and they all sound terrible. As literature they're very bare and sparse. You can pick out very bad lines and improbable characterizations, and yet they may be very effective on the screen.

What I liked most about this script was the structure and intention. It indicated a real effort to include very tough scenes from the book, scenes that I myself would have eliminated automatically if I had been doing the screenplay. If I'd been doing it, in fact, I think I would have made it into the type of movie I detest, because that would have been the easiest and safest way. It would have had lots of sex in it and lots of wisecracking, and it would have been very funny. The script I read did have a lot of that in it, but it also had very difficult and very strong and sobering scenes. It was also too long—185 pages.

Nichols and Buck Henry and I met at a midtown Chinese restaurant that they think is very good. Having Buck Henry there was extremely awkward. After all, Nichols wanted to know what I thought of the script and right there at the table was the guy who had written it. But I did make some suggestions, some general and some specific. I gave them my opinion that there was too much dialogue, too much extraneous transitional talk, and also that the first seventy pages or so had lots of action and lots of comedy but that nothing seemed to be happening in the way of developing either the story or Yossarian's character. Mike said, "Get up a list of specific suggestions and we'll talk about it some more. You'll be paid for it. I'll get back to you." I was halfway through the script, working up my list of specific suggestions, when I realized what "I'll get back to you" means. I stopped right then and there and never did send him my list of criticisms and suggestions. I still have my copy of the movie script, and someday, I suppose, I'll donate that to Brandeis University too—*after* I sell it to Columbia.*

They finally all went off to make the movie in Mexico. I had a kind of lukewarm invitation to come down but I didn't go because it wasn't Acapulco. Instead, they were in some godawful place none of them could stand from the day they got there. People started going crazy almost at once; there was a story somewhere on it—in *Newsweek* or the *Times Magazine*. Bob

---

*The final revised script for the movie version of *Catch-22* is in the Joseph Heller Collection at the Thomas Cooper Library, University of South Carolina.

Newhart went crazy one time or at least pretended to—nobody is absolutely certain which, but, either way, somebody finally rushed over and gave him an injection to make him happy again. Another reason I didn't go down there is that I'd been on a set where a movie was being made, and I knew that if a person isn't working he might just as well be on a torture rack, dying of boredom. Consider what happened to Jack Gilford. He started a scene, but for some reason they stopped and Nichols said, "Okay, we'll finish in a day or two." Seven weeks went by, and then Gilford mailed a letter to Nichols right from the movie set. It began, "Dear Mr. Nichols: You are in Mexico making a movie. I am in Mexico not making a movie. I have some acting experience and if you have a spot for me, perhaps to finish a single scene, I'd be happy to work for you." The next day Nichols got Gilford and they did finish the scene.

Then John Wayne arrived. He breezed into the hotel uninvited in a blaze of expectation, but nobody knew who he was or cared—these were all intelligent people—and he got angry and drunk and broke a foot.

Then Orson Welles came and intimidated everybody. His presence alone was enough to get everyone tense. But even the people on the movie who, by then, were not too happy to be working for Nichols say that Nichols showed his true genius in his tact with Welles.

Meanwhile the cost of the movie kept going up. Nichols is a perfectionist. I have a feeling he makes a movie pretty much the same way I write a novel. I might write one page four or five times and then decide that the first way was best, or I might write three pages twelve different ways and then decide a paragraph will do. I think Nichols may have gone through somewhat the same process with this picture. At the end almost everybody in the movie was unhappy with his role, which seems to me a tribute to Nichols. It's an indication he wouldn't let any actor take over the picture, or even a scene. Nichols had his conception of what he wanted his picture to be. This is not to say that his conception was perfect, but he worked his best to achieve it.

In time, a sneak preview was scheduled in Boston. At first I thought I'd go, but then I heard that every actor in New York who was in the movie was going, along with everybody from Paramount Pictures, which by this time was the lucky owner of the film, and I decided I didn't want to go. Instead, I went to a small town in Ohio to make a speech at a college there. Late in the evening I got a phone call from Mike Nichols. He said the sneak preview had gone well—he and Paramount both thought the reaction had been very good—and if I wanted to see the film he would stay over and show it to me and any friends I cared to invite. I said I'd very much like to see it. I went with just my wife and daughter—she was eighteen at the time—and we saw it in one of those little screening theaters.

I found it stunning, surprising, and overpowering, and when it was over I took Mike by the arm and said, "As far as I'm concerned, it may be one of the best movies I've ever seen." I meant it and he knew it and we were very pleased with each other and ourselves.

I'll admit there was one change in the movie that took a lot of adjusting to. I've seen the movie three times now and only by the third time could I get used to Mike Nichols' concept of Milo Minderbinder. It was a big change in characterization. But essentially, after that first screening, my wife and daughter and I found it a very grim and powerful and very engrossing and very disturbing movie. If a certain objective had to be striven for, I was pleased that it was a grim one, a melancholy one. The easy way would have been to emphasize the sex and the comedy.

I didn't react to the comedy in the film as strongly as the audiences apparently did. A lot of times there was a kind of nonsense dialogue going on which added nothing; it was just time-filling. There's a scene, for example, when Alan Arkin is trying to make love to Paula Prentiss on the beach. And she's just talking nonsense: "I'm the only girl on the base and it's so difficult." In that moment, I think it would have been better to have gotten in what's in the book, that she was breaking off a love affair of some meaning for him. She was, in fact, rejecting him, and it wasn't simply a kind of rape scene.

There was only one thing I missed from the book. I wish they had put into the movie at least one of what I consider the interrogation scenes or inquisition scenes or trial scenes. There were three in the book, three fairly full ones, but none in the movie. In the stage version of *Catch-22* I've just completed, this air of investigation and inquisition continues from beginning to end almost without interruption. And yet I can't think of anything in the movie that I'd take out in order to gain the five or six minutes that would be necessary for one of those trial scenes.

I guess the most effective scene to me is the one with Yossarian and the old Italian woman in the whorehouse. He comes back to the whorehouse, you remember, and it's empty and she's just sitting there smoking a cigarette. And she just answers, doesn't react. There's a kind of weary, age-old resignation in her remark. He is reacting to what she's saying with horror and surprise. And then she says, "Catcha 22." She realizes, that in the long view of history, this is how life is. She's not happy about it, but why all this surprise? That remains, for me, the most powerful of the scenes. The gory scenes are gory, and they make an impact, but I don't think they're as meaningful as that scene.

You may have noticed a strange occurrence in the scene in Major Major's office. Each time Major Major crosses in front of a photograph, the photograph changes. First it's Roosevelt, then it's Stalin, then it's Churchill. I would say that was an attempt at humor—whimsical, arbitrary humor. It's not something I would have recommended doing. There's another thing in the movie that Nichols told me his friends advised him to delete; that was the Richard Strauss theme that was used in *2001*. When Yossarian's eyes fall on Luciana that theme is played and the audiences, when I've seen it, do laugh. I laughed, and I haven't even seen *2001*. Nichols was told by certain friends: Don't do it, it's inside humor, it's self-indulgence. He said he wrestled with it and then figured that he's allowed a certain amount of self-indulgence. So he left it in.

When *Catch-22* finally opened, some reviews were ecstatic. Some were attacks, but only attacks on the movie, I'm glad to say. The book came through it all beautifully. I was surprised, in fact, to find that throughout the country there were so many reviewers who thought of *Catch-22* as a very good book. There certainly weren't that many when the book came out. For my part, I can't think of any American film I've seen before, or any I've seen since, that I would put on a higher level.

Well, *Catch-22* did very well at the box office those first few months. After that it did less well and currently shows a loss of some ten million dollars, which hardly indicates a need for a quick motion picture sequel. More importantly to me, it did even better on the book racks. During the summer after it opened I got a call from Dell Publishing saying that in the preceding six weeks *Catch-22* had been the fastest-selling book they'd ever produced. Over a million copies were sold in those six weeks and it made the *Times* paperback best-seller list. That made me happy. And it also amused me, in a kind of sadistic way, because I knew that many of those million copies had been bought by people who wouldn't be able to get past page six or eight. But that didn't bother me, because I get the royalties anyway—people don't have to read it, just buy it—and it's nice to get money from the people who make millionaires out of Harold Robbins and Jacqueline Susann.

I've also done *Catch-22* as a stage play—it's already been performed in East Hampton and it got a rave review in *The New York Times*—but because I don't like working in the theater I just sold the amateur and stock rights directly to Samuel French. Usually you go for a big commercial production and then sell the rights, but in this case production rights are available to anyone who wants them. The reason I'm not interested in working on productions of the play is that I don't like working with people. I don't have the patience for it—I like working alone—and rehearsals are tedious for me and I don't like rewriting even when I know what to rewrite and how to rewrite it. Another thing is that I don't like sitting and watching actors rehearsing and listening to their discussions. I'm not geared for it and I'm not stagestruck.

Anyhow, there isn't much relationship between a book, a motion picture script, and a stage play. A few people in movies know this, but most of them aren't all that intelligent. The ideal motion picture would be one that has no language in it at all— movies are essentially a nonliterary medium. In a play the architecture from the very beginning is based on language, dialogue. That's why in the stage version of *Catch-22* I'm able to cover ten times as much ground as the movie covered. Characters come on only when they're ready to speak, and as soon as they're finished they're whisked offstage. And changes of place are made very freely. If I have a character say, "I'm going to Rome," and then have him step across the stage and meet a girl dressed as a prostitute, the audience knows right away that the scene has shifted to Rome.

But despite everything—all this prosperity, fame, and success—I'm still unchanged, still wonderfully unspoiled by it all. Modesty remains my most flamboyant characteristic. I'm still just as corruptible as I was the day I sold *Catch-22* to Columbia and, God willing, I'll remain that way in all my dealings with motion picture people. I'm at work on a novel now and have been for several years. Most people who've read it think it's truly extraordinary—as extraordinary as *Catch-22* was. But even if it should turn out to be a terrible novel, which probably won't happen, it will sell a fantastic number of copies.

I don't know whether it will be made into a movie. These

days the motion picture business is such a devastated area it should be getting federal aid. But even if the book is made into a movie, I won't work on it, certainly not from the start. I'd step in and do rewrites and polishes, if I'm asked to and am overpaid at least as much as everyone else, but I would not want to work on a movie script from the beginning to the end. It takes too much time and too much effort if you're going to do it well. To have to go to meetings, and to have to agree with the producer and director on what approaches to take, and then to have to write the script all require the same amount of energy that goes into fiction writing, and I'd rather spend my energy in fiction writing. It's really the only kind of work I do that I consider serious writing. When I'm doing novels it's just between me and the paper. I forget the audience and problem of sales and the film rights and all other sorts of similarly irrelevant and debasing things. And that's the way I like it.

REELING IN *CATCH-22*

The concept of the novel came to me as a seizure, a single inspiration. I'd come to the conclusion that I wanted to write a novel, and moving back to New York after two years of teaching college in Pennsylvania sent the ambition coursing again. I had no idea what it would be about, however. Then one night the opening lines of *Catch-22*—all but the character's name, Yossarian—came to me: "It was love at first sight. The first time he saw the chaplain he fell madly in love with him."

My mind flooded with verbal images. I got up in the night and walked around, just thinking about it. The next day I returned to the small ad agency where I worked, wrote the first chapter in longhand, spent the week touching it up, and then sent it to my literary agent. It took a year more to plan the book and seven years to write it, but it remained pretty much the same inspiration that came to me that night.

I don't know where it came from. I know that it was a conscious assembling of factors, but the unconscious element was very strong, too. Almost immediately I invented the phrase "Catch-18," which would later be changed to "Catch-22" when it was discovered that Leon Uris's *Mila 18* would be coming out at about the same time as my book. Initially Catch-22 required that every censoring officer put his name on every letter he censored.

The Sixties, ed. Lynda Rosen Obst (New York: Random House/Rolling Stone Press, 1977), pp. 50, 52.

Then as I went on, I deliberately looked for self-contradictory situations, and artistic contrivance came in. I began to expand each application of Catch-22 to encompass more and more of the social system. Catch-22 became a law: "they" can do anything to us we can't stop "them" from doing. The very last use is philosophical: Yossarian is convinced that there is no such thing as Catch-22, but it doesn't matter as long as people believe there is.

Virtually none of the attitudes in the book—the suspicion and distrust of the officials in the government, the feelings of helplessness and victimization, the realization that most government agencies would lie—coincided with my experiences as a bombardier in World War II. The antiwar and antigovernment feelings in the book belong to the period following World War II: the Korean War, the cold war of the Fifties. A general disintegration of belief took place then, and it affected *Catch-22* in that the form of the novel became almost disintegrated. *Catch-22* was a collage; if not in structure, then in the ideology of the novel itself.

Without being aware of it, I was part of a near-movement in fiction. While I was writing *Catch-22*, J. P. Donleavy was writing *The Ginger Man*, Jack Kerouac was writing *On the Road*, Ken Kesey was writing *One Flew Over the Cuckoo's Nest*, Thomas Pynchon was writing *V.*, and Kurt Vonnegut was writing *Cat's Cradle*. I don't think any one of us even knew any of the others. Certainly I didn't know them. Whatever forces were at work shaping a trend in art were affecting not just me, but all of us. The feelings of helplessness and persecution in *Catch-22* are very strong in Pynchon and in *Cat's Cradle*.

Catch-22 was more political than psychological. In the book, opposition to the war against Hitler was taken for granted. The book dealt instead with conflicts existing between a man and his own superiors, between him and his own institutions. The really difficult struggle happens when one does not even know who it is that's threatening him, grinding him down—and yet one does know that there is a tension, an antagonist, a conflict with no conceivable end to it.

Catch-22 came to the attention of college students at about the same time that the moral corruption of the Vietnam War became evident. The treatment of the military as corrupt, ridiculous and asinine could be applied literally to that war. Vietnam was a lucky coincidence—lucky for me, not for the people. Between the mid and late Sixties, the paperback of *Catch-22* went from twelve printings to close to thirty.

There was a change in spirit, a new spirit of healthy irreverence. There was a general feeling that the platitudes of Americanism were horseshit. Number one, they didn't work. Number two, they weren't true. Number three, the people giving voice to them didn't believe them either. The phrase "Catch-22" began appearing more and more frequently in a wide range of contexts. I began hearing from people who believed that I'd named the book after the phrase.

One way or another, everybody is at the mercy of some context in the novel. I move from situations in which the individual is against his own society, to those in which the society itself is the product of something impenetrable, something that either has no design or has a design which escapes the boundaries of reason.

There is a dialogue early in the book between Lieutenant Dunbar and Yossarian. They are discussing the chaplain, and Yossarian says, "Wasn't he sweet? Maybe they should give him three votes." Dunbar says, "Who's they?" And a page or two later, Yossarian tells Clevinger "They're trying to kill me," and Clevinger wants to know "Who's they?"

It is the anonymous "they," the enigmatic "they," who are in charge. Who is "they?" I don't know. Nobody knows. Not even "they" themselves.

"I AM THE BOMBARDIER!"

When I enlisted in the Army Air Corps on the nineteenth of October, 1942, I was nineteen years old. Four of us, all from Coney Island, went to enlist at the same time. We went down to Grand Central Station and spent almost a whole day filling out forms. There was a long medical examination. We were inducted right then. Somebody said something, and you nodded, and you took a step forward—and you were in the Army. Ten or fifteen days later, we had to report back to Penn Station and we took a train out of Camp Upton on Long Island. Then we went to Miami Beach, where the Air Corps had taken over almost every hotel. Then we got on the train again and it must have been eight, ten, or twelve days to Lowry Field in Denver, a huge training center.

I loved Denver. It was winter, but it was a beautiful winter, the kind of winter you never see in New York. This was my first time out of New York except for maybe one trip to New Jersey as a kid. That was part of the excitement of it, the adventure. Also there was a feeling that you were doing something that was socially approved and esteemed. In Denver, and then wherever I went, there was always a list of families that wanted to have servicemen to dinner. They didn't care if you were from Coney Island. They didn't care if you were Jewish. They might have cared if you were black. Well, they might have cared if you were Jewish too. One of the things that surprised me was how courteous and generally how warmhearted people are outside New York. There's an affection and an optimism that New Yorkers are not accustomed to. And there's also very slow service in luncheonettes.

" 'I *Am* the Bombadier!' " *The New York Times Magazine*, 7 May 1995, p. 61.

Toward the end of my training I was told that they wanted aviation cadets. So I took a few intelligence tests and passed, and I was classified a bombardier and went to bombardier school. After that I was commissioned a second lieutenant, given a furlough and came home a hero in my aviation cap. I have photographs of me—I look like I'm six.

We flew overseas in B-25s, which were ridiculously small. We were assigned to a squadron on the west coast of Corsica. In ten months I flew sixty missions and my squadron lost two or three planes at the most.

I was not scared until my thirty-seventh mission. Until then it was all play, all games, it was being in a Hollywood movie. I was too stupid to be afraid. In the beginning I didn't know what flak was. You saw black puffs of smoke. And then on certain missions you would hear it explode. I had seen only one plane go down, and that was slow and beautiful. I saw a plane high above the others, with a beautiful plume, you know, an orange plume—wonderful. I remember I was bewitched, it was like a motion picture. It began to circle and I saw parachutes coming out, and then it began to spin all the way down. Three people were killed in that one.

On the day of the invasion of southern France I flew two missions. We bombed gun emplacements on the beaches of southern France in the morning, and in the afternoon we went to Avignon. We lost at least three or four planes, a lot for one group. The mission was planned to attack three bridges simultaneously. Before we turned to go in, I saw a plane destroyed for the first time. A few miles away I saw an engine on fire, and then I saw the wing fall off, and then I saw the plane drop like a rock spinning. Everybody in there was killed.

We went in and dropped the bombs—and suddenly I felt my plane dropping. I heard a shell explode, and right after that we began to drop. And I was paralyzed. That was fear. And I thought, *I'm going down, like that other plane over there.* And then we leveled out, and there was a ghostly silence. I looked down and saw that the earplug of my headset had pulled out of the connection. When I plugged it in, I heard a guy wailing on the intercom, "Help the bombardier!" So I said, "I *am* the bombardier!" The top-turret gunner in my plane was wounded in the leg and I had to give him first aid.

After that, I was scared even on the milk runs.

Almost all our bombing missions were bridges. I didn't think about the people on the ground. I would guess very few military personnel or civilians were injured by our bombs. But I would also say that if we had been bombing cities I doubt if it would have bothered me. It would bother me now. I was an ignorant kid. I was a hero in a movie. I did not believe for a second that I could be injured. I did not really believe that anyone was being injured. Until Avignon, the war was the most marvelous experience in my life. I wouldn't feel this way if I had been wounded. I certainly wouldn't feel this way if I had been killed. But for me—and I think for many people looking back—it was wonderful. I'm telling you, the war was wonderful.

The bomb dropped in August. I had been discharged in June. I remember where I was. I had been taken to the race track by a good friend of mine, and as we were coming out they were handing out newspapers—"Atom Bomb, Atom Bomb." Nobody knew what it was except it was a very big deal. I thought, *What a wonderful thing!*

Twenty-one years old. I had no idea what war was like until I read about the Vietnam War. That war was described much better than any other war I've read about, probably because the writers were in combat. Really in combat. I don't consider that I've been in combat with my ten months overseas. It looks like combat in the eyes of other people, you know? And the longer I live, the more it becomes heroic. Because I've survived so long— not because I survived the war.

CONEY ISLAND
The Fun Is Over

Coney Island is beautiful to children and ugly to adults, and, in this respect, it is often typical of life itself.

Most people, including many who have been there, are surprised to learn that families live in Coney Island and children are brought up there. The image they have is of a gigantic, enclosed amusement park that is locked up at the end of each season until the following spring. In fact, though, the amusement section occupies perhaps nine blocks of a seaside community that is nearly four miles long and perhaps half a mile wide and which, by contemporary suburban standards, is heavily developed and densely populated with year-round residents. Even back in 1929, when I was in kindergarten, there were enough families living in Coney Island on a permanent basis to overcrowd the two elementary schools—and each of these schools stood six stories high and a full block wide.

The schools were almost a mile apart, and one already had an annex, a series of bungalows one street away, for students in some of the lower grades. Before the end of the Thirties, a modern junior high school was built to absorb the upper grades. For some implausible reason, the new junior high school was given the name Mark Twain, possibly because Robert Moses (who re-

Show, vol. 2, July 1962, pp. 50–54, 102–3.

ally runs New York State and has done so from the day of his birth) was too diffident to name the school after himself, or possibly because Samuel Clemens was the only noncontroversial American left who had ever written anything of quality.

Coney Island is, of course, in Brooklyn, lying laterally along the southern rim of that borough and facing the Atlantic Ocean a few miles outside the mouth of New York Harbor. While not a slum, Coney Island was, and is, a depressed neighborhood and seems, from my present perspective, a bleak and squalid place. The older my mother grew, the more she detested it and regretted having to live there, particularly in summer, when the streets were filled continuously with people and noise. We were children from poor families and didn't know it. Everyone's father had a job, but incomes were low. It is a blessing of childhood to be oblivious to such conditions, and I do not think the circumstance of moderate poverty was too upsetting to our parents, either, nearly all of whom were immigrants. They worked hard and did not quarrel often. They did not drink or divorce, and, unless they were more circumspect than my own generation, they did not fool with the wives or husbands of their friends and neighbors.

There were apartment houses on every block in my section of Coney Island. All were buildings with three landings of apartments above the ground floor, which might have a row of stores or another hallway of apartments. None had elevators, and one of the painful memories I have now is of old men and women (in time, the old men and women were our own fathers and mothers) laboring up the steep staircases.

Scattered everywhere about the island, mostly toward the beach side, were those ingenious complexes of bungalows and frame buildings called "villas" or "courts" or "esplanades." They would lie empty for nine months of the year and then fill each June with families who rented the cramped housekeeping units for the summer and came pouring in with their bedding and baby carriages—almost all of them arriving on the same day, it seemed. They would come from other parts of Brooklyn and from the Bronx, Manhattan and New Jersey to spend the summer in teeming proximity that would have been intolerable to people more refined. And they would spend the summer happily, for the same families would return, with their bedding and growing children, to the same "villas," "courts" and "esplanades" year after year.

Back about 1927, some shrewd speculators decided to build a luxury hotel right on the boardwalk, the Half Moon, and promptly went bankrupt. What in the world led those crafty real estate operators to suppose that people with enough money to go elsewhere would ever come to Coney Island? Today, the hotel is a home for the aged, and this, though morbid, is an apt symbol for the old and decaying island itself. Since the War, with the exception of three city-financed housing projects, there has not (to my knowledge) been a single new residential dwelling constructed; and the amusement area of Coney Island, once as up-to-date as any, has not provided a significant new attraction since the parachute jump was borrowed from the 1939 New York World's Fair.

Coney Island has a boardwalk that seemed to me the largest and most splendid boardwalk in the world. It has a beach that is long and wide and of very fine sand: one has to stumble in shock upon the rocky shore-fronts of Nice, Villefranche and Brighton, England—and realize that these also are called beaches—to begin to appreciate the beach at Coney Island as a geographical feature. And Coney Island had those long, paved streets that were better playgrounds for us than anything any recreation engineer has ever devised.

The amusement area of Coney Island—that section containing the rides and the games, the food stands and penny arcades—was of greatest interest to us in the cooler days of spring and late summer, or on hot days when someone would give us free passes to Luna Park or Steeplechase. Luna Park and Steeplechase were the only two true amusement parks; every other attraction was an individual enterprise. Stauch's indoor arena was still standing, where championship prizefights had taken place and where marathon dance contests were then being conducted. And famous Feltman's was still there, grand and garish in structure but dying of neglect now that Diamond Jim Brady and other celebrated patrons of the past were gone. We did not know of Feltman's illustrious history, nor would we have cared. It served an inferior frankfurter, and that was all that mattered.

We learned early that a boiled frankfurter is not as good as one cooked on a griddle, and that no frankfurter is as good as Nathan's; that the Wonder Wheel was better than the Ferris Wheel but that both were for squares or for adults accompanying children who were squares; that the Cyclone was far and away the best of the roller coasters; and that it was futile to search anywhere in the world for a tastier potato knish than Shatzkin's. This was useful knowledge that trained us to expect value for money. Later we came upon a different principle that trained us toward cynicism, the fact that it is often impossible to obtain fair value. We learned this from the barkers who offered to guess your weight, guess your age, guess your name or occupation, the part of the country you came from or the date you were born, guess anything at all about you for a dime, a quarter, a half-dollar or a dollar, because here was a setup where the customer could never win. Phrased more accurately, while the customer might win, the proprietor could never lose, for the prize at stake invariably cost him less than the customer spent to win it. But a kid could win a coconut for a penny at the penny-pitch game, make a hole through the shell with a hammer and nail to get at the milk, then smash the whole coconut into a dozen fragments and distribute it liberally to everyone around. Today you can win a plastic comb or a paper American flag made in Japan.

There was rivalry between Luna Park and Steeplechase. Luna Park had the Mile Sky Chaser and the Shoot the Chutes, which was a pretty good ride. The Mile Sky Chaser was the highest roller coaster on the island (God, it was tall!) and I approached it the first time (at the age of eight in a Cub Scout uniform, I recall) in the same frame of mind with which I suppose I shall eventually face death itself—with the conviction that if other people could go through it without harm, I could, too. As it turned out, the Mile Sky Chaser was a cinch. It soon, in fact, became a bore, for, though high, it was not nearly as fast or exciting as the Cyclone, the Thunderbolt or the Tornado; after experimenting a few times in the front seat, the back seat, the middle seat, we could anticipate every twist and joggle of the Mile Sky Chaser with our eyes closed (we often did take the whole ride with our eyes closed as an additional variation). The only excitement the Mile Sky Chaser provided us was the opportunity to demonstrate to awed strangers how casually we disdained its apparent terrors.

Steeplechase, "the Funny Place," was always cleaner and more sensibly organized, and much of it was under a roof, away from the sun. For 25 cents you bought a pink ticket that entitled you to 25 rides. For 50 cents you bought a blue ticket that allowed you on 31; the added six were the best ones there. The trick was to get inside any way you could and then ask well-dressed ladies and other people who were leaving for the remainder of their unpunched tickets. In this way, you could accumulate enough tickets to go on every ride as many times as you wished. But most were rather tame. Of the 31, you soon figured out that all but a few went around in a small circle in one kind of seat or another and, so, were really only modifications of each other. Luna Park seemed the better of the two areas. And

Luna Park, of course, is now out of business. The most weirdly designed housing project I have ever seen stands in its place, so the spirit, at least, has managed to survive. Steeplechase has never looked better than it does today.

Each year after Labor Day, the traditional end of the season at most resorts, there is a week of parades that are quaintly called "Mardi Gras." If you hate parades as much as I do, you may love the Coney Island Mardi Gras, for it epitomizes everything about parades that is sordid, debased and synthetic. On the other hand, its purpose is more honorable than most: its purpose is profit, rather than anything demagogic. It is intended to draw crowds to the island for an extra week and keep business at a high volume.

We would go to the Mardi Gras every evening, although it was always really the same parade. One might be called "Boy Scout Night," another "Policemen's Night," another "Firemen's Night," and there would be heavier concentrations of these groups than the night before; but the floats were identical, the same monophonous brass and clarinet bands would go clumping by and there was always a goodly sprinkling of the ladies' auxiliaries of things—whatever *they* are. (To this day, I don't know what a ladies' auxiliary is, since I have never made the acquaintance of a lady who is a member of one.) People would buy confetti from vendors with gunny sacks and fling it into the faces of strangers. We would scoop up the confetti from the filthy sidewalk and use it secondhand in the same way. On Saturday afternoon there would be an utterly fantastic procession called "the Baby Parade," a spectacle, I believe, which has since been abolished by humane societies and which was too barbaric and grotesque even to contemplate in retrospect.

One night I saw Mayor La Guardia at the Mardi Gras, and I

am very glad I did, now that I can appreciate what an exceptional person he was. Nowadays it is standard campaign procedure for political candidates to come to Coney Island for a frankfurter and a smiling stroll on the boardwalk, introducing themselves to the populace. It really seems too much of a burden to impose on a neighborhood already afflicted with poverty. In past election years, we've had Wagner, Javits and Lefkowitz. One of the most vulgar sights in recent memory was a newspaper photograph of Nelson Rockefeller sinking his choppers into a hot dog. Even Henry Cabot Lodge has lent himself to the ritual, and one can only be amused by the inner repugnance he must have suffered as a result of his fastidious good taste, and hope some mustard dribbled down his sleeve. It is sufficient to have such men as public officials without having to endure their fellowship as well. None come because they like the place, and they would not walk through Coney Island smiling if they had to live there.

The years of our childhood were the years of the Depression when there were few automobiles, and we could play in our wonderful streets almost without interruption. Best of all, they were right outside our doors and windows, and we could see in an instant what kids were already out and what kind of game was about to start. During the day, we usually played one sort of ball game or another, or hockey on roller skates; in the nighttime, after dinner, the streets were ideal for "tag" and "ring-a-leavy-o," "hide-and-seek" (which we called "hangoseek") and "red rover, red rover, let Joey come over."

Possibly the most valuable resources we had as children were other children, great quantities of other children nearby to play with, enough children of all ages to organize any kind of activity and field any kind of team, even football. The streets were divided into segments by intersecting avenues, and each of these segments on every street contained enough children of all sizes to form a self-sufficient recreational community.

• • •

This, then, was "the block," a section of a street filled with all the companionship we needed, and our interests were centered exclusively on our own. Our best friends in school might be classmates from other blocks; but outside of school we seldom saw them and never had anything to do with them unless it was to challenge *their* blocks to a game of punchball or hockey. When a family moved from one street to another, the children almost inevitably attempted to maintain their affiliation with the old block and resisted assimilation into the new. Occasionally, two blocks would decide to have a fight; when that happened, we would mass our respective forces a safe distance apart, throw small stones at each other for a few minutes, and then depart and return to our customary diversions without antagonism, which probably had not even existed in the first place.

I suppose it was the beach that exerted the strongest influence on our activities. In autumn we played football there, which meant we were spoiled and tenderized by the soft sand and unfit for the game when the time came to play on hard terrain. (I take pride in the fact that not a single one of the fellows I grew up with ever amounted to anything as an athlete. It is also to our credit, I feel, that no one I knew in Coney Island ever attended a freak show or voted for Herbert Hoover.) Our favorite team sports were punchball, which was played with a rubber ball and is not too dissimilar to baseball, hockey, football and association, a game that is played in the street with a football and requires more dignity and technical skill than touch football.

There was a rhythm to our sequence of games that was both seasonal and instinctive. One day in spring the sun would come out, and suddenly kids on every block were punching grounders at each other, and the punchball season was on. There would come a certain moment after Labor Day when every boy would know that the summer had really drawn to a close and that it was time to start throwing footballs. The same was true of hockey; all over the island, on almost the same day and on every block, the footballs would vanish from the air and the grinding of roller skates would be heard in the land. In the summer, of course, there was the beach and swimming. Even at night the streets were much too busy for games, and we roamed the boardwalk for hours watching the gaudy, colorful world of grownups enviously, until our older brothers or sisters were sent searching to find us amid the strolling crowds and drag us home to sleep.

Considering how little we were watched and the late hours we kept and the vast influx of strangers into the island every summer, it is surprising how little harm befell us. There were few crimes or serious accidents in our neighborhood. I can't, for example, recall a single murder in Coney Island up until the time I left there to enter the Army at the age of nineteen. (Since the War, there have been two killings that I know of, both involving people mixed up in bookmaking and Shylocking.) I was never made aware of a single incident of rape or child molestation. Occasionally, one of my friends would be hit by a car and suffer a broken leg. One summer, when I was just into my teens, a young boy in my building was drowned. I knew his sister, and before a week had passed, he was almost forgotten. Before the summer was over, like that lovely, doomed girl in Antonioni's incomparable *L'Avventura*, it was as though he had never existed at all.

One year I was almost killed reaching persistently for a kite that had caught on a radio wire strung just out of reach beyond the low parapet on the roof of our apartment house—while my mother stood chatting with the neighbors on the sidewalk far below. (What a sight that would have been!) I was almost killed one night when I wouldn't come upstairs after I was called, and my brother Lee was sent down to get me. I was a swifter and trickier runner, and I led him a mischievous chase back and forth across the street. It ended with both of us stretched out against the bumper of an automobile that screeched to a stop just in time. I was almost killed, I think now, every time we played tag in the empty bathhouses and I leaped from the top of one row of lockers to the top of another. And I *know* I was almost killed every time I swam out to the bell buoy, even though nothing perilous ever happened to me.

The summer would begin officially, I suppose, on that day in late June we called "promotion," when we would come running home on that last day of school, waving our final report cards and shouting to everyone we knew that we had been promoted. By that time, though, we were already brown enough from the sun to be the envy of every pale adult, for we would have been swimming in the ocean and romping around in our bathing suits for over a month. The Coney Island beach, then as now, was packed inhumanely on Saturdays and Sundays, but that never bothered us as children, for we never looked for a place to sit. Instead, we were always in and out of the water, jumping off the wooden jetty or skipping nimbly out to the end of the breakwater of mossy rocks to rest or watch the strange adults who fished for hours and who never caught a damned thing.

It seems, now that I look back, that there was an inordinate number of young men who played the ukulele or guitar in those days. The sand burgeoned with them, and it was there at Coney Island, surrounded by the stout mothers with their thermos bottles and the men from the old country playing pinochle or *klabaitsch*, that I first heard songs like "Red River Valley." Today, I suppose, there are transistor radios and people Twisting. There were also a great many impromptu acrobats. I think I would go goggle-eyed today if I saw a man bend over and stand up on his hands. But then, anytime you looked, there were always at *least* two or three people walking around on their hands. God knows why! I don't know where these people have gone or what has become of them, and I don't care. I have not seen a person at a beach stand on his hands in years, and I hope I never see one again.

We learned to swim in shallow water by the age of seven or eight. The waves at Coney Island are seldom high, since the beach is shielded in part by the Rockaways and Sandy Hook and is not really exposed to the open ocean. From the day we discovered we could keep afloat for more than a stroke or two, we began preparing ourselves for the swim to "the third pole." This was not really to a pole, but to the heavy rope marking the outermost limit of the protected swimming area. The distance from the first pole, at the shore, to the third pole was perhaps no more than forty yards. At low tide we could walk more than halfway. But the day we did get to the third pole for the first time—no matter how—was a day on which we had accomplished a noble and heroic feat. To be able to swim there and back regularly was to possess definite status in the young masculine community. After that, the only sea challenge left was the bright red bell buoy, ringing and rocking back and forth endlessly on the water almost half a mile out.

It was not an especially dangerous swim, but I would not attempt it now for a million dollars. There was really no way to ease up toward it. A day would simply come when we felt we could make it, and we would just tag along with a group of other boys who had been to the bell buoy before and survived. Courageous as we were, and young, we were nevertheless too cowardly and too mature ever to try it alone. Harbor poles leaning left or right in the barely visible distance would tell us which way the ocean was flowing, and we would move up or down the beach three or four blocks so that the tide would carry us toward, rather than away from, the small, floating buoy that was our destination. The tide was usually very powerful that far out; and if we had ever miscalculated and missed the bell buoy, I think we would have drowned. We were only ten or twelve years old, and not nearly strong enough to make the trip out there and back without a substantial rest.

First, we would swim directly to the third pole and pause to replenish what little energy we had spent. Then we would start swimming straight out leisurely, doing the dog paddle mostly and a comfortable side stroke. We would talk a great deal as we swam—I forget about what—and gradually the bell buoy would come closer. It was not a strenuous challenge, really; it was more a matter of patience. You simply kept paddling and talking calmly, and, after a while, you were nearly there. The only moments of fear might come when you looked back at the dwindling and miniaturized shore and realized—if you had an imagination like mine—how far away help was. (Today, the mere memory of that sight is enough to make my blood run cold.) But, of course, help of a sort was always near in the friends we were swimming with. And all the while, the tide was carrying us closer. When we were fifteen or twenty yards away, we would turn over impatiently into the Australian crawl and swim the rest of the way as rapidly as we could. And when we arrived finally, we would haul ourselves aboard and clang that bell triumphantly.

The swim back never had that keen anticipation of danger that is often exquisite to a young boy taking a chance, mainly, I suppose, because each minute afloat brought us closer to safety. And this time our objective was a few miles of beach that would have been impossible to miss. One time, though, in a group of four, one boy tired suddenly and exclaimed that he did not think he could make it back. Without panic or a sense of danger, each of us simply took hold of a piece of him and towed him gently in, close enough to the rope at the third pole for him to go the rest of the way alone. I don't think any of us had an awareness then that we had just saved his life. Seven years later, he was killed in Italy by an artillery shell. His name was Irving Kaiser, and his death is more saddening to me now than at the time it occurred.

Puberty and World War II, in that sequence, produced explosive changes in our attitudes, responses and social groupings, and so did moving on to our high school, which was in Flatbush, miles away from Coney Island. For the first time, we found ourselves associating with people from other parts of the world, even if they were only from other parts of Brooklyn. A year's difference in age no longer meant merely a difference in class levels, but a difference in schools, with different classmates for acquaintances, different loyalties and different interests and activities. Old relationships began to dissolve and new friendships formed. Boys from different streets organized into clubs that were as interested in girls as in athletics. To the dismay of those who were younger, the old ties of "the block" were melting away.

And suddenly there were those former friends who belonged to no group at all: the boy without personality, the girl who was homely and could not live with that knowledge, the odd ones, the quiet ones, the crippled ones who could not play ball or dance the Lindy. These were the friendless ones who had been left behind, although they were still there to say hello to.

Life was turning cruel and ugly in other ways as well. Some boy we had grown up with would finally die of his "weak heart" or of a rare disease we had never heard of before. Another childhood friend would turn unaccountably mean and vicious and begin hanging around with hoodlums from another neighborhood. Girls we had never even wanted to kiss in kissing games would become pregnant and force boys several years older into unwanted marriages. The kid we had teased as a sissy back in elementary school would indeed turn out to be a homosexual. Many of us were already working after high school classes at jobs we liked only a little. Others were dropping out of school as soon as the law allowed to find jobs they did not like at all. We were staying up late enough in summer now to see the litter of watermelon rinds and chewed corncobs and to realize that Coney Island is a dirty place when the lights go out. In winter, we found it was a lonely, icy place for people too old to roller skate or play tag.

During the War, I came home on furlough once in winter and was so depressed after three days that I ran away to a hotel in the mountains to be with strangers. I was discharged from the Army during a beautiful week in spring, and ran down Surf Avenue in my civies looking for any old friend to rejoice with. Suddenly I spied Davey Goldsmith, whom I hadn't seen in over three years and who was still in his khaki uniform. We hugged each other jubilantly and hurried down to the amusement area in search of our childhood. We ate some hot dogs and knishes, and that was easy and it was just like old times. But when we went on the parachute jump, I was afraid. We went on the Cyclone, and I came off with a pounding headache and a wrenched neck, and all at once I realized it was over. I was twenty-two and knew I was too old. And, like someone very old, I felt that something dear had been lost forever.

That was seventeen years ago, and I have not been on a ride at Coney Island since, except to take my children on the carousel or the "dodg'em," those small, electric bumping cars that are always fun. When friends who have never been there ask to go, I lead them directly to Nathan's for a hot dog and then head for the Cyclone, which they can ride to their hearts' content while I wait on the sidewalk. After the Cyclone, which I explain is the best of the roller coasters, I head for the parachute jump. When they have had their fill of that, I try to get them out of the Island as quickly as possible, either back to Manhattan or to Lundy's in Sheepshead Bay, a huge, excellent seafood restaurant that never fails to astound anyone seeing it for the first time. When I go to Coney Island with people with children, I go directly into Steeplechase. Those same factors that were disappointing in the past make Steeplechase ideal now. The rides are all safe, and I can sit with the other fathers while the kids go running from one ride that moves around in a circle to another that does the same thing.

I almost never go there anymore unless it is to drive out to Nathan's to eat. Almost everyone I know from Coney Island has moved somewhere else. No one I know who has lived there wants to move back. It is almost as though we all share a common revulsion, and this in a way is strange, for we spent what I'm sure were happy childhoods there. On the other hand, the explanation may be perfectly simple: it may simply be that Coney Island is a poor and decrepit place, and we know that now.

Whenever I drive through, I am uncomfortable. Whenever I leave, it is with a sense of relief. But whenever I'm there, I am impressed by the children, by the great quantities of children I see on every block, by more children having more fun playing in the street than children I ever see anywhere else. But children can be happy anywhere.